## Was the dress cursed?
## Or simply magical…

A strange combination of apprehension and desire flooded Jenny's limbs, weakening her knees and weighting her feet. McBride's gaze never left her, not even when he interrupted his advance to move a ladderback chair standing in his path. A few feet away, he abruptly stopped. "You make a beautiful courtesan, Jenny Fortune."

She couldn't breathe. "It's the dress," she croaked.

He arched a brow. "Is it?"

Folding his arms, he walked around her in a circle, coming so close at times she could feel the brush of his body against hers.

"The dress is only the wrapping paper for the package. And your package…" He gave a soft, appreciative whistle. "I imagine a man would consider it Christmas every night."

# THE BAD LUCK
# WEDDING DRESS

## GERALYN DAWSON

HQN™

ISBN 0-373-77037-5

THE BAD LUCK WEDDING DRESS

www.HQNBooks.com

Printed in U.S.A.

# THE BAD LUCK
# WEDDING DRESS

I thank Kenneth W. Davis
and the University of North Texas Press for the use of
material from *Black Cats, Hoot Owls & Water Witches*
(edited by Kenneth W. Davis and Everett Gillis, 1989).

I also owe special thanks to Sharon Rowe,
Jeff Buehner and Karen Powell for their insightful
critiques and to Pat Cody and Linda Nichols,
my Monday-night buddies who came to the rescue
time and again. And I want to thank my sister,
Mary Lou Jarrell, for reading a romance when
she'd rather be reading a mystery.

For my father, John E. Dawson,
the greatest storyteller I know.
And for my mother, Pauline Dawson.
Thanks, Mom, for everything.

And as always, for Steve.
My own Texan hero.

*To cut out a dress on Friday and not
finish it brings bad luck.*

## CHAPTER ONE

*Fort Worth, Texas, 1879*

JENNY FORTUNE WATCHED the newspaper columnist descend
in a cloud of calico and spite and wished herself miles away.
Wilhemina Peters wrote the daily "Talk about Town" com-
mentary in her husband's *Daily Democrat*, and she considered it her civic and professional duty to sniff out every scrap
of gossip making the rounds in the frontier city. From the moment she spotted Jenny at the Tuesday-morning meeting of
the Fort Worth Literary Society, she'd been a bloodhound on
a scent.

Mother must have been up to her shenanigans again, Jenny
thought. Or perhaps this was about her father. Mrs. Peters
might have heard about Richard Fortune's most recent scientific paper and the controversial theories proposed therein.
Jenny bit back a sigh. Either one boded ill for her peace of
mind. After this latest fuss involving the Bailey daughters, she
didn't have the heart to deal with yet another scandal.

"Miss Fortune," Wilhemina said, her predatory smile displaying a particularly wide gap between her front teeth. "I'm surprised to see you here this morning. I know your work has kept you too busy to join us for the past few months. Ever since the first Bailey wedding, I believe." She shook her head and clicked her tongue, adding, "It just goes to show. These clouds do have their silver linings. Perhaps now we'll see you on a more regular basis."

Despite the cloying heat in the second-floor meeting room of the Cosmopolitan Hotel, a cold chill inched up Jenny's spine. She waited for Mrs. Peters to swoop in for the kill. It didn't take long.

"In fact, I'm so glad you've joined us today." Wilhemina lowered her bulk into a ladder-back chair, arranged her skirts, then set her fan to fluttering. "My efforts toward seeing to the establishment of public schools in town has me extremely busy right now. The opportunity to speak with you here this morning saves me a trip to your shop this afternoon."

Always thankful for small favors, Jenny's mouth lifted in a genuine smile. "How nice it has worked out this way. I came to watch Emma McBride recite her poem. Wasn't she wonderful?"

"Well…" Wilhemina nibbled at her lips in obvious indecision. Emma McBride, along with her sisters Maribeth and Katrina, made regular appearances in "Talk about Town," usually under the headline "McBride Menaces Strike Again."

Having broached the subject of the girls, Jenny fully expected Mrs. Peters to launch into one of her usual diatribes against the trio. But after a moment, the woman simply gave her head a shake and said, "Yes, Emma was fine."

Jenny knew then she was in trouble.

The matron's pitying little smile confirmed it. "I hate to do this, dear, but under the circumstances, I'm certain you'll understand." She raised her voice loud enough to carry. "I want to cancel my latest dress order."

Jenny's heart sank as every bonneted head in the room turned toward her. Mrs. Peters leaned forward, the air around her alive with anticipation, and Jenny sensed there was more at stake than the loss of a dress commission. She spoke quickly, hoping to get through the moment with as little damage as possible. "Very well. Consider your order cancelled, Mrs. Peters."

She rose to leave, but the other woman caught her arm. "You do understand, don't you? I mean, after the news about Ellen Bailey it would be foolish of me to take the risk."

*The news about Ellen Bailey.* Jenny definitely did not want to listen to Wilhemina Peters's friendly little bombshell. She shut her eyes and winced, longing for a way to close her ears.

"You have heard about poor Ellen, have you not? I was so distressed to learn the news. Imagine, a rider of her skill falling off her horse and breaking her leg."

By now a crowd had encircled them. Jenny gazed with longing toward the door.

"That makes three of the Bailey brides to suffer an accident, doesn't it, Jenny dear? All within mere months of their weddings." Wilhemina ticked off the names on her fingers. "First Electra with that hive of honeybees, then Margaret and the collapsing wall, and now Ellen. Why poor Mary Rose must be trembling in her slippers. She was the first to wear the dress at her wedding, wasn't she? The dress you made?"

Jenny closed her eyes awaiting the words which were bound to come next. She'd first heard the whispers weeks ago, but at the time she'd dismissed the silliness with a laugh. The Bad Luck Wedding Dress. Whoever heard of such a foolish idea as a dress causing the travails of the woman who wore it?

Half of Texas, she was beginning to fear.

Wilhemina Peters's voice rang out loud and shrill. "After this, I don't see how any lady will dare wear a dress from Fortune's Design, no matter how lovely it is. I'm afraid your business is doomed to failure, my dear." She touched Jenny's knee and added, "You must be terribly distressed."

Jenny clenched her fist to keep from slapping Mrs. Peters's hand away. She smiled tightly. "Fortune's Design will be fine, I'm sure. These murmurings about bad luck will fade in no time at all."

"Do you think so?" Wilhemina's face was a picture of innocence, a look that practically guaranteed the mention of the Bad Luck Wedding Dress in "Talk about Town" for all the citizens of Fort Worth to read.

"Yes, I do think so," Jenny lied. Standing, she continued, "Now, if you and the other ladies will excuse me, I've a half-dozen orders to fill before the end of the month and I simply must get back to work."

Two lies in two sentences, she thought ruefully as she eased her way down the row of chairs to the aisle. It must be a record of sorts.

She delayed her departure long enough to give Emma McBride a congratulatory comment for a job well done. "Thank you so much for coming," the young girl said, her eyes shining with gratitude.

"I wouldn't have missed it for the world. Thank you for inviting me."

While twisting a long auburn pigtail, Emma looked at the floor and said, "The other girls all have mothers in the audience. Since my mama is dead, you're the closest I have to one of those."

"Oh, Emma." Jenny wrapped her arms around the child and gave her a hug. In the two months of their acquaintance, Emma and her sisters had captured a piece of her heart. "I'm honored to stand in for your mother any time you like."

The girl's smile could have lit the sky. She hugged Jenny back, saying, "I'm so glad you moved your shop into my papa's building. We didn't have anyone before you came. You're wonderful, MissFortune."

Jenny's stomach sank at the way Emma ran her name together. All she needed was for Wilhemina to overhear and make a connection between the Bad Luck Wedding Dress and Misfortune's Design. "I think you're wonderful, too. Now, I must get back to work. Why don't you and your sisters stop by my shop this afternoon. I brought a plate of cookies from home and I need someone to help me eat them."

Wilhemina Peters sidled up next to them. "Miss Fortune, about that wedding dress—"

"Do excuse me, Mrs. Peters," Jenny interrupted. "I am running late. Isn't life simply too much of a hustle-bustle these days?" With her head held high and shoulders squared, she took leave of the Tuesday morning meeting of the Fort Worth Literary Society.

Once in the hallway, she stopped abruptly. She'd left her purse on the floor beside her chair. As she debated whether to retrieve the bag containing only a handkerchief and a solitary dollar, she heard Mrs. Peters's satisfied voice carry from inside the room full of women. "You know, ladies, as much as I like Miss Fortune, I believe it is my duty to warn the women of this city—and of the entire state, for that matter—about the potential danger. After all, the trouble may not be limited to the Bailey dress. There's no telling what harm might befall a woman who wears a Jenny Fortune gown."

"Now, Wilhemina," a voice protested.

"No, it's true, Delia. I had an interesting discussion about it with big Jack Bailey just last night."

"Big Jack Bailey is a superstitious fool," a voice said. "The man doesn't settle for eating black-eyed peas for good luck on New Year's Day. He eats them every morning for breakfast!"

Wilhemina sniffed. "True, he may be a bit peculiar about such things, but he is right about the Bad Luck Wedding

Dress. Look at the havoc it has wreaked so far. Look at his daughters, and even Miss Fortune herself. I certainly won't be ordering any more gowns from the woman. In fact, just to be safe, I'll no longer wear the ones I already own. Mark my words, ladies, within a month, Fortune's Design will have closed its door. One more victim of the Bad Luck Wedding Dress."

Forget the purse, Jenny thought, her limbs trembling with anger. Any more of this and she'd be written up in the *Fort Worth Daily Democrat* under "Dressmaker Assaults Prominent Citizen." Fleeing down the staircase, she exited the hotel.

It was summer in Fort Worth—cattle season—and the moist odor of manure hung on the air like an invisible fog. Although still early in the day, the heat was stifling. Nausea churned in Jenny's stomach as she walked the dust-filled streets, the busybody's words echoing in her mind.

Wilhemina Peters didn't know the half of it. More than her business was at stake. She'd made a promise to her father. If she failed in her attempt to make Fortune's Design a success, she'd sworn to return to Richard Fortune's East Texas home and resume her work as his research assistant.

That was absolutely the last thing she wanted to do.

Worry assailed her as she walked toward her shop. She hardly heard the bustle of the busy town—the whinny of horses, the rattle of wagons, the streams of conversation flowing past her. Jenny's thoughts were concentrated on her troubles. Was Mrs. Peters right? Would enough of her customers believe these ridiculous rumors and destroy her business as a result?

Maybe. Probably. Oh, bother.

A freight wagon pulled by a pair of giant oxen rumbled by, sending clouds of dust into the air. Jenny watched the brown dirt, picturing instead the lush vegetation of the Big Thicket where Richard Fortune made his home. As much as she loved her father, Jenny wanted more from life than to be his assistant, making notes on the plants and flowers he gathered on his treks through the forests and swamps. The study of medicinal herbs and plants was her father's vocation, his life. Just as art and the whirl of the Dallas social scene was her mother's.

A frustrated sigh escaped her lips as she turned a corner. She wanted her own life, her own dreams. Her gaze sought the sign on a building halfway down the block, the nameplate that represented those dreams—Fortune's Design.

As the only child of two such distinctive personalities as Richard Fortune and Monique Day, Jenny was a unique blend of scientific substance and artistic fancy. Designing dresses and dealing with customers offered her the perfect outlet to combine her talents.

Even more important, Fortune's Design provided her something few women enjoyed. Her business gave her independence. Security.

She couldn't bear the thought of losing it.

A lump of emotion hung in her throat, but she determinedly swallowed it. It wouldn't happen. She wouldn't lose her shop. She'd fight this ridiculous rumor for all she was worth and she'd win. She'd win despite the Baileys, and despite busybody women like Wilhemina Peters.

Thus fortified, Jenny's heart lightened. She even hummed a song beneath her breath as she walked the last block toward her shop. Drawing near, she spotted a heap of white lying on the stoop. A sheet? Had the younger McBride girls been hanging from the windows again?

She shuddered at the image. Their father had best get better supervision for the girls before they hurt themselves. Perhaps she should mention it to the man.

She pictured herself approaching Mr. Trace McBride with advice on how to raise his daughters. He'd likely throw back those broad, muscular shoulders, brace his large hands on his hips, and glare at her through narrowed, emerald eyes. A lock of wavy dark hair might fall across his brow. His voice would surely resonate with offense as he told her to mind her own business.

Grimacing, she decided that upon reflection, discussing the Menaces with their father probably wasn't a good idea. The saloon owner didn't appear to be the type to appreciate interference in family matters, no matter how well intentioned.

Jenny had met Trace McBride a little over two months ago when her business had outgrown the confines of the west-side cottage where she lived and worked since her arrival in Fort Worth some seven months earlier. Her search for commercial shop space had led her to the Rankin Building, a three-story structure on Throckmorton Street. At street level, an attorney's office occupied one-half of the building, while the other half had been available for rent.

Jenny had taken one look at the space and known it was perfect for her needs. She'd negotiated and signed a lease with the ruggedly attractive Mr. McBride before learning he was a widower and that he and his three young daughters lived above the shop in an upstairs apartment that occupied the second and third floors.

At the time she hadn't known whether to curse her bad luck or count her blessings.

Two months later, she found herself cursing the very idea of bad luck, but that had nothing to do with the girls or the secret fancy she harbored for their father. The sisters' near constant presence in her shop had proven to be a joy rather than the trial she first feared. Upon making the connection between the three little girls and the McBride Menaces so often mentioned in the *Democrat*, Jenny had been a trifle concerned. But they'd never given her a bit of trouble. Well, almost never. And could there be any nicer background music to work by than the laughter so often ringing from the upper floors? Jenny didn't think so.

Still, the man needed to do something about his daughters' mischievous streak. Although Trace McBride gave every appearance of being an excellent father in most regards, he failed miserably when the girls took the notion to display the Menace side of their natures. Lately, their pranks had gotten out of hand. These sheets-from-the-window incidents were a perfect example. Jenny worried the girls might end up seriously hurt.

I will talk with him, she decided. She'd brave his bluster for the sake of those precious girls. And it wasn't as if her actions would be ruining a budding romance; Trace McBride never looked at her twice. The important matter here was that she didn't want to arrive at her shop one morning and find one of the girls lying on the ground all broken and bloodied by a fall from the window.

But as she neared Fortune's Design, a closer look revealed that the cloth lying on her stoop was not a sheet after all. Not cotton—but taffeta, lace, and pearls.

Her tempered flared. *Oh, that blasted Big Jack Bailey!*

She lifted her skirts and hurried to the shop's front door. Crisp cloth rustled as she bent and scooped the gown into her arms. She read the vulgar note pinned to the bodice and choked back a cry of rage.

Wouldn't Wilhemina Peters love to get hold of this?

It looked as if Jenny stood to lose more than her business and her freedom. According to this note, the Bad Luck Wedding Dress threatened her very life.

THE AFTERNOON HEAT made Trace McBride long for winter as he wiped down the scarred oak bar at the End of the Line Saloon. But all thought of the oppressive heat disappeared when his seven-year-old daughter, Katrina, burst through the swinging front doors crying, "Papa, Papa, Papa!"

Immediately, he tossed down his rag and hurried around

the end of the bar. His heart seemed to hang in his throat as he knelt and scooped the child into his arms. "What's wrong, Kat? Are you hurt? Is it your sisters?"

"Oh, Papa, it's simply awful." Round, shimmering blue eyes gazed at him. "It's MissFortune!"

"Misfortune?"

"Miss Jenny Fortune!"

Trace's first reaction was relief, although guilt followed quickly on its heels. Jenny Fortune was a nice enough woman—quiet, plain, and polite. He sincerely hoped nothing terrible had happened to her. The girls would have a fit. "What's wrong with Miss Fortune?"

"She's crying. She's sitting in her store with that pretty white dress in her lap and she's bawling like a baby. I've never seen Miss Fortune cry, Papa. Something's wrong with her! Emma says Mama used to cry a lot. What if Miss Fortune is sick? I don't want Miss Fortune to die, Papa. Not like Mama. Oh, Papa, what are we going to do?"

Trace's mouth flattened into a frown as his arms tightened around his daughter. The familiar shame slithered down his spine at the mention of his daughters' mother, but he determinedly ignored it. He wouldn't think about Constance. He couldn't. "I'm sure she's fine, Katie-cat."

"Can you come see, Papa? Please?"

"Reckon I can." Standing, he looked toward the doorway and asked, "Are your sisters outside?"

After a moment's hesitation, Katrina shook her head. "I'm here by myself."

Trace closed his eyes and bit back the caustic, fear-inspired curse hovering on his tongue. "All right, Katrina," he said with a sigh. "While we're heading that way, you and I can have a little chat about breaking rules. You know you're not allowed in this part of town alone. Especially not now." He shot her a scolding look and asked, "What time is it?"

Katrina's lower lip poked out and trembled. "I dunno."

"Take a guess."

"Umm…noon?"

"It's nigh on to three o'clock and I'm certain you're aware of it. So, tell me when you're allowed to come into the Acre."

"Eleven to one."

Trace folded his arms and nodded. The End of the Line was located smack dab in the middle of the Fort Worth district known as Hell's Half Acre. The area was relatively tame during those hours—after the night folks had cleared out and before the early crowd arrived—and he knew the girls were safe enough visiting his saloon that time of day. Some of the good folk in town wouldn't agree, but he figured his children were better off with him than with the housekeeper—or alone, now that Mrs. Higgenbothem had thrown in her dust rag.

Katrina swiped her hand across her face, drying her tears. "I'm sorry, Papa. I'm just so worried."

Relenting, he gave her a wink and a smile. "I know, baby. Remember, though, that I have reasons for my rules. As much as you like Miss Fortune, this wasn't an emergency, and that's the only excuse I'll allow."

"I don't just like Miss Fortune, Papa. I *love* her."

"You *love* licorice."

"Miss Fortune's even better than licorice. Except for you, I love her the mostest."

In Katrina's vernacular, the mostest was saying a lot. Well, hell, Trace thought. That could be trouble. He knew his girls spent some time down in the dressmaker's shop, but he hadn't realized they were forming an affection for Miss Fortune. He'd have to put a stop to that. He would not have another woman in their lives to break their hearts when she…disappeared.

Damn. He shouldn't have rented that space to a woman. Not to any woman, and especially not that particular woman. Within moments of their first meeting, he'd realized he liked

Jenny Fortune. Maybe it was her determination to succeed or perhaps the aura of independence she wore like a crown. Likely it had something to do with her straightforward way of speaking. Whatever it was, it had sneaked past his defenses, and he'd acted against his better judgment and rented her the shop space.

Now it seemed his children would suffer for his indiscretion. *Acting true to character, McBride. True to character.*

Well, hell. Trace shook off the familiar guilt. He could chew on all this another time. The first order of business must be to get Katrina out of the Acre and back where she belonged. Lifting his daughter into his arms, he called instructions to the bartender and walked out of the saloon.

The streets of the Acre were filled with the flotsam of society that so often collected in railroad terminal towns. As Trace carried his daughter across the district, he noticed how the sights and sounds served to distract her from her worry, and he was mostly pleased at the prospect. Katrina's eyes brightened at the sight of nattily dressed adventurers and tinhorn gamblers. She timidly returned the grins of trail-dusty cowboys and wrinkled her nose at buffalo hunters who reeked of the rancid fragrance of their trade. She sang along with tinkling piano notes floating on the breeze and even called back to the barkers who stood in saloon doorways announcing the entertainments that gave Fort Worth its reputation as the "Paris of the Plains."

"Hello there, handsome."

Trace winked in reply to the well-dressed sporting house madam, then blocked his daughter's view of one of the woman's scantily clad employees. Knowing Katrina, she'd want a scarlet and canary yellow dress, too.

"Papa, I can see your sign from all the way down here," Katrina said with wonder.

"Yep, I do have a good spot, don't I?"

The End of the Line's location was one of the best in the Acre, Trace's furnishings were first-rate, and his liquor was the finest available. The saloon enjoyed a good reputation, and every night of the week customers flocked through its doors to participate in the entertainments.

After arriving in Fort Worth four years ago with little more than lint in his pockets, Trace had taken a lucky turn of a card and begun his efforts to rebuild his children's lives. Recognizing the potential of the saloon he won in a card game, he'd set about making it one of the premier establishments in the Acre. And he'd succeeded, in spite of the absence of an upstairs business. Miss Rachel's Social Emporium directly across the street serviced that particular need.

He'd survived both the good times in Fort Worth and the bad, acquiring the nest egg that would finance his ambitions. Now, four years after settling in town, six years since the nightmare began, he stood poised at the edge of the culmination of his goal.

The McBrides were going respectable.

"I do hope MissFortune is all right," Katrina said with a worried sigh.

He glanced down at the concern etched upon his little girl's face and realized the timing couldn't be more perfect. Part of his secret plan involved moving his family from the Rankin Building apartment into the nearly completed house of spectacular design he was having built on the west side of town. The change of residence would remove his daughters from daily contact with Miss Jenny Fortune, and considering the situation, it wouldn't happen a moment too soon.

Katrina bounced back and forth from her worry about the dressmaker to fascination for the adult delights of the Acre. By the time they reached the respectable part of town, Trace almost wished Katrina had continued with her sobbing the entire time. He worried his baby had enjoyed herself entirely too much.

*I'll need to make sure she finds the price of an untimely visit to the Acre too expensive to risk another visit.*

Trace did his best to protect his girls from the seamier side of life, therefore his strict rules on visits to Hell's Half Acre. Of course, in Fort Worth it was difficult to get away from violence and vice entirely. This frontier town was the end of the line for the railroad and the collection point for a number of stage lines. The Chisholm Trail ran one street west of Main. Here men outnumbered women at least ten to one, and as they passed through town, their needs were basic.

In the Acre, those needs were well met. A bath, a haircut, food, drink, and female companionship were readily available for the price of a coin. Hell's Half Acre was heaven to the men who rode into town with coins scorching the bottoms of their pockets.

Money—fast and plentiful—was the reason Trace had chosen to remain in Fort Worth to raise his girls. Money and the fact that the railroad didn't go any farther.

It was difficult for a man to continue running when he tagged three little girls along with him.

Wanting to get Katrina home as quickly as possible, Trace hailed the mule-drawn streetcar that hauled passengers up and down Main. As he settled into a seat, he asked his daughter, "Do your sisters know where you went?"

The girl shook her head.

"Where do they think you are?"

Katrina mulishly set her mouth and shrugged in reply.

Trace wasn't surprised by her lack of cooperation. Although the girls constantly bickered among themselves, they consistently presented a united front when facing any foe. A father bent upon discipline definitely counted as the enemy.

As the streetcar headed south away from the Acre, Trace's thoughts turned to Miss Jenny Fortune. Bawling like a baby, was she? Good Lord, he hoped she wasn't ill. The girls certainly didn't need that.

He reached over and tucked a stray auburn curl behind his daughter's ear. Chances were the dressmaker wasn't sick. She'd probably heard of the nonsense Big Jack Bailey was spreading around town. He had wandered through the End of the Line just last night spouting some nasty sentiments about Miss Fortune, going on and on about how his daughters had been brought low by the Bad Luck Wedding Dress. Then he'd shared his ideas on how to deal with the woman who'd created the gown.

At that point Trace had heard enough and suggested the wealthy rancher might be happier at the Red Light Saloon.

All in all, Trace wasn't overly concerned about what Big Jack had said. While the man was unpredictable, full of talk and superstitious nonsense, he'd never taken any of his threats farther than his tongue. Which looked to be a good thing for Jenny Fortune.

At the corner of Main and Eleventh, Trace and Katrina left the streetcar to walk the remaining two blocks to their home. He'd acquired the three-story brick structure from a liquored-up banker within months of arriving in town. It wasn't the best place for the girls to live, but it wasn't all that bad.

Heaven knew they'd lived in worse places before settling in Fort Worth. Much worse. He'd had just over two hundred dollars in his pocket the night they snuck out of Charleston and that hadn't lasted long.

The Rankin Building stood directly across from the Catholic church, and he waved a hello to one of the priests as he opened the door that bypassed the shops and led directly upstairs. Despite Katrina's protests, he'd see to his children before he dealt with Miss Fortune.

Once inside he sent Katrina to wait for him in the parlor, then he headed for the stairway. He expected to find the girls in their bedroom on the third floor. But before he reached the steps, he was stopped by the murmur of voices floating down the hallway. From his own bedroom.

"What are those hellions up to this time?" he muttered, following the sound.

At the doorway, he abruptly stopped. Both girls were on their hands and knees. Maribeth, his nine-year-old, had her face pressed against the floor. Her eleven-year-old sister, Emma, was nudging her shoulder and saying, "Well, what is it? What do you see now?"

Trace folded his arms. Summoning his most fatherly glare, he cleared his throat.

A pair of heads snapped up; two guilt-ridden faces lifted toward him.

"I'll hear your explanation in the parlor in two minutes."

"Oh, Papa," Emma said, her voice riddled with dismay.

"What are you doing home this soon!" Maribeth exclaimed.

Trace's brow rose. "You don't know?"

The girls shared a worried look, then Emma closed her eyes and said, "Katrina."

They hadn't even missed their sister. She'd been gone nigh on to an hour, and the girls had not noticed. Trace set his jaw. In a tight voice, he said, "The parlor. You're down to one minute, ladies." They scrambled to their feet and were gone in a flash.

A wave of frustration nearly drowned him. He knew that leaving the girls alone in the daytime wasn't the best of situations and he felt guilty because of it. But it wouldn't last much longer. And besides, was it too much to ask that the children watch over one another for a few days until he found a new housekeeper? Was it too much to ask that they refrain from scaring off every woman he managed to hire? What was their problem?

Trace raked his fingers through his hair, and his gaze caught on the place where his daughters had congregated. Up to more mischief, obviously.

His boots thudding against the pine floor, he crossed to the spot. A knothole. They'd been spying on someone in Miss Fortune's shop.

Telling himself he did this only for education's sake to discipline his daughters more appropriately, Trace hunkered down and peered into the opening.

He couldn't see a thing. He glanced toward the doorway, checking to see that the girls hadn't sneaked back to watch him. Then he knelt on his hands and knees and put his eye to the hole.

What he saw nearly blinded him. Miss Jenny Fortune stood directly beneath him, the Bad Luck Wedding Dress in her hands. She was stripped down to her corset.

Good God. How the hell had he ever thought her plain?

*If you put one sock on inside out,
you must set it right before taking a single
step to avoid bad luck.*

## CHAPTER TWO

SOME DAYS WERE SWEET as ginger cookies, Jenny thought, gazing into the dressing room mirror.

Today was buttermilk gone bad.

Her eyes felt gritty from all of her weeping, and her nose glowed as red as a porch light in Hell's Half Acre. She hated to cry. She considered it a surrender to weakness. Or, to a trait even less admirable.

Jenny had grown up watching her mother use tears to manipulate those around her. She had promised herself long ago never to stoop to such feminine wiles.

Weeping in private wasn't quite the same thing, she tried to reassure herself. And after the scene with Mrs. Peters, then finding the dress on her doorstep and reading the threatening note, crying had seemed the natural thing to do. She'd carried the gown inside, locked the door, and proceeded to all but ruin the fabric with her tears.

To top off her day, at that point her mother had shown up.

"I've a train to catch," Monique Day had said, breezing into the shop on a trail of spicy French perfume. "I'm off to visit your father. I've only a few minutes to spare, but I wanted news about these rumors I've been hearing."

"Rumors?" Jenny had repeated, curious as to what non-sense had reached her mother's ears. Monique lived thirty miles east of Fort Worth in Dallas. Richard Fortune lived another hundred miles east from there. The trip to Fort Worth had not been a casual visit, no matter how abbreviated the stop.

"The seamstress in Dallas has been telling the local ladies something about bad luck."

*Ethel Baumgardner.* Jenny had silently cursed the woman's name. Central Texas was big enough for two dressmakers. Ethel didn't have to go out of her way to hurt Fortune's Design.

"Well?" Monique had demanded.

Jenny appreciated her mother's concern, but even more welcome was the news that the stay would be brief. Monique could be as taxing as hundred-degree heat.

After filling her mother in on the details, Jenny had acquiesced to the demand to see the infamous dress modeled. "Blast Ethel Baumgardner, and blast Wilhemina Peters, too," she now muttered, stepping into the skirt of the exquisite white silk taffeta gown. "At least Ethel has a reason for spreading rumors. Wilhemina simply has a gossiping tongue. I hope she bites it. I hope her husband replaces that column of hers in the newspaper with a cattle report."

"Now, dear. No need to moo on about it," Monique called from outside the dressing room curtain. Laughter at her own joke filled the small shop.

Jenny sighed. Her problems weren't Mrs. Peters's fault, or Ethel Baumgardner's either. They hadn't coined the term now being used for this dress. That was all Big Jack Bailey's doing.

Monique was right, and her daughter found the fact profoundly annoying.

"I need help with the buttons, Monique," she called as she

pushed her arms through the sleeves of the two-piece dress. Tugging the material over her shoulders, she smoothed the bodice, then stared into the mirror. The gown had survived both the Baileys' mishandling and her own waterworks with little obvious damage. It *was* a lovely dress. Her masterpiece.

Jenny's laugh echoed hollowly in the tiny room. Her nightmare, more to the truth.

"What is it, child?" her mother asked, pushing back the curtain and stepping inside.

"It's the Bad Luck Wedding Dress." Jenny lifted her hand and her fingers trailed over the chiffon trim and seed-pearl-beaded fringe, then across the swag of pearls down the skirt front panel. "I billed Big Jack Bailey five hundred dollars for this gown—enough for a small farm—and although he fussed about it, he paid the price."

Monique withheld comment as she fastened the row of pearl buttons up the back. She stepped away and both women studied the results.

Elegant simplicity was the look Jenny had intended, and she'd achieved it with this design. This dress should have secured her reputation and her future. She stood on tiptoe, lifting the hem from the floor, and a wry smile touched her lips. The dress was giving her a reputation, all right.

Her gaze caught on the pearl-trimmed rosette at the neck. The wedding gown was perfect, as beautiful as any Worth, himself, might have designed. A sense of purpose filled her and chased any lingering sadness from her eyes. "I'll tell you this, Mother. I refuse to allow these silly rumors to ruin my future. I'll save Fortune's Design if it's the last thing I do."

Arms folded and a tender smile on her lips, Monique nodded. "The gown is everything I heard it was. My congratulations. You obviously get your flair for design from me. So, what do you plan to do?"

It went without saying that Monique would support her

daughter as best she could. It also went unspoken that Jenny preferred to deal with her problems herself, experiences of her youth having taught her the advantage of such a course. One should not depend on others. They would fail a person when she needed them the most. Independence must be the ultimate goal.

That way, the only person able to fail you is yourself.

"I don't know," she told her mother. "I don't know what to do."

"Well, you must decide. You must have a plan."

Minutes passed as Jenny stared at her reflection in the mirror, considering and discarding different methods of dealing with these ruinous rumors. "I'd like your advice," she said finally. "Converting difficulties into advantages is one of your specialties, after all."

Monique's smile was almost wicked. A sculptress of renown in Europe, Monique and Dr. Richard Fortune had been the source of so much scandal that the pair had fled their home in England, eventually landing in Texas a year before Jenny was born. Texas proved to be a good place for Monique to live and work. The state attracted all sorts of strange characters, so the outrageous artist and her single-minded lover had fit right in.

At least, for a time. Texas grew more conservative with every year that passed; Monique Day's reputation kept pace in the opposite direction. She thrived on scandal, and the proof of it now glimmered in her eyes. She thoughtfully tapped a finger against her lips, then said, "You should take the Bad Luck label and turn it into something women covet."

"I want the entire subject to fade quietly away," her daughter grumbled.

"But that will never happen, will it?"

Jenny shrugged. Although she took after her mother with her penchant for autonomy, she also was a realist, a side of her nature she inherited from her father. As surely as the dress in the mirror was white, this rumor wouldn't go away without help. So, what was she going to do about it?

Jenny turned sideways, eyeing the profile of the dress. Simple and elegant and too tight in the bust. Those Bailey girls were flat-chested women. "If I were to wear the dress, I'd need to let out the seams in the bodice and take them in on the skirt. I'd need—"

Monique clapped her hands. "Wait. Don't say another word." She gazed shrewdly at the dress and said, "Yes. It's perfect!"

"What's perfect?"

"Why, for you to wear the dress, of course. What better way to disprove this silly idea that a dress can create bad luck than to wear it yourself? Preferably at a wedding. Your own wedding."

For just a moment, Jenny considered it. Then she sadly shook her head. "It wouldn't work, Monique."

"Certainly it would," her mother replied. "Trust my judgment in this. After all, didn't you just ask for my advice?"

"But—"

Monique interrupted with a martyred sigh. "That's the story of my life. She asks and then she never listens." Lifting her nose into the air, she exited the dressing room in a whirl of petticoat and perfume.

Jenny followed, searching for the words to convey both her appreciation for her mother's efforts and her doubts about the outcome of such a plan. Monique took a seat at her daughter's worktable and flipped through a stack of designs. She pointed to a sketch of a ball gown with a plunging neckline and said, "I'd like one of these. In yellow, I believe. For the Christmas Ball."

"Yellow in December?"

Her mother gave her a droll look. "Jenny, you forget to whom you are talking."

"No, I don't." Despite her troubles, a smile tugged at the

corners of Jenny's mouth. "I'm fully aware that you could wear a costume toga to a formal ball and still be the belle of the evening."

Monique nodded, taking the compliment as her due.

"But I have a bolt of emerald silk perfect for you," Jenny continued. "I love sewing for you, Monique. You do my designs better justice than any other woman in Texas. Although, now that I think about it, for your figure I believe I should alter the line of the—"

"Whatever." Monique grasped her daughter's hand. "I trust your judgment where fashion is concerned, Jenny. But in other areas…" She gave the fingers a squeeze. "I've been waiting for you to marry for years. Not for grandchildren, mind you," she added with a shudder. "I'm not that old."

"Monique, I'm happy by myself. I don't need a man."

Her mother dropped Jenny's hand, held her own hands palms up, and lifted her face toward the heavens. "That a daughter of mine would actually put voice to such drivel."

"Mo-ther."

"Sit down, Jenny."

"But—"

"Please?"

Jenny sat.

Monique smiled gently and said, "I understand your feelings toward marriage. I know you think I don't, but you are wrong. I hate to see you living alone. I want you to know the joy a woman can find with a man—the right man. A bliss such as what I've found with your father."

"Bliss?" Jenny scoffed, rubbing her forehead with her fingers. "Monique, you've divorced him three times."

Monique waved a hand. "Don't confuse me. I'm attempting to make a point here."

Jenny stopped herself from rolling her eyes. "And what point is that?"

"I believe you are waiting for love, am I right?"

Jenny didn't want to talk about this with her mother any more than she'd wanted to talk about the Bailey girls with Wilhemina Peters. "Mother—"

"That's your problem; you can't expect too much too soon. True love isn't something that occurs overnight. True love takes time to build—time and shared experiences to strengthen the bond between two people."

"Like the true love you built with Papa?" Jenny asked sarcastically.

"That's what I'm trying to tell you. Of course we didn't have true love from the first. We had great passion. Love grew from that."

"I don't think we should be discussing this."

The older woman gave a frustrated snort. "And who better to discuss such matters with than your own mother? Listen to me. This is important. You do not need love to lust for another, Jenny, and sometimes lust can lead to something deeper. You are twenty-three years old. Have you ever surrendered to a man?"

Jenny's back snapped straight. "No, Mother, and I never will."

Monique waved a hand. "Perhaps surrender was a poor choice of words, but you know what I'm asking. Jenny, are you a virgin?"

"What a thing to ask your daughter!"

"Well, you asked for my advice, and I'm simply trying to help. Marriage is the ideal solution to your problem and you've always been so set against it. I'm thinking a little experience might prove to you what pleasures you are missing."

Jenny hung her head. This conversation was a perfect example of just how different her upbringing had been. Most young women were cautioned against surrendering to passion by their mothers; Jenny was being encouraged. She closed her eyes. "I appreciate your point, but I'm afraid I can't view marriage and love and…relations with a man in the same light as you. I've never been the free spirit you are."

"Your father's influence, I fear," the artist replied, sniffing with disdain.

Conviction rang in Jenny's voice. "Nevertheless, I'd rather be a spinster than be trapped in a loveless marriage." With that, she stood and walked regally to the dressing room, suddenly feeling the need to be free of both the wedding gown and her mother.

"Ah-hah." Monique followed her, shaking a finger. "But that's not the question, is it? The question is whether you would rather be your father's assistant living at Thicket Glen than be married and run your own business."

Jenny grimaced. "I'll solve my problems another way."

"Marriage would be the easiest."

"Marriage is never easy. I'd think you of all people would admit that. And it would not work. A marriage made for such reasons is bound to fail."

"Now, Jenny—"

"I know what you're going to say," she interrupted, her frown deepening as she noticed a tear in the dress's trim. The taffeta rustled as she lifted the skirt to check for damage. "You know how I feel about divorce."

Monique waved her hand. "Oh, all right. I don't have time to waste time with that old argument, anyway. I do have a train to catch, you remember."

"I can fix this," Jenny murmured, then breathed a sigh of relief that had nothing to do with the rip in the trim. She simply didn't have the energy to debate the merits of divorce with her mother this afternoon. As the product of such an on-and-off-again union as that of her mother and father, Jenny's views on divorce differed substantially from Monique's. They'd argued the question on numerous occasions.

The older woman's brow lifted as she gave her daughter a pointed look. "You did ask for my opinion."

"My mistake," she muttered under her breath.

"I heard that, and I want to say you are being terribly unkind to a mother who wants only the best for her child. Proving the dress to be free of bad luck is a good idea, and I think you are foolish to dismiss it out of hand."

Jenny knew she'd hurt her mother, and she felt guilty because of it. Adopting a conciliatory tone, she said, "You're right, Mother. I'm sorry." She worked the buttons on the left sleeve. "I'll admit your idea has some merit, but I'm afraid it's a moot point. I don't have a beau."

"Oh, dear." Her mother groaned. "Not one?"

Jenny lifted her shoulders in reply.

Monique laid her hand against her chest. "I am scandalized. Simply scandalized. My heavens, you may have my features, but you certainly have more of your father in you than what is healthy. It's bad enough that you disguise your beauty with that silly chignon and the dull colors you choose. You know I never have agreed with your idea that a modiste shouldn't outshine her customers. It seems to me that you should be your own best advertisement."

She hooked her thumb over her shoulder toward the worktable where a pair of wire-rimmed spectacles lay beside the sketches. "And those eyeglasses! Perhaps they do help prevent eyestrain while doing stitch work, but you wear them in public. Like armor...unattractive armor at that."

She shook her head in wonder. "I don't understand you, daughter, I simply don't. It's difficult enough to accept that you don't have a husband, but how can you not at least have a beau? Didn't you learn anything growing up? Why, you were raised at the petticoats of the best flirt in Texas!"

That much was certainly true. It was also the reason Jenny had long ago chosen not to attract attention to herself by dress or manner. Something inside her rebelled against her mother's flamboyant ways.

"Men and I seem to want different things," she said defensively in a soft voice as she unfastened the buttons on the right sleeve. "I've yet to meet a potential husband willing to allow me to keep Fortune's Design. I see no reason to waste my time being squired about by a man when we have no future together."

Monique tsked. "See what I mean? If you were not still a virgin, you'd know better than that."

"Mother!"

"I'm certain there must be at least one man in Fort Worth who would serve your purposes. Your business is at risk today. Unless you come up with a brilliant idea of your own, I think you must at least consider mine and identify the man you would target. Surely there's someone in Fort Worth who interests you?"

Jenny had a sudden vision of her landlord sweeping his youngest daughter into his arms, both their faces alight with laughter.

Just because she found the man attractive didn't mean she'd consider marrying him. And so what if she indulged in daydreams involving him from time to time? The man had never looked twice at her.

"No, Mother." She shook her head decisively. "I appreciate your help, but I don't think this is the answer. Besides, I'm not certain wearing the dress myself would do the trick. Fort Worth would simply hold its collective breath waiting for 'bad luck' to happen to me. They'd probably publish odds on how and when it would happen in the *Democrat*, just like they do for the horse races."

While people all over the world had strange ideas about luck, Fort Worth, being a gambling town, seemed to have stranger ideas than most. Folks here made bets on everything from the weather to the length of the sermon at the Baptist church on Sunday. Jenny theorized that this practice contributed to a dedicated belief in the vagaries of luck, making it easy for many to lay the blame for the Baileys' difficulties on the dress.

Monique shrugged. "Well, I think you're wrong. Give it a try, dear. It's a perfect solution. And you needn't be overly concerned with your lack of a beau. Despite your father's influence, you are still my daughter. The slightest of efforts will offer you plenty of men from whom to choose. Now, I think you should start with this."

She pulled the pins from Jenny's chignon, fluffed out her wavy blond tresses, then pressed a kiss to her cheek. "I'm so glad I was able to help, dear. Now I'd best get back to the station. Keep me informed about the developments, and if you choose to follow my advice, be sure to telegraph me with the date for the wedding. I'll do my best to see that your father drags his nose from his studies long enough to attend."

"Wait, Monique," Jenny began. But the dressing room curtains flapped in her mother's wake, and the front door's welcome bell tinkled before she could get out the words, "I can't undo these back buttons myself."

Wonderful. Simply wonderful. She closed her eyes and sighed. It'd be just her luck if not a single woman entered the shop this afternoon. "The Bad Luck Wedding Dress strikes again," she grumbled.

Of course, she didn't believe it. Jenny didn't believe in luck, not to the extent many others did, anyway. People could be lucky, but not things. A dress could not be unlucky any more than a rabbit's foot could be lucky. "What's the saying?" she murmured aloud, eyeing her reflection in the mirror. "The rabbit's foot wasn't too lucky for the rabbit?"

Jenny set to work twisting and contorting her body, and eventually she managed all but two of the buttons. Grimacing, she gave the taffeta a jerk and felt the dress fall free even as she heard the buttons plunk against the floor.

While she gave little credit to luck, she did believe rather strongly in fate. As she stepped out of the wedding gown and donned her own dress, she considered the role fate had played in leading her to this moment. It was fate that she'd chosen to make Fort Worth her home. Fate that the Baileys had chosen her to make the dress. Fate that the brides had suffered accidents.

The shop's bell sounded. "*Now* someone comes," she whispered grumpily. "Not while I'm stuck in a five-hundred-dollar dress and needing assistance." She stooped to pick the buttons up off the floor and immediately felt contrite. She'd best be grateful for any customer, and besides, she welcomed the distraction from her troublesome thoughts.

Pasting a smile on her face, Jenny exited the dressing room and spied Mr. Trace McBride entering her shop.

He was dressed in work clothes—black frock jacket and black trousers, white shirt beneath a gold satin vest. He carried a black felt hat casually in his hand and raked a hand nervously through thick, dark hair.

Immediately, she ducked back behind the curtain.

*Oh, my.* Her heart began to pound. Why would the one man in Fort Worth, Texas, who stirred her imagination walk into her world at this particular moment?

She swallowed hard as she thought of her mother's advice. It was a crazy thought. Ridiculous.

But maybe, considering the stakes, it wouldn't hurt to explore the idea. Jenny had the sudden image of herself clothed in the Bad Luck Wedding Dress, standing beside Trace McBride, his three darling daughters looking on as she repeated vows to a preacher.

Her mouth went dry. Hadn't she sworn to fight for Fortune's Design? Wasn't she willing to do whatever it took to save her shop? If that meant marriage, well...

Wasn't it better to give up the dream of true love than the security of her independence?

Jenny stared at her reflection in the mirror. What would it hurt to explore her mother's idea? She wouldn't be committing to anything.

Jenny recalled the lessons she'd learned at Monique's knees. Flirtation. Seduction. That's how it was done. She took a deep breath. Was she sure about this? Could she go through with it? She *was* Monique Day's daughter. Surely that should count for something. She could do this.

Maybe.

Trace McBride. What did she really know about him? He was a businessman, saloonkeeper, landlord, father. His smile made her warm inside and the musky, masculine scent of him haunted her mind. Once when he'd taken her arm in escort, she couldn't help but notice the steel of his muscles beneath the cover of his coat. His fingers would be rough against the softness of her skin. His kiss would be—

Jenny started. Oh, bother. Had she lost her sense entirely?

Perhaps she had. She was seriously considering her mother's idea.

What was she thinking? He'd never noticed her before, what made her think he'd notice her now? What made her think he'd even consider such a fate as marriage?

Fate. There was that word again.

Was Trace McBride her fate? Could he save her from the rumor of the Bad Luck Wedding Dress? Could he help her save Fortune's Design?

She wouldn't know unless she did a little exploring. Was she brave enough, woman enough, to try?

She was Jenny Fortune. What more was there to say?

Taking a deep breath, Jenny pinched her cheeks, fluffed her honey-colored hair, and walked out into the shop.

*If you break your washpot, you will
have twenty years bad luck.*

## CHAPTER THREE

TRACE STOOD AWKWARDLY between a rack of ribbons and lace
and a naked dressmaker's form. He'd been in the shop before
but always with his daughters. Something about all the frou-
frou and furbelows in this place made his neck itch. He didn't
want to think it might be the woman.

Jenny Fortune wasn't his type at all. The question of plain
or pretty aside, she was respectable and acquainted with his
girls—reason enough for him to maintain his distance. Trace
had a firm rule to remain on a nodding-acquaintance-only
basis with any woman his daughters might consider a prospec-
tive mother. He wouldn't have them hurt, and since he'd
never—under any circumstances—marry again, he didn't
want them getting their hopes up.

Despite all his good intentions, when the woman in question emerged from the back of the shop, he found himself
fighting a strong surge of lust. Must be the tears, he tried to
tell himself. He'd always been a sucker for a lady's tears.

Except Jenny Fortune wasn't crying. Oh, her face showed

signs of an earlier bout of blubbering, but she certainly wasn't teary at the moment. The dressmaker had her hair down and she was smiling. It threw him off balance.

As did the memory of his peephole vision.

This Jenny Fortune was pretty. Bordering on beautiful, in fact. A tawny gold complexion, bright blue eyes. More curves than a barrel of snakes.

Damn him for a fool. Why had he allowed spectacles and a forthright manner to distract him? How could he have never noticed? If he'd taken one good look at the woman, he'd have rented this shop to the doctor who wanted the space. It didn't matter that he'd liked her or that he'd appreciated her contract negotiating skills. Trace would never have done business with a beautiful, respectable woman.

He'd learned the hard way they couldn't be trusted worth beans.

"Good afternoon, Mr. McBride," she said, warmth glowing in her eyes. "What can I do for you?"

She had a Tennessee sipping-whiskey voice, mellow and rich. A surprising number of answers to her question flitted through his mind. He cleared his throat before saying, "I want a dress."

"I see." Humor added a spark to her eyes that Trace found captivating. And distracting. He hardly took note of what she asked. "Will this dress be for a particular occasion or for everyday?"

"Everyday." It was more than just beauty. Something about Jenny Fortune's manner was different this afternoon, too. He couldn't quite put his finger on it, but whatever it was, she simmered with it. It made him simmer more than a little, himself.

"What sort of materials do you prefer?" With a graceful sweep of her arm, she gestured to a stack of cloth bolts lying atop a counter.

Bold, that was part of it. She had a boldness about her today, from the look in her eyes to where she positioned herself in the room—just a tad too close but not near close enough. "Materials?"

She lifted a tape measure from a basket. "Percale, cashmere, bouclé…?"

His stare fastened on her lips. Full and pouty. He imagined them soft, sensuous. "Silk."

Her gaze swept him head to foot and she took the tiniest of steps backward. Then, curiously, she inhaled a deep breath and stepped forward once again. "Silk it is," she said, nodding. "And the color? Do you have a preference? I have a beautiful bolt of arctic blue, or a primrose might be nice."

He shrugged, forcing himself to drag his thoughts back to the matter at hand. Forget about her looks. He'd promised his daughters he'd make sure their Miss Fortune wasn't dying of some dread disease, and that was all he was here for. Now, if he could only figure how to go about it.

Hell, maybe he should just ask her. Sometimes folks appreciated these things being met head-on. "Miss Fortune…"

"Yes?"

He hesitated, then said, "Blue will be fine."

Her lips twitched with a smile as she lifted a tape measure from a table and said, "You'll look divine in blue, Mr. McBride."

The fog cleared from his brain and he realized the direction in which she'd taken this conversation. Why, the little tease. Lord help him. Beautiful, smart, and a sense of humor. The most dangerous kind of woman.

Knowing that, yet still unable to stop himself from baiting her back, Trace lifted his arms wide, held his hands palms out, and drawled, "Y'know, insecurity would make a lot of men run from a woman with a tape measure in her hand. Personally, I've never had the worry."

Twin spots of color stained her cheeks and she retreated a few steps.

Trace took his first good breath since she'd entered the room. At least the exchange had yielded information, he told himself, feeling the need for an excuse. Miss Fortune was the type to badger a man, but only up to a point. He was glad. He wouldn't want his daughters charmed by a tart.

Bad enough to find himself tantalized by a tease.

"Forgive me, Mr. McBride," Jenny said, offering an apologetic smile. "I should never have indulged my tendency to jest. I fear it's one of the penchants I've inherited from my mother."

He opened his mouth—to protest or agree, he wasn't sure—but she barged ahead.

"I forgot we are basically strangers. It's just that your daughters speak of you so often that I feel as if I've known you for years." Her tone became brisk and businesslike. "Now, I take it you are here to order a dress for one of the girls. Emma perhaps? Her birthday is close."

He nodded and she continued. "May I suggest that the blue silk would not be an appropriate everyday dress for a girl her age? What about calico? I received a new bolt last week in colors that would be perfect for Emma."

Trace blinked. He'd had no intention of buying a dress when he walked through the door. He'd already purchased a frilly new doll for Emma's birthday gift, and he didn't want to give her two presents. That would set a bad precedent with the other girls. "Fine. Whatever you think."

Jenny's smile was stunning. "Emma will be so pleased. She's been talking to me about her birthday. I compliment you on being aware of her wishes, Mr. McBride. She seems to think you've not noticed how grown-up she's become, and she's afraid you'll give her another doll."

Trace barely managed to keep the scowl from showing on his face. "Yes, well, I know better than that. She'll be twelve years old after all." Guess he could save the doll for Kat's birthday. Surely *she* was still young enough for baby dolls.

Lifting a book from the desk that sat against the wall, Jenny jotted down some notes, then asked, "Do you want to keep this secret from Maribeth and Katrina, too? I could use their help in getting Emma's measurements."

Measurements. Trace's gaze slipped to the dressmaker's bodice and the wayward thought occurred that it might have been worth the embarrassment of ordering a dress for himself just to get her hands on him.

He forced himself to look away, and he wasn't too pleased that his stare landed on the naked dressmaker dummy. What was the matter with him? He'd never looked twice at this woman before, and today she had him pole-axed. "You can let Maribeth in on it if you need to, but Kat can't keep her mouth shut. Now, if that's all you need, I'd best get back to work."

"This will do. For now, anyway."

Her low-pitched voice and the soft look in her eyes sent a wave of heat washing through him. Then she startled him— shocked him—when she crossed the room and took his hand in hers. Her touch had a kick like hundred-proof moonshine.

"Thank you for your business, Mr. McBride." She gently pumped his arm and the faint spice of her perfume filled his senses. "And thank you for sharing your daughters with me."

Before Trace quite knew how it had happened, she had ushered him to the doorway. He stared down at the hand that clutched the doorknob, his skin still warm from her touch. How curious. He glanced over his shoulder. "Why did you do that?"

Her look was all innocence and fire. "Do what?"

"Shake hands with me. Just like a man."

She looked him straight in the eye, telegraphing messages he thought he surely must be misreading. "Why did I shake your hand? It's something my mother taught me to do."

Trace was halfway back to Hell's Half Acre before he realized he'd forgotten to find out why, earlier that afternoon, Jenny Fortune had been crying.

ON HER HANDS AND KNEES in the front parlor, Emma McBride watched through a knothole as one floor beneath her, Miss Fortune collapsed into a nearby rocking chair following Papa's exit. Her sister, Maribeth, sat against the parlor wall, a loose chimney brick at her feet, her ear fitted to the hollow space as she listened intently. Katrina paced the floor between her siblings.

"I can't do this!" Jenny groaned, loud enough for all the girls to hear. "I don't have it in me to act like Monique. It was a silly idea, anyway. It never would have worked. I'll simply have to come up with a solution of my own."

Emma saw Jenny's chest lift in a heavy sigh; Maribeth heard the soulful sound. Minutes passed without further action. Finally, Emma lifted her head and looked toward her sister, thinking that the entertainment was over. She realized she'd missed something when Maribeth's eyes rounded and her mouth dropped open in shock.

"What?" Emma demanded, putting her face to the knothole once more. Miss Fortune continued to rock in her chair, her pretty face a picture of sadness. Emma glanced at her sister and asked, "What did she say?"

Maribeth bent, scooped up the brick, and returned it to its spot. She stared at her sister, excitement sparkling in her eyes. "It's working. Oh, Em, I think it's working."

"What?" Katrina asked. "Y'all are too mean to me. Next time I get a peephole, too."

"Hush, Kat." The eldest sister pushed to her feet and glared at the other two. "And Mari McBride, if you don't tell me what Miss Fortune said I'll put grass burrs in your sheets!"

Maribeth's wicked smile was a copy of her father's. "She said, 'What foolishness made me think I could make a man like Trace McBride take notice of me.'"

"It's working!" Emma flew across the room and swept her

sisters into a quick, but fierce, hug. "Oh, Mari, you were right. I didn't think Miss Fortune listened to any of our talk about Papa, but I must have been wrong."

"What about me?" Katrina's lips pursed into a pout. "I'm right, too."

Emma and Maribeth shared a rolled-eye look, then the latter lifted a superior chin and said smugly, "I told you so. Twice this last week I saw that peculiar look on Miss Fortune's face when we got to talking about Papa. She likes him. I just know she does."

Emma began to pace the room, her expression gathered in a thoughtful scowl as she contemplated the latest developments. Shortly after the three of them decided they wanted Jenny Fortune to be their mother, they'd launched an all-out effort to convince the dressmaker that their father would be a perfect husband for her. "Something we said must have made a difference."

"I bet it was the part about Papa sewing up the rip in my dolly's arm," Katrina observed solemnly. "She must really like people who sew."

"Maybe, Kat. You never know," Emma replied. She turned to Maribeth. "I'm ever so sorry about whatever happened to make Miss Fortune cry, but it turned out splendidly for us. You know how Papa gets about tears. Did you see his face when he was talking to her? I think he finally realized how pretty Miss Fortune is. This is wonderful."

"Wonderful? I wouldn't go that far." Maribeth snorted in disgust and glared at Katrina. "We ended up in major trouble because of it. You got back way too soon, Kat. You could have hollered or something and warned us that Papa was here. You could have ruined everything."

"That's not my fault!" the youngest sister protested before popping her thumb in her mouth.

"You did fine," Emma, the peacemaker, said.

"No, she didn't; she got us in trouble! I didn't think Papa would ever end that lecture." Maribeth folded her arms in a huff. "It will take us two days to wash all the baseboards in the house. Oh, Kat, how come you didn't slow him down? Emma and me didn't beat y'all home by more than five minutes." Glancing at her older sister, she added, "I told you we shouldn't have waited for her to get inside the End of the Line before we left."

Emma shook her head. "Absolutely not! We couldn't leave Kat alone in the Acre."

"We're getting punished for doing just that."

Katrina's voice sounded mushy as she spoke around her thumb. "Mari McBride, you're a mean sister."

The squabbling continued for a number of minutes while Emma bent her mind to the task of how next to proceed. "We must work on Papa," she announced during a lull in the action. "We've primed the pump with Miss Fortune. Now it's time to prove to Papa how badly he needs a wife."

Katrina stuck out her tongue at Maribeth one last time then asked, "How we gonna do that, Emmie?"

"That's what I want to know," Maribeth chimed in. "We can't talk to him about it. Anytime one of us brings up the idea of getting a new mother, he gets that look on his face. I don't like that look, Em. Don't forget we need to be sneaky about this."

The eleven-year-old's eyes gleamed with mischief. "First, I think we'll give Katrina that reward we promised her for crying to Papa about Miss Fortune."

Clapping her hands together, Katrina beamed at her sister. "You're still gonna buy me my dill pickle at the mercantile?"

Maribeth frowned and opened her mouth to voice an obvious protest, but Emma forestalled her by saying, "No, I'm not."

Maribeth gave a cat-and-cream smile while her younger sister wailed, "Why? I did what you told me to!"

Emma nodded. "That's right, you did. And I do plan to get

you your pickle, only we're not going to buy it. We are going to steal it."

"What?" Maribeth and Katrina gasped in unison.

"It's the next part of my plan. It's how we'll go to work on Papa. We'll steal pickles from the mercantile, and we'll make sure we get caught doing it."

"Oh, Emma, you're naughty." Katrina's eyes grew as round as a barn owl's.

"Yeah," Maribeth agreed, her eyes shining with delight. "And smart, too. Nothing needles Papa more than an appearance by the McBride Menaces." Her grin faded as she added glumly, "He'll have us scrubbing the ceilings for sure."

Emma pointed toward the floor and the woman who worked on the street-level shop. "But won't it be worth it?"

They all nodded.

ONE WEEK LATER when Marshal T.I. Courtright arrived for what was becoming a daily visit to the End of the Line Saloon, Trace had a shot of rye whiskey poured and waiting for him. He preferred bourbon himself.

Courtright drained his glass before he spoke. "You're going to have to do something, McBride."

He *had* done something. In seven days he'd been through three more housekeepers. This morning he'd hauled his girls across the street so the nuns could deal with them. He should have known holy women had no chance of controlling holy terrors. All this nonsense was playing hell with his plans to go respectable. Making a place for his daughters in Fort Worth society would be difficult enough considering his soon-to-be-former occupation. No way would the good women of Fort Worth accept his daughters as one of their own if they continued with these pranks. Trace closed his eyes and asked, "What did they do today?"

"They've crossed the line this time. This ain't no pickle swiping or even turning mice loose at the Baptist Ladies' Benevolent Society meeting. This is out-and-out criminal activity. Punishable, I might add, by—" he pulled a paper from his pocket, donned his spectacles, and read "'branding, lashing, a one-thousand-dollar fine, one-year imprisonment, and restoration.'"

Trace, having a passing acquaintance with the laws of crime and punishment in Texas, took a long swig of bourbon, then croaked, "Are you telling me my girls stole a horse?"

"Two of 'em." Courtright took off his spectacles and returned them and the paper to his pocket. "From the nuns at Saint Stanislaus Kostka Church."

"Good God."

"I reckon you'd better hope so. We did recover the horses, at least. Little Katrina told us where to find 'em." A reluctant grin tugged at his lips. "They tied them up over behind First Baptist."

Trace dropped his chin and shook his head in defeat as Courtright continued, "You're gonna have to do something and fast. Folks around here won't put up with that sort of behavior out of young'uns. Especially girls. You've been living on borrowed time as it is, all the mischief they've caused in the past year or so."

Trace clamped his mouth shut as anger—at the marshal, his daughters, the entire world—threatened to burst into words. But how could he be mad at Courtright? The man was right. The girls were out of hand. Horse thieves, by God!

He finished off his drink and asked, "Where are they?"

"Jail."

"What?" Trace shouted, shoving to his feet, heedless of the chair that clattered to the floor.

"I had to do something with them, McBride. Only have one prisoner today, and he's sleeping off his drunk. Figured a dose of cell time might get through to 'em. You sure as hell haven't."

Trace was out of the front door in a flash. His long strides ate up the ground as he hurried toward the jailhouse, conveniently located at the far end of the Acre. That sonofabitch had put his little girls in jail!

That sonofabitch had put his little *hoodlums* in jail.

"What am I doing wrong with those girls?" he muttered. If they were boys, he'd know what to do. Same thing his father used to do to him—the three W's. Words, work, and woodshed. In the past week or so, Trace had served up the first two on a regular basis. He'd worn out his tongue lecturing and worked his girls until the house sparkled. But he simply couldn't bring himself to haul them to the woodshed. He didn't believe a man should ever hit a woman, no matter how young that woman might be.

So what did a father do with daughters who stole horses from nuns?

The summer heat bore down relentlessly as he made his way toward the calaboose. The odor of whiskey slapped at his senses and made him think of the locked-up drunk. He silently cursed the marshal. What had the man been thinking of, putting three little girls in jail? They'd be frightened. Kat would have nightmares for weeks. What if one of the deputies brought in a criminal before he got there? Trace sprinted the last hundred yards to the Fort Worth City Jail.

Deputy Rufus Scott sat at one desk, cleaning his fingernails with a knife. He looked up as Trace burst through the door, saying, "I want my girls now."

The deputy laid down his blade. "They ain't here."

"What?" Trace's gut clenched.

"That dressmaker came and got 'em. Said she was taking them to your place. Talked me up one side and down the other, she did. Hell, wasn't my doin's putting them here. Marshal Courtright decided that all on his lonesome."

Jenny Fortune. Trace breathed a long sigh of relief. How

she had found out about these latest shenanigans, he didn't really care. She had taken care of his girls for him and that was all that mattered. Without another word to the deputy, he turned and left the jailhouse, headed for home.

He made quick work of getting there. When he turned the corner of Throckmorton and Eleventh, he spied the trio of nuns lying in wait along the garden fence of Saint Stanislaus. Well, hell. Trace slowed his steps, knowing the time to demonstrate repentance was at hand.

"Mr. McBride!" Sister Gonzaga called, blue eyes glaring beneath her wimple, her round cheeks flushed with heat or maybe anger. Probably both. "Mr. McBride, we have serious trouble here."

Trace cleared his throat, but before he could speak, Sister Janette Louise asked, "We trust you have heard the news?"

"Yes, ma'am. I'm real sorry about—"

"Sorry isn't good enough, Mr. McBride." Sister Agnes sniffed with disdain. "Those girls of yours are completely out of control!"

Trace set his teeth. He'd about had enough of other folks criticizing his children. It was one thing for him to do it, but quite another for someone else to open their mouth—nun or not. He reached into his pocket and pulled out his wallet. "Listen, Sister, I'll make a nice donation to the church. That should—"

Sister Gonzaga swiped the money from his hand and deposited it in her pocket even as Sister Janette Louise said, "It's the girls we are concerned about, Mr. McBride. These pranks are a cry for help."

"They're crying for something, all right," he grumbled.

"Those girls need female influence in their lives. They need a mother, Mr. McBride."

"They had a mother," Trace snapped. "She's dead."

Sister Janette Louise smiled beatifically. "Dear Maribeth

has told us that their mother died some years ago. You need to put your grieving aside and provide for those sweet little angels."

Grieving? Not likely. "Those sweet little angels stole your horses, Sisters. You have my apologies, and as soon as I'm through with them, you'll have theirs also. Now, if you'll excuse me." He turned to go.

Sister Agnes snorted. "Angels, hah! I wouldn't be surprised to see horns and a tail on any of them. Especially that Maribeth. A dervish in petticoats, that girl is."

Trace shot a look over his shoulder but forced himself to keep his mouth closed. Damn, but he'd like to tell those women off. His daughters were doing fine without a mother. Just fine. He could take care of his own, by God. He could—

Reaching for the door to his home, Trace stopped. Hell. The worst lies were the ones a man told himself.

The girls weren't doing fine. Like a springtime Texas twister, they had cut a swath of mischief a mile wide through the center of town. Even the mayor had stopped by the End of the Line to complain.

Trace heaved a weary sigh. What was he going to do?

*You could send them home. Grandmother would teach them to be ladies.*

Trace closed his eyes as his mouth flattened into a grim line. It's what he should do. It'd be the best thing for them. He could hire someone to take them east, and within a year, his grandmother would have drummed the devilment out of them. Perhaps in time and with her help, his girls could overcome the stigma of being Trace McBride's daughters. Except for that to happen, he'd have to give them up.

*I can't do it. I need them. I can't let them go.*

Besides, he'd be damned before he allowed Katrina within a hundred miles of his dear brother Tye.

He entered the building, his troubles adding weight to his

boots. He hated having to discipline his girls. They'd never believe it, but the giving of these lectures and chores was much worse than the listening and doing. To add insult to injury, all the lectures and chores were proving ineffective. But he couldn't allow these incidents of mischief to continue. Unless he broke them of this habit, one of these days the McBride Menaces would land themselves in serious trouble.

Trace didn't intend to allow that to happen. *But what the hell am I going to do?*

He forced himself to climb the stairs. Jenny Fortune's voice drifted from above, the scolding notes striking an already sore nerve. Who did she think she was? What right did she have to talk that way to his girls?

Trace followed the sound, righteous indignation churning in his gut. He conveniently forgot how she'd befriended his daughters, going so far as to rescue them from the calaboose. He refused to remember all the praises sung by his girls on this woman's behalf.

The woman was trouble. He'd known it for days. Half the time the girls called her MissFortune, running the two words together. Trace thought it a particularly appropriate name.

*Well, before I'm through with her, Miss Jenny Fortune is going to wish she'd damn well kept her nose out of my family business.*

He prepared to enter the parlor with both barrels blasting, but the sight that met his eyes upon reaching the room unloaded the words from his mouth. His daughters, all three of them, sat perched on the settee, their hands clasped in their laps.

They gazed up at Jenny Fortune, their expressions brimming with repentance.

They had never, ever, looked that way at him. Not even when he had them scrubbing the inside of the fireplace. Witnessing such a look here and now served to edge his temper right on up past boiling.

How did she do it? What had the woman said to get through to his daughters? No one had noticed his arrival, so Trace decided to listen a minute and maybe learn what magic the modiste possessed. The delay might just stop him from killing someone. He crossed his arms, leaned against the doorframe, and silently fumed.

"You are right, Miss Fortune," Emma said. "I guess we never looked at it that way before. We *do* want to be ladies, it's just that we don't know how. Papa tries; he truly does. But he isn't good with girl things. I'd never have finished my sampler if you hadn't taught me."

Maribeth piped up in defense of her father. "True, but Papa taught us to play poker. That's better than silly old embroidery anytime."

Trace nodded smugly until he noticed Emma and Jenny Fortune sharing one of those knowing-women looks. A pang of emotion gripped his chest and time seemed to stop. *Emmie's growing up so fast.* He hadn't really noticed before. His little girl was becoming a young lady and there wasn't anything he could do to stop it. A near silent groan escaped him as another thought occurred.

Monthlies. Oh, Lord. How the hell was he going to handle that?

When he tuned back into the conversation, Jenny was speaking. "...can see practicing arithmetic skills by playing poker. Certainly it's a novel approach. But what you girls must learn is that some things are simply not appropriate endeavors for young ladies. Hiding horses from nuns most definitely falls in that category." She tugged a chair near the settee and sat down beside them, an imploring note in her voice as she spoke. "Oh, girls, you touch a special place in my heart. I see so much of myself in you."

Katrina took her thumb out of her mouth long enough to say, "It's 'cause our eyes are mirrors. Sister Agnes told me that."

Maribeth snorted. "That's not what she meant, goose. She was saying our souls are mean 'cause we were giving her the evil eye when she took away our cards."

The evil eye? Trace thought.

"The evil eye?" Jenny asked. "Oh, dear." Then she shook her head and said, "What I meant is that I understand what it's like not to have a mother to teach you feminine skills."

"But you have a mother," Emma interrupted. "We've met her. She's beautiful!"

"Yes," Jenny said with a sigh. "But she's an artist and they are very different. It's almost like your father teaching you poker. I'm afraid my mother taught me a number of skills, but not many of them are proper for a girl who wishes to be a lady."

"Papa says we're ladies," Maribeth said. "He lots of times calls us his little ladies."

"That's good." Jenny reached up and smoothed a gentle hand over Maribeth's hair. "But you see, a woman cannot just say she's a lady and be one. She must act like a lady." That scolding note reentered her voice as she added, "Stealing from the mercantile and playing pranks on unsuspecting people are not the actions of a lady."

"But how do we learn?" Emma asked, gazing tearfully up at Jenny. "The housekeepers Papa hires are too busy cooking and cleaning to teach us anything."

Maribeth groaned. "Who wants to learn anything from them, anyway. They're all—"

"Mari…" Jenny warned.

Katrina said. "I want you to be our teacher, Miss Fortune. I want you to be my mama. Except you can't cry anymore. I don't like it when you cry."

*I want you to be my mama.* The sentence ricocheted in Trace's mind like a slug from a Colt .45. Guilt bubbled in its wake, and as the woman reached out to wrap Katrina in a hug,

Trace reacted with heated, almost savage fury. He marched into the parlor, demanding, "Jenny Fortune, what the hell have you done to my daughters?"

*It is bad luck to spin a chair around on one leg.*


## CHAPTER FOUR


JENNY'S MOUTH dropped open in shock. Twisting in her seat, she gazed up at Trace McBride, noting in a glance the irate set of his mouth and the furious rage in his eyes. He charged into the room like an angry bull—big and powerful and intent on doing damage—and Jenny had the notion to run for cover. Instead, she drew herself up straight, lifted her chin, and fixed him with a chilly look. "I beg your pardon?"

He halted in the center of the parlor, his hands braced on his hips. His gaze swept over his daughters before settling on her, and the picture in Jenny's mind altered from angry bull to predatory wolf.

"It is not your place to scold my girls. They are *my* responsibility." Trace thumped his chest with his thumb. "*My* concern."

A few choice replies regarding responsibility and concern hovered on her tongue, but she bit them back. The man was obviously overwrought. Understandably, she thought, considering his daughters had been ensconced in the local jail. Taking his worries into account, Jenny was inclined to give him the benefit of the doubt.

Then he opened his mouth again.

Clipping his words, Trace said, "And I'll thank you, Miss Fortune, to refrain from putting ridiculous notions into their heads."

"Ridiculous notions?" she repeated, defensiveness creating a rise in her voice.

The cords in his neck strained as he shouted, *"You are not their mother!"*

His words echoed in the sudden silence.

That does it, Jenny thought. How could she ever have found this pigheaded, unappreciative man attractive? She pushed to her feet, saying, "You are correct, Mr. McBride, I am not the girls' mother. *My* daughters would have the benefit of sufficient supervision so as to avoid landing themselves in the city jail on a summer afternoon."

Hands on hips, she walked toward him as she stated, *"My* daughters would enjoy the benefits of effective discipline. *My* daughters would have been taught to act like proper ladies, and *my* daughters would not have learned to use the love I feel for them to wrap me around their mischievous little fingers!"

Emma gasped and Maribeth muttered grumpily as Jenny halted a few short feet from the man. She defiantly held his gaze, waiting for his attack. In his eyes she saw fury and something else, some brittle emotion she couldn't name.

Then Katrina's innocent little voice filled the moment. "Oh, MissFortune, I wish I were your little girl. I want a mama so very bad."

Trace swayed as if he'd been struck, and in the instant before he closed his eyes, Jenny identified the feeling she was seeing in their depths. Grief. Overwhelming, all consuming, grief.

Poor man. He must have loved his wife so deeply.

At that realization, a tide of compassion for Trace and for

his dear little Menaces washed away her anger. Jenny drew a deep breath, licked her lips, and said in a low, even voice, "If I have overstepped my bounds with Emma, Maribeth, and Katrina, then I apologize, Mr. McBride. Let me assure you, however, that I have never intended to offer them more than my friendship."

When he looked at her again, his stare was empty. He remained silent as she nodded first at him and then the girls before turning to make a dignified exit from the parlor.

The last remnants of Trace's anger faded along with the click of the dressmaker's steps against the stairs. She had hit it on the nose. He was handling his girls all wrong. They needed something he wasn't giving them and that had to change.

The thought sneaked in like an unwelcome guest. *They need a mother.*

Trace set his teeth against the vicious curse that burst from his very heart. There had to be another way. He'd be damned if he'd marry again to provide the girls a mother.

*Right, McBride, as if you aren't damned already for what you did to the one they had.*

He looked at his daughters, and the disapproval in their gazes laid him even lower. Emma heaved a sigh. Maribeth shook her head and said, "You treated Miss Fortune worse than Kat treats her peas."

"I smush my peas," Katrina said seriously. "I don't like peas. You shouldn't have hollered at Miss Fortune. I'm 'barrassed."

Great. Wonderful. Trace heard the front door bang shut and felt a bit bare-assed himself.

Emma stood and walked to the parlor window, pushing back the curtains. As she gazed down into the street, her teeth nibbled worriedly at her lower lip. Then she said, "You'll have to apologize, Papa. That's the only way."

Trace dragged his attention away from Jenny Fortune. His

Menaces were trying to do it to him again—manipulation by way of distraction. This time he wouldn't let it happen. "Whoa, there, girls. Let's back this buckboard right on up. I don't believe the dressmaker is the issue here." He quirked a finger at Emma. "Sit back down, Emmaline Suzanne."

As his eldest hastened to do as instructed, he allowed the anger he felt over his daughters' criminal capers to show in his expression. Gratified to see the uneasy looks they exchanged, he questioned, "Did you really believe I'd forget my little girls had taken to stealing? Did you think it'd slip my mind that you landed yourselves in the calaboose?"

Emma and Maribeth shared a look. Kat popped her thumb in her mouth, her eyes round and worried.

"Nuns, for goodness' sakes!" he exclaimed, throwing out his hands. "You stole from nuns! What kind of daughters am I raising?"

After a quick glance at her sisters, Emma lifted her chin and shrugged. "Maybe we've made a few mistakes, Papa, but we haven't done anything you haven't done before."

"What!"

Emma smoothed the skirt of her yellow gingham dress, every inch the young lady as she said, "We've listened to your bedtime stories all our lives, Papa. The ones about the mischief you used to make when you were growing up. During the day when we're here alone and wishing for something to do, we remember all the fun you had. We're just taking after you."

Trace was flabbergasted. As the father of the McBride Menaces, he'd listened to more than his share of nonsense. This bit, however, blew the meringue right off the pie. "I never stole horses from any nuns!"

"You swiped a pig from a preacher," Maribeth noted matter-of-factly.

Katrina nodded quickly and took her thumb from her

mouth long enough to add, "Horses are easier to catch than pigs, Papa. We decided. They don't make bridles for pigs."

Bridles for pigs. What he needed were bridles for three young girls. Trace hung his head, rubbing the bridge of his nose with thumb and forefinger. He'd never have guessed that repeating the tales of his youthful escapades could cause this much trouble. Those stories had become one of the little rituals between them as they traveled. The girls had always begged for stories, and once they wore out the pages of the storybook he'd carried from home, he'd taken to repeating instances of his past.

Besides, he'd missed his family something fierce. His brother's name flashed in his mind and he corrected himself. He'd missed most of his family, not all of it. Talking about them to the girls had sometimes helped to dull the ache. He never guessed they would mimic his mischief. Why, none of his sisters would ever have dreamed of tagging along on one of the boys' escapades; they wouldn't have wanted to get their dainty little hands dirty.

Of course, Grandmother would have nagged them silly if they had. After the death of her eldest son and his wife in a carriage accident, Mirabelle McBride's main goal in life appeared to have been teaching her granddaughters how to be prissy. He and Tye had often complained....

Trace set his jaw, furious at the thought. That was twice within the span of a minute the name had popped into his mind. It had to stop. His brother was dead to him, had been since that bloody night in Charleston. He wouldn't allow him into his thoughts.

*If I can't bury him for real, I can at least bury him in my mind.*

So done, Trace lifted his gaze and studied his girls, one after the other. Only on Emma's face did he see any evidence at all of prissy. Did they need it? Was it important? He scowled. So what if his grandmother had spent so much time on it? His girls would be all right without it. Surely. He didn't necessarily like that feminine trait anyway.

Trace felt better until he recalled that every last one of his prissy sisters had grown up to marry well and happily.

"What are you going to do to us, Papa?" Maribeth asked, portraying her normal impatience.

Angrier now and not certain why, Trace's glower deepened. Not a one of the girls appeared the least bit repentant for their actions. Apprehensive, yes. As well they should be. They had to know their punishment would be severe for this particular prank.

But damn, he hated to do it. Sure as shootin', they would turn those puppy-dog eyes his way and make him feel even worse than he already did. It happened that way every time, and nothing could get to him quicker. If they had a mother—

*Damn. I won't think that way. I won't.*

"What am I going to do to you?" he repeated, beginning to pace the room. "Well, I reckon that's a good question." He didn't have a clue, actually. The girls had already cleaned the place from top to bottom. He'd have to get creative with his punishment. He rubbed the back of his neck, saying, "If your Miss Fortune hadn't stepped in, I'd have left y'all in jail."

Maribeth looked at Emma and rolled her eyes.

Trace set his teeth. He didn't scare them one little bit. Maybe it was time to see if someone else could put the fear of God into them. "As it is, I reckon I'll turn you over to the folks most inconvenienced by your actions."

It took a moment for Emma and Maribeth to catch on. When they did, Emma murmured, "Oh," and hung her head. Maribeth cried, "Aw, Papa, you can't!"

He smiled. "C'mon, girls. It's time to pay a visit to Sister Gonzaga."

THE PACKAGE on the shelf was wrapped in plain brown paper but tied with hair ribbons in nine different colors. Next to it sat a dress box containing a young woman's gown made of calico, designed with a careful eye and sewn with loving stitches. Today was Emma McBride's birthday.

Jenny hadn't seen the girls except in passing for the past ten days, ever since the clash with their father upstairs. "Talk about Town" reported that their time was divided between the Catholic and Baptist churches, doing odd jobs and for the most part staying out of trouble. She hoped for Mr. McBride's sake that was true. He'd certainly appeared at the end of his patience when he stormed into the parlor that memorable afternoon.

She could empathize with the feeling. She was reaching the end of her own patience with the superstitious citizens of Fort Worth.

With every day that passed, the outlook for Fortune's Design grew bleaker. Nothing she tried made a difference. She'd cut her prices and placed an advertisement in the *Democrat* to alert customers to the change. She'd had broadsides printed and passed out to people on the streets. She'd attended every pie supper, quilting bee, and church social in town, but no one appeared willing to take the risk of wearing a Jenny Fortune design.

Her gaze drifted to the ribbon-wrapped box. Except for Trace McBride, that is. He had not canceled his order for Emma's dress. Neither had the Widow Sperry, bless her soul.

Jenny had work to do today because of that kind lady. The last order on her book was a cool-weather dress in black bombazine. Rilda Bea Sperry, an elderly woman whose wealth was the direct result of having married and buried four husbands, had scoffed at the idea of being felled by bad luck if she patronized Fortune's Design. As she happily proclaimed while ordering the gown, what some perceived as bad luck, others knew to be a windfall. Jenny wished Fort Worth had more people like her.

Before the latest Bailey bride's mishap and the subsequent

mention of the Bad Luck Wedding Dress in the *Democrat*, Jenny had been forced to turn away work. Nowadays if her shop's welcome bell rang at all it was more likely a gust of wind than a customer. Even the McBride girls hadn't shown their faces inside the store since the trouble with the nuns' horses.

The McBride girls. Jenny wondered how the drama upstairs had ended. Their father had been so upset, so angry. She'd have changed her opinion of the man entirely had she not seen his concern for his daughters and sensed his grief for his wife. It must be exceedingly difficult for a man to raise three daughters alone. Look at all the trouble her own father had encountered, and there had been only one of her.

She fluffed out the bombazine, eyed the length of hem yet to be sewn, then resumed her stitching. She really shouldn't try to compare Trace McBride and her father. The saloon-keeper wasn't anything like Richard Fortune.

*Lucky for the McBride girls.*

Jenny dropped her needle at the mean-spirited thought. Guilt rolled over her in waves. Richard Fortune wasn't a bad father, not at all. He simply expended so much energy on his science and her mother—the two great loves of his life—that there wasn't a lot left over for his daughter. She understood; she truly did.

There wasn't a doubt in Jenny's mind that her father cared deeply for her. He always wanted what was best for her. Why, the argument that had led to her parents' second divorce had begun as a disagreement over her education. And he wouldn't be insisting she return to Thicket Glen if he didn't care.

And yet he did it all from a distance. For all of the love they shared, she and her father had never quite bridged the space between them. She'd wanted hugs and he'd patted her head, when he remembered she was around.

Trace McBride hugged his girls all the time.

Jenny sighed in self-disgust as she put the final stitch in the dress hem, then reached for her scissors and snipped the thread. She shouldn't indulge in uncharitable thoughts. It was selfish of her to wish she had a father who was more...demonstrative. Someone like Mr. McBride.

An image shimmered in her mind, she and Trace McBride, his actions demonstrative and not at all fatherly.

"Jenny Fortune!" she exclaimed, slamming her scissors against the worktable. She began yanking pins from the bombazine's hem and stabbing them into the pin cushion. These fantasies involving her and that man popped into her mind with disturbing frequency. What had gotten into her lately? Her thoughts had become downright, well, lusty.

It must be the wedding dress. All her other problems could be laid at its skirt—the wedding dress's skirt and her mother's mouth, that is. She couldn't quite forget the idea of wearing that gown at her own nuptials or the embarrassing talk about the delights of lost virginity.

But even if she seriously entertained her mother's idea, Trace McBride wouldn't do for a groom. She'd tried to flirt and failed. The man simply didn't like her.

She might be her mother's daughter, but she feared she took after her father when it came to matters of the heart. Clumsy was the word that came to mind.

Swiping at a pin in frustration, Jenny managed to drive the point into her palm. "Ow!" She lifted her hand to her mouth, silently cursing her carelessness. Clumsy. It should be her middle name.

Just then, the bell sounded and she looked up. Trace McBride's emerald eyes gleamed. His mouth quirked in a roguish smile as he looked at her and said, "You want me to do that for you? I'm awfully good at kissin' away ouches."

*Oh, goodness.* The temperature in the room went up a good ten degrees.

Jenny gawked speechlessly as Trace's daughters filed in behind him. She was struggling to find a reply when the odor hit her, bringing tears to her eyes. "What in the world?" she said, trying not to breathe.

Emma's look was sheepish, Katrina's unconcerned. Maribeth offered a feminine replica of her father's mischievous grin. "We've been working in the sisters' stable. Papa said we were expert at mucking things up, we ought to try mucking something out."

Katrina added, "But we're all done now, Miss Fortune. It's Emma's birthday, and we gets to go swimmin'. We want you to come with us."

"Papa allowed me to choose." Emma's eyes shone. "He's taking the whole afternoon and night off from work, and I got to pick to do whatever I wanted. It's swimming and a picnic, Miss Fortune, and you have to come or else it won't be perfect."

Maribeth nodded. "It has to be perfect. Today's her birthday."

Jenny's eyes were beginning to water at the smell. "Swimming?" she asked doubtfully.

"And a picnic," the girls all said at once.

Trace's voice was an intriguing combination of challenge and amusement. "We've found us a nice, safe swimming hole just a short ride from town. We'd like you to join us, Miss Fortune. I figure that if you have trouble accepting my apology for my less-than-gentlemanly behavior last time we spoke, you can always push me into the creek."

THE SUN BORE DOWN mercilessly upon the occupants of the buggy heading northwest out of town. The heat during August was miserable as a rule and this summer was no exception. Not a breath of air stirred the leaves of the oak trees that stretched across the lazy waters of Quail Creek.

The girls led the way along the familiar path to where a curve in the creek created a pool perfect for swimming. Trace toted a picnic basket and a tapestry satchel containing changes of clothing.

Jenny Fortune carried a pair of blankets.

Despite his best intentions, Trace's gaze dropped to the gentle sway of her skirts as she followed his chattering daughters toward the swimming hole. She hadn't wanted to come along. Some of her excuses had been silly, some of them inspired. None of them had worked. The girls had chewed on her like pups on a steak bone, and eventually the dressmaker had given in.

For the first time in weeks Trace was glad of his daughters' cussed stubbornness. He needed to deal with the dressmaker on his own terms, and Emma's birthday outing was his first effort in that regard. At the reminder, he tore his gaze from the dressmaker's skirts.

After the confrontation in his parlor, he'd devoted some thought to the situation that, like it or not, had landed in his lap. His girls had developed an affection for Jenny Fortune, one she apparently returned. He'd been too late in catching on to the developing relationship to do anything to prevent it, and experience had taught him that short of locking the Menaces in their room—which probably wouldn't work worth a damn anyway—he'd be wasting his time trying to put a stop to it at this late date. Moving into the house wouldn't likely solve the problem now. Trace knew without a doubt they'd find a way to visit the woman.

At that point he realized he'd have to make this connection between his daughters and Miss Fortune work for him. Working for him meant putting the boot to this mother talk and to the unsettling effect Miss Fortune was having on his senses.

The dressmaker got prettier every time he saw her. That business over the girls had made it even worse. Throwing all that sass in his direction had caused her eyes to shine, her cheeks to glow, and that bountiful bosom to lift in an admirable way. Ever since the skirmish he'd had a devil of a time forcing the image from his mind.

So he'd bent his mind to the task of developing a strategy on how to deal with Miss Jenny Fortune. Once he realized that she'd not become a problem for him until he allowed her to cross that mental line between business and personal, Trace had known what tack to take. He'd made the first move by allowing the girls to invite the woman along on the birthday celebration. Before they left Quail Creek this evening, he intended to have the job done and the problem of Jenny Fortune solved.

"Miss Fortune," Emma called, glancing over her shoulder. She gestured toward a patch of grass nestled among a collection of flat rocks lining the creek bank. "This is where we usually spread the blankets. Papa can sit here and watch us all while we're swimming. Katrina plays where it's shallow off to the left, while Mari and I swim where it's deeper over on the right."

Katrina turned round, solemn eyes toward Jenny. "I like the shallow best, but I know how to swim where it's deep," she said. "Little Louise Who Is An Angel couldn't swim and so Papa made sure to teach us all first thing."

"Oh, I see," Jenny replied, her questioning look toward Trace showing that she didn't see at all.

He explained. "The girls had a cousin who drowned. I want them to know how to handle themselves in any situation. In fact, I'm hoping we'll have the chance to talk about that for a bit this afternoon."

"Talk about swimming?"

"No, I was thinking more along the lines of quilting bees."

"You've lost me, Mr. McBride."

He gave her a slow, easy smile. "No, Miss Fortune, I think I've found you."

Jenny's heart fluttered at the look. Of course, it had been in near constant quiver since Trace McBride sauntered into Fortune's Design a little over an hour ago. The man confused her. She'd rented shop space from him for months, and in all of that time, he'd never acted the least bit interested in her as a woman.

Firmly, Jenny dismissed the speculations. She probably just imagined the heat in his eyes. She obviously read meanings he didn't intend into the words he spoke. One more silly idea, that's all it was. Funny how a single little intimation by her mother had managed to put all of these suggestions in her mind.

Intimations. Intimate. Oh, goodness.

Jenny focused her attention on the girls as she spread the blankets where Emma had indicated. Giggling and frolicking about, they stripped to their shifts and made a beeline for the water. The resulting splash sent droplets of water raining down on Jenny and Trace.

"That feels good," she said, smiling as she wiped the wetness from her cheeks.

"Yeah. It's hot enough to wither a fence post, all right. I imagine you'll get to wishing you'd brought that swimming costume of yours after all."

Jenny shrugged and reached for her parasol. She wasn't about to try and explain why the idea of an innocent swim with the McBride family sounded so wicked. "I'm content to be away from town, Mr. McBride. The herd fording the Trinity today is extra large, and I can't say that's my favorite time to be in Fort Worth. The noise, the dust."

"The smell."

"Yes, there is that." She grinned ruefully and added, "Although the ride out here wasn't exactly a perfumer's delight."

Trace nodded as he settled himself on one of the blankets, his long legs stretched out in front of him. "They did stink something fierce. I still can't figure how Mari managed to get that mess behind her ears. You were a good sport about it, Miss Fortune, and I appreciate it. I'm afraid I couldn't see making them go through the effort of bathing when we were headed toward the swimming hole."

Jenny smiled, and because she needed something to do, artfully arranged her skirts. She put up a valiant struggle to ignore the way his clothing outlined the rugged length of his body as he reached down to tug off his boots, but in the end, she failed.

That annoyed her. It was all her mother's fault. She'd never noticed Trace McBride until her mother had mentioned lust. *Liar,* her conscience declared.

All right, so she'd noticed him. Quite a lot, in fact. But not near as much as now. Now she couldn't seem to *stop* noticing him.

He called out cautious instructions to his daughters, then looked at her and said, "Don't be shy about getting your feet wet, Miss Fortune. I wouldn't want you to get overheated." He yanked off his socks and wiggled his toes, then proceeded to roll up the bottoms of his trousers to midcalf.

Jenny thought the temperature must have gone up ten degrees again. She dug in her bag for her fan, flipped it open, and waved it in front of her face. "I knew I shouldn't have come," she grumbled beneath her breath.

He must have the hearing of an owl, because he looked at her and remarked, "You didn't stand a chance against them, you know. Once those girls decided they wanted you at Emma's birthday do, they were willing to do anything and everything to make certain you'd accept."

Exasperation filled Jenny at his words. "They shouldn't have that power. I shouldn't have allowed them to manipulate me that way. For that matter, neither should you. At risk of treading on a sensitive subject yet again, I fear I must advise you to teach your daughters a modicum of control."

"Modicum of control," he repeated, nodding thoughtfully. "I do like the sound of that. Tell me, Miss Fortune. How do you propose I go about it?"

Just then, Katrina's feet slipped out from under her, and she fell hard against the creek bottom. Jenny started forward immediately, but Trace laid a hand against her arm. "You all right, Katie-cat?"

She sat in no more than a foot of water. "I can't decide if I should cry or not."

"Does it hurt?"

"Not really."

"Then why would you want to cry?"

"'Cause I want you to come play with me, and I know you will if I cry."

"You know I'll come play with you anyway. I always do, don't I?"

"Uh-huh."

"So what's the fuss?"

"I want Miss Fortune to come play, too. I don't know about her. Would it be better if I cry?"

Trace turned to Jenny. "Modicum of control, right? No more manipulation. I'd love a demonstration, Miss Fortune."

It was a challenge that struck at the core of her beliefs. Pulling away from his touch, Jenny gave him a significant look and nodded. Then she glanced at Katrina. "Come here, sweetheart. I'd like to talk with you."

"Are we going to play?"

"That's what we are going to talk about."

The older girls paddled toward the bank and Katrina stood and sloshed her way over to Jenny, who gestured for the child to sit in her lap.

"She'll get you all wet," warned Maribeth.

"I won't melt. I'm not sugar."

"I don't know about that," Trace observed in a wry tone.

Katrina plopped into Jenny's lap and spoke around the thumb she stuck in her mouth. "I'm here, MissFortune."

"Good. I want to ask you a question. Do your sisters ever try to trick you?"

She nodded. "Lots of times."

"Are they sneaky when they do it?"

"Uh-huh."

"Do you like it when they trick you?"

Beneath her dark brown bangs her little brow furrowed. "No. It makes my lip go bloop."

Jenny leaned away from the child, a confused smile on her face. "Makes your lip go bloop?"

Katrina demonstrated by sticking out her lower lip. "Bloop is what my daddy calls it."

Biting the inside of her cheek to prevent the laugh that threatened, Jenny risked a sidelong glance at Trace. He winked and she felt it clear to her toes.

"I see. Well. Bloop it is then." Jenny shifted Katrina's weight and soon felt a wet chill seep through the layers of cloth dividing them. "So, here's another question. Don't you think that pretending to cry to get me to come play with you would be the same as tricking me? You tricking me is not a lot different than your sisters tricking you."

Katrina's eyes went wide. "Did I make your lip bloop, MissFortune?"

Jenny displayed a pout and nodded.

"I'm very sorry."

"I accept your apology, Katrina. Just try not to act that way again, all right? Adults call it manipulation, and it's not a nice way to treat others. Will you try to remember that?"

Katrina nodded. "I promise."

Jenny smiled warmly and lifted the girl to her feet. "Good. Now, run play. Maybe you can find some frogs to chase."

"Let's do that," Maribeth chimed in. "We could catch 'em and have races. We did that last spring, y'all remember?"

"Yuck." Emma wrinkled her nose and splashed water at her sisters. They retaliated, and soon the air was filled with the sound of their squeals and laughter.

Trace turned to Jenny. "I have to hand it to you. You knew just what to say, Miss Fortune. I'm impressed."

Jenny lifted her chin, accepting her due, as a part deep inside of her basked in the warmth of his approval.

"That never happens to me, you know," he continued, idly reaching to pluck a straw from the grass. He stuck the end in his mouth and chewed it thoughtfully, never taking his gaze from his daughters who were now busily hunting frogs. "You were right the other day, carrying on so about my letting the girls run roughshod over me."

"That's not exactly what I said." Jenny frowned, not liking the way he made her sound almost shrewish. She hadn't carried on. Not really.

"Problem is, I don't know what to do different." In a graceful, fluid movement, he stood, the motion attracting Jenny's gaze to the rugged flex of muscles beneath the white cotton shirt and dark trousers. He tossed away the straw he'd been chewing and added, "It's a hard job for a man to parent all by himself."

His words struck a sympathetic chord inside of Jenny. It hadn't been easy for her father, either. How many times had Richard Fortune admitted to wishing Monique were around to help manage problems that arose between father and daughter?

Before she could frame a reply, Trace called out, "Hey, you little tadpoles, quit pestering those poor frogs." After rolling the legs of his trousers even higher to just below the knees, he stepped into the water and rumbled in a threatening tone, "You have bigger game to worry about now."

That, to Jenny's surprise, elicited a trio of high-pitched squeals.

"It's the Giant Throw-Fish!" Katrina gasped, bringing her hands dramatically to her chest. The very picture of fear, she ruined the effect by bursting into giggles as her father made a roaring lunge in her direction.

What followed was a game of such joyous abandon that Jenny got a lump in her throat just watching. He launched them one after the other, roaring out monstrous threats amidst their squeals of delight. Within minutes he was as soaked as his daughters, and Jenny wondered why he had even bothered to roll up his pants. She resisted the girls' entreaties to join in the game, despite the fact that the wetter their father became, the hotter Jenny felt.

He called for a break in the action and stood, hands on hips, his chest rising and falling as he worked to catch his breath following the exertion of their play. Watching him, Jenny was reminded of one of her mother's sculptures. The beauty of the human form. Man at his peak. Perfection.

Only Trace McBride was no artwork made of clay, but a living, breathing man.

She imagined her hands acting the sculptress, sliding over shoulders and down the corded planes of his back. Molding themselves against the ripple of muscle....

Heat flushed her cheeks and she gratefully shifted her gaze when Katrina called her name. "Yes?"

"Come play with us. Please, MissFortune?" Katrina begged.

"Yeah, Miss Fortune. We'd love for you to come play." Noting the look that accompanied Trace's words, Jenny wouldn't have been surprised to see the creek go to steaming.

"Not now, Katrina," she said, trying unsuccessfully to look away from Trace's blatant gaze. Had he guessed what she was thinking? Did he sense the wanton turn her thoughts had taken? He watched her closely, seeming to read her very soul, and a tingle crept up her spine. Mortification, she told herself. "I don't want to get my dress wet."

"It's already wet." He chuckled softly and took a step toward her.

Jenny stood and backed away.

Maribeth called, "Come on, Miss Fortune!"

"What do you know, Maria-berri." Trace's mouth lifted in a slow grin. Another challenge. "I think Miss Fortune might just be...afraid of the Giant Throw-Fish."

Tension charged the air between them. Jenny suddenly wanted to fight, to fight Trace McBride and these feelings he brought to life inside her. Lifting her chin, she smiled and threw his challenge right back at him. "Afraid? I hardly think so. I happen to know that Giant Throw-Fish are nothing to fear."

Emma shook her head in warning. "Uh-oh. You shouldn't have said that, Miss Fortune."

Although Jenny's concentration was fixed on Trace, she could see Maribeth and Emma off to one side, sharing a grin, their eyes gleaming. Think this is funny, do they? Ornery little girls, in some ways they were just like their father. He had now arched a brow and was smiling more like a shark than a make-believe fish.

"Nothing to fear? Oh, really?" He took another step.

"Really."

"And why is that?"

Jenny decided the McBrides were all too smug for their own good. So, now that he'd moved to within her reach, she boldly lifted her hand and removed the limp weed clinging to his shirt. Tossing it back into the water, she said sweetly, "Because, it's a well-known fact that throw-fish are always on their best behavior around ladies."

Humor, and something warmer, flashed in his eyes. "What does that have to do with you, Miss Fortune?"

"Are you inferring that I am not a lady, Mr. Giant Throw-Fish?"

"Not in the least," he replied, a husky note to his voice.

"You are every inch the lady, Miss Fortune, but I'm afraid you are mistaken about throw-fish. Ladies tend to get beneath their gills, so to speak. Throw-fish need to prove just who rules the stream."

Making the move she had anticipated, Trace McBride grabbed for her. Jenny gave an exultant laugh as she employed a move taught to her by one of her mother's cousins. Shifting her weight, she turned her body and used Trace's own momentum against him to throw him over her shoulder.

His yell changed to a gurgle as he landed with a splash in the clear, cool waters of Quail Creek.

*If you forget something and have to go
back in the house, sit down and count to
ten or you will have bad luck.*

## CHAPTER FIVE

TRACE CAME UP SPUTTERING.

Somehow he'd gotten a mouthful of silt. Treading water, he spat out the metallic-tasting mud, then rinsed his mouth. He barely heard his daughters' gasps and giggles, as both his gaze and attention remained focused on Jenny Fortune.

Her sun-kissed hair was a tumble of lost pins and loosened braid, her complexion a triumphant rose. She calmly dusted her palms, her blue eyes shining, her mouth lifted in a smug grin. She was a self-satisfied imp, proud of her victory.

And desire roared through Trace like a summer storm. *Ah, Jenny Fortune, how did I ever think of you as plain?*

But on the heels of desire came displeasure. What the hell had he been thinking, baiting her like that? He'd brought the woman along on this outing for the express purpose of establishing a business relationship. Instead, like a cake short on leavening, he'd fallen to the dressmaker's heated looks.

They had been scorchers. Twin blue flames that inched across his skin, kindling a corresponding heat within him everywhere they touched. Who'd have thought it of prim and proper Miss Fortune? In fact, what the hell had happened to prim and proper Miss Fortune? He wished she'd come back. Quickly.

He cleared his throat and said the first thing that came to his tongue. "Didn't have you pegged for feisty, Miss Fortune."

"Feisty? I don't know that I agree to the term." She dipped to lift her parasol from the blanket. "I simply decided to take you up on your invitation."

"My invitation?"

"To push you in the creek."

"Oh, I see." He recalled his quip that accompanied his invitation this afternoon—accept his apology or toss him in the creek. Ten bucks said she'd only remembered it herself after he went in the drink. "Does this mean you don't accept my apology?"

"No. It means I seldom refuse a challenge. It's one of the few traits shared by both my parents, so it runs quite strong in me, I'm afraid."

"Really?" He swam to the shallow part of the creek and sloshed his way toward Jenny. "I reckon that's good under the circumstances."

Wariness shone in her eyes, but her reply was interrupted as the girls found their voices. "Papa," Katrina said, giggling, "you looked so silly. Your eyes went as big as a bullfrog's."

In a voice filled with wonder, Maribeth asked, "How did you do that, Miss Fortune? You flipped him right over your shoulder."

"You have a clump of leaves on your head, Papa," Emma pointed out.

Trace brushed the mess from his hair, paying scant attention to Jenny's explanation of how a cousin of her mother's, a circus acrobat and clown visiting for a time in Texas, had taught her a few tumbling tricks and throws. It was time to get down to business. Past time, considering the provocative looks Jenny Fortune had been throwing along with everything else. When a woman like her got to watching a man like that, her mind invariably went to thinking weddings and bridal gifts. That would never do.

*Be honest, McBride, you're doing a bit of the same kind of looking, yourself.*

Trace watched her laughing with his daughters and did his best to ignore both the beauty of such a picture and his conscience. His success in getting her to talk to Kat about manipulation had set the scene well for his proposition. Now it was time to get the job done.

When he reached the satchel lying beside the blanket he fumbled inside for the bar of soap. He had a sudden mental image of his hands all slicked up and slippery assisting Miss Fortune in her bath.

Damn. This had to stop. Otherwise he was making a serious mistake. Surely this problem would go away once he actually hired the woman for the job. After he had shoved Miss Fortune back across that mental dividing line between business and personal, certainly his mind would leave her there.

*Keep talking, McBride. You might convince yourself by next spring.*

Disgusted, he tossed the bar of soap to Emma, saying, "Enough laughing at your Pa, you three. I know it's been fun, but my pride can't take anymore. Besides, it's time to get cleaned up and dried off. My stomach is telling me it's nearly suppertime, and I have a notion Emma might be wanting her presents."

He glanced at Jenny. "I'll go after wood for a fire if you'll keep an eye on them while they bathe."

She nodded her consent, and he started up the path that led away from the swimming hole. Just before he disappeared behind a clump of honeysuckle vine, he turned back and said,

"I like the way you talk to my poor, motherless Menaces, Miss Fortune. You know when to laugh and when to be serious. If they were in your care, I imagine you could teach them to be ladies. You would make them a terrific—" he paused as if searching for the proper word, then finished "—teacher."

Jenny watched him disappear from sight, her heart pounding, her breathing shallow and fast. In a daze, she looked toward the children sharing a bar of soap as they lathered away any clinging remnants of the day's labor in the stables.

*Poor, motherless Menaces. You could teach them. Make them a terrific...teacher.*

Her knees felt weak. Something about the way he had looked. The light she had seen in his eyes. The way he hesitated before completing his sentence. She thought he'd had another word in mind. Not *teacher.*

*Mother.*

Could it be? Did he want her to be a mother to his children? Would Trace McBride ask her to be his wife?

Surely not. None of her problems were ever solved so easily.

Besides, was marrying Trace McBride even something she wanted? What about Fortune's Design? Was he the type of man to tolerate a working wife?

Jenny simply didn't know.

Having removed her shoes and stockings and knotted her skirts to just below her knees, Jenny waded into the shallow waters of Quail Creek to help Trace's daughters wash their hair. Her mind half on the task, half on her musings, she worked lavender-scented lather through Maribeth's auburn curls.

She was being silly, surely. How desperate she had become, reading marriage into his innocent remark. The jump in logic was indefensible. He wasn't about to ask for her hand. Why, he'd never once come courting.

She paused, staring at the soap bubbles clinging to her fingers. Unless that's what today was all about.

"Miss Fortune, aren't you done yet?"

Jenny nodded absently and stooped to rinse her hands. No, today was Emma's birthday. She had been invited to attend the celebration at the girls' request. Hadn't she?

"Emma, I want to thank you for inviting me to join you on this special day. Since it is your birthday, I assume it was your idea?"

Emma had washed her hair without assistance. Seated in clean, dry clothes on a nearby flat rock, she combed tangles from her curls. "No," she replied. "Actually, it was Papa's idea to invite you, but I was ever so happy when he suggested it. We've been so busy being in trouble lately, we've hardly had the chance to see you."

Their father's suggestion? Jenny was shocked. What did it mean?

She'd best mull that one over. In the meantime, the youngest McBride looked to need some help. "Katrina, you're about to get soap in your eyes. May I help you?"

"Please." The girl sloshed into position in front of Jenny, who briskly rubbed the bar of soap. This job required extra suds. Little Kat's hair was even dirtier than her sister's.

Jenny tried to put any speculation about their father's motives from her mind as she scrubbed the young girl's scalp. She hummed beneath her breath as she worked. Of the three sisters, Katrina's hair was closest in color to her father's. Dark and wavy, it was thick and smooth as silk. Jenny dreamily wondered if Trace's would feel the same.

Her cheeks flushed from embarrassment. Silly ideas. Her mind was filled with them. Perhaps she should dunk her head and wash away these thoughts herself.

"I'm hungry. I can't wait to eat," Maribeth declared. "Papa packed the best birthday basket, even down to Emma's favorite dessert."

"And he brought plates, too," Katrina added, laying her

hands atop Jenny's in an effort to participate in the washing of her hair. "We don't normally bring plates on our picnics. He brought them just for you. I know 'cause I asked."

"That was nice of your father." Jenny couldn't help but wonder if she'd had the right idea before. Maybe this *was* the way Trace McBride courted.

It made a measure of sense. From everything she had heard and observed about the man, he spent as much time as possible with the girls. Other people in town remarked on it, so unusual was the occurrence. Of course, other people's children didn't require quite as much supervision as the McBride Menaces.

Knowing this, Jenny could see where a man like Mr. McBride just might bring his children along on a courting call. He would consider his girls' opinions in the choosing of a wife.

*That's in my favor. The girls have already said they'd like to have me as their mother.*

"Wait a minute." She unintentionally spoke aloud. What difference did it make to her whether the McBride daughters liked her or not? She wasn't looking for a husband, despite Monique and her ridiculous ideas.

Was she?

*You've tried about everything else to combat the bad luck rumor. A husband might be just what you need.*

"What? Wait a minute what?" Katrina asked. "I was standing still, MissFortune. I don't want to get soap in my eyes."

"No. No, of course not. I'm done now. You can rinse." Distracted, Jenny retrieved the soap from Katrina's hands and began to work up more soap lather, even though all three girls were through washing their hair.

What if he did ask her to marry him? What did she want? She didn't love Trace McBride, not at this moment. Why, she hardly knew the man.

*According to your mother that doesn't matter. Remember what she said? Lust before love?*

Jenny thought of her dreams; she did have a head start in that regard.

But she didn't want a husband. She wanted Fortune's Design and the autonomy it provided. She'd been only a little older than Emma when she first realized she wanted to be someone in her own right. Always Richard Fortune's daughter or Monique Day's little girl—how she had dreamed of being just Jenny Fortune.

It was only as she grew older that she came to realize what she truly wanted was her independence. Her security.

Security. Being sent from her father's home to her mother's every autumn, then back again in the spring, Jenny had not grown up knowing an overabundance of security. Fortune's Design had offered that and more.

Now the Bad Luck Wedding Dress threatened to take it all away.

The question became one of how far she would go to hold on to it. If Trace McBride proposed marriage and agreed upon the conditions she'd request, would she go through with it?

*You said you'd do anything to save Fortune's Design.*

That was her answer, wasn't it? She waited for her stomach to sink, but instead she experienced a tingle of anticipation. Well, fancy that.

"Come on, girls," she said to the two younger McBrides. "We'd best get you out of the water and dried off."

Maribeth called, "Last one out and dressed has to kiss a fish."

Jenny absolutely refused to think about Mr. Throw-Fish.

TRACE HAD BUILT a fire more from habit than need. They'd brought a cold picnic supper in a pair of wicker baskets—fried chicken, potato salad, a jar of green tomato pickles, peaches, and Emma's favorite cake. He eyed the contents, then looked down the hill toward the creek, wishing the females would hurry. He was hungry.

The spot he'd chosen for their picnic was away from the creek and the hum of gnats that swarmed over water in the late afternoon. The grass here was thick, the breeze pleasant. He fed cedar sticks to the fire, the spit and crackle of the wood pleasing to the ears, the aroma of the smoke olfactory ambrosia.

He loved getting away from town, its crowds and noise and foul-smelling streets. Gazing below toward the gap in the cottonwoods hugging the creek bank, he watched a cardinal dip then rise, a splash of red paint against the bleached sky. Someday he'd own land like this. Maybe even this land itself. He'd give his girls space to grow up in. He'd give them a place to lie on their backs and name pictures in the clouds, a place with room to think and dream and plan for the future.

A place like Oak Grove where he had been given those same opportunities.

Damn. Trace kicked at a tuft of grass. He had to quit thinking of home. He didn't need it. He *wouldn't* need it. The house in town would provide all the room the girls needed. And Jenny Fortune would give the girls the mothering they required. He planned to secure her agreement to do so right after supper.

To that end, after the five of them feasted on Emma's favorite dessert of lemon jelly cake and the girls scattered to play ball, he turned to Jenny and casually brought up the topic of the Bad Luck Wedding Dress. "I guess business has fallen off for you quite a bit since the trouble with the Bailey girls' dress."

Undoubtedly, the sour look that came to her face had little to do with the tartness of the cake filling. "Fallen off isn't quite the right term. Disappeared would be more accurate."

She looked cute when she got snippy, Trace observed, then wished he hadn't. "It's a bunch of foolishness, in my opinion. The notion that the wearing of a dress had anything to do with the Bailey girls' troubles. It's amazing, really, what nonsense people will believe."

"Mr. Bailey is quite superstitious."

"Big Jack Bailey is a fool."

Jenny didn't contradict him. Instead, she nodded toward the box that held the birthday gift Trace had commissioned for his daughter. "Thank goodness not everyone listens to rumors. I hope Emma likes the dress, although I must admit I am certain she will. Over the years I've sewn more young ladies' frocks than I can count, and I believe this is one of my better designs." Sincerity shone in her eyes as she added, "I want you to know, I do appreciate your support, Mr. McBride."

He felt the urge to hear his given name on her lips. But before he could open his mouth and ask her to call him Trace, better sense prevailed. Good God, what was he thinking? Domestic help simply didn't call their employer by his first name. *This is business, McBride. Business.*

A ball bounced in front of his face and he reached out and caught it. "You're side-arming again, Maribeth," he called, throwing the sphere back to his daughter. "Remember, come over the top."

As the girl practiced her throwing motion, Katrina asked, "Is it time to open presents, Papa? Emma can't hardly wait."

It was obvious his youngest daughter was just as excited as the birthday girl herself, and Trace shared an amused glance with Jenny as he answered, "Almost Katie-cat. Let us finish up our cake, here, and then we'll get to the important stuff. Is that all right with you, Emmie?"

"Yes, Papa." Emma rolled her eyes at the childish nickname she'd repeatedly asked him not to use.

Trace chuckled as he looked at Jenny. Lowering his voice to where the girls couldn't hear him, he said, "She's growing up way too fast. They all are. But I'm sure she'll love the dress." He fingered the ribbon on the gaily wrapped package. "I regret I didn't get down to see it before you had it all boxed up. I meant to, but seeing to my work while keeping those girls of mine in line has kept me moving so fast you'd swear I was twins."

Jenny laughed. "They have been a handful lately."

He scoffed. "Handful? I reckon you calling the McBride Menaces a handful is like me saying your business has fallen off. Speaking of which, I'd expected an invoice for the dress by now. You must have finished it some time ago."

Her gaze slid away from him. "I thought to ask you to apply it toward my rent. I guess I might as well go ahead and tell you, I'm going to be a little late with the rest of it."

Trace couldn't ask for a better opening. He searched for a delicate way to put it, but ended up asking, "Having financial difficulties?"

She nodded. "It's only temporary, I'm sure. The Harvest Ball will be here before we know it. I feel certain that the ladies of Fort Worth will rethink their groundless fears when faced with attending the city's premier fall event in last year's ball gown."

"There's a dressmaker in Dallas, isn't there?"

Jenny's lips stretched into a grim line. She didn't reply.

Trace folded his arms and observed her. "Miss Fortune, this may be none of my business, but as your landlord, I believe I have a stake in the answer. That dance is what, two months away? That's a pair of rent payments due, not to mention other details like food. Do you have enough to tide you over until then?"

He saw the color creep up her cheeks. Squaring her shoulders and lifting her chin, she said, "Thank you for your concern, Mr. McBride, but I think that's a bit too personal of a question."

"No, actually it's business. I have a proposition for you, and it would help for me to know just how bad a bind you're in."

She grew deathly still. "A proposition?"

"Yes. I have a problem, ma'am, and I think you are just the lady to solve it." He captured her gaze, his own solemn and serious. Jenny's eyes widened, then as he opened his mouth to speak, she jumped to her feet and began gathering the plates that lay scattered over the blanket.

The girls snapped to attention like pups at feeding time. "You're done!" Katrina cried, diving for the smallest package. "Emma, open mine first. Please, oh, please!"

"She can't, Kat. She promised me," Maribeth stated as she lifted another box from the blanket.

Frustration at the interruption swelled inside Trace. But then he saw the excitement shining in his daughters' expressions and he knew his discussion with Jenny Fortune must wait. He put a stop to the bickering by stating in a firm voice, "Rest your mouths, women. I'm the father, I get to settle this." He lifted his package and handed it to Emma. "Me first, Emmie. Please?"

Jenny burst out laughing as Emma shook her head and said, "Papa you are so silly." And then she was gasping, "Oh, Papa. It's beautiful."

Emma was the picture of a young woman's delight. She jumped to her feet, held the dress out for a good look, then brought it up to her shoulders to measure the size. "It's perfect. Absolutely perfect. And so grown-up. Oh, Papa, how did you know to get me a dress?"

Grown-up? He should have made time to go see the damned dress. Eyeing the calico with a skeptical eye, Trace shrugged and said, "I knew what you wanted for your birthday. I'm your father; these things come natural."

He ignored the smothered snort coming from the dressmaker.

The festive atmosphere continued as Emma opened her sisters' gifts. Family tradition dictated the presents between sisters be offerings of time and effort rather than objects purchased with coin. The practice had begun that first year when the McBrides fled home and family with little more than the clothes on their backs, and although Trace now made it a practice to buy his daughters' birthday gifts, they continued the exchange of favors among the girls. From Maribeth, Emma received two weeks of dishwashing and a promise of a three-week respite from being begged to play ball. Katrina's gift was bed making for one week and the vow not to cry and embarrass her sister on the first day of school.

Then it was Jenny's turn to offer a gift. She lifted the package tied with hair ribbons and handed it to Emma with a smile and good wishes. Trace leaned forward, curious as to what the dressmaker had chosen. He'd been surprised earlier when he saw the package for his daughter ready and waiting on the shelf in her shop. Her thoughtfulness about Emma's big day both touched him and reinforced his decision to hire Jenny Fortune to be a stand-in mother for the girls.

"Be careful, now," Jenny warned as Emma lifted the lid from the box. "It's made for show rather than play."

"Oh, Miss Fortune!" Emma exclaimed, lifting the item from the box.

Trace's jaw gaped. "A doll? You gave her a doll?" He couldn't believe it. That's what *he* had wanted to give her, and Jenny Fortune had been the one to tell him not to do it. Of all the nerve. He folded his arms and scowled. "I can't believe you gave her a doll."

The tolerant grin that appeared on her face ruffled his feathers even more. "It's a *fashion* doll, Mr. McBride. A dressmaker's tool."

"See, Papa?" Emma said, fingering the tiny skirt of green foulard. "This is a model of a visiting dress."

"I made that one for Wilhemina Peters." Gesturing toward the box, Jenny addressed Emma. "I included a few other samples if you'd like to study them and see how they're put together."

"You gave her a dress-up doll with doll clothes," Trace declared, the peevishness he was feeling seeping into his tone. *Her* doll was somehow all right for a twelve-year-old, but the baby doll he'd bought for Emma wasn't?

Jenny gave him a puzzled look, then said, "The doll and samples are just things to look at. My real gift to you, Emma, is similar in nature to your sisters'." Leaning over, she removed a miniature pinafore from the box. "I'm offering to teach you how to make this, if you'd like."

"You'll teach me how to sew?"

Jenny nodded.

"Just like a real mother," Maribeth breathed.

The words hung on the early evening air. "That's it," Trace said, standing abruptly. The time had come to get this matter settled. "Girls, I'd like to talk for a bit with Miss Fortune. Can y'all keep yourself occupied for a few minutes while we take a walk?"

Emma and Maribeth exchanged a look Trace couldn't quite interpret, and then the older girl said, "Certainly, Papa. You go on. I'd like to try the other costumes on the doll, and I'll let Mari and Kat help me choose which ones."

Katrina stuck her thumb in her mouth and said, "No. I want to go with Papa."

Maribeth eyed her father, then said, "I'll bet we could have seconds on cake if we stay behind."

Trace nodded, settling the question in everyone's mind. Everyone's but Miss Fortune's, that is.

She ignored his outstretched hand and bent her attention to brushing a nonexistent smear of dirt from her skirt. "It's getting late, Mr. McBride. I think it would be best for us to head back to town."

He nodded. "We'll go soon, I promise. But first, I'd enjoy a little walking and talking, and besides, the girls told me they left their shifts drying on a bush and we need to get them before we leave." Reaching down, he grasped her hand and gently pulled her to her feet. She didn't protest as he led her down the hill, back toward the creek and the swimming hole.

Jenny had difficulty breathing. He was holding her hand, just like a suitor. She thought her heart must surely be lodged in her throat and her thoughts were in a whirl. She hadn't been this nervous since Mother took up with that Italian following her third divorce from Richard.

A proposition, he'd said. Not a proposal. But a proposition could be a proposal. Or, a proposition could be something less honorable. But Trace McBride appeared to be a man of honor. Didn't he?

Jenny couldn't take the uncertainty anymore. Jerking her hand away, she planted her feet beside a large rock and blurted out, "What is this proposition, Mr. McBride? I want to know now, please."

He stopped, frowned, and rubbed the line of his jaw with his hand, and Jenny braced for the question she fully expected to come. What would she say if he declared his love? She didn't love him, not yet. She thought she could grow to love him, but for now, what would she say?

He hoisted himself onto the rock. "All right, Miss Fortune. I'll come right out and speak what's on my mind. Lately I've had problems controlling my girls." He paused and his mouth twisted in a rueful smile. "But then you know that already, considering you near to beat me over the head with the fact."

Jenny nodded and plucked at the leaves of a sunflower that dipped across the path. Why didn't he just get to the point?

"Anyway, in the past few months we've gone through enough housekeepers to keep a palace up to snuff, and I've pretty well given up on the idea of a cook-and-clean type of woman to keep my daughters in line." He propped one boot atop the rock and wrapped his arm around his bended knee. Flashing a grin, he added, "Guess they take after me more than I'd like."

"Mr. McBride," she began, her voice pitched high with impatience.

He ignored her interruption. "I realize I need more than a housekeeper. My girls need a mother."

That was it. Jenny closed her eyes and drew a breath. He'd marry to provide a mother for his children. He was saying it right out, no declaration of love or even affection, just the straight truth. She should feel relieved and appreciative of his honesty.

Then why was she feeling insulted?

Trace continued, "They need to have a woman they respect in their lives, a woman they'll listen to and mind. And they need someone who can teach them how to be ladies. With Emmie getting older, it's easier for me to understand that it's something important and something that has been missing."

He paused for a moment and looked toward the creek, a pensiveness lingering in his eyes. Then he shrugged. "After our set-to the day my Menaces landed in jail, I got to thinking. You obviously care about my daughters, and they sure as hell care for you. They pay attention when you talk. You proved that earlier when you had that chat with Kat. And offering to teach Emma to sew is exactly the type of thing I'm looking for in a mother for my children."

Jenny's nervousness faded with his speech, and before he finished, she was well on the way to vexed. She plucked the bloom from the stem, then tossed it away. Her pride had taken a direct hit. The receiving of a marriage proposal was an event a woman remembered for the rest of her life. It wouldn't hurt the man to be a little more…romantic. He treated the moment like a business proposition.

Trace McBride needed a reminder that she was a woman.

Jenny thought of her mother. She recalled her own less-than-successful efforts at flirtation with this man just a few weeks ago. She'd always made it her practice to learn from her mistakes, and she believed herself better prepared this time.

Subtly, she shifted her stance. Pulling her shoulders back, she leaned forward, toward him, her breasts brushing the boulder just beside his dangling leg. Then, she slowly, deliberately licked her lips.

His eyes narrowed and his nostrils flared slightly.

A sense of power ripped through Jenny, and in a soft, seductive tone, she stated, "Then I guess you do need a woman, don't you, Mr. McBride."

His gaze fastened on her mouth, he slowly said, "Uh-huh."

Jenny knew a triumphant grin would ruin it, so she firmly squelched the urge. Instead, she sent Monique a silent message of thanks for having imparted the intricacies of such a useful skill as flirting.

In a barely audible voice, Trace repeated, "Oh, yes."

He closed his eyes, shook himself, and slid down from the rock. He stepped a few feet down the path before he stopped and turned.

His gaze was direct and emotionless, his voice brisk and businesslike. "I want your help with my daughters. I'm willing to forego your rent and pay you ten dollars a week."

Jenny swallowed abruptly. "Excuse me?"

Sunlight highlighted streaks of red in Trace's dark hair as he shrugged and said, "I think it's a fair wage considering you won't be doing any household chores. I might be willing to negotiate a bit, but you need to keep in mind that I'm not made of money."

Silence hung between them, broken only by the trill of a mockingbird perched in a nearby oak. Something wasn't right here. Not even an unconventional man like Trace McBride would use the word "wage" in a marriage proposal. She searched his expression for a clue to his thoughts, but he might as well have been playing poker for all she could tell.

Suddenly, she had enough of his posturing. The rate he was

going, they'd be here until dark. "Are you, or are you not, trying to ask me something, Mr. McBride?"

He nodded, reached for her hand once more, and pulled her down the path toward the creek. "I realize this idea might strike you as strange at first. Folks usually take other avenues to reach an agreement like this. But if you'll just give it a chance, I'm sure you'll see the arrangement has its merits. Don't forget that a little earlier you confessed you'd have trouble making the rent."

He gave her a sidelong look, waiting. When she nodded, he continued. "Well, throwing in with us would solve that particular problem. And considering the state your business is in, you should be grateful to have the work."

The idea of charging his wife rent was bad enough, but the reference to Fortune's Design poured salt into a wound. "Job?" She lifted her chin. "Well, I don't doubt that marriage to you would be a job, but let me tell you right up front, Trace McBride, *no one* is going to make me close my business."

"Marriage!" The word exploded from his mouth and his boots kicked up a small cloud of dust as he backed away from the threat. "Who the hell said anything about marriage?"

"You did," she snapped.

"I did not," he scoffed. "I never will. I'll never marry again. The very idea makes me want to lose my dinner." He marched the last few feet to the creek. Swiping two of the white cotton shifts from the branches of a bush, he reached for the third, then stopped dead cold. "Good God, Miss Fortune. Surely you didn't think I was asking you to marry me!"

Lose his dinner at the thought of marrying her? Jenny almost swooned from the injury.

Thankfully, pride came to her rescue. "Of course not," she jeered, sweeping Katrina's little shift from beneath his outstretched hand. "I'd have to be a fool to think such nonsense. I'm simply trying to get you to make your point so that we can return to town. It's been a tiring day, Mr. McBride. I'm ready to go home."

"Oh? I thought I'd spelled it out, but maybe not." He appeared both puzzled and relieved.

Foolish man.

"I'm offering you a position in my household, Miss Fortune. I want to hire you to be a substitute mother for my daughters. I want you to take them in hand and do all the mother things they are missing out on. Things like teaching them to sew. I want Emma, Maribeth, and Katrina to grow up to be ladies. Truth be told, I'm not having much luck teaching them myself."

Heat stung her cheeks as embarrassment washed through her. How stupid of her to think of marriage; how mean of him to phrase his words and actions in such a way that led her toward that conclusion.

She began wringing the water from the shift, heedless of the fact that the cloth was nearly dry, and nearly a minute passed before she emphatically stated, "No."

Turning around, she hurried up the path.

*You can tie out bad luck by tying a
string around a broom.*

## CHAPTER SIX

"HUH?" TRACE WATCHED her flee, bewilderment washing over
him. What the hell had happened? "Miss Fortune? Hold on
there a minute, would you?"

She hiked up her skirt and began to run. Trace muttered a
curse and followed. Twice he heard the rattle of gravel as her
footing slipped, and he increased his speed fearing she'd fall
and hurt herself. He caught up with her beside a bank of honeysuckle vines. "Slow down, there," he said, grasping her arm.

She jerked, trying to pull away. "You have a lot of nerve,
McBride. And quit manhandling me! Every time I turn around
you are grabbing at me." She waited, glaring up at him until
he dropped her arm, then she scuttled beyond his reach.

Trace lifted an exasperated gaze to the heavens. How she
could look both so wounded and so angry at the same time
was beyond him. "Do you want to tell me what happened back
there?"

"I turned down your job."

"That much I figured," he grumbled. Damn, but she looked

pretty—all eating fire and spitting smoke. Her blue eyes burned like flames in a gas lamp; her cheeks glowed pink as a prairie sunset. Shutting his eyes, he dropped his chin to his chest. *Keep your mind on business, McBride.* Thoughts like that weren't getting him anywhere he cared to be.

Inhaling deeply, he raked his fingers through his hair. Then, he lifted his head and pinned her with his gaze. "Why? Why did you turn it down? You didn't give it a chance; you hardly heard me out."

"I didn't need to hear anymore, Mr. McBride. You managed to say plenty."

If she lifted that chin any higher, she'd break her neck. "What's the problem? I thought you liked my daughters."

"I *do* like your daughters," she stressed. "I like them well enough never to risk doing them harm by participating in this ridiculous scheme."

"What do you mean, harm? As long as I am careful about the woman I choose, how the hell could I harm my girls by giving them a mother?"

"Mr. McBride." She said his name like a curse. "You are missing a basic truth with this little plan of yours."

Trace clenched his jaw. Maybe he'd been wrong about her. Maybe he didn't want her around his girls after all. In a snide voice, he replied, "And what, pray tell, is that?"

The flames in her eyes flared hotter, and he spied the flex of tendons as she briefly clenched her fists. Apparently, the woman didn't like snide.

Making an obvious effort to summon control, she spoke slowly and evenly. "I'll do my best to explain it to you. The way I understand it, you believe that the reason your girls have committed ample mischief to be dubbed the McBride Menaces by the people of Fort Worth is because they don't have sufficient womanly influence in their lives. Am I correct?"

"That's right. They need a mother's influence."

She nodded. "So, the way I understand your proposition, you want me to provide that influence by fulfilling such a role."

"Yes. Exactly." Trace folded his arms. "The arrangement would benefit us both. I tried to be kind about all that bad luck business, but the truth of the matter is, Fortune's Design is obviously on a fast slide downward. Until the rumors die away, you'll have a hard time keeping the door open. If you come to work for me, I'll even allow you to sew a little on the side, if you'd like. Make a little extra income."

"You'd *allow* me?" she said, her voice rising in a squeak.

"Sure. I don't see what it would hurt. I don't believe you'd neglect the girls. Face it, you need me and I need you. It'd be foolish not to help each other out."

She closed her eyes. "What is foolish, McBride, is your idea that I'd give up my business, not to mention the notion that it is possible to hire a mother."

"Now Miss Fortune. Jenny—" Trace began.

Shaking her head, she glanced his way. "Let me explain, at least about your inaccurate perceptions of motherhood." She reached for a honeysuckle blossom, plucked it from the vine, then twirled it between her fingers as she spoke. "I spent half my childhood physically apart from my mother, and no matter how wonderful my father's hired help, not a one of them came close to duplicating the relationship I shared with Monique. You see, I could teach your girls to sew. I could teach them manners and deportment and any other feminine skill you'd like them to learn. But those things do not make a mother."

She tossed the blossoms to the ground and said flatly, "You cannot buy love, McBride. You cannot hire someone to love your daughters as a mother would. Love is a gift that comes from the heart, freely given. You are wrong to try and purchase it."

Her words pricked his skin, giving rise to defensiveness. He snapped, "Are my children so unlovable?"

"Of course not. I could easily love your girls. I'm halfway there already. But can't you see the potential harm your plan might cause, to both me and the children?"

He gawked at her. "No. No, I can't. Seems to me that we'd all win, unless you spend all day acting snippy like you are now, that is."

She gave him a killing glance, then promptly looked through the trees where the girls were playing. "All right, McBride, let's just say for the sake of argument that I went along with your notion and gave your daughters my love. Say I played the mother's role. What happens when you give them the real thing? What happens when you bring home a wife?"

It was a verbal punch to the gut. Trace snapped his reply. "I told you I'll never marry again!"

Her wan, weary smile presaged her words. "I've heard it before. My father said the same thing each time he divorced my mother. At least I was lucky in that he chose my mother to remarry time and again. Had each of his marriages been to a different woman, I could have had up to four mothers by now. Imagine that."

"Look, Miss Fortune. I'll be damned if I marry again once, much less four times. We're not talking about the same thing here."

"Yes, we are. Mothers are not interchangeable, Mr. McBride. You cannot buy one like a new bonnet or rid yourself of one like an old shoe."

"You want to bet on that?" The words were out of his mouth before he could stop them. It didn't matter though. She had no way of knowing the impetus behind the words.

After giving him a look of pure disdain, the dressmaker said, "If you want your girls to enjoy the advantages of having a loving mother in their lives, I suggest you provide for them in the normal manner. Get married. Give them a mother who can't be fired or replaced short of divorce."

Trace gazed back toward the campsite where his daughters waited. "Or death," he murmured softly.

Jenny's look was sharp, but compassionate. "I know you want what is best for your girls, but this idea of yours isn't it. Those girls want and need a permanent tie. I can't be that for them."

"You can if you'll only allow it."

She shook her head. "Even though you might have sworn off marriage, I have not. I like to believe that someday I'll meet a man and fall in love. What happens then if he wants to move away? Are you going to allow your daughters to come with me?"

"Of course not."

"You need a permanent tie, Mr. McBride. Get married. That's the way to give your children a mother." She took a few steps up the path, then glanced back over her shoulder to say, "It's getting late. Take me home, please. All in all it's been an enjoyable day, and I thank you for including me."

"Can't we just talk—?"

"I think I've made myself perfectly clear. I will not be a party to such an ill-conceived notion. Not now, or ever."

Trace yanked a sprig of honeysuckle from the vine. What did he do now? How could he convince her she was wrong?

He tried the only thing he could think of. "I'll let you keep Fortune's Design if you want," he called after her. "I'll even advance you some cash to tide you over. How about it?"

Miss Fortune didn't reply.

JENNY AND THE GIRLS chatted amiably on the ride back to town. Trace was unusually quiet. As he pulled the horses to a halt in front of the dressmaker's cottage on a quiet residential street not far from downtown Fort Worth, he bade the girls wait while he escorted Miss Fortune to her door.

"No need to do that, Mr. McBride," Jenny said hastily. Despite her protest, he was there to assist her from the carriage.

"I may be a saloonkeeper, but I was raised a gentleman, ma'am." With a bow of his head, he gestured toward the walk. Jenny gave a little shrug, then proceeded up the path.

Trace's gaze gravitated to her dress below the waist, making a lie of his claim to gentlemanly behavior, as he scrutinized the swish of her skirts up the porch steps. Watching her backside was getting to be a habit, he silently acknowledged.

Then Jenny pulled up short. "Oh, no. Not again."

He followed the path of her gaze, and a curse burst from his lips. A dress form draped in white linen hung by a hangman's noose from a beam on the right side of the porch. Light glinted off the surface of the handles of a pair of scissors protruding from the figure. A wet red stain streaked the white fabric. A woman's nightgown, Trace realized. "Go back to the wagon, Jenny. Get the girls and head over to my place."

She shook her head, pushing around him to approach the dangling obscenity, lifting a finger to touch the splotch of color. "It's from the shop." In her trembling voice, Trace heard fear, but also a trace of anger. "The gown is mine. They've been in my home, too." Bringing her hand to her nose, she sniffed. "Paint. It's only paint."

Trace's boots scuffed the porch as he reached for her arm, tugging her away. "I'll check it out. Go on, Jenny, go on back to the wagon."

"No," she said flatly. "This is my house. My concern. A lamp is on next door at the Littys'. Send the girls over there. Mary will gladly keep an eye on them."

"You're not going in there. Whoever did this may still be inside!"

She spared him a glance. "Whoever did this is gone. I can

feel it. Take care of the girls and I'll wait for you. But only for a minute."

Cursing beneath his breath, Trace dashed for the wagon, saw his daughters safely next door, then hurried back to Jenny. As he sprinted up the front walk, she marched into the house, Trace right on her heels.

He damn near ran over her, so abruptly had she stopped.

Jenny moaned softly. Trace whispered, "Sonofabitch."

Furniture in the parlor had been overturned, books and papers lay strewn across the floor. Leaving her standing dumbstruck in the parlor, he moved to search the premises. The tiny kitchen showed similar signs of abuse as did a bedroom she apparently used as a sewing room.

He assumed the last room must be her bedroom. Walking on near silent feet, he approached the open doorway. At first glance, all he noticed was the pool of red.

The sight struck a chord deep within him. He remembered another night and another room. Only that night, the pools of red had not been paint, but blood. Real blood. His wife's blood. "Good Lord, lady," he said, his voice a croak. "What sort of trouble are you in?"

THE FOLLOWING MORNING Jenny woke with the roosters. She rose from her bed filled with purpose, ready to follow through with the decision she'd made last night while cleaning her home, mopping up and throwing out reminders of her unwelcome visitor.

She'd be darned if she'd let this incident frighten her or cause her to cower in any way at all. With dress orders to solicit and a business to save, she had no time for more of these upsetting pranks. Big Jack could take his silly superstitions and feed them to his precious cows for all she cared.

And she intended to tell him just that.

Jenny washed and dressed and left her house. The weather

this first week of September could be summed up in a word—blistering. With a glance toward the cloudless sky, she snapped open her parasol and marched toward downtown.

On this first Monday of the month, she had every confidence she'd find Big Jack Bailey at the Tivoli Restaurant near the courthouse. The city council was scheduled to meet today at noon. As a rule, all issues to be voted on later that day were decided over breakfast at the Tivoli by a handful of Fort Worth's most powerful citizens. Big Jack counted himself among their number.

Jenny's anger was a powerful force itself. Last night's shenanigans, combined with her upset over Trace McBride's proposition, had pushed it past its limits. She couldn't do anything about McBride, but she could darn well have a chat with Big Jack. She should have confronted the rancher weeks ago when the rumors first surfaced. She should have taken that very first threatening note and slapped his face with it.

Town was bustling this morning. Hammers pounded at a new building going up on Seventh Street. Wagons rattled by filled with freight. A young boy on his way to school accidentally bumped Jenny with his lunch pail. Smiling, she accepted his polite apology and thought of the McBride girls. Yesterday Maribeth had glumly informed her that she and her sisters were due to start at Blackstone Academy today.

She wondered if Miss Blackstone was ready for the McBride Menaces.

Eyeing the Tivoli Restaurant sign, she wondered if Big Jack Bailey was ready for Jenny Fortune.

Peering through the plate-glass window, Jenny spotted Bailey, the mayor, two of Fort Worth's most prominent attorneys, and three of its most successful businessmen at a large rectangular table near the back of the restaurant. She took a deep, fortifying breath then walked inside.

The room smelled of fried eggs and Cuban cigars. Jenny

smothered her reaction to the odor and greeted each man politely by name. Turning toward a scowling Jack Bailey, she said, "I'm sorry to interrupt, but may I have just a few moments of your time?"

Cold gray eyes glared from beneath bushy salt-and-pepper eyebrows. "What for?"

"I'd prefer to explain to you in private."

He shook his head. "No, I'm doing business here. I don't—"

"Aw, go ahead, Big Jack," one of the attorneys said. "See what the little lady wants."

The little lady would like to tell you off for calling her a little lady, Jenny thought. Instead she offered a smile as sweet as spun sugar and waited silently for Big Jack Bailey to lumber to his feet.

"Outside," he instructed. "At least I'll get a breath of fresh air out of this."

Jenny was pleased at that idea herself. She nodded toward the gentleman, then exited the restaurant. Turning right, she walked beyond the window before she stopped, not wishing to be observed by the men inside.

Big Jack hooked his thumbs through the armholes of his vest. "Make it quick, Dressmaker."

"I'll be pleased to keep it brief." Jenny faced him and demanded, "These pranks must stop."

He frowned. "Pranks? What the hell are you talking about, girl?"

"I'm talking about the dead roses on my pillow. I'm talking about the black drapes over the mirrors in my house. I'm talking about the fact I found every pair of shoes I own under my bed last night!"

Shock widened Big Jack's eyes, and his hand went to his neck to grasp the gold rabbit's foot pendant he wore on a chain. "Good Lord, you shouldn't do that. Shoes under a bed bring bad luck!"

"I'm aware of that superstition, Mr. Bailey." She folded her arms, her voice tight. "But what, pray tell, is red paint brushed across my sheets and walls supposed to bring? Other than cleanup work, that is?"

"I don't know what the hell you're talking about. I didn't play any pranks on you."

"Don't lie to me, Mr. Bailey!"

His brow lowered and his eyes snapped. "You'd best watch your mouth, Seamstress. I don't cotton to folk who have done me wrong—man or woman—and heaven knows you've done me more harm than most. I've held off doing anything about it, but you're pushing me now."

He lowered his voice and took a step toward her. "I'll make you pay. I'll make you pay ten times over for every hurt done to each of my girls."

His tone brought a shiver to Jenny's skin, and she thought she may have made a mistake by confronting Big Jack Bailey. Had temper encouraged her to recklessness? It wouldn't be the first time she'd acted like her mother. Perhaps it was time to employ the more prudent side of her nature inherited from her father.

She set her mouth in a determined line. "I'm not trying to push, Mr. Bailey. I simply wish to make my point. You may threaten me all you like—with notes or telegrams or dead roses in my bed—but I cannot undo anything that has happened to your daughters. I am not at fault for their accidents."

"Yes, you are. You and that damned Bad Luck Wedding Dress. Listen to me well. I suggest you stay out of my sight for a good little while. I'll be less likely to give you the trouble you deserve if I don't find you in my face all the time."

Jenny set her teeth. More threats. She was sick to death of threats. "I'll make you a deal, sir. You stay out of my way and I'll stay out of yours. No more vandalism, or I'll go to Marshal Courtright."

His scowl was ferocious. "Are you attempting to threaten me?"

She shrugged. "I simply want us to have an understanding."

"Well, understand this. I suggest you go home and yank those shoes out from under your bed. Turn your socks inside out and wear 'em that way until noon. Double check all the beds in your house to make sure nobody's left a hat on them. In other words, Miss Fortune, do every goddamn thing you can think of to bring you good luck and ward off the bad."

He leaned toward her and said, "Because believe me, you don't want any more troubles to visit my daughters. Especially Mary Rose. Up until now, she has avoided the bad luck—the only Bailey bride to do so. You'd better hope to hell it stays that way."

He turned to leave, then paused and drilled her with his gray-eyed gaze. "'Cause otherwise, I'll kill you. So help me, I'll kill you."

THE WHISKEY tasted bitter going down and rested in Trace's stomach like glowing coals. "I can't believe she did that. Are you certain about this, Courtright?"

"Saw it myself," the marshal said, nodding. "Miss Fortune all but shook her finger at Big Jack Bailey."

Trace groaned. "Dammit, I thought she had more sense than that. You need to do something, Marshal, before this thing gets out of hand."

"Now, McBride." Courtright swirled the amber liquid in a crystal glass. "I can appreciate your concerns, but there is really nothing I can do. You didn't see anyone; we can't know for a fact that Bailey was behind this."

"Oh, he was behind it all right. Who else but Big Jack Bailey has a motive for leaving 'gifts' like the ones left for Jenny Fortune?" Trace took another sip of his drink and recalled what he'd found in her bedroom the night before. A frilly pink-and-white room shrouded in black crepe. A white satin eiderdown soaked in blotches of red. Withered red roses gathered in a bridal bouquet and tied with black ribbon lying on her pillow.

"Big Jack has always been a bit crazy," the marshal began. "One time he damn near killed one of his cowhands for stomping on a spider in the ranch house parlor. Said it was bad luck."

"See what I mean? He's tormenting Jenny Fortune because of that blasted wedding dress. He's crossed the line. I made her tell me about it last night. He's left her notes, sent her telegrams. Now this. I'm telling you, Marshal, you need to have a chat with Big Jack."

Courtright rubbed a palm across his grizzled cheek. "This was the first I'd heard about any notes. Maybe she's making it all up? Maybe she did up her house like that herself, trying to get a rise of sympathy out of folks."

"No, Jenny wouldn't do that."

The marshal's craggy brow lifted. "That dress shop of hers is in a bad way, according to the newspaper. I wouldn't put a scheme like that past Miss Fortune, considering who her mother is. Have you ever tangled with that woman...Monique Day? She could break a man like a matchstick." He punctuated the thought with a quick gulp of whiskey.

Jenny must take after her mother, Trace thought. He had the feeling she could snap half the men in Fort Worth in two with not much more than a bat of her eyelashes if she put her mind to it. "You're wrong, Marshal. Jenny Fortune is telling the truth about these threats, and if you don't do something, she's liable to end up dead."

"Hell, McBride, that's a bit of a stretch, don't you think? Even if Big Jack is behind this business, he hasn't done anything other than scare her a little bit."

"Yet." Trace finished his drink and set the empty glass on the bar with a bang.

The marshal waved a hand. "You're overreacting. Besides, for all his superstitions, nasty notes and dead roses don't sound like Big Jack to me. Just can't picture him playing a few harmless pranks."

"These are not harmless pranks. The woman is scared out of her mind."

The lawman shook his head. "Nope, I can't see that. Miss Fortune doesn't strike me for scared. Braving Big Jack Bailey before breakfast at the Tivoli isn't the act of a fearful person."

"Stupid is the word that comes to my mind," Trace replied glumly.

"Why are you so concerned about the dressmaker's problems, anyway?" Courtright inquired, his eyes sparked with interest. "Is something going on between you two?"

"No. Nothing but the rent, that is. It's my property she's renting for her shop, you know, my building Bailey broke into to steal the dressmaker's form. Not to mention the fact that my defenseless daughters live one floor above. I reckon I have a stake in what happens to Jenny Fortune."

"Defenseless daughters?" Courtright chuckled. "That's the funniest one I've heard all day."

Trace averted his gaze, unwilling to listen to any more of the marshal's jabs. The sight of a boy sallying up to the bar brought a scowl to his face.

"One bottle of gin, please," Casey Tate asked the bartender, his boy's voice sounding sadly out of place in the surroundings.

Casey Tate was almost thirteen years old. He lived next door at Miss Rachel's Social Emporium where his mother made her living on her back, while he earned his keep playing step-and-fetch-it for the madam. When Trace first took notice of the boy, a few discreet questions had assured him Casey played no role for Rachel more unsavory than that of delivery boy. A visit with both the madam and the mother insured it would stay that way.

In his most authoritative voice, Trace called, "Casey Tate. Haven't I told you to stay out of the End of the Line? A saloon is no place for a kid."

"Yes sir, Mr. McBride," the boy answered with a freckled-faced grin. "But then, neither is a whorehouse. Miss Rachel is wanting to fix a fancy drink for a visitor of hers, and we ran out of gin about an hour ago."

"Did she send any money with you?"

Casey shook his head. "She said to put it on her tab."

Standing, Trace said, "Excuse me, Marshal. I'd best see to business." Rachel's tab hadn't been paid in over three months, and Trace had cancelled her credit two weeks ago. As much as he liked the madam, she was dipping into his pocket. He needed every cent he earned to pay for the completion of his children's new home.

He gestured for the bartender to give him a bottle of gin, then said to the boy, "Tell you what, squirt. I need to visit with Miss Rachel. How about if I deliver this for you."

Disappointment flickered across Casey Tate's face. "Hell, Mr. McBride. I didn't think you diddled the whores."

Trace shook his head. "I'm not going there to 'diddle,' Casey. Not that it's any of your concern." His mouth lifted in a rueful smile as he pushed open the End of the Line's front doors. He did very little "diddling" these days, what between his fatherly duties and his general distaste for whores.

Maybe that's one reason Jenny Fortune kept popping to mind, he told himself. Maybe he just needed to get diddled.

The wail of a train whistle and the distinct odor of cattle met them as they stepped into the warm September sunshine. Trace led the way across the wide dirt street, carefully dodging a freight wagon going north and a drunked-up cowboy on a spindly legged paint headed mostly south with a few weaving detours east and west.

Miss Rachel's Social Emporium lay directly opposite the

End of the Line, and as they entered the establishment, Trace nodded to a pair of trail-dusty cowboys intently debating whether to spend their last bit of coin on a "nooner" or a steak. After telling Casey to grab some lunch, he climbed the stairs to Rachel Warden's room.

The boy should be in school, Trace thought, watching Casey scamper toward the kitchen. He'd speak with Miss Blackstone about it. Perhaps she had something in the way of scholarships available. People here in the Acre likely would help with the boy's tuition. Everyone liked Casey Tate. Besides, chances were good assistance wouldn't be needed for long. It looked like the city was finally ready to get off its butt and finance public schools. Not a moment too soon, to Trace's way of thinking.

Upon reaching Rachel's room, he knocked twice and waited. Etta Norris, a raven-haired voluptuous woman considered to be the most talented of Rachel's girls, answered the door. Trace held up the bottle, winked, and said, "Delivery."

Etta crooned in a husky, southern voice, "Ah, sugar, remind me to start drinking gin." She swung the door wide and gestured Trace inside. He pressed a kiss to her cheek as he stepped into the room, surprised to see so many of Rachel's "ladies" within. "What's going on? Looks like—" He broke off midsentence.

His mouth went dry as West Texas in July. The air rushed from his lungs. The bottle of gin slipped from his hand and shattered on the wood floor, the eye-watering vapors rising from his feet in an invisible cloud.

Jenny Fortune. In black-and-scarlet striped satin. With a neckline cut halfway to China, and a hemline hiked damned close to heaven.

*Good Lord, look at the legs on that woman.*

Trace had a vague awareness of the fuss and fluster over the broken bottle as he locked gazes with the dressmaker.

Myriad emotions flashed through those sapphire depths—surprise and embarrassment uppermost among them.

Glass crunched beneath his boot as he approached her. Almost against his will, his gaze swept her once again. Dressed like this, Miss Fortune showed off womanly charms enough to make every painted lady in the Acre weep with envy.

Jenny Fortune in a whorehouse. Surely she wasn't—no, he didn't believe that. But look at all that lace. What the *hell* was she thinking?

From out of his past came the answer, and it ignited a long-buried fury. Almost a full minute passed before he spoke, his words all the more threatening for their soft-spoken tone. "Rachel, I need to speak with Miss Fortune privately."

The madam took one look at the light in Trace's eyes and shooed her twittering trollops away. "I'll be charging you rent for the room, Trace."

He ignored her, waiting like a panther for his prey, until the door clicked shut and he and Jenny Fortune were left alone. Jenny watched him, her gaze apprehensive but unafraid.

Neither had Constance been afraid all those years ago.

Trace's hand snaked out and clenched her elbow. He gave it a shake and asked in a low, angry voice, "What do you think you are doing?"

She glanced down at her arm, then glared up at him. "Let me go, McBride."

His grip clamped tighter and he demanded an answer with a steely gaze.

"Let me go!" Jenny repeated, clawing at him. Only because he allowed it, she wrenched free, scratching his hand in the process. He heard frustration in her voice as she added, "How many times do I have to tell you? Quit manhandling me!"

Trace's smile was ugly as he held up his hand and wiggled his fingers, calling attention to the scrapes. Manhandling? *She* was the one whose talons had drawn blood. The stinging scratches were nothing; the temper they fed was imposing. "You're one to talk, Dressmaker."

Boldly holding his gaze, Jenny didn't reply.

Trace's lip curled. "But I guess I understand. You want to set the price first. I can live with that. Hands off until we come to terms."

"Set the price?" she repeated, her voice rising.

"Keep in mind I'm cash poor, but I reckon I'm willing to pay a little more than the going rate for one of Rachel's whores."

Her hand lashed out to slap him, but he caught her wrist scant inches from his cheek. "Hands off, remember?"

Her emotions were written on her face. She fumed. She boiled. She silently raged.

But rage had its claws in Trace, too. He had no call to speak to her that way, but the picture of Jenny Fortune, dressed like a working girl in a bordello bedroom, brought to mind another woman, another room. Another man.

He couldn't think straight when he was thinking about them. He could only feel, and those feelings were mean.

Trace loosened his grip and she pulled away, this time fleeing clear across the room. From there she faced him, arms folded, and head held proud.

God, she was beautiful.

Just like Constance.

His wife. The whore.

*It is bad luck to burn the wood of a tree
that has been struck by lightning.*

## CHAPTER SEVEN

JENNY WANTED to scream. When he first appeared in the doorway, she thought she'd die of embarrassment. But then his gaze had swept over her, blatant and hot, and she'd known a heady sense of power new to her experience. He'd stolen the feeling with his words and rough touch, and now all she felt was anger.

Just who did he think he was, coming in here and acting this way? What business of his was it where she went or what she did? The arrogant, domineering, overbearing cad. Let him think the worst of her, she didn't care.

With a sugary drawl, she repeated his question. "What am I doing here? You said it yourself, McBride. I've come to sell my wares, of course. What do you think? Am I worth the coin?"

He reacted with sudden and total stillness, but for the fire burning in his eyes.

Jenny licked her lips. For the first time in her life, she knew the meaning of the phrase "living dangerously." Her heart pounded so hard she was sure he heard it, maybe even saw it. He was, after all, staring intently at that general area of her chest.

The goading words she'd hurled didn't seem as clever now as they had just a few moments ago. She wasn't afraid of him, not exactly. It was just that the Trace McBride standing before her shared little resemblance with Mr. Throw-Fish.

He gave her a slow, sweeping look. "Ah, such a question. Are you worth the coin?"

Jenny's skin burned beneath his scrutiny. "Not me," she hastened to say, taking a step backward. "I meant my dress. I need rent money. I need new customers, and the society ladies are afraid. This is a sample, you see."

He nodded, and stepped forward. "Oh, yes, it's definitely a sample."

A strange combination of apprehension and desire flooded Jenny's limbs, weakening her knees and adding weight to her feet. His gaze never left her, not even when he interrupted his advance to move a ladder-back chair in his path. A few feet away, he abruptly stopped. "You make a beautiful courtesan, Jenny Fortune."

She couldn't breathe. "It's the dress," she croaked.

He arched a brow. "Is it?"

Folding his arms, he walked around her in a circle, coming so close at times she could feel the brush of his body against hers.

"The dress is only the wrapping paper for the package. And your package..." He gave a soft, appreciative whistle. "I imagine a man would consider it Christmas every night."

A whimper escaped her lips.

His look was knowing. "You like that, hmm? You like the power? To know you can make a man ache. To know you can make him want. Want, even though he knows he shouldn't."

She shook her head. The words and his manner had a hard edge that made her uneasy. When he moved to close the gap between them, she backed away. For every forward step of his, she retreated an equal distance. Soon she felt the ridges of flocked wallpaper against her bare shoulders.

He laid his palms flat against the wall, effectively trapping her between his outstretched arms.

Jenny swallowed hard. "You said hands off."

His smile was slow, predatory. "I don't intend to use my hands, Jenny. Don't need to. Every good whore knows that."

Emerald eyes drilled her, making promises, making accusations. And then he bent his mouth to hers.

She'd anticipated anger in his kiss. Instead, he gave her gentleness. His lips brushed hers like the softest satin, the lightest silk. Jenny's eyes drifted shut as the liquid sensation returned. Her limbs grew heavy—pliant—as he increased the pressure of his mouth on hers. Her lips parted with a moan and he swallowed the sound, then ventured inside with his tongue. Stroking the slick sides of her cheeks and the rough surface of her tongue, he offered her a taste of whiskey and of the forbidden.

He made her forget everything but the need to feel his hands upon her. The need to touch him in return.

Lifting one arm, she tentatively brushed his shirtfront. He made a sound low in his throat, then escalated the intensity of the kiss. Now came the heat. The passion. He pushed his body hard against her, and Jenny felt the unmistakable evidence of his desire.

*Oh, Trace.* A thought hovered in the back of her mind, a vague shadow she couldn't grasp in the heat of the moment. Her fingers slipped upward, tracing his jaw in a gentle caress.

"Goddamn you, Constance," he murmured against her mouth.

Jenny stiffened, his words acting like a pail of ice water on molten emotions, and Trace went still. She tasted his fury just before he wrenched his head away.

He backed up, his harsh breaths echoing in the unnatural

silence. He stared at her from eyes that hinted of untold agonies until, with a blink, they shuttered, and his expression smoothed into an unreadable mask. "I beg your pardon. Now, get dressed. We're leaving."

Jenny's heart seemed to lodge in her throat. What had just happened here? Who was Constance? His wife? Had Trace been kissing her and thinking of a ghost?

Insulted at the thought, Jenny lifted her hand and wiped her mouth. "I beg your pardon? That's all you have to say? And what do you mean 'get dressed'? I am dressed."

"Not enough. Not to go out in public." He went to stand beside the window where he pushed aside the filmy red curtains and stared outside.

She folded her arms and waited for him to explain. Before long, it became obvious she waited in vain. "I'm not going anywhere, McBride," she goaded. "I'm not through with my business."

His manner cold as the winter prairie, he glanced around the room and asked, "Where's the dress you wore down here?"

"I wore this!"

He gave a disgusted shake of his head. "You wore that outfit on a public street? What's the matter, Dressmaker. Isn't it enough to have one person stalking you? You want a herd of trail-dusty cowboys after you?"

Wonderful. As if she didn't feel bad enough already, he had to go and bring up Big Jack Bailey. "I have a cloak," she snapped.

"Get it on then. I'm taking you home."

"No, you're not." She didn't want to go back to her cottage. Not yet. Knowing someone had been there and had gone through her things gave her the shudders. She'd stay at the hotel again tonight even if it did mean squandering the coin. "I won't go home."

"You're sure as hell not staying here."

"Who do you think you are to tell me what I will or will not do?"

He drew a deep breath in an obvious effort to hold his temper. "My daughters care about you, Miss Fortune. They'd be devastated should any harm befall you. After the incident last night, and the one you instigated this morning at the Tivoli, I don't like the idea of your wandering around Hell's Half Acre alone. No telling what trouble you'd be setting yourself up for. I cannot go home and face my girls until I know you're safely away from here."

His speech took the wind right out of her sails. He was considering his daughters' feelings. How could she argue with that?

Still, she wasn't ready to go home. "You may escort me to my shop, Mr. McBride. I need to work. I was given two dress orders before your untimely arrival."

He shrugged. "The shop then. That's better for me, anyway. Blackstone Academy began classes today, and I want to be home when the girls arrive. It's Katrina's first day, after all. So, is that all right with you, your highness?"

She gave him an evil glare and snapped, "That's fine."

"Fine," he repeated, marching toward the door.

The working girls at Miss Rachel's Social Emporium didn't think it was so fine. They met Jenny with dress orders in hand as she descended the stairs. Trace grumbled incessantly for the next hour and a half as measurements were taken and money exchanged, but he ignored each of Jenny's requests for him to leave, even when school dismissal time came and went.

When they finally left the Acre, he spent the entire trip to the shop asking Jenny questions about the Baileys. Had she noticed Big Jack hanging around since the notes and such started? What about the sisters, any of them giving her grief?

"The Bailey daughters all moved away following their weddings. I think Mary Rose is in Louisiana, the others somewhere in south Texas."

He continued to grill her, and Jenny sighed in relief when she finally saw the Fortune's Design placard. She'd had about all she could stand of Trace McBride for one day. "Tell me, McBride," she said as he took the shop key from her hand. "Have you always been this domineering, or is it a recent development?"

"Sarcasm doesn't become you." He turned the lock and pushed open the door. "Stay here while I check the shop."

She followed him right inside. "I am not your responsibility, you know. I've been taking care of myself for quite some time."

"I told you to stay outside."

She shrugged. "That was a sure way to get me to come on in."

"Contrary as a mule," he declared, sweeping back the curtain of the fitting room.

"You don't need to do this, McBride."

He stopped and gave her a measured look. "Things were troubling enough before the stunt you pulled this morning." He paused, then almost against his will added, "I'm worried about you."

She didn't know what to say. She simply couldn't mesh the reality of the Trace McBride now conducting a thorough search of the premises, with the Trace McBride who'd kissed her nearly senseless and treated her so meanly in one of Miss Rachel's bedrooms a short time ago.

Taking the order list from her handbag, she crossed to the worktable where she sat and opened her permanent record. She rummaged around for a pencil, then commenced recording the information she'd gathered from her newest clients. She did her best to ignore McBride, but when he finished his search and propped a hip atop her table, obviously waiting for something, she laid down her pencil and looked up. "What is it?"

"Aren't you frightened at all?"

"Of you?" she scoffed.

He scowled. "I'm talking about Bailey."

"Oh. I see." She paused, then said, "I'm not really frightened. Nervous might be a more accurate word. Big Jack is as full of superstition as an egg is of chick, but I doubt he's the type to do physical harm."

"The man hanged a paint-soaked dummy on your front porch and left dead roses in your bed! You don't think that's a warning?"

Jenny's smile was rueful. "He says he knows nothing about it."

"And you believe that lie?"

"No. Well, maybe I believe that there's more to it than I previously thought. I may be wrong, but I believe the mess last night was an attempt to protect against danger, not a threat of it. I think he was trying to get rid of my 'bad luck.'"

"What gives you that idea?"

"Something he said. He told me to do all these different things to change my luck."

Trace picked up her pencil and rapped it against the table. He shook his head. "I don't know. That might be some risky thinking on your part. Sometimes men with strange ideas like Bailey's are the most dangerous. You need to be careful."

"Oh, I'll be careful," Jenny replied. "In fact, I intend to stay at the Cosmopolitan again tonight and give my cottage a little more time to air out." With a grim smile, she added, "I noted a certain sense of…viciousness in the atmosphere last night."

He snorted. "I smelled a rodent."

Jenny fiddled with a button on her cloak, searching for the right words to make the point she believed he needed to hear. "There is something you should understand about me, Mr. McBride. I take after my father in that I am tenacious about something I want. I want Fortune's Design, and I refuse to allow Big Jack Bailey to take it away from me with either rumors or threats. I appreciate your concern, but I am determined to carry on as if nothing happened. Because, in truth, nothing of consequence has occurred. I won't be bullied." She sharpened her stare and added, "By anyone."

One side of his mouth lifted in a crooked grin. "You talk a good game, I'll grant you that. Foolish, but a good game."

"I mean it," she snapped right back. "Now, I have work to do, and you'd best go on upstairs and see to the girls. Who is staying with them after school?"

His grin faded, and was replaced by a grimace. "The housekeeper of the week is a woman named Wilson. I expect she might last till Friday if I'm lucky."

He pushed off the table and sauntered toward the front of the shop. "I'll keep an eye on things as best I can, whether you want me to or not."

"Why?" she asked, throwing out her hands in frustration. "Surely you don't still expect I'll accept your job offer."

He shrugged but didn't really answer. "Guess I'm right tenacious myself."

It wasn't enough. She couldn't say why, she just knew it wasn't enough. "That's no answer, Trace McBride."

At the door, he hesitated. "I'll do it for my girls. Everything I do, I do for my girls."

Jenny's question came low and soft and without forethought. "Is that why you acted the way you did at Miss Rachel's? The kiss? Was that for the girls, too?"

Her words seemed to echo through the shop. She held her breath. Her heart pounded as if her entire fate rested on his reply.

Trace stood frozen, his back to her, his hand gripping the doorknob. Abruptly, he turned. Mockery lengthened his drawl as he said, "Hell, no, Miss Fortune. I learned a lesson a few years back and I'll never forget it. Any time I kiss a woman, I do it for me. All for me. Take it as a warning."

With that, he left her shop.

TRACE STEERED CLEAR of the dressmaker for the next few days, relying on the attentions of others to reassure him Jack Bailey had been leaving her alone. Every time he remembered what had transpired between the two of them in Rachel Warden's bedroom, he wanted to kick himself. He'd been a real bastard. The lady had gotten to him and he'd hit back—quick and fierce and mean.

But truthfully.

He could salve his conscience with that. Any woman who thought to dangle her lure in his direction needed to know he'd steal the bait and dodge the hook. Jenny Fortune had definitely been dangling.

And he'd come closer to being hooked than he had in years. Six years, to be exact.

He'd wanted her. Badly. She'd set his senses afire, erased all rational thought from his mind. He'd sunk into pleasure so pure it was torture, and all from a kiss.

God knew what bedding her might do.

Determined to put the incident from his mind and meeting with only limited success, he managed to avoid any personal contact with Jenny Fortune for the next few days. That ended when a note arrived from Miss Harriett Blackstone, the girls' teacher, requesting a meeting to discuss mischief Maribeth had hatched at school the previous day. Upon arriving he was startled to find Jenny Fortune also in attendance. The meeting that followed proved to be an exercise in humiliation, and one of the longest half hours of Trace's life.

As they left the building a blush stained Jenny's cheeks, and he thanked God for the summer tan that hid proof of his own embarrassment. He yanked on his hat and grimly set his teeth. If he had a nail he'd be chewing on it. "When I get my hands on that girl I swear I'll dust her feathers."

Jenny wouldn't meet his gaze. "I'm certain she meant no

harm. And Miss Blackstone realized the…uh, stories…Maribeth told about us couldn't be true."

"She's only nine years old, by God! I haven't taught her about…that. Where did she learn it? Who told her? That's what I want to know."

They walked together toward the wagon Trace had driven to the school, having delivered four cases of whiskey to a private home on his way to the meeting. Beside the buckboard, he paused. Unwilling to appear ungentlemanly on the heels of his daughter's devilment, he offered Jenny a ride back to the Rankin Building, half-hoping she'd decline.

She accepted. He refused to acknowledge the ripple of rightness he felt at having her seated beside him.

She smelled like soap. Nothing fancy, just clean and fresh. He'd noticed it first in Miss Blackstone's classroom amidst the autumn odor of chalk and children. Her scent teased him, luring his thoughts in a direction they didn't need to go.

She made a couple of attempts at conversation, but Trace wasn't in the mood to chat. They completed the trip to Fortune's Design with an uncomfortable silence hanging between them.

His tenant had recently added awnings to the front of her shop, and the green-and-white striped canvas flapped in the breeze as Trace jumped down from the buckboard. As his boots hit the dry red dirt on Throckmorton Street, Katrina shouted from an open window upstairs. "Papa, oh Papa," she cried, leaning farther out than was safe. "We're so glad you're home."

Emma's head joined her sister's. "Please hurry, Papa. We have something important to tell you."

Trace had a few things to say, himself. He called up to his daughters. "Y'all back away from that window. And tell your sister I said to meet me in the parlor. In fact, I might as well talk to all three of you."

"But Papa!"

The welcome bell in Jenny's shop sounded a tinkle. Trace turned his head to see a stunning woman dressed in a stylish traveling suit of royal-blue serge step from inside. "Well. There you are. No wonder your business is failing if you leave it unattended all the time."

"Mother?" Jenny said incredulously. "What are you doing here?"

*Her mother.* So this was the infamous Monique Day. Trace's gaze swept the older woman, taking in at a glance the fine bone structure, radiant complexion, and curvaceous figure. He should have recognized the lady immediately. Jenny looked just like her.

He glanced from the woman to the upstairs window where now all three of his daughters leaned dangerously over the sill. He lifted his hand to wave them back inside at the same time a man stepped from inside the shop.

Younger than Trace and impeccably dressed, the tall man smoothed a finger over his dark mustache, smiled warmly, and said, "Hello, Jenny darling."

*Jenny darling?* Trace looked at the dressmaker. Was that surprise he saw in her expression? Shock? He tied the reins to a hitching post, his gaze flicking between Jenny and the dandy who called her darling.

She finally cleared her throat, nodded, and replied, "Hello, Edmund."

Edmund. So, his name was Edmund. Trace's mouth suddenly tasted sour. Who the hell was Edmund?

"You're surprised to see me here, are you not, my dear?" Edmund moved forward, lifting a hand to assist Jenny from the wagon.

Trace stepped right in front of him, grabbed the seamstress around the waist, and swung her to the ground

The stranger's eyes flashed a protest. "I say, man!"

"Nothing I imagine I want to hear," Trace drawled.

As the two men squared off like bantam roosters, Monique glanced eagerly from one to the other. "My goodness, Jenny. Who is this man? This situation has shades of one of my dramas. Perhaps we should all go inside before—"

Jenny made brief introductions all around. Trace learned the man's surname. Wharton. Edmund Wharton. Wharton Shipping was a big concern out of Galveston. Did this dandy have a connection with them?

Dismissing the men, Jenny frowned at her mother. "Did you and Edmund cross paths here in Fort Worth?"

"No, he traveled with me. We've just arrived from the coast."

Trace didn't miss the way Jenny's mouth dropped open in surprise as she asked, "You're traveling with Edmund now?"

Monique gave her a look. "Don't be gauche. I am being faithful to your father during this marriage. I have told you that." Then she flashed Wharton a smile. "Edmund has been such a dear. We have plans, Jenny, grand plans. And they involve you."

"Why is it I don't want to hear this?" Jenny questioned of no one in particular.

At that moment the apartment's front door banged open and a trio of petticoats and pigtails burst onto the scene. "What's taking you so long, Papa?" Maribeth asked, folding her arms and looking downright peevish.

Katrina flung herself at his knees, and Emma hung back, wringing her hands. "Don't be mad, Papa. We simply couldn't stay upstairs any longer. You said not to leave until you came home, but you're home now so we shouldn't be in trouble, right?"

"Never mind trouble, Emmie," Katrina said against his shoulder. "We have a 'mergency."

Trace looked at his two older daughters, noting their fearful expressions. "Emergency?"

"Yes!" the three girls exclaimed as one.

The dressmaker stepped toward them. "Girls? What has happened?"

"It's awful, Miss Fortune." Maribeth glared at Edmund Wharton.

"Truly terrible," Emma agreed, fastening her unforgiving stare on Monique Day.

"The most terrible awfullest worstest thing," Katrina cried, wrenching herself from her father's arms. With her flare for the dramatic, she stepped forward, put one hand on her hip, and extended the other arm, her finger pointed at Edmund Wharton's face. "That man has come to steal you away from us. We heard the whole story."

Emma nodded and grasped Jenny's hand. "He says he's come to Fort Worth to marry you!"

*It is bad luck to have a rabbit cross
your path from right to left.*

## CHAPTER EIGHT

AN UNUSUAL, yawning ache spread outward from Trace's heart, catching him by surprise as he turned to Jenny.

She said, "Oh."

That was all.

Then the girls all began talking at once. They protested, challenged, and generally acted extremely upset. As the situation deteriorated, Trace stood woodenly through it all, assaulted by the vague sensation that he was about to forfeit something he hadn't realized he wanted.

After giving Trace a curious look, Monique Day took charge by shooing Wharton and Jenny inside the shop. But when Trace made to follow, his daughters trailing like three little ducklings at his heels, Monique blocked the doorway, her smile gracious but the light in her eyes unyielding. "Family business, Mr. McBride. I'm certain you understand."

He understood, all right, and he didn't like it one little bit. Jenny's dazed expression made him downright uncomfortable. "Mrs. Fortune," he began.

"Day," she corrected. "Monique Day. Please call me Monique. I do feel badly about rushing you away. Perhaps you and your family would care to join us for dinner later this evening at the Cosmopolitan Hotel?"

Trace hesitated. This was a school night; he should put the girls to bed early. But they needed supper one way or the other. What would it hurt? "Thank you, ma'am—uh, Monique. I accept the invitation."

He ushered his daughters upstairs, hating to leave Jenny in the hands of this fancy-man Wharton who called the dressmaker "darling."

The moment the shop's front door shut behind Trace and his children, Jenny looked from her mother to Edmund Wharton, then back to her mother again. "Would someone care to explain just what is going on?"

Monique's smile blossomed like a peach tree in spring. "It's perfect, dear. I've taken the germ of an idea and nurtured it into a full-blown scheme."

Jenny leaned against her worktable and stifled a weary sigh. This was just like her mother.

"Your mother and I have solved your problems," Edmund's voice resounded. "Our plan is simple and to the point. We need only your agreement to put it into motion."

"That's right." Monique opened the door of Jenny's display case and removed a silk fan. Studying the butterflies painted on its face, she explained, "Edmund needs to marry, too. After I left here last time I remembered a conversation I had with his mother. I fear there's been a scandal of some sort involving him and..." Her mouth dipping in a frown, she sought the name from her memory.

"Elizabeth Randolf," Edmund supplied with a laconic smile.

"That's right. The Randolfs are in banking, I believe. I've met the family on a number of occasions. The daughter is a beauty, but that mother of hers has woefully neglected her teeth. Why, if I were her, I'd—"

"Moth—er," Jenny protested.

Monique batted the fan and wrinkled her nose at her daughter. "Anyway, Edmund's moth—er explained that her son's scandal involving the shipping magnate's daughter threatened the Wharton family's personal fortune. His father has issued an ultimatum: Find a wife and settle down or risk disinheritance."

Jenny looked at Edmund. Leaning against the wall, his arms folded across his chest, he lifted a shoulder in a casual shrug. She wasn't surprised by his predicament. It fit with everything she knew about the man.

She had met Thomas Edmund Wharton III last year while visiting her mother in Galveston. He had declared himself smitten within hours of their first meeting, and he had pursued her from that moment on. Jenny had found his attentions flattering at first, but her opinion changed following an incident during the second week of her visit.

While her mother was busy taking the island society by storm, Jenny had sneaked off to a secluded beach to be alone and contemplate the proposition she intended to pose to her father the next time she saw him—the idea of moving away and starting her own business.

The day had been warm, the gulf waters inviting. Believing herself to be quite alone, Jenny had indulged in a swim, dressed in only her chemise and drawers. She'd been gliding along in chest-high water when she met up with the shark named Wharton.

Flashing an enormous smile, he informed her that Monique had sent him to bring her daughter back to Wharton mansion for afternoon tea. He urged her to continue her swim, stating that they weren't in a hurry and that he'd enjoy the opportunity to spend time with her. He swam in circles around her, offering views and opinions of popular topics of conversation. Although he acted the gentleman, Jenny found herself eyeing his back for a dorsal fin. She'd headed for the beach as quickly as possible. He'd sworn to avert his eyes as she exited the water, but the heat of his gaze was tangible as she gathered her clothes and dashed for the cover of the dunes.

From that moment on, she could not look at Edmund Wharton III without picturing him as a shark who swam on land. Over the months that followed, he'd continued his pursuit every time circumstances placed him and Jenny in the same location at the same time. This was the first time, however, he had migrated to the waters of Fort Worth, Texas.

Jenny found herself glancing around the shop for a harpoon. She addressed Edmund. "You don't mind my mother telling this story?"

"Not at all."

Jenny pulled out her work chair and sat down. She had the distinct feeling she'd best save her strength to get through the remainder of the day.

Monique continued. "Once I remembered Edmund's trouble, I realized I had the perfect solution for you both. I telegraphed him and here we are." She snapped the fan shut with a flourish.

"And your 'perfect solution' for me is marrying Edmund?"

"Isn't it wonderful?"

"Wonderful is hardly how I'd describe it, Mother."

Edmund pushed away from the wall. "Monique has told me how important your dress shop is to you, and I've agreed to do what I can to help you keep it. I suggest we live together long enough to satisfy my father's edict and reverse the townspeople's fears about the Bad Luck Wedding Dress. After that, we may enjoy a more liberal, less restrictive marital state."

"It's how your father and I structured our second marriage," Monique informed her. "It worked fine for a time.

Had Mr. Montgomery not become so…proprietary, I believe the experiment would have had a more satisfactory outcome."

Mr. Montgomery, a south Texas cotton planter, hadn't understood the dynamics of Richard and Monique's arrangement, and Jenny remembered the duel between her father and the gentleman to this day. Thank God they both were such pitiful shots.

For a few minutes Jenny sat and thought about her mother's idea. A more liberal, less restrictive married state, he'd said. She knew firsthand just how unfair such an agreement was on children. She wouldn't dream of bringing a child of hers into such a situation. Was she willing to give up future daughters or sons for the sake of Fortune's Design? A few weeks ago, she wouldn't have hesitated to say yes.

But a few weeks ago, she hadn't grown to love the McBride Menaces.

"I appreciate the effort to which both you and Edmund have gone," she said. "I'll need time to think about it." Standing, she continued, "Now, if you'll excuse me, I'd like to check something in the back."

What she wanted to do was escape for a bit. That and change her clothes. She'd made it a practice to keep a few things here at the shop, and now she was glad she did. Before the meeting this morning she'd donned her most stylish day dress in the hopes of gaining the schoolteacher's patronage. Her choice, she silently insisted as she entered the dressing room, had nothing to do with the fact that she'd be seeing Trace McBride.

"Lot of good it did," she muttered. The teacher obviously didn't give a fig for fashion.

And Trace had walked away without looking back.

As Jenny yanked at the buttons on her bodice, her mother's voice intruded. "Now, now. For a seamstress you're being horribly rough with that fabric, Jenny. Please don't be so careless."

"Monique, I'd appreciate a little privacy."

"You don't need privacy; you need a husband. Tell me what the problem is so I can see to solving it."

Jenny sighed. "I can't tell you what the problem is because I don't know what it is myself." She might suspect, but she wasn't about to admit it.

"Is it your father? Have you changed your mind about living with him?"

"No," Jenny said without hesitation. "I do want to remain in Fort Worth. I want to restore the reputation of Fortune's Design and make it the success it once was."

"Then why aren't you happier about the solution I—at great trouble I might add—have offered?" Monique paused and gave her daughter a considering look. "Don't tell me you've managed on your own. Have you done it, Jenny? Did you find your own man to marry? Could it be this Mr. McBride? He'd a look about him. Possessiveness. It clung to him as nicely as that shirt he wore."

Jenny heard Trace's words echo through her mind. *Surely you didn't think I was asking you to marry me,* he'd said. *I'll never marry again.*

"No, Mother. I have no marital prospects at the moment."

Monique tapped a finger against her mouth. After giving her daughter a long, considering look, she shrugged and said, "Yes, you do have a marital prospect. You have Edmund! He's perfect. He needs you as much as you need him."

*Trace McBride needs me.* The thought flashed through Jenny's mind as she stared at her reflection in the mirror. It was true. He did need her. For his children, and maybe even for himself. He was simply too big a fool to realize it.

*He might need me, but he certainly doesn't want me.*

Monique continued to talk, reiterating her arguments. Jenny listened, growing colder by the moment, and a grim smile spread across her face. She had more pride than to pursue a man who didn't want her. It was time to forget about Trace McBride entirely, forget her foolish dreams.

Marriage to Edmund wouldn't be all that bad. She'd regain her professional reputation. She'd have Fortune's Design. Certainly, her fate could be worse. She could return to East Texas and work as her father's research assistant.

Marry Edmund and save Fortune's Design. Save her independence, her autonomy. Monique was right. It was a perfect solution.

If it made her want to cry, so what?

She exhaled the breath she had been holding and exited the dressing room. Edmund leaned against her worktable, flipping through a sketchbook. When he looked up, Jenny nodded and said, "All right. I'll marry you, Edmund. As soon as possible, if you don't mind."

He flashed a mouthful of teeth and walked toward her. As Edmund's mouth swooped down on hers for a kiss, she shuddered and wondered, *Dear Lord, what have I done?*

AFTER LEAVING Fortune's Design, Trace sent the girls upstairs while he unloaded foodstuffs from the back of the wagon. Returning the conveyance to the wagonyard could wait, he decided, hoisting a pair of boxes into his arms. Experience had taught him that leaving the girls alone for more than a few minutes when they were this upset invited trouble.

Besides, he sort of wanted to keep an eye on the situation downstairs.

As he climbed the steps to his apartment, his thoughts focused on Edmund Wharton. Trace didn't like the look of the fellow one bit. His eyes were too close together, and he had an oily look about him. A fellow like that couldn't be trusted.

Trace knew men like Wharton; he made his living off men like Wharton. They came to the Acre to drink away their troubles, gamble away their money, and throw away their marriage vows by bedding the whores.

Jenny Fortune deserved better.

Trace entered his apartment, dumped the boxes on the kitchen floor, then headed straight for his bedroom where his daughters were already in position, monitoring the events taking place in Fortune's Design.

Emma lifted her eye from the knothole in the floor and begged, "Papa, don't make us leave. Please. This truly is an emergency. You won't believe what's happened."

Trace shook his head. "Scoot over, Emmie."

"But Papa!"

"Hush, sweets. We won't be able to hear a thing if you keep yammering." With that Trace dropped to his hands and knees and put his eye to the spy hole.

What he saw made him seethe.

Thomas Edmund Wharton III was kissing Jenny Fortune.

FORT WORTH had seen more than its share of strange sights over the years. In a rowdy town of buffalo hunters and whores, cowboys and tycoons, bizarre incidents often proved the order of the day. But the sight that got the town to talking, the event that created more wind than a west Texas dust storm, was the gathering that took place in the restaurant of the Cosmopolitan Hotel that evening.

Mr. Thomas Edmund Wharton III, dapper in gray pinstripes, entered the dining salon with a beautiful woman on each arm. On his left walked the talented, notorious sculptress, Monique Day. On his right was Monique's daughter, Jenny, infamous as the creator of the Bad Luck Wedding Dress. They took their seats with quiet aplomb, and the gentleman made a show of ordering a bottle of the Cosmopolitan's best champagne.

As appealing as the two women proved to be, it was another sight entirely that stopped people on the street. A crowd gathered, pointing and murmuring as they gazed through the plate-glass window into the hotel dining room.

Trace McBride had brought his Menaces to dine in public.

"If a man didn't know better, he might label those three pretty little girls angels," a portly gentleman observed. "All dressed up in ruffles and bows, they certainly look the part."

"Table manners!" a matron noted, shaking her head in disbelief. "Who would have ever thought."

Finally Trace asked the waiter to see that the window curtains were closed. "I feel like a monkey in a cage," he whispered to Maribeth.

"In a circus wagon, Papa," Katrina piped up. "Did you hear the news? P. T. Barnum is bringing his circus to town. Isn't it exciting?"

Jenny, in the first natural action Trace had seen in her that night, offered Katrina a conspiratorial smile. "Yes, it is. I can't wait. The animals. The acrobats. It sounds so exciting."

"I want to ride an elephant." Katrina turned to her father. "Can I, Papa? Can I ride an elephant? Will you take us to the circus, please?"

Trace gazed around the table. "Don't have to, Katie-cat," he said in a loud whisper. "We're already there."

Jenny laughed into her napkin, pretending a cough.

Katrina's eyes clouded with worry. "But Papa…"

"I'll take you, sweetheart. Don't worry." He winked at his youngest daughter, who clasped her hands joyfully together.

Her face beaming, she asked, "Can Miss Fortune go with us? We'd have ever so much fun."

"I'll be Miss Fortune's escort, young lady," Edmund Wharton said. He dabbed at his mouth with a pristine napkin and gave Jenny an intimate smile. "Ah, the circus. Mr. Barnum puts on quite a show, I'm told. The bareback riders are said to be unbelievably daring."

Trace glanced around the table. No one but he seemed to have noticed how the light in Jenny's eyes dimmed as she nodded in response to her fiancé's comment.

Her fiancé. Memory of that kiss Wharton planted on Jenny had haunted him all afternoon. First thing tomorrow he intended to patch that damned spy hole in his bedroom floor.

Trace stabbed his beefsteak with his fork. Why had he come here tonight? Why was he putting himself and his girls through this? After Emma informed him that Jenny had accepted Wharton's proposal moments before the kiss he witnessed, he'd decided not to go anywhere near the Cosmopolitan Hotel that evening. But as the girls took to hammering him about stopping Miss Fortune's wedding, he'd decided the best thing for them—and possibly himself—would be to demonstrate how he supported the dressmaker's decision to marry.

The problem was he didn't support it. Not one bit. Not to this fellow.

He lifted a bite of meat to his mouth and observed Edmund Wharton while he chewed. The man was a snake, a sharper. Trace couldn't imagine Jenny Fortune married to a man like that. She needed someone scholarly, someone more reserved and cerebral.

Wharton would give her physical.

The steak's flavor turned sour at the thought, and Trace forced himself to swallow. His hand clenched around his fork as he imagined his fist crashing into the pretty boy's face.

The violence of his reaction—both this afternoon and again this evening—had shown him the necessity of supporting the dressmaker's decision to marry. He realized he was dangerously close to falling under the woman's spell himself. A wedding ring around her finger would put an end to that, thank God.

Trace didn't mess with other men's wives. He knew just how destructive such an action could be.

Watching Jenny smile at something Maribeth said, Trace reminded himself that marriage between Wharton and the seamstress would also mean the finish of the foolish fantasies his girls had indulged in concerning him, the lady, and marriage vows. What a blessing that would be!

Ever since Emma's birthday picnic, the Menaces had wrenched up the harassment. That foolishness with their teacher was but a small part of it. Hell, they'd done everything but book a church and preacher.

He lifted his water glass to his lips as Monique turned to him and said, "Before I forget, allow me to compliment you on the quality of spirits you serve at the End of the Line, Mr. McBride. I was quite impressed with the entire establishment, in fact."

Trace damn near choked on his drink. Clearing his throat, he said, "You've visited my saloon?"

"Yes. I accompanied Jenny this afternoon while she visited the whorehouse across the street." Emma's and Maribeth's heads jerked up and their mouths fell open. Before Trace found his voice, Monique forged ahead. "The madam and I had a long chat about you, and I wanted to see your place of business. I will caution you to watch the bartender named Bob. I believe he was watering the whiskey. Peter, however, poured a nice strong drink."

When his older daughters shared a scandalized look, Trace smothered a groan and turned his attention to containing the damage. "Girls," he said, offering his daughters a pointed smile, "you may be excused."

"But, Papa, we're not ready to leave yet." Emma's gaze darted from her father to Monique, desire to hear more written all across her face.

"That's right," Maribeth added. "We can't go yet. Look at Katrina's peas. All she's done is smush them. She hasn't eaten a one and you said—"

"*Now*, Maribeth." Trace's tone brooked no argument. "Mrs. Raines is upstairs in her apartment waiting for your visit."

With one look at her father, Maribeth's mouth snapped shut. She scooted from her chair without another word, as did her sisters. The Menaces knew not to push him any further today.

He'd given them plenty of warning. Before they left home he'd laid out his expectations concerning their behavior at dinner. No whining, no back talk, and absolutely no shenanigans or they would suffer dire consequences.

As they politely said their good-byes, Trace was thankful he'd previously made arrangements for his daughters to go upstairs after dinner to visit with the hotel proprietor's invalid mother. The girls liked the elderly Widow Raines and usually enjoyed the weekly visits that had begun following an incident involving a rock, a window, and a bruise on Mrs. Raines's head.

At this particular moment, he wished he had a rock to chuck at Edmund Wharton. The oily bastard was sipping at his drink, his lips twitching in smug amusement.

Like well-mannered young ladies, his daughters filed from the room. They spoiled the effect somewhat by making a mad dash up the staircase clearly visible through the French doors that separated the dining area from the hotel lobby.

Monique's eyes were wide with innocence as she said, "Oh, dear, did I speak out of turn?"

"Of course you spoke out of turn, Monique," Edmund drawled, lifting his wineglass toward Trace in mock salute. "Few men care for their dealings with whores to be discussed at the dinner table. Am I right, McBride?"

"Now, Edmund, I wasn't referring to Trace's sexual exploits. Rachel Warden mentioned those only in passing." Monique gave Trace a wink and continued, "Mainly we talked about his financial exploits. He is quite the success story according to Rachel. His End of the Line is considered the best saloon in town, despite the fact he has no abovestairs business. I was quite impressed, actually."

She freed a dazzling smile and addressed Trace. "That's another reason I was so glad you accepted my invitation here tonight. I had an idea that might help Fortune's Design through these difficult times until the wedding restores her reputation. Your saloon has the perfect place for a stage, Mr. McBride. If you were to host a floor show, my daughter could design costumes for the dancers similar to some of the dresses she's fashioned for Rachel's girls. Why, you'd have to add to your building to serve all your customers." With a quick glance to Edmund, she said, "You must see this one gown she's made. It's striped black-and-scarlet satin, and cut all the way to—"

"I've seen it," Trace said flatly, Monique's words recalling the image to his mind.

"That's right." Monique waved a hand. "Silly of me to forget. That's what gave me the idea to begin with. Rachel said you took one look at my daughter and—"

"Mother!" Jenny put down her fork, obviously embarrassed. "Please. I'm not designing any dresses for any floor show."

"I should say not," Edmund agreed. "You won't have time because you'll be too busy sewing a trousseau." Lifting her hand, he pressed a kiss to her palm and added, "I think I'll request five ensembles, my dear, all similar to this black-and-scarlet striped silk."

Trace shoved to his feet. "Excuse me. I'm afraid I've developed a bad case of indigestion. It's time I fetched my girls on home, anyway. Can't keep them out too late on a school night."

He heard Edmund Wharton's self-satisfied chuckle as he walked away. Monique Day sputtered on about wedding plans, and Jenny remained silent. Upon reaching the doorway into the hotel lobby, he couldn't resist a glance back.

She was watching him, her eyes dimmed with an emotion he didn't want to name. Fragile, he thought. As if a stiff wind could snap her in two. Not at all like his Jenny Fortune.

*His Jenny Fortune. Well, hell.*

Trace slammed the French door behind him.

*Charleston, South Carolina*

WIND BUFFETED the lone figure standing on the second-floor veranda of the stately home overlooking the Ashley River. A dark gray haze hung low in the sky, swallowing the treetops and lending an appropriate sense of isolation to the morning.

Tye McBride's lips curled in a bitter smile. He didn't need weather to provide the perception of solitude. He was used to feeling alone, even when surrounded by people. Especially then, in fact, because the crush of bodies in a crowd made him feel his loss more intensely.

His loss. That made it sound like a death, and in a very real way it was. All his life he'd shared a bond with another soul, his other half, his twin. Distance had not affected it, neither had war. Even in the darkest days of Reconstruction politics, when they were pitted against each other in a vicious battle of words, the connection had never been severed.

Until that god-awful night seven years ago when a woman had succeeded where all else had failed.

Since then, Tye had been alone. Bitterly, guiltily, miserably alone.

Rain spat from the clouds, splattered against the cobblestones, and advanced upon him like a harsh, cold death. The wind whipped and swirled, sending a loose shutter somewhere above him flapping against the wall. Tye stood his ground, braced against the wind, facing the decision he had avoided a good portion of the day.

He glanced down at the newspaper clenched in his fist. Waterspots had left darkened splotches across the yellowed pages but failed to obstruct the letters of a masthead. D-E-M-O. For the *Fort Worth Daily Democrat*, a Texas newspaper dated April 18, 1879, and delivered to him by the investigator earlier that day.

*Texas. Why the hell Texas?*

On page 3 under "Letters to the Editor" the owner of a local saloon had chided the city fathers for their crackdown on the entertainments offered in a place the writer called "the Acre." The letter read in part:

Mayor Beckham has gone beyond the public mandate to control the lawlessness in the entertainment section of our fair town. With the cattle season beginning, I implore the city leaders to rescind the ordinances that have closed so many of our amusements, keeping the cowboys on the prairie with their herds and their monies still in their pockets. Fort Worth's economic survival depends on it.

The letter was signed "Trace McBride, Proprietor, End of the Line Saloon."

Tye drew back his arm and threw the rolled newspaper as hard and as far as he could. Weighted by the rain and blown by the wind, it landed atop a flower planter almost directly below.

"Damn. A bartender." The injustice of it, the irony of it, made him want to scream. Years ago, alcohol had damn near killed Tye, and his brother had saved him. Trace had left his home, his family, and his flourishing career as an architect to spend three months drying out his hostile and sometimes dangerous brother.

When it was over, Tye had sworn never to touch the stuff again. He'd broken the vow once, and it had cost him everything.

"Thackery," a soft voice called from behind him. "Come inside. You're getting drenched."

Turning around, he smiled at his grandmother. At seventy-four, Mirabelle McBride was still a beautiful woman. White hair crowned a face lined with age, but time had yet to dim the vividness of her emerald eyes. She held out a hand. "Help me, Thackery. This stormy weather seeps into my bones."

Tye immediately moved to do her bidding. He would not fail Mirabelle. If she needed him in any way at all, he'd be there to help her. Pressing a kiss to her temple, he took her arm and offered her his support. Just as she had done for him and Trace and their three sisters since the day they buried their parents.

"Help me to the rocker by the fireplace, dear, and add more wood if you don't mind. It's chilly in this parlor. Too chilly for an old woman."

"Grandmother, you'll never be old." Tye settled her into the seat, then took a log from the woodbox and tossed it onto the low burning flames. Sparks rose up the chimney and within moments the wood caught fire. He lifted a brass poker and moved the logs around. As he returned it to the stand, Mirabelle spoke.

"What will you do now, Thackery?"

He shut his eyes. Though he stood mere feet from the now crackling fire, he felt cold inside. Brittle. "I don't know. I haven't decided."

She tsked. "You decided four years ago when you began searching for your brother."

The Westminster chime of the mantel clock struck the quarter hour. "I don't have to go myself. Anyway, I don't want to leave you, Grandmother."

"I will not be used as an excuse, Tye," she said pointedly. "I am quite capable of watching out for myself. It isn't as if I'd be alone, not with your sister living here now."

"What about the plantings? I need to—"

"Correct me if I'm wrong, dear, but isn't that why you

asked your sister to move home? That husband of hers is an
excellent manager. Ellen and Scott and I can take care of Oak
Grove just fine, and if we need any help, your other sisters
are only a day away."

"But—"

"No 'buts,' Thackery. You must settle between you face-
to-face. You owe him that much."

He did owe his brother. He owed an explanation and an
apology for a start, but neither one would ever be enough to
make up for his betrayal, to replace what he had stolen.

*What he had stolen.* The words were thorns in his heart.
For all his villainy, Tye wasn't the only one who had stolen.
Trace had stolen from him, too. Something irreplaceable.
Something precious.

Guilt fed the anger that flared, fierce and hot inside him. He
whirled away from the fire and began to pace the room, fists
clenched at his sides. "You're right, Grandmother. I have to go,
don't I? This situation must be resolved, one way or another."

Mirabelle tugged on the lap robe draped over the back of
her rocker, then spread it across her legs. "I know it will be
difficult for you, Tye, and it will be difficult for Trace, also.
When he left here he was hurt and angry and grieved, but six
years is a long time. He'll be ready to listen now."

"I don't know, Grandmother. He hates me still." He brought
his fist up to his heart. "I feel it here."

The elderly woman shook her head. "No. Trace isn't like
that. Once he listens to your side of—"

"*If* he listens." Tye caught sight of his reflection in a gilt-
framed wall mirror. He saw the traitorous guilt etched in
permanent lines across his brow. He saw his brother, horror-
stricken and bowed by grief. Memory provided the image of
a third figure. Beautiful. Bewitching.

Bloody.

If he'd had anything at all in his hand he'd have flung it at the mirror. "He wouldn't listen six years ago. If our places were reversed, I doubt I'd want to set eyes on him the rest of my life. I betrayed him, Grandmother," Tye said, his voice rough. "I betrayed him—my own twin brother—in the worst possible way."

"Come here, dear," Mirabelle said, holding out her hand.

He wanted more than anything to flee the room, but he would not deny his grandmother anything. Steps dragging, Tye crossed the room to stand beside the rocking chair. She took his hand, gave it a squeeze, and brought it to her lips for a kiss. "Other than you, I know Trace better than anyone. He'll forgive you, Thackery. And once he does, perhaps you'll be able to forgive yourself."

He closed his eyes. He wanted that. God, how he wanted that. In the very core of his soul, he ached for his brother's forgiveness. Emotion clogged Tye's throat. "It'll never happen."

"It will. I am certain of it."

Tye's smile was weary. "You believe that, Grandmother, because you don't know all the facts. You see, there's something I've never told you about that night."

Concern furrowed Mirabelle's brow. "Thackery?"

He stared into the fire, remembering the hell of that night long ago. "She was dying. Trace held her in his arms. Tears flowed down his face. Constance looked up at him and smiled. She looked so beautiful, Grandmother. Radiant, like an angel. She told him—"

His teeth clenched. He swallowed hard.

"What, dear? What did Constance say?"

Tye spoke in a broken whisper. "Ah, Nana. She told him about the baby."

*You will have bad luck if you look at
the moon through trees or bushes.*

## CHAPTER NINE

WITH THE WEDDING DATE set a scant three weeks away, Monique plunged into a flurry of anxious planning. Jenny, unable to shake the aura of melancholy hanging over her, paid scant attention to her mother's arrangements and participated only when forced.

While Monique labored to provide the most elegant wedding Fort Worth had ever seen, Edmund hobnobbed with the city's elite and communed with the sinners down in Hell's Half Acre. Three or four times a week he arrived on her doorstep to escort her to various social events. He purchased the best seats in the house for P. T. Barnum's One and Only Show on Earth, then put on a courtship show as entertaining to the crowd as the performances inside the rings. At picnics, soirees, and dance club socials, they played the happy couple, and soon the pending wedding was the talk of the town, fueled by the snippets of gossip provided in the *Daily Democrat* by Wilhemina Peters.

Amid all the commotion, the bride-to-be devoted most of her attention to Fortune's Design.

Her situation was getting downright desperate. In filling orders from the ladies of Miss Rachel's Social Emporium, she had depleted her supplies. Her cash reserves remained woefully small because the majority of those orders had been made on credit, the recipients scheduled to make weekly payments on account.

Jenny knew one word to Monique would replenish her coffers, but Jenny wanted to do this on her own. She needed to do it on her own. She was confident a little conservation here and a little stretching there would carry her through the lean times until her marriage erased the reputation of the Bad Luck Wedding Dress from the minds of the citizens of Fort Worth.

The McBride Menaces took to visiting her shop every afternoon, providing a well-appreciated distraction from her troubles. She found their attempts to dissuade her from her intended course of action both creative and heartbreaking.

They talked about Trace constantly, expounding at length about his good qualities, glossing over his less attractive traits—such as his taste for green peas. Even more telling, the girls acted like angels. They abandoned all their pranks and took up doing good deeds—going so far as to assist Sister Gonzaga in the nuns' garden. As the wedding date grew closer, they intensified their efforts. They made wild promises, swore vows of good behavior, pleaded their case with tear-filled eyes and a sense of drama that affected Jenny more than they guessed.

Their objective was obvious. They wanted Jenny to marry their father. Short of telling them Trace had sworn—quite forcefully—never to marry again, Jenny did everything within her power to convince them to abandon their hopes. She stated clearly and often that her wedding to Edmund Wharton would take place as planned, at the same time assuring the McBrides that her marriage would not interfere with the friendship they shared.

But Emma, Maribeth, and Katrina refused to give up. The day before the wedding, Jenny arrived at her shop to find Maribeth McBride seated on the stoop. "We've a holiday today," she said.

"So soon?" Jenny unlocked the front door and stepped inside. Maribeth trailed in after her.

"It's sort of an emergency holiday. There was a big fight at school yesterday, and Miss Blackstone declared a day off to allow everyone time for tempers to cool. You should be proud of us, Miss Fortune. Emmie, Kat, and I sat off to the side and watched. We weren't involved one little bit. Miss Blackstone could hardly believe it."

"I can imagine."

"You should see Sally Franklin, though." Wonder filled the youngster's voice. "Biggest shiner I've ever seen. Sally will be black and blue for weeks."

Not wanting to comment on acts of violence in the classroom, Jenny changed the subject by posing a question about the newest housekeeper employed by Trace McBride.

"We've decided to be nice to Mrs. Wilson," Maribeth replied. "She bakes the best green apple pie we've ever tasted. Don't tell Papa, but it's because of the brandy. She adds a scosh of brandy to the recipe."

"A scosh of brandy, hmm?" Jenny stifled a smile, hiding her amusement.

"Yep. Papa would probably have a fit if he knew. You know how he is about drinking."

Jenny remembered the taste of whiskey in his kiss and said, "No, I don't. What do you mean?"

"Well." The child paused dramatically and accepted a molasses cookie from a plate Jenny offered. "It's because he owns a saloon, you see. He tells us he sees some very wicked things that arise from a person's overindulgence. He wants us to know we never have to worry about him doing anything wrong because of John Barleycorn."

"John Barleycorn," Jenny repeated. "Your father said that?"

Maribeth nodded and chomped her cookie. "Papa never touches the stuff."

*Why, the big liar.* Jenny sat at her worktable, thoroughly disgusted. She knew very well Trace McBride had been drinking the day he came to Miss Rachel's room. Was he trying to protect his daughters from the knowledge of his vices? While she might understand it, she refused to condone it. Lying was never a good excuse for the truth. If she were the girls' mother, she'd make certain—

Jenny broke off the thought. She wasn't going to think that way. She wasn't their mother. She never would be their mother.

After wiping crumbs off her face with her sleeve, Maribeth said, "Miss Fortune, can I talk with you about something?"

"Certainly."

The girl straddled a chair next to Jenny, heedless of a bold display of petticoat. Her expression turned somber and her eyes glazed. "It's about the wedding. You must listen to us, it's very important. Kat and Emma and I are convinced you shouldn't marry Mr. Wharton."

Jenny sighed. She'd anticipated this talk for days now, and she'd planned a nice, clear explanation the girls would understand. "Now, sweetheart, I want you and your sisters to know that nothing will change between us once I'm married. You'll still be welcome here; you'll still be my friends. I'm doing what I must do."

"No, Miss Fortune, you're wrong. Haven't you noticed how good we've been lately? We haven't done a single bad thing. We'd be *wonderful* daughters."

Ah, so that's what this was about. Jenny reached across the table and tilted up Maribeth's chin. "I'd like nothing more than for y'all to be my daughters. But honey, the fact is—"

*Bang, bang, bang.* The back door rattled from the force of the knock.

Maribeth hopped up and ran to answer it. Hinges creaked as the door swung open. "It's Mr. Starnes from the railroad, Miss Fortune."

"Howdy, ma'am." The burly deliveryman stood beside a wagon, invoice in hand. "I have a shipment for you that's come all the way from Europe. Imagine that."

Immediately Jenny forgot all about weddings and explanations and excuses. Her fabric had arrived! She'd placed this order months ago, when Fortune's Design looked to be a resounding success, long before Wilhemina Peters and Ethel Baumgardner started spreading their clothesline talk. Excitement sparked to life inside her. "Oh, I've been waiting for this shipment. There is a particular bolt of cloth I'm dying to work with. It's a midnight-blue silk shot with gold and silver threads."

Starnes mumbled something, obviously unimpressed. Jenny didn't care. With this shipment of yard goods, she'd create gowns the likes of which this state had never seen. She clasped her hands to her chest, her smile as big as Texas.

"What is it, Miss Fortune?" Maribeth peered up at the crate with interest.

"Oh, Mari, just wait till you see. It's—"

The deliveryman interrupted with a paper for her to sign, saying, "Put your John Henry here, pay me the $321.75 you owe, and it's all yours."

Jenny's hand stilled in midsignature. "Three twenty-one seventy-five?" she repeated.

She didn't have the money. She'd used the cash held in reserve for this order to pay the July rent when the first of the bad-luck rumors had surfaced and cut into her business. The payments from Miss Rachel's girls wouldn't make a dent in this bill. "I thought I'd have time. I didn't think it would drag on this long," she mumbled, closing her eyes in distress.

"What's that, ma'am?"

"Um, Mr. Starnes, I have a slight problem." What followed was a ten-minute discussion that degenerated into begging and pleading on Jenny's part, to no avail.

"It's gotta go back to the railroad, Miss Fortune," the deliveryman eventually pronounced. "My hands are tied."

A heavy sense of defeat weighted her shoulders. She desperately needed this shipment. One look at her designs for these fabrics would have the women of Fort Worth racking their brains for an excuse to order dresses. Her donning of the Bad Luck Wedding Dress for her own ceremony would provide that excuse.

The timing was perfect. Jenny couldn't afford to allow this opportunity to pass.

She'd borrow the money from her mother.

"Mr. Starnes, I'll obtain the funds later today and have them for you tomorrow. If you'll leave the fabric—"

"Sorry, ma'am. This order is COD. I can't leave the goods without the cash." He glanced down at his form. "I have a standing order for all goods refused at this address, and I'm obligated to see that the goods are delivered there. Sorry Miss Fortune." He heaved the crate back onto the wagon.

"Standing order?" Confusion dulled her mind. "What standing order?"

Touching a finger to his cap, he climbed into the wagon. Grabbing up the reins, he glanced down and said, "From a woman in Dallas. Miss Ethel Baumgardner. I'd best hurry along if I'm going to get this delivery back to the station before the next train pulls out." The wagon rolled forward, leaving Jenny standing stiff with shock in its dusty wake.

*Ethel Baumgardner. Ethel Baumgardner!*

"That witch," she whispered. "That underhanded, talentless, green-eyed biddy." Fury pounded through her as she stared after her departing dreams. Wasn't it enough that Ethel Baumgardner had capitalized on the Bad Luck Wedding Dress fiasco and stolen all her customers? Did she have to steal the fabric right off her bolts, too? Angry tears swelled in Jenny's eyes and spilled down her cheeks.

She felt a tiny hand slip into hers and she looked down.

"Don't cry, Miss Fortune," Katrina's sad voice implored. "Please?"

Jenny glanced around to see Maribeth and Emma standing behind their sister, watching her with somber faces. She tried to smile, but knew it was a sorry effort at best. "When did you and Emma come down?" she asked Katrina in a tremulous voice.

"About the time the grumpy man started carrying on about money. Maybe you should have paid him in kisses, Miss Fortune. That's what I always do with my papa."

Jenny swallowed the hysteric laughter that bubbled up at Katrina's innocent comment. Then Emma spoke, her soft voice filled with concern. "I'm sorry about the yard goods, Miss Fortune."

"It's not fair!" Maribeth stared down the alley, arms folded as she fumed. "It's the stupidest thing, him not waiting one little day. That Ethel woman shouldn't get your cloth!"

"It doesn't matter, girls. Let's go inside."

"It does too matter! I've met that Dallas dressmaker before. The dresses she makes are ugly. She'll ruin your fabric!"

Jenny closed her eyes and sighed. Maribeth was right. That fabric would be wasted on a designer of Mrs. Baumgardner's talents.

"Never mind Ethel." She gathered the girls in her arms and gave them a big, group hug. "I want to talk about you three. Y'all are my very best friends, do you know that? Your support means so very much to me."

Katrina wrapped her arms around Jenny's legs and hugged tight. "We love you, Miss Fortune."

Emotion clogged Jenny's throat. "I love you, too." Taking

a deep breath, she swiped at the tears on her cheek and stepped away. "Now, don't you think you should get back upstairs? It's almost lunchtime, and Mrs. Wilson might have some of that green apple pie waiting for you."

Acknowledging Jenny's point, the McBride daughters hurried upstairs. After gulping down their lunch, they settled down in their attic bedroom to complete the extra schoolwork assigned to make up for the unexpected holiday. At least, that's how they made it appear should Mrs. Wilson check on them.

Katrina mouthed her way through the alphabet. Emma whipped through an arithmetic lesson, and Maribeth stared out the window, her expression glum. "It didn't work, Emmie. The wedding is tomorrow, and I was just working into my argument when Mr. Starnes knocked. Now Miss Fortune's too upset to listen to anything we'd have to say."

Katrina wrinkled her nose. "That mean Miss Baumgardner, I don't like her. I wish we'd said no to Monique's idea."

"Me, too. I think Miss Fortune's feelings are going to be hurt when she sees us in those dresses. Besides, they're ugly. They're better suited for a garden scarecrow than us." She paused, her forehead knit in wrinkles. "We have to do something."

Emma looked up. "We will. I have it all figured out. Obviously, our acting good all the time hasn't done the trick."

"It's the hardest thing I've ever done," Katrina observed, plopping her thumb into her mouth.

Emma continued. "It's all right, Kat. That's all over with now. The McBride Menaces are about to return. With a vengeance."

Katrina's thumb left her mouth with a pop. "What are we going to do?"

"Are we gonna get her fabric back?" Maribeth inquired.

"Yes, we certainly are. We'll get that fabric. Then, we return it to her in such a way that Miss Fortune will cancel the wedding."

"How?" the younger sisters chimed.

"It's simple, really." Emma offered an angel's smile. "First, the McBride Menaces are going to rob the train."

EMMA PLANNED the assault like a West Point general. After listening while her sister outlined their strategy, Maribeth nodded. "Sounds good to me, Emma. Casey Tate will be glad to help us. He's good at that sort of thing. Papa will kill us, of course, but I reckon it'll be worth it."

Katrina nodded seriously. "It's a good plan, Emmie. We're lucky you're the thinker in the family like Papa says."

"He says that?"

"Yep. You're the thinker, Mari's the doer, and I'm still trying to make up my mind. I do know two things, though. I don't want Miss Fortune to marry that man, and I don't want that old Ethel lady to get Miss Fortune's cloth."

Emma nodded slowly and shifted her gaze toward the mantel clock. "The train leaves here at eleven-thirty."

"Yep," Maribeth said. "They changed the schedule last week."

"Good. And the wedding is at four tomorrow afternoon, so we should have plenty of time to arrange everything."

"If we hurry." Maribeth jumped up and headed for the stairs.

"It won't take more than five minutes to sneak the crowbar we need from the blacksmith's," Emma replied, motioning Katrina to come along as she followed Maribeth downstairs. "We might have trouble finding Casey, though. Especially if we have to go into the Acre to look for him."

Maribeth groaned. "The Acre! Papa will really kill us."

"That's stupid, Mari. What difference is there between killing and really killing?"

"The number of blisters on our backsides."

"Oh."

The girls peered cautiously around a doorjamb, then darted

past Mrs. Wilson, who was busy dusting the parlor furniture. Once outside, they headed first toward the Tivoli Restaurant where they hoped to locate Casey Tate. The owner of the Tivoli often provided the boy a meal in exchange for work.

They found Casey munching on a plate of fried chicken, and Emma outlined their plan without delay. Casey was able to provide both the crowbar and a quilt to hide it in, and soon the three girls were hurrying through the streets toward the Texas & Pacific depot at the far south end of town. They had a close call at the intersection of Fourteenth and Houston, when they nearly ran right into Mrs. Wilhemina Peters. Thankfully, the editor's wife looked in the opposite direction, staring with disapproval at a painted lady headed toward the Acre.

The sisters reached the train yard without further incident, and as they drew to a halt near the massive, hissing iron engine, Maribeth leaned over and said, "There's a bunch of freight cars. Where do we start looking?"

Emma's brow wrinkled in thought, then she said, "I think we should try the last one. It makes sense that goods to be unloaded at the first stop would be in the last car, don't you think? They might just unhook it and leave it behind."

Maribeth agreed, and the two older girls turned to their younger sister. Emma pointed toward the front of the train and murmured, "You know what to do, Kat?"

The little girl nodded. "I'll do a good job."

"We know you will," Emma replied, smiling. "Good luck."

Katrina's eyes shone with anticipation as she skipped toward the front of the train. Then, with a last glance toward Emma and Maribeth, she turned her back, lifted her face toward the sky, and wailed at the top of her lungs.

Immediately, all eyes around the train depot turned in Katrina's direction. Maribeth and Emma used the diversion to clamber into the boxcar nearest the caboose on the train departing for Dallas and points east at eleven-thirty.

Their sister's cry built to a crescendo as they went to work, and they paused just long enough to share a smile. "She'll be an actress when she grows up, sure as shootin'," Maribeth stated.

The open door on the boxcar provided plenty of light to see, but the sheer number of crates made it difficult to move around. To complicate matters, many of the boxes looked strikingly similar to the one for which they searched. "This is gonna take forever," Maribeth grumbled.

Emma ignored her, checking the address markings on each crate she came to. "Here's one for Dallas. Hand me the crowbar, Mari." She held out her hand as her sister retrieved the tool from near the door.

"Well, is that it?" she asked impatiently as Emma worked to open the large square box.

Emma lifted the lid and peered inside. "Nope. It's leather goods. But here." She passed her sister the crowbar and pointed toward a crate in the corner. "I think I see a Dallas stamp on that one. Try it, all right?"

The second box failed to yield their treasure, as did the third, fourth, and seventh boxes. But the eighth time they pried up a lid, their eyes lit at the sight of rectangular bundles wrapped in brown paper. Emma reached into the crate and tore a slit in the covering, exposing a swath of delicate pink lace. "Mari, we've found it!"

Carefully, they unloaded bolt after bolt, inspecting every one until they discovered the midnight-blue silk. "Oh, it is beautiful," Emma marveled, unwrapping a length of the cloth. "No wonder Miss Fortune wanted this so badly. Look, Mari, see how the light catches the metallic threads and makes it shine?"

Maribeth had only a moment to see the feature her sister pointed out. With a shuffling roar, the boxcar door slammed closed, plunging the girls into darkness.

"Oh, my!" Emma squawked.

A whistle blew two long blasts, then slowly, the train began to move. "Heck fire, Emma," Maribeth groaned. "We've stepped in the cow chips now."

THE NOONTIME SUN pounded down upon Fort Worth, unusually warm for a late-September afternoon. Taking inventory of her shop's dwindling supplies, Jenny fanned her face, frowning as she attempted to recall when she had used the last of her pumpkin-colored thread. It wasn't like her to fail to replace her stock.

"But then it isn't like me to count pennies in order to buy spools of thread, either," she grumbled. She plunged her fingers into a button tin, rattling the contents in a fruitless search. She had not misplaced what she needed; she simply didn't have it. No pumpkin-colored thread.

And no European shipment.

That blasted Ethel Baumgardner. Jenny wouldn't put anything past that woman. She'd out and out copied some of Jenny's designs and tried to pass them off as her own. She'd been pea-green jealous when the Bailey daughters chose the Fort Worth designer to create their wedding gown. Shoot, if not for Big Jack's superstitious nature, Jenny would suspect Ethel of inventing the Bad Luck Wedding Dress myth. The woman certainly had done her share of spreading the tale. Of that, Jenny had no doubt.

*She's a poisoned-mouth old biddy—even if she is not more than five years older than I am.*

Jenny was replacing the buttons on the storage shelf when a child's fearful shriek sounded just outside her door. She jerked toward the noise, her hand bumping a box in the process, and a dozen spools of white thread spilled from the container and clattered to the floor. They rolled in every direction, but Jenny paid them no mind as she flew out of her shop.

Katrina McBride was yanking open the door that led upstairs, yelling at the top of her voice, "Papa, Papa, Papa!" Yellow ribbons trailed from rich brown pigtails as the young girl climbed frantically toward the family rooms above.

Jenny called, "Katrina, what's wrong?"

The girl glanced over her shoulder but didn't slow down. "Help, MissFortune. I have to find my papa." She pushed open the door and disappeared inside the McBride home.

Filled with apprehension, Jenny followed Katrina up the stairs. Trace was never home this time of day. "Isn't your father at work?" she asked as she went inside.

"I want him to be home! I have to tell him! He has to hurry to catch them." She ran through the parlor and the kitchen, then back to her father's bedroom, crying, "Papa, please be here!"

A wide-eyed Mrs. Wilson trailed Katrina from the kitchen, wiping wet hands on a dishrag. The two women shared a brief, worried gaze before Jenny caught up with Katrina as she made a turn back through the parlor, headed for the stairs and the attic.

"Whoa, there, sweetie," Jenny said, kneeling before the panicked child. "I want you to tell me what's wrong."

Tears spilled down rosy cheeks. "You have to take me to Papa's saloon, Miss Fortune. I prayed he'd be here because I mustn't go there on my own. He has to save them!"

"Save whom?"

"Emma and Maribeth. The train took them away!"

With a little more coaching, the story poured from the young girl, and as Jenny held her and listened, she had to stifle a groan at the implications of the tale.

They'd done this for her. For her! A wave of emotion washed through Jenny, a peculiar combination of love and guilt. Those foolish, reckless, wonderful children. She wrapped Katrina in a fierce hug and said a silent prayer for the safety of the sisters. Poor Emma and Maribeth. They must be so afraid.

Immediately, she planned her course of action. First she spent a few moments assuring a sobbing Katrina that she'd find Trace and help him return the older girls safe and sound. Next she hurried to Main Street where she hopped the trolley for the fastest transportation to Hell's Half Acre, only to discover a closed sign and a locked door at the End of the Line Saloon.

Where was he? Jenny banged on the door, then on the window. She paused to peer inside to the gloomy interior. Nobody was there.

"Of all the times for him to go missing," she muttered as she crossed the street to inquire after him at Miss Rachel's Social Emporium. Having no luck there, she checked the saloons on either side of the End of the Line, but again came up empty.

She stared frantically up and down the street. Where was he? What kind of father was Trace McBride to up and disappear when his daughters needed him? A responsible parent would always be available in the case of emergency.

*Now, Jenny, be fair,* her conscience scolded. She had to acknowledge the difficulty of such an aim, especially when a family had but one parent. And Trace *was* trying. She couldn't forget his offer of a job. A hired mother.

She chuckled humorlessly. Trace McBride didn't have to pay her to worry about his girls.

The image of Emma and Maribeth, frightened and alone and trapped inside a dark, swaying railroad car played over and over in her mind. Jenny knew then what she must do.

Purpose fired her blood as she hurried away from the Acre and made three quick stops: her home, the McBride's home, and the wagonyard, where she rented the fastest horse and buggy available.

When Trace stopped to inquire after her almost an hour later, he was told by the proprietor, "That crazy woman lit outta here like a prairie fire with a tailwind. What the hell is she up to?"

A faint smile played about his lips as he replied, "That crazy woman is trying to save my girls."

TRACE RODE ALONGSIDE the parallel troughs carved over time by the wheels of hundreds of wagons that had traveled the thirty-mile stretch between Fort Worth and Dallas. The past two hours had near worn him to a frazzle, and his day was far from over.

The Menaces had struck again, and this time if not for a little luck, the consequences could have been disastrous. Thank God that as of an hour ago—when he'd saddled up and headed east out of town—Emma, Maribeth, and Katrina were safely ensconced in their bedroom with strict instructions not to set so much as a big toe across the threshold until school the next morning. In light of today's events, he felt reasonably sure that they'd mind him. This time, at least.

As he scanned the golden grasses of late summer stretching across the prairie, Trace was still a little woozy from all of the worry. He felt certain he would remember until the day he died that moment when Emma and Maribeth had burst through the doors at the End of the Line with scraped hands and knees and a tale that had turned his knees to water; Kat missing from the train depot, Em and Mari banged up from jumping off a moving train.

He'd probably aged ten years between that moment and when he rushed into his kitchen and spied Katrina sitting at the table drinking a glass of milk. In those next few moments, his body had gone limp as a dishrag put through the wringer and hung out to dry.

He didn't feel much better than that now. Giving his mount a little kick, he spurred him to speed. He needed to hurry if he intended to catch up with the dressmaker in time to bring her back to Fort Worth before dark. And Trace had every intention of doing so. It'd be asking for trouble to spend the night, just the two of them alone on the prairie beneath a star-filled Texas sky.

As he eyed the sun's position, his brows lowered in a frown. He gave his horse an extra kick.

Crazy woman. The fellow at the wagonyard had been right. The day before her wedding day, Miss Fortune forgets all about herself and rides off to rescue his children. Of course, it shouldn't have come as any great surprise. He'd known she was that kind of person when he offered her the job. She'd done what any good mother would have done under the circumstances.

She wasn't anything like Constance.

Shame curdled in his gut like sour milk every time he thought of his actions that day at Rachel's. And he thought about it a lot. He couldn't seem to forget it. Not the way she'd tasted or the way she'd fit so perfectly in his arms. He especially couldn't forget the little sigh she'd made when she touched him.

Damn. He had to stop this. The woman was getting married tomorrow.

Marriage. That's what she'd been fishing for that day at the swimming hole. He had been slow to pick up on it, true, but he wasn't stupid.

Or maybe he was stupid. He'd actually considered it. Only for a second, true, but the fact that the idea had even entered his thoughts made his skin crawl. "Good Lord," he muttered, gigging his horse. He was acting as absurd as Big Jack Bailey.

It must be the fatigue. His bones ached with it. As grateful as he was to Jenny for trying to rescue his girls, he'd rather be back at the End of the Line getting drunker than a hoedown fiddler than chasing after her with the news that the rescue wasn't needed. Not this time anyway. Between the worry and the hard gallop across the prairie, he was near to being played plumb out.

At least one good thing had come from today's debacle.

Reaching down, he gave his horse's neck a pat. For the first time in a long while, he didn't feel guilty for having indulged his passion for fine horseflesh.

He'd bought the roan gelding Maribeth had named Ranger shortly after arriving in Fort Worth, and he'd spent more than he could afford at the time. Living in town, he didn't actually need a horse, but owning one was a habit too hard to break. Riding a horse like Ranger was the lone pleasure in this chase after Miss Jenny Fortune.

He muttered a curse as the words *pleasure, riding,* and *Jenny* brought to mind an image that suddenly made his seat in the saddle downright uncomfortable.

He rode for another ten minutes, trying hard to change the direction of his thoughts. He contemplated the liquor order he needed to place for the End of the Line. He ruminated on the curiosity demonstrated by the townspeople concerning the identity of the owner of the "fancy new palace goin' up on the west side." But despite his best efforts, mental images of the dressmaker continued to hound him.

Trace scowled and leather creaked as he shifted his position. He couldn't blame it all on fatigue; he might as well admit it. He'd made a valiant effort to bury his attraction to Jenny Fortune, but he'd failed miserably. Even worse than being physically tempted by the woman, he'd actually come to like her. Really like her. How could a man not like a beautiful woman who races off to rescue his daughters on the very eve of her wedding?

"She's trouble," he grumbled to Ranger. "I should have seen it sooner."

Topping a rise, Jenny tugged on the reins, calling, "Whoa, boy." The buggy creaked to a halt.

Relief washed through her, warm and sweet. Below her, a ribbon of black rose from the smokestack of a train bearing bright gold markings: Texas & Pacific.

Puzzlement followed right on the heels of relief. Why was the train stopped in the middle of nowhere? She'd never thought to catch up with them, instead hoping to get to Dallas as soon as possible following their arrival.

Jenny scrutinized the scene for any sign of trouble. The only movement she observed was the vapor rising from the smokestack. What had happened? Could the engine have suffered a mechanical failure?

She winced at the thought of all those people stranded so far from town. How far were they from Arlington? Five miles? Eight? A long walk most certainly. Surely though, once the train was overdue someone from the railroad would be sent out to check on the problem.

In the meantime, she'd take advantage of the Texas & Pacific's misfortune and retrieve the McBride Menaces, minus their youngest member, from the boxcar.

With a flick of the reins she signaled the horse, and the buggy began to roll forward. Because the track ran south of and parallel to the road, Jenny was forced to leave the trail to approach the train. The carriage bounced and rattled across the uneven terrain, but after a few moments, she neared the rails. For the first time the angle of her approach allowed her to see the opposite side of the train.

Oh, no. Fear raced through her. Up near the engine, a man on horseback held the reins of five other mounts. He wore a kerchief pulled over his face and his hand rested on the butt of a gun.

Desperadoes. Train robbery.

*Oh, dear Lord, Emma and Maribeth!*

Quickly, Jenny wheeled the buggy around, putting the train between her and the rider in order to hide from his view. Her breath came in shallow gasps as she considered what to do.

Would the girls be in more or less danger if she tried to effect their escape while the bandits were aboard? Uncertain, Jenny's gaze fixed on the train.

Katrina had said Emma and Maribeth had climbed into the last boxcar. The man holding the horses was twelve, maybe fourteen cars away. Chances were good the robbers would work their way toward the back. She could smuggle the girls out of the boxcar while the bandits were stealing from the paying passengers a distance away.

It could work, she thought, knowing she had no time to waste. Decision made, she started the buggy forward, intending to pull alongside the train.

Then a man stepped out of the caboose. He stood in the shadows, his hat pulled low on his brow, and he pointed a shotgun toward her heart.

"Well, well, well," the vaguely familiar voice declared. "Look what we have here. If it isn't the creator of the Bad Luck Wedding Dress." He gave a menacing chuckle, then stepped out into the sun. "This must be my lucky day."

Big Jack Bailey. Butterflies of dread fluttered in her stomach. Meeting up with a train robber was bad enough; meeting up with a train robber who held a personal grudge against her made the situation even worse. Her mouth went as dry as a Texas July.

"Aren't you going to say hello, little lady?"

She lifted her chin and spoke with surprising calm. "Good afternoon, Mr. Bailey."

Lifting a finger, he pushed his hat back on his head. His dark eyes gleamed with amusement. "What brings you out this way? Hoping to see a train wreck?"

Tension made her body almost rigid as her hands tightened on the reins. Bailey's look of amusement was downright scary.

He motioned with his gun. "Get on out of the buggy."

Jenny's pulse raced as she climbed slowly from her seat. The composure she displayed was pure false bravado, because her knees had turned to water. Another man stepped out onto the platform, distracting Big Jack and giving her the opportunity to seek shelter of a sort behind the buggy.

"There you are, Pa," the newcomer said. "I've been looking for you. Sorry I got caught up talking with the senator. I know folks must be anxious to leave."

Big Jack's expression tilted in a sly smile. "No, I wanted you to visit with Senator Charles. He's someone you should know. Besides, once I saw who was driving this buggy, I knew we were in luck. This is somebody else I want you to meet, son."

Jenny nervously licked her lips. Pa. Son. This must be the Bailey girls' brother. The gunslinger brother who couldn't attend the weddings because he'd been in jail.

The Bailey son pushed back the brim of his hat. He was tall and lanky with a cookie-duster mustache and a scar that marked his cheek. As his dark-eyed gaze drilled her, a shudder of fear ran down Jenny's spine.

Big Jack chuckled. "This here is Miss Jenny Fortune, Frank. She's the one who made the dress."

"My sisters' dress?"

"Yep. The Bad Luck Wedding Dress."

Frank Bailey put his hands on his hips, just inches away from the guns riding low in their holsters. His measuring gaze swept over her. "Comely little thing. You didn't tell me that about her, Pa."

He shrugged. "She's prettied herself up lately. Who knows, maybe she's after a man."

An evil smile stretched across the younger man's face. "Well, now. Ain't that handy."

The unstated threat hung on the air like a foul odor and Jenny gasped. A weapon. She needed a weapon. She needed the Colt she had stashed inside her satchel along with her nightgown and the change of clothes she'd packed anticipating an overnight stay. She always carried a gun when she traveled from town, but she'd never before had need of it.

*Next time, leave it somewhere easier to reach than wrapped up in your petticoats.*

She prayed there would be a next time. Cautiously, she reached for her bag as Big Jack Bailey and his son climbed down from the train.

Jenny wrapped a hand around the satchel's leather handle while the men covered half the distance between the buggy and the caboose. Then the drum of approaching horses interrupted them.

A rider called, "Boss, the train is ready to move out."

Wonderful. She'd be left here alone with Bailey and his men. Could this situation get any worse?

She told herself to look on the bright side. Obviously this was not a train robbery. If the father and son were criminals, they wouldn't have been so quick to reveal their identity. That man with the kerchief over his nose could have been protecting his face, not hiding behind the bandanna. And what was it Frank Bailey had said about speaking with a senator?

The whine of a whistle and groan of an engine warned that the train was pulling away. Her thoughts momentarily distracted, she gazed helplessly toward the boxcar that carried Emma and Maribeth even farther from home. She'd come so close to helping them. But better they be on that train than here to witness whatever wickedness the Baileys intended.

With the departure of the train the men on horseback surrounded her. She began to believe she'd made a grave error of judgment by not taking Big Jack's threats more seriously. Frank Bailey stepped within arm's length, circling around her, looking her over good. "That's a little package to cause so much trouble, Pa. Maybe we should unwrap her, see what's inside."

Big Jack shrugged. "I warned her to stay out of my way."

When pushed too far, a streak of recklessness inherited from her mother surfaced in Jenny. Today was no exception. With a toss of her head, she glared from Big Jack to Frank and snapped, "I may be small, but I can slap you a new hat size if I must. It might do you well to remember that."

Slipping her hand inside her satchel, she felt through the layers of muslin for the cold hard metal of her pistol. She gripped the butt—not crazy enough to draw—but ready to protect herself as she waited for Frank Bailey's reaction.

"You hiding a weapon with your corsets, Dressmaker?" he asked.

"Yes."

Big Jack's brows rose. "Shit. That's bound to bring bad luck."

"You ever shot a man before?" Frank inquired.

"No. But I could in self-defense."

The gunfighter's dark eyes glittered as he winked at his father and drawled, "I do so like spunk in a woman. I reckon I'm right happy I decided to come on home, Pa. Glad you let me in on what's happening around here."

Her grip on the gun tightened. She welcomed the anger churning in her stomach, because it helped to mask the fear. "I attempted to explain this before. You people are fools if you think I'm in any way responsible for those accidents. What is it I'm supposed to have done to that dress? Sewn it with enchanted thread? Put a curse on the beads? Really, Mr. Bailey, I'd have thought a man of your experience would be a bit smarter than that."

Beneath the dark brim of his hat, Frank Bailey's brows arched in surprise.

"There's a rider coming, boss," one of the men on horseback called. "Fast."

Big Jack leveled an ugly stare upon Jenny and said, "Let's go, Frank. We'll have another opportunity to…converse with this dressmaker. Let's head home."

Frank gave Jenny a wink, then sauntered toward one of two riderless horses and swung into the saddle. The men gigged their mounts and started off, all but Frank, who tipped his hat and said, "It's been a pleasure, darlin'. I'll look forward to furthering our acquaintance."

Jenny's energy melted like chocolate on an August afternoon as she watched Frank Bailey canter off on a bay mare. Still too afraid to feel relieved, she didn't move an inch until the pound of horse's hooves behind her made her start.

Whirling, she yanked the gun from the bag. She pointed it toward the rider and shouted, "Stay away from me you—"

Trace saw his identity register on her face. Her lips silently shaped his name. Then, still in the saddle, he watched helplessly as Jenny Fortune collapsed in a faint, the gun falling harmlessly beside her.

*It is bad luck to put a hen to set
on Sunday.*

# CHAPTER TEN

TRACE SPIED the rough-edged rock partially veiled by the spread of golden tresses. His stomach sank. Had Jenny hit her head when she fell? She lay still and silent, her skin as pale as a late-morning moon, her chest rising and falling in shallow breaths. "Damn," he muttered, easing his hands beneath her. The scrape of the stone against his knuckle was an ugly contrast to the silky caress of her hair across his fingers. Gently, he lifted her head and searched for a wound. Finding no obvious cut or lump, he worried all the more. A bruise inside the skull could be perilous.

What had happened here in the minutes before his arrival? He'd seen the crowd of riders surrounding the buggy, but he'd not noticed Jenny until the men rode away. She turned on him like a wildcat, then faded to a kicked kitten in the blink of an eye.

It left a bad feeling in his gut. A real bad feeling.

Trace hurriedly secured both horses, then retrieved his canteen from his saddle. Dragging a handkerchief from his pocket, he sluiced it with water and wrung it out. He sat cross-legged beside the unconscious woman and gently eased her head onto his lap. "C'mon, Jenny," he said, dabbing her pale cheeks with the wet cloth. "Wake up. You've caused me enough trouble as it is. Don't make it worse by doing something stupid like being hurt bad, all right?"

He stroked her gently. "You need to wake up. I need to tell you something. What you did for my children…" His voice trailed off as emotion choked his throat.

How long he sat with her head in his lap he wasn't certain. It felt like forever, but it was likely less than five minutes. He felt the change in her before he could see it—a transformation in the dead air surrounding them and a subtle tightening of her limbs. Slowly, her eyes fluttered open, and Trace lost himself in the unfocused depths of her mystical, blue-eyed gaze.

"What…?" Jenny murmured, her voice barely above a whisper.

"You fainted." He drew a gentle finger across her cheek. "Are you hurt? Does your head hurt?"

"No. Well, maybe a little." She paused, and after a beat her eyes widened. Her pupils, large and unfocused when she woke, shrank to a pinpoint and she jerked upright. "Emma and Maribeth! They're on the train."

He shushed her, easing her back down onto his lap. His hand continued its soothing caress as he explained, "They're safe, Jenny. Em and Mari jumped off the train before it worked up to speed."

Questions and concerns bloomed in her expression.

"They weren't hurt," he reassured her. "But it scares me half to death to think about it. You should have seen the way my knees wobbled when Emma said in that haughty little voice of hers, 'We jumped before the track makes the bend to cross Sycamore Creek.' Then Maribeth made it even worse by shrugging and saying, 'It was barely rolling, Papa.'"

Horror sharpened her tone. "They could have fallen beneath the wheels!"

Trace grimaced. "Helluva thing, isn't it? God must have been watching over them when they leaped. They cleared the wheels and came away with nothing more than a few scratches." He brushed her hair back from her brow and asked, "But what about you? Did you hit your head when you fainted? Where do you hurt?"

She licked her lips. "I'm all right. I think."

"Maybe you should lie here for a little bit."

"Yes," she said breathlessly, snuggling against him.

Knowing he'd best turn his thoughts from the intimacy of their position, Trace asked, "Are you feeling up to telling me what happened? Who were those riders?"

At that, she stiffened. When she attempted to rise and move away from him, Trace held her in place with the slightest pressure of his hands. "Relax. I don't want you getting up too fast and passing out on me again, all right?"

After a moment's hesitation, she settled back against him. But instead of addressing his question, Jenny asked one of her own. "Did Emma and Maribeth come home? We must have crossed paths."

Trace nodded. "By the time they brushed themselves off and ran back to the depot, Katrina had disappeared. They were afraid something awful might have happened to her. I'm forever warning them about going around town alone because little girls aren't always safe." He gave Jenny a shrewd look and added, "But then, neither are big girls, are they?"

She closed her eyes and didn't answer. After waiting a moment, Trace continued his story. "Anyway, Em and Mari came straight to End of the Line from the depot. I shut the place down and went looking for Kat."

"That's where you were when I came looking for you. You must have been so worried."

"Terrified." Trace smiled grimly at the memory. "I found someone at the station who remembered seeing her, and by talking with him and Mrs. Wilson, I've been able to piece together what happened."

He threaded his fingers through her hair as he spoke, allowing the honeyed strands to slip through his hands like the finest of silk. "Apparently, after causing a scene that allowed Em and Mari time to sneak onto the train, Katrina waited inside the depot where she watched for her sisters' signal. She was supposed to well up with another distraction once the girls found your fabric. Anyway, when the train pulled out, she started crying for real."

"Poor Katrina."

Trace rolled his eyes. "There's nothing poor about that little actress. I'm hoping this will teach her, and her sisters, a lesson." He paused for a moment as a fresh wave of frustration washed over him. "Anyway, she waited a little while after the train pulled out, hoping her sisters had slipped off when she wasn't looking. Finally, though, she ran home looking for me."

"But found me instead."

Jenny made a token effort to sit up, but once again he prevented it. She appeared stronger now with more color in her cheeks and more life in her eyes. But frankly, Trace was enjoying the opportunity of holding her, and she didn't put much effort into objecting.

"Yep, Katrina found you, and it must have been about the time Em and Mari arrived at the saloon. We lit out for the depot, which is why you and I missed each other, both at the End of the Line and at home. By the time I managed to get all my daughters in the same room and wade through the waterworks trying to figure out just what was going on, you had already set out to rescue my Menaces." He put his hand on her shoulder and gave it a squeeze. "I thank you for that, Jenny. From the bottom of my heart."

"I was glad to do it, Mr. McBride."

"Trace."

"Trace." Her eyes drifted shut, and in a breathless voice, she said, "But they didn't need rescuing after all, did they? So you set out to rescue me."

A comfortable silence fell between them, broken only by the calls of a mockingbird hidden in a nearby tree. The scent of cedar sweetened the breeze that cooled the afternoon. Trace stroked her hair, savoring the peace of the moment amid a tumultuous day and relishing the sensation of cradling Jenny Fortune in his lap.

Even when he knew he shouldn't.

The thought brought him back to reality. "And did you need rescuing, Jenny? I want to know what happened here, and I believe you've put me off long enough."

She made another effort at evasion by looking up at him and asking, "Where are the girls now?"

Her eyes sparkled like jewels in the sunlight. Wishing he hadn't noticed, Trace tore his gaze away. "I made arrangements with Mrs. Wilson to stay overnight. I wasn't certain I'd catch up with you in time to ride back to town tonight. The girls are confined to their room until I return."

"You trust them to stay there?"

He laughed without amusement. "This time I do. They're too scared to get into any more mischief. They know they crossed the line today." He slanted her a glance. "Tell me what happened. Why did you faint?"

Jenny took a deep breath. She didn't want to think about it. Neither did she really want to move. His hand never stilled, stroking her hair ever so gently. Soothing and sweet. It was the kind of touch she imagined he offered his daughters, the type of tender caress she'd always wished from her father.

Jenny appreciated the comforting touch after the fright

she'd received, so she left her head in his lap, ignoring the seed of conscience that told her it wasn't proper. "It was Big Jack Bailey."

Trace's muscles tensed. His hand stilled. "Did he hurt you?"

"No."

He pierced her with his gaze.

"He never touched me."

"Tell me what happened." Trace's hand resumed its soothing strokes. "Start at the beginning."

In a low, soft voice, she granted his request. At times during her story she sensed his anger, but always the fingers in her hair continued to soothe. Peace crept over her like a gentle dawn. Trace McBride had unwittingly reached out to the little girl deep within her who had longed to be held, but whose parents had never noticed.

"I thought the train was being robbed. But Frank said something to his father about speaking with the senator, so now I wonder if it wasn't a prearranged meeting. The train stopped not far from the Lady Luck Ranch's main house."

"Frank?" Trace's hand stilled. "Are you telling me Frank Bailey is back in town?"

"I don't know about town, but he was on the train."

He released a whispered oath, and beneath her head his thigh muscle went taut. Rock hard. Distractingly hard.

And in that moment, Jenny forgot all about comforting, fatherly touches.

The mood had changed. Where before she found his touch soothing, now she found it stimulating. He smelled of horse and sweat and leather and tobacco. Manly. She found she wanted to touch him, to glide her fingers along the firm length of muscle. She wanted to grasp his chambray shirt and pull him down to her for a kiss.

She shocked herself. This was ridiculous. She'd never before felt this way about a man. She should be ashamed, she knew. She had no business lying here like a wanton with her head in Trace McBride's lap.

But she wanted to lie here forever.

She stared up at his mouth. She watched his lips move, but she didn't hear his words. Silently, she willed those lips to lower. In that moment, she wanted Trace McBride's kiss like she'd wanted few things in her life.

He glanced down. His eyes widened slightly. His breathing seemed to still as he paused an interminable moment, his gaze shifting to her lips.

Jenny wetted them with her tongue, waiting anxiously.

Then, with a blink, his eyes shuttered. He looked away, and worst of all, put his hands beneath her shoulders and lifted her out of his lap. Once she was sitting up, he stood and walked over to his horse.

Jenny schooled her features to hide her dismay. "Tell me the rest of it. I want to know about Frank." Trace snagged the gelding's reins and tied them to the buggy, a needless gesture considering the obviously well-trained animal hadn't moved since he dismounted.

Feeling rather huffy, Jenny lifted her hand to probe at the knot on her head. Then in a clear, calm voice she condensed the events by explaining how she'd whirled around ready to shoot, only to see him riding to her rescue. "I don't make a habit of fainting, I assure you. I apologize if I caused you undue concern."

"Undue concern? Undue concern!" He narrowed his eyes. "Frank Bailey is a gunslinger. A cold-blooded killer. The only reason he's not in jail is that Big Jack has bribed enough lawmen to get him out. Did either one of those men threaten you, Jenny?"

She shifted her gaze away and Trace muttered an oath. He demanded in a flat voice, "Tell me exactly what was said."

Some of it was too embarrassing to tell. Jenny wouldn't repeat on a bet what Big Jack had said about her "prettying her-self up to catch a man." Fixing her gaze on a tuft of weeds at her feet, she said, "It wasn't what was said so much as the look in their eyes. Big Jack seems halfway crazy." After a pause, she added, "Frank Bailey has cold eyes. Dead eyes."

"And? What else happened?"

"Nothing else. Not really."

He shot her a disbelieving look. "Tell me."

She offered him exasperation in return. "He called me dar-lin' and said something about furthering our acquaintance."

A muscle worked in his jaw. "Frank Bailey is more than a killer, Jenny. He's been known to assault women. Thank God I got here when I did."

Her temper flared and she pushed to her feet. "You didn't ride to the rescue, Mr. McBride. I rescued myself, thank you very much."

He snorted and muttered something beneath his breath.

"What was that?" She folded her arms. "Did I hear you mention my gun?"

He scowled. "It was a stupid thing to do, lady. In fact, this entire afternoon has been filled with a series of stupid actions on your part. First you hightail it out of town without a thought to your own safety. Next, you insert yourself into the middle of what might well have been a train robbery. Then you—" He broke off his tirade abruptly.

"Then I what?"

"Never mind."

Never mind? Not hardly. He'd all but called her stupid. Jenny would admit to being many things, but stupid wasn't one of them. Fuming, she advanced on him. "Please, Mr. McBride, do go on. Tell me what else I did that was"—she put her hand against his chest and tried to push him as she said—"*stupid.*"

His hand whipped up and grabbed her wrist. Their gazes

connected, and for a long moment, they stared at each other. Then Trace's eyes caught fire. "You lay with your head in my lap and you begged me to kiss you."

Jenny sucked in a breath, her knees turning to water as her mouth went dry. In those emerald eyes she saw a man's hunger, naked and intense. In his body, she saw a battle for control, a raging tempest of will against need.

In that moment, for the first time ever, Jenny gloried in the power of being a woman.

Weakness turned to strength. She lifted her free hand and touched his cheek. "Trace, I…"

Abruptly, he released her and stepped away. "Don't," he whispered harshly.

Jenny hesitated. She licked her dry lips. Need washed through her like hot, melted honey and she took a trembling breath. The wise thing, she knew, would be to allow the moment to pass. To act as if it had not happened. To pretend her world hadn't tilted on its axis.

But she couldn't do it. Not here and now. She didn't want to do it. Not when Trace McBride had looked at her with such naked desire. Not when her own body echoed his need.

The air seemed thick and heavy, as if the forces of nature were gathering for a storm. In that moment, Jenny wanted nothing more than to be caught up in it, to lose herself in the fundamental energy pulsing around her, within her.

What was stopping her?

The question trailed like a velvet ribbon through the sensual haze in her mind. What *was* stopping her? Wasn't she her mother's daughter? Hadn't she poured her talents and treasure into Fortune's Design just so she could make her own decisions? What good did independence do her if she never used it?

*Independence is the freedom to do what I want.*

And here, on the wildflower-dotted prairie beneath the unending Texas sky, Jenny Fortune knew how she wanted to exercise her freedom.

She wanted Trace McBride.

TRACE WAS RIDING a wild mustang and doing his level best to hang on.

He smelled her scent, a whisper of roses, on the air. He shut his eyes, but still he saw her, imagined her, naked and wanting beneath him. His hands, though fisted at his sides, reached for her. Every fiber of his being hungered for her.

He flinched when she touched his arm.

"Trace?"

Her fingers burned a path from his wrist toward his elbow and he had to think to breathe. He spoke through his teeth. "Leave it alone, Jenny. Leave me alone."

"I can't." Her voice rippled across his senses. "You make me…ache."

The mustang bucked and Trace lost his grip.

He yanked her against his body and kissed her. He took her mouth roughly, savagely. He kissed her like a man too long without a woman, like a man who hated himself for succumbing to temptation.

It was his most honest action in years.

His legs spread, widening his stance, as his hand slipped down her body to cup her rump, lift her and pull her closer. The groan rumbled from deep inside him and was answered with a breathless sigh against his lips—a breathless, responsive, desire-laden *ah*. He'd never heard a more erotic sound.

He trailed wet kisses up along her jawline, nipping gently at her ear. So long. It'd been so damned long since he'd felt anything like this for a woman. Not since the early days with Constance. "Damn you, Jenny Fortune. Why this? Why now?"

She leaned away from him then, her blue eyes soft with passion and another emotion he refused to recognize.

"I've waited so long," she said, her voice beckoning.

The words melted past his driving hunger to steal into his soul. She'd waited. Ice cold water couldn't have cooled his ardor any faster.

*I'm five buttons and a couple of petticoats away from taking a bride the day before her damned wedding.*

He put his hands on her shoulders and firmly pushed her aside. "Haven't you forgotten something? Like your fiancé?"

She froze, her eyes rounded, her lips forming a silent "oh." By the looks of it, the dressmaker had forgotten all about her fiancé.

Which was just like a woman. Jenny Fortune was no different from all the others. "Get in the buggy, Miss Fortune. We're going back to town. If we ride hard we should make it back by dark."

She didn't reply, just climbed silently into the rig, her cheeks stained pink like a Parker County peach.

Trace rode his horse rather than join her. They rode west, into the afternoon sun, and he tried to force his thoughts in any direction but toward her.

He managed, for the most part. Except for the niggling truth that returned time and time again. The thought that he'd accused her wrongly. Jenny Fortune wasn't like all the others.

And that, he feared, was the biggest problem of all.

It was Friday night in Hell's Half Acre, and dives, dance halls, and dens of iniquity seethed with violence and vice. Cowboys in herds of twelve to fifteen rode from area ranches to drink and gamble and whore away their wages. Railroad workers in from the westward camps shared card games with no-goods who had hitched rides on inbound freight wagons. By eight o'clock all four policemen on Marshal Courtright's force had been summoned into service, and the jail was filled near to bursting.

In the midst of it all at the ever-popular End of the Line Saloon, Trace McBride sat sipping from a bottle of the house's best whiskey. It was Friday night in Hell's Half Acre. Tomorrow afternoon in First Methodist Church, Jenny Fortune would stand before God and Fort Worth, Texas, and marry Thomas Edmund Wharton III.

He couldn't get the damned wedding off his mind. All the way back to town he'd struggled against thinking about it. He'd endured verbal bombardment on the subject from the moment he hit his front door. The girls had yammered on about MissFortune's wedding even while being disciplined. After banishing them to bed, he'd come to work only to be assaulted by the headline in the damned newspaper: "Dressmaker Vows to Put Bad Luck Wedding Dress to the Test."

He lifted the glass to his mouth and gulped back the rest of his drink, but the whiskey failed to burn the taste of her from his mouth. Grasping the bottle to pour himself another hit, he eyed the newspaper lying beside it. The words printed on the page seemed to leap out at his eyes. "Wedding of the decade set for tomorrow afternoon."

For the past couple of weeks the *Democrat* had been chock full of reports on the wedding preparations. Tonight's edition even included an interview with both the bride and groom. The tone of the articles had provided a big step toward changing public opinion of the dress. Trace had even heard the gown referred to as the Not-So-Bad Luck Wedding Dress. "Looks like you'll get your wish, Dressmaker," he murmured softly.

One of her wishes, anyway.

*You make me ache.*

*Well, hell.* Clamping down on his wayward thoughts, Trace pushed to his feet. He strode around the barroom scrutinizing his customers on the sly, hoping to find a cheat at one of the card tables or a fellow trying to stiff the house on his tab.

He felt mean as hell with the hide off, and he was looking for a fight.

Not finding the relief he sought at the End of the Line, he left. Instinctively, his feet turned west, away from the Rankin Building.

Toward Jenny Fortune's cottage.

EARLIER THAT EVENING while Trace was at work, an early season norther had swept into town with blustering winds and a spattering of rain. Temperatures dropped thirty degrees in an hour, sending people scurrying for blankets and winter coats.

Trace turned up the collar of his jacket, then stuck his hands in his pockets as he walked along the shadowed lanes beyond the boundaries of Hell's Half Acre. Muted pools of light from gas lamps at street corners stabbed at the gloom but did nothing to banish the bitter chill.

Trace welcomed the cold. It helped clear his head and damper his nasty mood. That, of course, allowed an opportunity for fatigue to set in. He was bone tired—worn down, run over, and wrung out. It was damned foolish of him to be out this time of night in this kind of weather.

So why the hell did he feel compelled to walk by Jenny Fortune's cottage at three o'clock in the morning on her wedding day?

Trace kicked a loose stone illuminated by a streetlight. He wanted to check on her, that's all. He wanted to make sure no Baileys lurked in the shadows.

*And that no Wharton prowls in her bedroom.*

He wanted to kick himself at that thought. *Let it go, McBride. Let her go. She's not yours. You don't want her.*

"What a crock," he muttered, turning the corner of Jenny's street.

The white pickets of her fence shone with a pearly glow beneath the moonlight. Eyeing her darkened cottage, he noted that all appeared in order. Indulging the need to make certain, he quietly slipped the latch on the gate and stepped into the yard. He made his way along a path between the cottonwood and the front porch until the unmistakable sound of a gun being cocked stopped him in his tracks.

"Take another step and I'll blow a hole through your heart." Hidden by the shadows of the porch, Jenny's voice sounded deceptively soft. "If you don't tell me who you are and give me a good reason for being here, I just might do it anyway."

Bloodthirsty little thing. And what was she doing awake and outside in the cold at this time of night?

Trace asked the question uppermost in his mind. "Are you alone, Jenny?"

"McBride!" The chain on a porch swing rattled. "You frightened me half to death. I thought you were a Bailey. What are you doing?"

"Are you alone?" he repeated.

She gave a frustrated groan. "And what business is it of yours, may I ask?"

It wasn't his business. He knew that. Frustration ate at his soul. "That Wharton character is a skunk, lady, and I'm not certain you realize it."

"A shark."

"What?"

"He's a shark, not a skunk, and no, he's not here. I kicked him out of my parlor hours ago. By the way, he said to tell you to find someone else to chase after your Menaces once he and I are married."

At least she hadn't said her bedroom. "If he has something to say to me, he can say it to my face. Are you still holding a gun on me, Jenny?"

"No, I set it down," she replied, sounding disgusted. "I probably shouldn't have. You haven't yet told me why you're skulking around my house in the middle of the night."

Trace ambled up the front steps. "I'm on my way home from work."

"Then you're obviously lost."

"Walking helps me get to sleep. Some nights I need more help than others."

"Hmm," she replied, noncommittally.

Trace stared into the gloom and finally made out her form huddled at one end of the porch swing. "I thought I saw something in the shadows," he lied. "I figured it best to make certain the Baileys weren't causing any trouble."

He crossed the porch and propped his hip on the railing opposite the swing. "Why are you sitting outside in the dark in the middle of the night? It's freezing."

But not too cold to mask the clean scent of roses that washed his way with every sway of the swing.

"I'm more chilly inside than out, I'm afraid," she murmured softly. "I couldn't sleep."

She'd been damned hot this afternoon. Trace grimaced and gave the swing a push with the toe of his boot. The near complete absence of light lent an isolation to the scene, an intimacy that stripped away the layers of pretense between them. Trace was too tired, too soul weary, to fight it. "Jenny, you can't marry Wharton."

Cloth rustled as she shifted her position. "It's not your concern, McBride."

"Yes, it is." He sighed heavily. "It's like I said before, the man's a skunk. Hell, Jenny, he may spend his days with you, but he spends his nights in the Acre."

"Well now, Mr. Saloonkeeper," she sarcastically drawled, "there's a reason to think badly of a man."

Damn but the woman had a mouth on her. "You're a cold woman, Jenny Fortune." Propelled by a need he didn't stop to analyze, he pushed off the porch rail. His boots landed against the wooden floor planks with a thud. "It makes me realize I'm iced up myself. Scoot over and share some of that blanket with me, would you?" He moved as he spoke, so before she had the opportunity to refuse, he'd appropriated a spot on the swing. Then he tugged on the quilt.

"McBride!" she protested, yanking back.

He abandoned his efforts with the cover, instead reaching for her hand and pulling her against him. She struggled half-heartedly.

Trace said, "Come here, Miss Fortune, and tell me why you're really awake in the middle of the night."

"I'm not telling you anything. I'm angry with you. I don't owe you anything."

"I know." She resisted for another moment, then the starch seeped out of her spine and she surrendered. Trace wrapped his arm around her. She rested her head against his chest and a peaceful sensation of contentment stole over him. It felt right, holding her close like this, and that scared the hell out of him.

He cleared his throat. "I've been thinking about your situation, and I've come up with an alternative solution for you." Jenny's limbs began to stiffen and he hurriedly explained, "There's a man I know. Name of Wright. He's an upstanding young man, and he cleans up nice—if you look past the size of his nose. He'd make you a much better husband than that skunk Wharton. Why don't you have him stand up with you instead? He'd agree in a heartbeat. I'm certain of it."

She held herself so very still that had he not known better, he'd have thought she'd drifted off to sleep. Finally, she said, "You have more audacity than any person I've ever met."

"I appreciate the compliment."

Her sniff radiated disdain.

They swung for a few minutes in silence. Then Jenny asked, "Samuel Wright, the boy who works at M and M Produce?"

"You know him?"

"I've met him. I recognized the description."

Sam Wright's nose was rather famous in town, Trace thought. "He's a good fellow, Jenny."

"Yes," she agreed. "He's kind and he's gentle." Jenny sighed. "He's just like my father."

"Well, that's good, isn't it? You love your father. I've always heard a woman looks for a man like her father when she marries."

"Poor Emma, Maribeth, and Katrina."

"Witch." Trace leaned his head back against the swing and shut his eyes, soaking in the impression of the night, the place, and the woman in his arms. Despite the cold, he felt warmer than he had in years.

She was silent for a long time. "My father is a very good man. His research may one day offer humanity a great advancement. However, I've never dreamed of having a husband like Richard Fortune."

Trace waited, but she said nothing more. "Wharton's a user, Jenny. He's after something. I can tell it by looking at him. He'd hurt you."

She shook her head. "No, Trace. I know what to expect from Edmund. I have no illusions where he is concerned, and he does have his appeal."

"So he's pretty," Trace said with a snort.

She smiled against his chest. "Edmund is willing to give me what I want. Marrying Edmund will allow me to keep Fortune's Design."

*And I'll have to watch her parade around town as Mrs. Thomas Edmund Wharton III.* The thought made him sick to his stomach. "Is business all that matters to you?"

Jenny didn't respond to the question. Instead she asked one of her own. "Doesn't anything matter to you, Trace?"

"What do you mean by that?"

"I'm getting married this afternoon, and you stop by in the

middle of the night to tell me you've found a more appropriate groom than the one I already have."

"Hey now," Trace protested. "Your mother found Wharton, which by the way, is something I'll never understand. He's totally wrong for you. Why shouldn't I try to help?"

Frustration filled her voice. "*You* try to help? Be serious, McBride. We both know you're no help at all."

"Why the hell do you say that?" He'd been a lot of help to her. He'd protected her from the Baileys for one thing.

"I say it because you're being pigheaded, McBride."

"Pigheaded!"

"Yes, pigheaded."

His spine stiffened, but instead of drawing away from him, Jenny burrowed closer. "I don't know what your reasoning is, but the fact that you're doing this to your daughters purely drives me crazy."

"Doing *what* to my daughters?" he demanded roughly.

"Don't you ever listen to them? Do you have any idea how upset they are? They visit me every day, begging me not to marry Edmund. That's what was behind this train business today, you mark my words. They have some scheme up their sleeves. They don't want me to marry Edmund or any other man. They want me to marry you!"

His muscles tensed. For a breathless second, he didn't respond. When he finally spoke, ice coated his words. "A woman who uses children is lower than silt."

"Oh!" While she pulled out of his arms he was shoving her away. "How dare you accuse me of such a thing." She struck out blindly, the thwack of her hand against his face sounding like a gunshot in the dark.

"Goddammit, you hit my nose."

"I hope I broke it."

"Bloodthirsty wench."

"Don't call me that!"

"It's kinder than what I'd like to call you," Trace shot back, his voice dripping with disgust. "Trying to use my daughters. You should be ashamed."

"I'm ashamed of nothing!" she said, scrambling off the swing. "You know I haven't tried to manipulate your daughters. *You're* the one who is using them—using them to hide behind. You don't want me? Fine. Just go, then. Go home." She drew a deep, shuddering breath. "Go home. Now. Just go and leave me alone. Why did you have to come here anyway!" With that, she marched inside, slamming the door behind her.

Trace stood on the porch, his chest heaving with his anger. But it was more than anger. It was pain and heartache and jealousy and lust all rolled into one.

She was marrying Edmund Wharton.

The idea made him furious. He crossed to her front door and shoved it open. Then he followed the light to the back of the house and her bedroom. She'd slipped off her robe and was climbing into bed. Tears spilled down her cheeks.

The sight made him livid. Guilt and defensiveness put the words on his tongue. "You think I hide behind my children?" he asked, his manner making the question a threat. "Maybe you're right. But I stayed away from you for their sake, even when that was the last thing I wanted to do. So, maybe I have been using my girls."

She stiffened. "Get out of my bedroom, McBride," she said, swiping the tears from her cheeks. "Go away. You shouldn't be here."

He gave a bitter laugh. "You think you're telling me something I don't already know?"

"Trace, please—"

"You asked me why I came here tonight. Do you really want to know? You think I don't want you?" He gave a gravelly laugh. "Well, Miss Fortune, think again. I came here because I do want you."

He stepped forward. She looked as if she wanted to flee, but she didn't move her feet. The air between them crackled, and as he advanced another step, he saw the shudder sweep over her. He recognized it for what it was. "And you want me, too."

She met his gaze, and he saw a thousand agonies shimmering in her eyes. Her mouth opened, then closed, as she stared at him. The seconds dragged by until finally, she softly cried, "But you don't want to marry me."

"It's better this way, Jenny."

She gave him a contemptuous look.

"It's true. There are things you don't know about me. Things I haven't told you. As much as I hate the idea of you marrying that skunk, the fact remains you're better off with him than me."

The words lay between them like a corpse.

Trace drew a deep breath. He was faintly aware of his fists clenching at his sides. *Do it, tell her the rest of it. Not just for her sake, but for yours, too.*

Trace summoned his courage to speak. He tried—God, how he tried—but he couldn't make his mouth form the words. Now he was a coward on top of everything else.

"Lock the door behind me, Jenny. And for God's sake, get that gun off the porch and put it safely away." He turned to leave.

A floorboard creaked as she followed him from the bedroom. When he reached for the handle on the front door, she stopped him with one softly spoken word. "Why?"

His throat closed and sweat formed on his upper lip.

"Tell me *why,* damn you. Tell me why so I can forget you!"

For a long moment, the only sound to be heard was the rhythmic tick of the clock. The anguish in her voice gave him the strength he needed, because he found he could no longer bear the thought of her pain.

Trace's mind flashed back to another time, another place, before betrayal had stolen his world. He swallowed hard.

"You want to know why won't I marry you? Because I can't, Jenny, I can't."

"Is your wife still alive? Have you lied about being a widower?"

Trace unleashed a bitter laugh. Turning around, he faced her and said, "Oh, no, Miss Fortune. Constance is very dead. I'm certain of it, and that is why I won't marry you."

He burned her image into his mind. Gowned in white, her golden hair mussed. Achingly beautiful. Wanting him. Caring about him. He'd remember her like this, before she knew. Before she hated him.

"You see, my dear, I'm the one who killed her. I murdered my wife."

*If you put on a garment wrong side out,
you will have bad luck unless you let a
left-handed person change it for you.*

## CHAPTER ELEVEN

HE KILLED HIS WIFE.

Jenny sucked in a breath as the horror of it washed over her.

But on the heels of horror immediately came doubt. This was a man who to her knowledge never carried a gun. This was a man who made his daughter eat her peas. This was Mr. Throw-Fish.

This was no murderer.

While Jenny worked her way to this conclusion, Trace left the cottage. The front door banged shut, and she was staring at the empty room. A tide of frustration rose within her. The man was always running from something.

He'd marched halfway down the front walk before she caught up with him. Cold stung her bare skin as she tugged at his jacket. "Don't you dare leave like that! You can't make such a claim, then walk away."

He shrugged off her touch and kept on going.

Jenny blew an exasperated sigh, picked up the hem of her nightgown, and ran after him. "Trace McBride, you wait right there."

He kept on walking, his long strides eating up the ground. Her foot came down hard on a rough-edged pebble and she winced in pain as she stopped to brush the offending stone away. "Darn you, McBride," she called after him, "I'm in my nightgown and it's cold out here!"

"Go home, then."

He had reached the street corner before she caught up with him again. "Trace, please! I'll follow you home if I have to, and I'm barefooted. If I catch pneumonia it'll be on your conscience."

He stopped abruptly. "Goddammit, Jenny. I tell you I murdered my wife and you still think I have a conscience?"

Somber now, she placed her hand against his arm. "I know you do."

He stood stiffly for a moment, then swore a snarling oath and whisked her up into his arms. Toting her back toward her house, he muttered, "Barefoot and in your nightgown. Stupid. I never would have guessed it of you, but time and again today you've proved me wrong. Didn't you get the hint, lady? I'm dangerous. I killed my wife! You should not be chasing after me!"

She rested her head against his chest, soaking up his warmth. He was right about one thing. She shouldn't have chased after him without grabbing her robe first. "I want to know how it happened. I want to know why."

He didn't speak again until he'd carried her back inside her house, to her bedroom, where he deposited her on the bed. "Get some sleep, Jenny. You want to look good for the wedding."

"It was an accident, wasn't it? You loved her so much and you accidentally killed her, and the guilt you feel is crushing."

At the doorway to her bedroom he paused. His hands reached out and clutched the doorjamb. "One more time, Miss Fortune. I hated my wife. I shot her."

Jenny studied him closely and repeated his words in her mind. What he *hadn't* said provided her an answer. Smiling sadly, she told him, "I knew it was an accident. You may have killed, but you are no killer, Trace McBride. What you are is a coward. You're afraid of something—yourself, me, the phases of the moon, for all I know. And you've allowed that fear to dictate your life."

His eyes closed, and for the briefest of seconds she saw a world full of pain in his expression. When he looked at her again, his deep green eyes were shuttered.

"Good-bye, Miss Fortune."

As he took a step away from her, Jenny was compelled to add, "I believe in you, Trace, and I wish you could have believed in me, too. I'd have been a good wife to you. I could have loved you."

Trace stiffened, but didn't respond. This time, the door closed with a whisper.

MONIQUE DAY glanced at the wall clock inside the small room off the vestibule of Fort Worth's First Methodist Church and frowned. Where was that girl? Jenny had agreed to meet her here at noon to supervise the decorating. Now almost three o'clock, Monique was more than a little worried.

Had she made a mistake by not staying at her daughter's home for the duration of the wedding festivities? Monique liked her privacy, and she had wanted Jenny to have hers—just in case Mr. McBride decided to do something to stop this wedding. She paused, tapping her finger against her cheek. Maybe that was it. Maybe Trace McBride had finally made his move.

In that case, this would be a beautiful wedding after all.

A faint grin hovered on Monique's lips as she surveyed the interior of the church. White roses and English ivy twined around the arch that stood at one end of the long center aisle, white and blue ribbons cascading down the sides. A white cloth runner stretched toward the second, identical arch at the altar. There, more roses and ivy, dozens of potted plants and ferns, filled every available space and barely left enough room for the minister, bride, and groom.

"Excess," Monique murmured with a wrinkle of her nose. Excess almost to the degree of gaudy. Not at all her daughter's style.

Fort Worth would love it.

Doubts came back to plague her. If Fort Worth saw a wedding performed here today, that is. Jenny's delay might well have nothing to do with McBride. Knowing her daughter, she might have decided not to go through with the marriage to Edmund. The girl had enough of her mother in her not to be entirely predictable, and Monique found that worrisome. Would she bail out on the plan entirely? Monique simply couldn't say.

At first she was surprised by Jenny's apathy toward the idea of making arrangements for her wedding to Edmund. But after Trace McBride's stirring defense of Jenny the night of their dinner at the Cosmopolitan Hotel, Monique had begun to suspect the reason. The snooping she had done since then had proved her suspicions correct.

Her daughter had developed a tendresse for the saloon-keeper, and Monique suspected Mr. McBride wasn't immune to her, either. The events of yesterday had proved it. First Jenny went tearing off after those girls, regardless of her expected attendance at the prewedding festivities. Then Mr. McBride hightailed it after her, even though all his chicks were safely in their nest. Even Edmund, as apathetic as he was about this marriage of convenience, had looked askance at that.

Monique had kept her fingers crossed all afternoon and had felt real disappointment when Jenny rode back into town, her status unchanged. Still, Monique wouldn't give up hope until the vows were said. She still had her secret weapon to fire.

Maybe it wouldn't come to that. Perhaps the reason Jenny hadn't arrived at the church on time was because she was being detained by Trace McBride. "I can only hope," Monique said, rearranging a crooked blue satin ribbon bow.

Such hopes were also the reason she'd decided to indulge her penchant for troublemaking and do everything within her power to ensure this wedding reached its preferred conclusion. So was born her secret weapon. She'd concocted a sly, yet extreme, last-ditch effort to force her daughter and the man she fancied to confront the future they might forfeit due to their stubbornness.

She'd invited the McBride Menaces to serve as bridesmaids at Jenny's wedding.

Unable to appreciate the subtlety of her plan, the girls had at first objected. But Monique, being Monique, had refused to accept their protests. Forging ahead, and with silent apologies to her daughter, she had commissioned a Dallas seamstress, a dill pickle of a woman named Baumgardner, to create three attendants' gowns. Twice during the past three weeks she'd arranged for the girls to be excused from school for a pair of clandestine dress fittings. The secrecy had appealed to the McBride children and finally garnered their cooperation.

While she wouldn't go so far as to say the girls looked forward to the wedding, they did admit their presence at the ceremony would guarantee their father's attendance.

Monique planned to take it from there.

Assured that all was in readiness at the church, Monique left to make the short journey to Jenny's house. A cool wind stung her cheeks while she walked, and Monique tried to tell herself the tears collecting in her eyes resulted from the chill.

It wasn't true, of course. Monique was feeling emotional for a number of reasons, not the least of which was the message she shortly must convey to her daughter. "Maybe Jenny and Mr. McBride have eloped," she said, her hopes lifting. It would be a miracle, she knew, but it would save her from having to share a piece of news she desperately wished to keep to herself.

Richard hadn't made his train. Jenny's father wouldn't be here to escort his daughter down the aisle. She'd be brokenhearted.

Monique wanted to strangle the man. He must have lost himself in his work one more time. Richard and his foolish experiments—she had half a notion to divorce him again over this one. No matter who the groom turned out to be, Jenny could have used her father's support today of all days. But once again, Richard Fortune wouldn't be there for her when she needed him.

Monique hoped Trace McBride wasn't a similar type of man.

Reaching the waist-high picket fence that surrounded her daughter's yard, Monique's steps slowed. She took a deep, bracing breath, then flipped the gate's metal latch. The hinges squeaked as the door swung wide, and Monique stepped toward the front porch.

*Please don't be here. Please have eloped.* She entered the cottage without knocking. "Jenny? Oh, Jenny! Are you here?"

She walked straight to her daughter's bedroom, where she breathed a sigh of disappointment. Jenny stood before her full-length mirror, the Bad Luck Wedding Dress fastened halfway up her back.

*Well, we still have my secret weapon. And if McBride lets us down, at least she'll still have Edmund. She'll have Fortune's Design, which she says is all that matters.*

Monique knew differently, of course. But Jenny was young yet. She'd learn. Being a loving mother, Monique hoped her daughter could avoid the pain of education.

She gazed at her offspring and smiled. "Oh, my. Don't you make the most beautiful bride. We need to hurry, though. We're almost out of time. The wedding is scheduled to begin in less than an hour."

TRACE LAY FLAT on his stomach on the cold attic floor, one arm stretched beneath Maribeth's bed as he searched the smooth, wooden planks for her shoe. His gritty eyes slowly closed, and he seriously considered never moving again. He was tired enough to sleep on barbed wire. The few hours of fitful sleep he'd managed weren't nearly enough to keep a man going.

"Is it there?"

He opened his eyes to see Katrina kneeling beside him, her white organdy skirt hiked high in the effort to keep it off the floor. How the hell had the Menaces slipped this one past him? Bridal attendants.

At a wedding he wanted no part of.

Dust brought on a sneeze that caused him to hit his head on the bed. A thought sneaked in with the pain, and he realized he'd rather the Menaces choose another train to rob than carry the rose chain for Jenny Fortune and Edmund Wharton. Trace groaned.

"Can't you find it, Papa?"

He turned his head and eyed his youngest daughter. Anxious furrows dotted Katrina's brow. In that moment she reminded him of his grandmother, and a bittersweet smile touched his face. Wouldn't Grandmother love to see the girls today? All dressed up in ruffles and ribbons. So beautiful, so spirited. So ornery.

No wonder his Menaces held Jenny Fortune in such esteem. They were so much alike.

His hand brushed a lace. "Here it is, Katie-cat." He pulled the white leather slipper from beneath the bed and gave it to his youngest daughter.

"Oh, Papa. You're the bestest." Clutching the shoe to her heart, her eyes shone as she added, "I looked and looked and looked and looked. I couldn't wear my black boots in MissFortune's wedding. You saved me, Papa. You're my hero."

Leave it to Kat to dramatize a lost shoe, he thought wryly. But damned if it didn't feel good to be somebody's hero.

Jenny Fortune needed a hero.

Trace shut his eyes. He wished like hell he could roll under Katrina's bed and hide for a month or two or twelve. The woman had been right. He was afraid. He'd been afraid for six long years. Jenny only knew half of the story.

*But you don't want to marry me.*

Damn fool woman. Didn't she have a lick of sense? Apparently not.

Trace wanted to hit something. He wasn't up to watching Jenny Fortune take wedding vows, not today and probably not ever. And why was it happening? Because of that damned dress. She was tying herself to a no-good scoundrel in the hopes of saving her business.

*Hell, she could have done that with me.*

The thought struck like a hailstone and left him reeling. He rubbed his temples with his fingertips as if he could massage away the notion. Good Lord, what had gotten into him?

"Papa?" Concern laced Maribeth's voice.

He looked up. Emma and Mari stood at the top of the stairs gazing from him to Katrina and back to him again.

"What's the matter, Papa?" Emma asked in a serious tone.

Maribeth added, "You were scowling something awful, and we haven't done one thing bad yet today."

"I'm sorry I losted my shoe." Katrina patted his head comfortingly, right atop the knot where he'd bumped it a few minutes earlier. "I'll try real hard not to do it again."

A wave of love rolled through Trace at the sight of a trio of bright but worried faces. His mouth crooked upward in a smile as he stood. Brushing the dust from his trousers, he gave his daughters a wink and said, "I was thinking about how pretty you girls looked in these fancy dresses, and it made me start to worry about boys coming to call."

Katrina giggled, Maribeth snorted with disgust, and Emma's cheeks stained an appealing pink. Observing his eldest daughter's reaction, Trace realized there had been a grain of truth in the excuse he'd given.

They were growing up so fast. In so many ways no longer girls, but young ladies. *I would have been a good mother to your children.*

Trace's heart began to race. Sweat broke out on his brow. Katrina grabbed his hand and tugged him toward the stairs. "We'd better hurry, Papa. We don't want to be late. MissFortune would never forgive us."

Trace reached out to straighten the blue-and-white bow decorating his Katie-cat's curls. "We wouldn't want that, now would we? But I don't think you need to worry, girls. Miss Fortune strikes me as just the type of woman who forgives and forgets."

As the foursome left the house and headed for the church, Trace glanced up at the clear blue sky and murmured, "In fact, that's something I'm counting on."

IN THE VESTRY of the First Methodist Church, Monique Day clicked her tongue as she arranged the veil atop Jenny's head. "I do wish you'd tell me what is wrong, dear. It's as clear as the nose on my face that something is the matter."

Jenny shook her head. "I'm fine, Monique."

"You don't look fine," the sculptress said with a sniff. "You've a look about your eyes I do not like. I've told you half a dozen times already this afternoon, but I'll tell you again. If you want to back out of this wedding, you have my blessing. I admit I've had second thoughts about Edmund. Perhaps we could solve this bad luck problem another way."

Jenny shivered with a cold so deep even the steaming hot bath she'd taken hadn't warmed her. "Redeeming the dress's reputation will solve my troubles, Monique."

Monique patted Jenny's shoulders. "Well, you know what's best. Although, I will worry about you."

"I know."

"I want you to be happy."

"Of course you do."

Monique kissed her cheek, then checked her own appearance in the mirror. "La, would you look at that. I have a smear on my dress. I'll be right back, Jenny. I must see if I can locate a bit of water to—" She was still talking as she exited the room.

Jenny inhaled a deep breath and wondered why she wasn't nervous. She wondered why she didn't feel anything at all. Shrugging, she studied her reflection in the mirror and examined the Bad Luck Wedding Dress with a critical eye. Even Worth himself would be envious of this gown, she decided. She still had her talent. She shouldn't forget that.

A little flush of pride washed through her, and she welcomed the warmth.

She'd felt cold for too long, ever since Trace McBride's visit. The extremes of emotion of the previous day—and night—had numbed her. The "train robbery" and its aftermath; Trace's early morning visit with his shocking announcement and abrupt departure.

Murder. Jenny didn't believe it for a second.

Well, what she thought didn't matter now, did it? In a few minutes she'd march down the aisle to marry a man she didn't much like, ending any possibility, slight though it might be, for a future with the man she truly loved.

*Love?* Jenny closed her eyes in misery. Love. That word. That tiny four-letter, world-rocking word had slipped in despite her best efforts to hold it at bay.

God help her, it was true. She did love him; she had for some time now. She loved Trace McBride, and she was marrying Edmund Wharton.

*Oh, Jenny, Trace was right. Stupid. How stupid can you get?*

She stared into the mirror as if by looking hard enough, she could find the answer in her image. The mantel clock sitting on a small carved oak table against the west wall tolled the hour. Funny, she thought, it sounds almost like a death knell. Someone needs to fix the clock. Her brittle laugh echoed in the small room.

The door opened and Monique poked her head inside, a mischief twinkling in her eyes. "Your bridal attendants await."

Jenny's brows lifted. "Bridal attendants? What bridal attendants?"

Monique swung the door wide and three angels dressed in organdy with circlets of white roses in their hair stepped inside.

"Surprise, MissFortune," Katrina declared. "We're your bridesmaids. Aren't we beautiful?"

The McBride Menaces dressed as angels? Jenny's head, already muddled, began to swim.

Maribeth shrugged and said, "Kat just likes all the ruffles. The dresses are all right, but they're not as pretty as what you'd have made us. Papa says he's never seen dresses as pretty as those you make."

Trace. The name twisted Jenny's heart.

"What do you think he'll say about our halo?" Katrina asked, lifting a hand to touch the ring of flowers in her hair.

Emma added, "He hasn't seen our flowers, yet. Your mother gave them to us when we got here."

"Papa will probably faint when we walk down the aisle," Maribeth said with a giggle. "After all, the McBride Menaces wearing angels' haloes is a pretty shocking sight."

"When you walk down the aisle," Jenny repeated stupidly. "Your father is *here*?"

"Yes," Emma replied. "I don't think he really wanted to come, but he couldn't very well miss our grand entrance."

Monique motioned the girls back out into the vestibule. "Everyone appears to be seated. I'll signal the pianist to begin." She handed her daughter a bouquet of roses, then adjusted the filmy white veil over her face. "It's a beautiful dress. I hope it brings you the best of luck."

Jenny swallowed an hysterical laugh. "It's the Bad Luck Wedding Dress, Mother."

"Yes, but you are Jenny Fortune."

The opening strains of the wedding march sounded, and Monique led the way toward the center aisle. Jenny looked around and saw row after row of curious faces, their eyes alight with anticipation. A sense of approaching doom descended on her like a cloud.

What was she doing here? She couldn't marry Edmund, not like this.

Not when she loved another man.

The truth was a hard slap to the face. The music drowned out her groan. Dear Lord, why now? Why not ten minutes ago? Ten days ago?

She couldn't marry Edmund. "Mother!" she said in a loud whisper. "Mother, I can't—"

But Monique was already down the aisle, taking her seat as the mother of the bride. Jenny stood frozen, staring at the McBride girls. She loved Trace. She loved him, and she'd given up on him way too easily. Who was she to have accused him of being afraid? Wasn't that her trouble, too? Hadn't she been too afraid of being hurt to really try and win him?

Katrina started down the aisle, followed quickly by Maribeth. Emma hesitated, looking over her shoulder as she said, "I hope you don't mind too much, Miss Jenny. We did what we felt we had to do."

What? What did she mean by that? Panic rose within Jenny. What was she going to do? She couldn't marry Edmund Wharton!

Standing still as a fashion doll at the end of the aisle, she viewed the congregation from the periphery of her vision.

Smiling faces, curious faces, judgmental faces. Oh, help. Her gaze slowly focused on the altar and her groom.

She wished he'd turn around. She could signal him to bolt. That way she'd save him the humiliation of being left at the altar. Because she wouldn't marry him, she couldn't. *Oh, Edmund. I'm sorry. I never intended to embarrass you.*

Jenny took a step forward. She pasted a smile on her face and stared hard at the black-jacketed back of her groom, willing him to look at her. Why wasn't he turning around? That's the way it was done, wasn't it? The groom watched the bride walk down the aisle.

Maybe Edmund didn't want this any more than she did. Wouldn't that be wonderful?

She caught a glimpse of Rilda Bea Sperry seated in one of the back pews. The widow did look grand in that royal-blue serge. Where would she purchase her wardrobe once Fortune's Design had closed?

Jenny's step faltered. She couldn't deny it. What she was about to do would undoubtedly mean the end of her business. The Bad Luck Wedding Dress's reputation would live forever.

Swaying, she stepped forward and only then noticed the McBride Menaces had stopped dead-center, halfway up the aisle.

Less than a foot from the trio, Jenny clearly heard the whispers from their huddle.

"What'll we do now?"

"Where's Casey? Can we stop him?"

"Mari, this is all your fault."

"It was your idea, Emmaline Suzanne."

"Papa's gonna paint the walls with us this time for certain."

The scent of roses, beeswax, and trouble hung over the church like a cloud. Jenny touched Maribeth on the shoulder. "Girls?" she calmly asked. "What are you doing?"

"Oh, Miss Fortune," Maribeth said, "this is awful. Wonderful, but awful. We didn't know!"

"Please forgive us," Emma added.

"For what?"

"It's Casey."

"Casey Tate?"

"Maybe if we hurry we can stop him," Katrina interjected.

The two older sisters looked at each other, then made a dash for the altar.

Jenny eyed them with concern and a good measure of hope. Had the McBride Menaces been at it again? Would they inadvertently save her? Please, yes. Let her have just one bit of good luck to go along with all the bad.

As her bridesmaids reached the front of the church, Jenny glanced from left to right, peering through the lace of her veil, looking for Casey Tate. He was obviously involved in whatever mischief they had planned, but Jenny didn't see the boy. She did notice Wilhemina Peters, pencil and notebook in hand, and it appeared as if the entire roster of both the Fort Worth Literary Society and the Ladies' Benevolent Aid Organization had turned out for the big event. They stared at her dress as if waiting for it to explode. Although Jenny's customers and their husbands lined the pews, she spied not a glimpse of the boy.

Or the McBride daughters' father.

Then she was at the altar. Taking her place beside her groom, Jenny looked straight ahead. If the girls didn't come through for her, maybe she should pretend a faint. That might allow both her and Edmund to escape with a bit of grace.

The congregation quieted as the minister's voice boomed, "I welcome you all on this most solemn and joyous occasion. We congregate here today in God's presence to witness as this man and this woman are united in holy matrimony."

Her stomach turned at the words.

As the clergyman continued his remarks, Jenny's attention wandered. She unobtrusively lifted her hand and adjusted her veil so as to keep a closer watch on the McBride trio. Or, she should say, the McBride duo. Maribeth had disappeared.

Emma and Katrina were as white as their dresses, and—Jenny stifled a cry of distress when she saw this—tears rolled down the elder sister's face.

Oh, no. Whatever they had done must truly be awful. But why would they have changed their minds midaisle, so to speak?

The reverend's voice droned on, and when Jenny saw the girls share a look of alarm, she concentrated on what the man was saying. "If anyone knows a reason why this marriage should not take place…"

She braced herself, praying for a most welcome distraction. But the moment of silence following the minister's question passed without incident. She breathed a heavy sigh of despair and leaned toward her groom. "Edmund, be prepared. I'm going to faint."

The squeals began toward the back of the church at the same time the minister instructed the bride and groom to join hands. She moved to look over her shoulder as Edmund grabbed her hand and held it tightly. "Edmund," she protested.

From the back of the church came a woman's screech. "Mice!"

A second voice cried, "Dozens of them!"

Dresses rustled and shoe leather scuffed against the pews as the groom's grip tightened painfully upon Jenny's hand. She turned to glare at him.

Emerald eyes.

Jenny didn't move. The world stood still.

The man standing next to her wasn't Edmund Wharton.

She dropped both her chin and her bouquet as the minister said, "Do you, Trace McBride, take Jenny Fortune to be your lawfully wedded wife?"

"I do!" he declared about the time a pair of cats streaked past him.

The minister peered over the top of his wire-rimmed spectacles. "I wasn't finished yet, Mr. McBride."

Trace made hurry-up motions with his hand as Maribeth and Casey Tate darted past them, chasing the cats.

Jenny whipped the veil back from her face and simply stared, numb with amazement. Trace was here, standing beside her and reciting marriage vows. If repeating "I do" over and over again counted as recitation.

The church, the people, and the melee of children and animals faded to the periphery of her awareness. Nothing could distract her from the man at her side.

Why? What had changed his mind? She couldn't read the answer in his eyes. Now he refused to look at her. "Where is Edmund?"

"It doesn't matter," he whispered fiercely. "You're marrying me, not him."

"I don't understand!"

"You don't need to understand, just tell the preacher yes."

"Miss Fortune?" the reverend asked. "*Do* you take this man to be your husband?"

She got the impression it wasn't the first time he'd asked the question. Trace gave her hand a little shake. "Do it, Jenny. Now. All hell is breaking loose in here."

"In church?"

"My daughters are in church."

A warm bubble of joy swelled within her. Yes, the McBride daughters were here, as was their father. The family she'd always craved waited right here before her. All she had to do was reach out and grab it.

Following a particularly loud yelp from one of the dogs, the preacher suggested, "Perhaps we should call a halt to the proceedings."

"No!" Jenny and Trace said simultaneously. He finally looked at her, impatience glittering in narrowed green eyes. "Get on with it," he insisted.

She addressed the minister. "What do I do?"

"There, she said it," Trace insisted.

The preacher sighed. "Repeat after me. I, Jenny Fortune, take you, Trace McBride, to be my lawfully wedded husband."

She waited until Trace met her gaze once more, then firmly repeated her vows. Although chaos reigned around her, the world narrowed to just her and Trace as she swore to love, honor, and cherish. He watched her keenly, as if against his will, as she promised to be true and faithful. Jenny poured both heart and soul into her words, offering him everything.

When the minister asked for a ring, Trace shook his head. "Sorry, Jenny, I didn't think about a ring."

"I don't care," she insisted, blinking back tears of happiness. "You're here, that's all that matters."

"Me and the other animals," he said, one side of his mouth lifting in a rueful grin.

Jenny laughed. "The legend of the Bad Luck Wedding Dress lives on." And she didn't care one whit.

The minister interrupted, "Let's finish this up, shall we? I'd like to clear the church before the Widow Sperry injures someone with that parasol she's wielding."

Shortly, he declared them husband and wife. She grinned at Maribeth's loud *yahoo* even as Trace pulled her into his arms for the customary kiss. And then, she forgot everything else.

This was no peck on the cheek or polite buss on the lips. He wrapped her in a tight embrace and devoted himself to the task like Michelangelo at the Sistine Chapel. The kiss went on and on and on. Jenny heard a rushing in her ears. The din in the church receded until she and her brand-new husband were the only two people in the world.

The commotion actually did subside. People forgot about

the mice and the cats and the dogs as, one by one, they noticed the duration and intensity of the kiss. While the animals escaped through the open doors at the back of the church, the congregation grew silent. Speechless. Ceremony-ending kisses never lasted like this one.

Finally Wilhemina Peters expressed the thought running through many people's minds. "Why, I do declare," she said loudly, fanning her face with her notepad. "It looks as if that wedding dress has seen a change of luck!"

As the congregation cheered, Trace finally pulled away from his bride. Monique's face beamed with delight as she rushed toward the altar and grasped him by the lapels, yanking him toward her. Jenny laughed at her new husband's wide-eyed expression when his brand-new mother-in-law planted a kiss directly on his mouth and said, "Welcome to the family, you handsome thing, you. Welcome to the family."

*When a new home is built, the first fire
to be made in the fireplace should come
from a happy and prosperous home to
bring good luck to the new home.*

## CHAPTER TWELVE

THE HOUSE ROSE majestically atop a hill on the west side of
town. The back veranda overlooked the Clear Fork of the
Trinity, while the view from the front balconies offered a
scene of downtown Fort Worth, the railroad depot to the south,
and the broad prairie beyond, where, in season, cattle herds
waited to ford the river.

It was to this mansion on the hill that Trace planned to take
his bride.

The house had set Fort Worth tongues to wagging since the
beginning of its construction months ago. Through stealth and
carefully placed bribes, he'd managed to keep the owner's
identity secret. Now, with the house finished and the sale of
the End of the Line nearly completed, the time had arrived to
announce the resumption of his profession.

If all went as planned, public admiration for his house
would lead to commissions for other residential designs.
Those, in turn, would lead to bids for commercial buildings.

But Trace's professional concerns had little to do with

bringing Jenny to the new house after their wedding reception. It was the privacy that appealed to him. Privacy and the bed he'd purchased at the railroad's unclaimed freight auction a little over a month ago.

The bed was huge, the mattress firm, and he'd imagined Jenny lying on it a hundred times since he said "I do."

He gave his bride a sidelong look. She sparkled. She glowed. She acted as if all of her dreams had come true.

Damn it all, they needed to talk.

As much as Trace desired a wedding night with this woman, he could not in good faith proceed with it unless Jenny understood the situation. This was no fairy-tale marriage where "I do" meant happily ever after. He couldn't be that dishonest with her. In many ways this marriage would be similar to the arrangement she'd planned with Wharton, the oily bastard.

From the looks of her now, all pretty and bubbly and shining, she expected something more.

Her voice echoed in his mind. *I could have loved you.*

Damn. They needed to talk about that, too. He didn't want her love, and God knows, he would never love her. He liked Jenny Fortune McBride way too much to do that to her.

Jenny noticed his regard and offered him a shy smile. "All right, I give up. Just where is it we are going?"

*To bed,* he wanted to say. "You'll find out when we get there," he told her instead, snapping the reins to signal the horse to speed.

They rode in a coal-box buggy Monique had decorated with flowers and ribbons for the traditional Grand Parade around town following the reception. Instead of a Grand Parade, Trace had orchestrated a quick and quiet disappearance from the gala his new mother-in-law had hosted at the Cosmopolitan.

There, he'd had all the fun he could stand within the first half hour. Wilhemina Peters had dogged the newlyweds' heels like a bloodhound on the scent, recording every exclamation, felicitation, and proclamation uttered. Trace anticipated the devotion of an entire page in the *Democrat* for a recounting of all the wedding gossip. Two pages, if she went into any detail about the encounter she'd witnessed in the hotel lobby between the newlyweds and the former bridegroom.

Trace had been dancing with Jenny when Wharton steamed into the ballroom all but foaming at the mouth, his accusations loud, ugly, and for the most part true. Shrugging, Trace had refused either to confirm or deny the charge that he'd waylaid the groom, although he did quietly express surprise that Wharton had managed to escape the bondage room at Miss Rachel's.

While the guests at the reception speculated about the bruises on Wharton's face, Trace had advised him to lower his voice, congratulate the bride, and catch the evening train out of town.

He considered it unfortunate that the skunk then raised a stink, and he was forced to grab the man by the scruff of the neck and escort him from the hotel. The vicious, if empty, threats he murmured in Wharton's ears apparently did the trick. His complexion blanched as white as the stripe down his back.

Just to make certain, Trace had slipped Casey Tate five dollars to keep an eye on Thomas Edmund Wharton III until the man actually boarded the train. He'd welcomed the news a short time later when the boy returned to the party and announced, "He polled his freight and left!"

In the meantime, Mrs. Wilson, God bless her, had distracted the guests by launching herself at Trace and wrapping him in a boisterous embrace. She'd conducted a loud, extended expression of congratulations, then smacked a congratulatory kiss right on his lips, after which she wrapped Jenny in a smothering hug and suggested she stay with the girls for an entire week so the newlyweds could enjoy a proper honeymoon.

For his wife's sake, Trace couldn't decline her offer. The transformation of the wedding dress from bad to good had begun. Publicly refusing an opportunity for newlywed privacy might have placed the process at risk.

Besides, when it came right down to it, Trace hadn't wanted to refuse.

So, after promising his daughters that he'd think long and hard about an appropriate punishment for the day's mischief, he had kissed them good-bye and ushered his bride to the waiting buggy.

The ride from the Cosmopolitan had taken them fifteen minutes, and by the time Trace turned into the drive that led up the hill to the house, the setting sun speared the western sky with beams of pink, vermillion, and gold.

Jenny glanced at him, her brows arched in surprise. "Trace?"

A fierce sense of pride filled him as he said, "It's mine. We're all moving in next week."

Jenny's chin dropped. "*You're* the one building this place?"

Grinning at her surprise, he gazed toward the red-brick Georgian Revival style house. "Actually, I designed it. Someone else built it. I was the architect."

"Architect? But you're a saloonkeeper."

"Not anymore. I'm selling the End of the Line."

"You've sold the saloon?"

The gasp filled her lungs with air, lifting her breasts. Trace damn near dropped the reins. "I have a buyer. We'll sign the papers as soon as the lawyers finish their bickering."

Jenny plopped back against the buggy's seat. "I had no idea!"

"Nobody does. Not even the girls. I wanted to keep it a surprise for them until the time was right."

She closed her eyes, shaking her head back and forth. "The last twenty-four hours have been absolutely bizarre." After a moment's pause, she added, "I have so many questions, not the least of which is why you changed your mind about marrying me, but I find I'm afraid to ask them."

He tugged on the reins, bringing the horse and buggy to a halt in the middle of the circular drive. He thought of the bed upstairs and knew he had to speak. "We need to talk, Jenny."

Almost a minute passed before she replied. "I know." Then, meeting his gaze, she asked, "But, couldn't we put it off for just a little while? I have a nasty feeling we're bound to argue, and I truly don't think I'm up to it." She placed her hand on his knee. "It could wait until tomorrow, couldn't it?"

He gave her a sidelong, skeptical look.

"Please?"

The woman's smile packed more punch than moonshine. Sighing dramatically, Trace nodded and hopped down from the buggy, then moved to assist his wife. His hands lingered at her waist as he lifted her down, and he tried not to think about his easy capitulation.

He knew he'd taken the coward's way out. He'd seized on her excuse in order to enjoy a wedding night.

Grabbing her satchel from the buggy, he escorted her up the front steps and inside the house. She stopped abruptly, gazing around, and his hand clenched the bag's handle as he awaited her reaction.

"Oh, Trace!"

*Oh, Trace?* He wanted more than that. It had been a lifetime ago since anyone's opinion of his work had meant this much to him. Of course, it had been a lifetime since he'd done any work, period.

A crystal chandelier hung from the entryway's vaulted ceiling, and Italian white marble tiled the floor. With no carpets and few furnishings, Jenny's steps echoed as she walked toward the centerpiece of the house—the grand spiral staircase that led to the horseshoe balcony surrounding the second-floor landing. She stared for what seemed like days.

Finally, she glanced back over her shoulder. Wonder lit the depths of her summer-sky eyes as she said, "It's fabulous, Trace. Simply gorgeous. Show me the rest, please?"

He released a pent-up breath. "There's not much to see," he said gruffly. "The only furniture I have is some stuff I picked up from the railroad, and it's not all that special. Except for one piece, that is. I poured all my money into the house itself; my reputation depends on the design, not the sofas."

She started nodding before he finished speaking. "Of course. This house is a grand display of talent. People have known that for months. And once they see the inside..." She beamed at him. "You'll be the most famous architect in the state."

"Fame isn't important; commissions are. The girls need—"

"You'll have your choice of commissions, Trace McBride," she interrupted. "Believe me." An impish light entered her eyes as she added, "I knew I married a talented man, but I had no idea just how extensive those talents were."

Her reaction filled him with pride and something even more basic. Hell, he thought, as warmth pooled low in his belly, why not have a wedding night to remember? She had one coming to her; Wharton damn sure would have given her one. Before Trace locked the bastard in that room at Rachel's, Wharton had confirmed Trace's suspicion that "marriage of convenience" to him meant a convenient bedmate. That was the last thing he'd said before Trace threw the knockout punch and took the skunk's place at the altar.

Now he wanted to claim his own place in the nuptial bed. "You've only scratched the surface of my talents, Mrs. McBride." Decision made, he couldn't wait. "C'mon, I'll give you the two-bit tour. We'll start upstairs, all right?"

As they climbed the steps he enjoyed a renewed burst of energy. A short time ago he'd been feeling the effects of last night's minimal amount of sleep. Funny how a good dose of lust could kick the tired right out of a man's bones.

"This way," he said motioning to the right at the top of the stairs.

At the door to the master bedroom, Jenny stopped abruptly, a peculiar look crossing her face. Trace set her satchel beside the bed. "What is it?"

She rubbed the bridge of her nose. "I guess the events of the last couple of days are catching up with me. I'm more tired than I thought."

Trace tried to keep the disappointment from his voice. "You're tired? *Too* tired?"

"No, not *too* tired." Her cheeks flushed with color as she added, "It's not that. I guess I just now realized that we, uh…that we'll…that we're *married*."

She wasn't turning him down. Immediately his spirits lifted, and he reached out, pulling her to him. "You're hard on a fella's pride, Wife," he growled. "Have you forgotten that kiss we shared at the altar?"

"What kiss?" she breathed, her limbs trembling beneath his touch.

"Witch." Bending his head toward hers, he said in a rough, low whisper, "Guess I'll have to remind you."

She moistened her lips with an innocent, sensual swipe of her tongue. "Guess you will, McBride."

Heat filled him fast and hot as he crushed his mouth against hers. So soft, so sweet. Like the candy mints Monique had served at the reception.

Even as his tongue stroked the velvet of her mouth, his fingers wandered across the lustrous folds of taffeta, searching for a way inside.

She felt so damned good; she fit in his arms so perfectly. When she sighed her pleasure against his lips, a sizzle coursed through him, and he groaned aloud.

Good Lord, he wanted her. His body pulsed, the elemental need battling for control over his will. He didn't want to rush this. Not this first time. Their first time. He lifted his head and drew a ragged breath. She smelled of roses and something more—the deeper, more exotic scent of arousal.

He touched his lips to her temple. "Come to bed, Jenny. Please, come to bed with me."

Lifting her hand, she brushed back a curl from his forehead and teased, "Before the two-bit tour?"

"We'll start it with the bed." He turned his head and nipped at her fingers. "The longer tour costs fifty cents."

She answered with a little smile that betrayed her nervousness, and Trace discovered he disliked seeing the sentiment. "Don't be afraid, Jenny."

"I'm not," she said, shaking her head. "Not of you. Never of you."

Her declaration touched that gaping void within him and warmth filled the hollowness. He was humbled.

Her faith made him feel like a man again.

"Let me change?" she asked in a shy voice as she stepped away from him. "I made a gown for tonight. I'd like to wear it."

"No." The fierceness of his reply surprised them both. "You made it for Wharton. It doesn't belong in our bed."

She shook her head. "I did not sew this gown for Edmund. I made it years ago to keep in my bridal chest in anticipation of my wedding night."

"You'd have worn it for Wharton," Trace said, feeling downright peevish.

"No, I don't think so. I designed this gown to please the man I loved. It's true I packed it with my things, but I don't believe I would have worn it. Not for Edmund. But I'd like to wear it for you, Trace. May I?"

*To please the man I loved.* And she wanted to wear it for him? Oh, hell. As much as he didn't want to do it, they were going to have to talk. He held up his hand, palm out. "Jenny, wait a minute. Before we go any further, we need to get something straight—"

She placed a finger across his lips. "This is our wedding night, Mr. McBride, and wedding nights are not for talking. We have the rest of our lives to talk, but we only have one wedding night."

God, he could drown in those eyes. Well, hell, he'd tried. And she did have a point. Wedding nights only happened once. They'd talk tomorrow, and he'd make damn sure she enjoyed tonight.

Trace nodded toward a door on the side wall. "The dressing room is through there." Then, hoping to ease the tension he noted in her eyes, he added, "Hurry, all right? I'm anxious to begin the tour."

She lifted her satchel and walked toward the door, throwing an uncertain look over her shoulder as she did so. He winked at her and she answered with a slow smile. Then, as if gathering her courage, she raised her chin just a mite. In a brave, sassy tone, she teased, "Oh, I'll hurry, Trace. I'm eager for you to show me your—"

He gave her a sharp look.

"—house."

Trace was still grinning when, after stripping naked, he crawled into the bed. Stacking a pair of pillows against the headboard, he sank back into them. Then, considerate of Jenny's modesty, he drew the sheet and blanket up waist high. "I do love this mattress," he said with a sigh, wiggling his toes. Elbows outstretched, his fingers laced behind his head, he waited, erotic images running through his mind.

*Hurry up, Jenny.* It seemed to be taking forever. As his imaginings grew even more explicit, his eyes drifted shut. The better to see his fantasies as he waited for reality, he thought.

The mattress cradled him. The blanket warmed him. The lack of sleep caught up with him.

After only ten minutes, Jenny returned to the bedroom wearing a diaphanous midnight-blue silk gown that revealed more of her charms than it hid. But instead of the heated look of lust she expected from her groom, she was met at the door with something else altogether.

Her husband's snore.

Silently, she approached the bed, a tender smile stealing across her face. Her hero. Her savior.

Her love.

He hadn't wanted to marry. He'd sworn he never would again. She had a hundred questions to ask, and she wondered just how many answers he would give her.

*Not as many as I'd like, I suspect. Oh, Trace, I'll make our marriage good for you. I promise I'll make you happy. I'll help you forget.*

Then Jenny joined her husband in their marriage bed, curled herself against him, and went happily to sleep.

"I DON'T BELIEVE THIS," the raspy voice muttered in Jenny's ear.

She opened her eyes to the hazy light of dawn, rested and warm and spooned against her husband. Never in her entire life had she ever felt so content. Her lips lifted in a sleepy smile as she snuggled back against him, her eyes drifting shut as sleep beckoned once more.

Then his hand began to move, trailing upward from her waist to cup the weight of her breast, and a stab of yearning chased away all thought of slumber. "Trace?"

"I truly don't believe this," he repeated, his voice indignant and just a little embarrassed. He flicked the pad of his thumb across her nipple as he added, "I fell asleep on you."

His touch sent warm honey running through her veins, and she felt so good, so wonderful, she couldn't help but giggle, just a little. "Not exactly *on* me."

He growled, rough and low, and tugged on her shoulder,

rolling her onto her back. He loomed above her. "Are you laughing at me, Wife?"

"Oh, no, Trace. I'm laughing at us. I'm laughing for us." She lifted her hand to caress the stubbled skin of his face and put her heart into a smile. "I feel like the luckiest woman alive."

His eyes narrowed, passion flaring within their depths. "God, you're beautiful."

Her breath locked in her throat. When he looked at her that way, she thought her heart might burst. Anticipation filled her, fed by the love she felt for this man. "Make love to me, Trace."

He lowered his head to press a quick, gentle kiss to her lips. "I don't think anything could stop me this time." He rose above her, bronzed and naked, and she caught her breath at the proof of his desire. Then he touched her, stripping away her gown to leave her bare to his heated gaze, and Jenny lost the ability to think. All she could do was feel.

He stroked her, suckled her, teased her with his breath. He spoke to her with his eyes and voiced words she'd never heard before. Seductive words, erotic words, carnal words that embarrassed and excited her. Words that made her ache with a need beyond all experience.

Jenny writhed in his arms. "Please, Trace."

"Please?" He nipped at her neck. "Yes, sweetheart, I'll please you. I'll please you so well and so often you'll never leave my bed for another's."

She heard the words, but did not note them, so lost was she in the sensual haze he had created. He found the core of her womanhood with his fingers, stroking and stretching her. With every movement, tension inside her heightened. She held him by the shoulders, her hands tightening, nails digging into his flesh. Her head rolled restlessly as she moaned and pressed against him, seeking relief.

"That's it." His voice was raspy and rough. "Give it to me. Give me your pleasure."

She was poised at the edge of a high precipice, aching to tumble over, fearing the drop. Opening her eyes, she sought reassurance.

Trace held her gaze, both fierce and tender at the same time. "Go ahead and fall. I'm here to catch you. I'll always be here to catch you."

With a small cry, she gave herself up to the feeling. She rose, soaring, her husband holding her tightly all the way. "Oh, Trace," she breathed.

"I know, honey." He pressed a kiss to her lips and positioned himself between her thighs. She knew a moment of pain as he made her his wife, but its memory was lost as he filled her with his heat.

Each sensation imprinted itself on her mind. The sheen of sweat covering his skin, the musky fragrance enveloping them, the contrast of hard against soft. When she heard his groan and felt his body shudder as he poured his life force into her, Jenny knew an emotional pleasure as powerful and intense as the physical one of moments ago. Tears stung her eyes.

Her rescuer, her knight in shining armor. Her hero. This was love.

If only Trace could see it.

LATER THAT MORNING Trace once again attempted to instigate a "talk." Jenny wanted no part of it. She suspected such a discussion would lead to strife.

She decided she could wait to learn about his first wife and the accident that killed her. And what was the rush in learning why he had changed his mind and taken Edmund's place at the altar? They had plenty of time to discuss what to expect from this marriage.

She was living in a fool's paradise, she knew, and the questions must be asked and answered. But what was wrong with a few days of happiness? What would a few days of pretending hurt? Shoot, Monique pretended for years at a time, and it didn't seem to cause her any harm.

For now, Jenny was happy. Their lovemaking had been all she'd dreamed of, lacking only the declaration she knew not to expect. She wanted to enjoy the moment for as long as possible, and that enjoyment would surely end with the commencement of Trace's "talk."

Jenny loved Trace McBride, and she knew he didn't return the feeling. Knowing something was difficult enough; her heart didn't need the grief of hearing him say it. Not today. Not until after their honeymoon, however long she could make it last.

Distracting Trace from his purpose proved easy enough. Her talents in that regard, though never before used, were obviously something she'd inherited from Monique. She eventually got her two-bit tour, though not in a way she would have imagined. By the end of the day, Trace had made love to her in every room upstairs except for the girls' bedrooms. He promised to show her the downstairs the following day, predicting she would develop an extra strong attachment to the dining room and its wide mahogany table.

For three days they enjoyed an idyllic honeymoon. While they didn't have that "talk," they did enjoy conversations, and Jenny was pleased that he listened with genuine interest to her opinions about public and personal issues. He spoke with her at length about his plans to resume his profession. He was open and honest about his financial situation. He expressed a real interest in Fortune's Design, going so far as to offer advice on how to capitalize on the notion of "bad luck turning good."

"Use what Wilhemina Peters said at the wedding," he suggested on the afternoon of the third day. Sparks flew as he tossed another log onto the fire in the master bedroom fireplace. "Quote her in a newspaper advertisement. She'll love it."

Jenny dragged her gaze from the arresting sight of the flex of his bare muscles. "What are you talking about?"

"What she said when we kissed. You know, 'Looks like that dress has had a change of luck.'"

"She said that? I didn't hear her say that."

Glancing back over his shoulder, he unleashed a wicked smile. "Guess you were concentrating on my kiss."

Jenny almost groaned aloud. "Guess I was."

"Want to do it again?"

"Guess I do."

Half an hour later while stroking his finger softly up Jenny's bare midriff, Trace casually mentioned her wedding gift should be arriving sometime that afternoon.

"My wedding gift?" Jenny was both shocked and delighted. When had he found the time to purchase her a gift?

He grinned, his jeweled eyes twinkling, but he wouldn't say more despite her constant questions.

Trace had no way of knowing how much his action touched her. Her father's wedding gifts to her mother had always been a source of delight. Throughout Jenny's childhood, she'd spin fantasies about the next item to be added. Each time her parents married, Richard Fortune gave Monique a whimsical favor—a clown statue, a paper fan, a painted rock. The items occupied a place of honor among Monique's possessions, and they fascinated her daughter. Thus, wedding gifts from groom to bride came to hold a special significance to Jenny.

That Trace would even think of giving her a gift, much less actually do it, made her heart sing.

By the time a wagon rolled up the hill at half past three, Jenny all but trembled with excitement. Standing at an upstairs window, she peered intently through the glass. "That's Mr. Starnes, isn't it? He's bringing us something from the railroad?"

Trace was all mischievous innocence. "Well, I wonder what it could be?"

Jenny gave him a sidelong glance and was reminded of his

daughters. Laughter sputtered up inside her. "Come along, Mr. Head Menace. Let's go find out."

The air outside was crisp and clean-scented. Standing on the front porch, Jenny rubbed her arms, half from chill and half from excitement. Wood scraped against wood as Mr. Starnes tugged the crate stamped Texas & Pacific from the wagon bed onto a dolly.

"Howdy, Trace," he said. "Sure was surprised to see your name at this address. Surprised to be deliverin' something other than spirits, too. Where you want this?"

Trace eyed the crate, then gave Jenny a nonchalant glance. "The front parlor will be fine, Ray. Mrs. McBride will want room to spread it all out."

The deliveryman nodded to Jenny. "Best wishes, ma'am. Your wedding is the talk of Tarrant County. Dallas County, too, now."

"Dallas County?" she repeated.

"Sorry I couldn't help you with this, ma'am. Ain't it lucky ol' Trace here has been providing the liquor to the Fort Worth and Dallas offices of the T and P since the rails hit town?" He scratched his beard and chuckled a moment before adding, "That Ethel Baumgardner squealed like a stuck pig when your husband's telegrams snatched this crate right out from under her." He tilted back the dolly and rolled the box toward the house.

Jenny's heart seemed to stop. Her eyes widened and she steepled her hands over her mouth. "My European shipment?" She whirled on Trace. "That's my European shipment in that box?"

Trace folded his arms, nodding smugly. "Including the bolt Emma and Maribeth took off the train. It's dark blue with—"

"Midnight-blue silk with silver and gold threads," she said softly, as Mr. Starnes tugged the crate up the front steps and into the house. Following the men into the parlor, she blinked back tears and stared at the large wooden box. When she made no move toward it, Trace touched her arm. "I'll get a bar to pry it open, all right?"

She nodded, vaguely noting his curious look as he escorted Mr. Starnes outside.

A few minutes later his boot steps echoed in the entry hall. She heard him enter the parlor, but all she saw was a blur because of the tears pooled in her eyes. Metal scraped and wood creaked as he pried the top from the box.

Jenny gasped. Silks, sateens, lawn, and lace. Arctic blue, smoke gray, primrose, and heliotrope. Dots, plaids, Scotch tweed. Trims to make any woman gasp with pleasure.

Her tears overflowed.

"Jenny? What the hell—"

"Oh, Trace." She threw herself into his arms. "Thank you. Oh, thank you!"

The stiffness drained from his body and he wrapped her in a hug. "I take it you like your gift?"

"I've never…nobody ever…." Surrounded by his strength, his security, words erupted from the depths of her heart. "Oh, Trace, I love you."

She knew immediately she'd made a mistake. He grasped her shoulders and set her away from him. "Don't," he said flatly. "Jenny, don't."

"But—"

"No!" His eyes were shards of green glass, his jaw made of granite. "It's not that way for you and me. It's no different than it would have been with Wharton. I married you to take care of my daughters; you married me to save your business. That's all it is. A convenient marriage for both of us. Don't expect any more. I won't allow it. I don't *want* it."

A chill crept through her on spider's legs.

"Goddammit, Jenny, don't look like that!" He raked his fingers through his hair. "I tried to tell you. I wanted to talk."

She closed her eyes, reeling from the blow. It was true. He'd wanted to talk, and she wouldn't let him because she knew this would be the result. *Oh, Jenny, why didn't you just keep your mouth shut!*

He said quietly, "Look, this need not change anything between us. We've been getting along fine, haven't we? This marriage is working. Better than I expected, to be truthful."

A bitter note crept into her voice. "That's because you're getting everything you want."

"That's not fair," he said coldly.

She wasn't feeling very fair. She was feeling childish and discouraged and brokenhearted. She whirled around, pacing the room in agitation. Trace stood in the center of the parlor like a stone monolith, and Jenny was seized by an overwhelming desire to send him toppling. The thick-headed man.

The honest man.

He'd never made her any promises. She'd known that from the moment she said "I do," and that was why she'd resisted having this conversation. She'd wanted to pretend for a little while, to make believe that her dreams had come true. She'd had three days and that was more than she would have had if they'd talked on their wedding day.

Abruptly, the fight drained out of her.

She drew a deep, shuddering breath. "You're right, Trace. I apologize. I'll keep my feelings to myself from now on, and I hope you'll find that more…convenient."

Lifting her chin and squaring her shoulders, she swept regally from the room. In the doorway, she paused. "Thank you for my fabrics. I'll take them to the shop first thing tomorrow. I believe our honeymoon is over, don't you agree?"

A muscle ticked on the side of his jaw. "I'll fetch the girls after school."

"Good. I'll make certain their rooms are ready."

"Look, I intend for Mrs. Wilson to stay on," he said, his

voice betraying a slight bit of exasperation. "You won't have to worry about cooking and cleaning and that sort of stuff."

She offered him a false smile. "That's convenient."

Halfway up the stairs, she heard his curse. It was virulent, vivid, and distinct, and it gave her pause.

Jenny clutched the banister as emotions gave way to thought. Wait a minute. Perhaps she was being hasty here. He might not love her, but he wasn't indifferent toward her. Trace felt more for her than sexual desire alone. He cared for her. He'd shown her in many different ways. If she gave him time, gave them both time, could that caring deepen to love?

She continued up the stairs, her mind whirling. Out of the blue she recalled a conversation with one of her mother's more recent suitors. The man broke horses for a rancher in central Texas.

"Horses are no different than people," he'd told her. "You can't teach a kid to read if he don't know his letters. You have to teach a horse basic fundamentals first. You don't teach one to stop from a run. You do it by steps. First, you teach him to walk and stop; then trot, walk, and stop; then lope, trot, walk, and stop. Finally, unless you ruin his mouth or something, it all falls into place and he'll stop from then on."

Was there a lesson in there for her? Could she compare marriage to training a horse? *Trace already has the stud part down.*

Continuing up the stairs, Jenny didn't feel as badly as she had before.

She entered their bedroom and the bed drew her gaze like a magnet. She crossed the room, her heels clicking against the hardwood floor. She reached out and brushed the downy satin of the coverlet. *We've been getting along fine,* he'd said. *This marriage is working.*

Trace was right. Her ill-timed confession hadn't changed the situation. She hadn't lost his love with her declaration. A woman can't lose something she never possessed.

That horse trainer had said something else. "If you push a horse too hard, too young, you're likely to ruin his legs. If a horse doesn't have good legs, he don't got nothin' 'cause he needs good legs for the long haul."

Jenny wanted Trace for the long haul.

"I just have to be patient." Patient and persistent. She knew how to be persistent.

All her life she'd fought for what she wanted. Fortune's Design was proof of that. Well, her marriage deserved no less.

Despite her many unanswered questions, one thing she'd figured out on her own. Trace's love for a woman had hurt him in the past, and he'd learned to protect himself. Making this marriage a success was not an impossible task, just a difficult one. A challenge.

Jenny was good at challenges. She'd follow the horse trainer's example. She'd start slow, be patient, and work on one step at a time.

Her gaze swept the length of the bed and she grinned. She had her own version of a corrective bit.

After all, she wasn't Monique Day's daughter for nothing.

When Trace finally entered their darkened bedroom late that night, having spent the intervening hours shut away in his first-floor office, he was surprised to discover his wife in their bed. Well, hell. If she thought to banish him to one of the girls' youthfully short mattresses, she had another think coming.

A lamp flared. Jenny sat up, the sheet slipped down, and Trace damn near fainted dead away. "What the hell?"

"Midnight-blue silk shot with gold and silver threads," she said in a smokey whisper. "I thought you should see what a superior fabric can do for a lady."

"Hold on a minute. I don't understand. What is this?"

*Today's lesson, McBride. Walk and stop.* She smiled a siren's promise. "Why ruin the part of our marriage that's working? Come to bed, Trace."

TRACE WAS STILL off balance the following morning as he hitched up the buggy to go for his daughters and bring them back to their new home. He could not for the life of him figure his wife out. She'd been hot enough to melt diamonds in their bed last night when he'd expected her to be cool as November well water. And now this morning she was acting…friendly.

For some reason, friendly made him nervous as hell. That and the fact she reminded him of her mother today.

She told him at breakfast she'd decided to wait one more day before reopening Fortune's Design. She wanted to help the girls settle in, she'd said. If he didn't know better, he might think that he'd imagined yesterday's fight.

Trace put his worries from his mind as he halted the buggy in front of the Rankin Building. He'd missed his girls. They'd never before spent this much time apart, not since leaving Carolina.

Calling a hello toward the open windows, he hopped to the ground, then lifted Jenny down beside him. Three petticoated whirlwinds burst through the front door and he grinned, opening his arms wide.

They went to Jenny first.

She caught his disgruntled look, and between kisses, smiled at him and said, "It's the novelty of having a mother, Trace. Don't fret."

He didn't. Not really. But he was fiercely glad when the Menaces flew into his arms.

Two hours later, the novelty of being reunited had long worn off. Trace winced as a flash of calico came sailing down the polished mahogany banister. "I knew I should have built a one-story house."

Maribeth hopped to the floor. "Papa, I love this house. I love my bedroom and the playroom and this banister is the very most fun." She flew into his arms and gave him her hardest hug. "But the secret passageway...oh, Papa...that's the best of all."

Grinning, he stroked her hair. "You like that, do you?"

She nodded fiercely. "It's so much fun. The secret entrance in the playroom is hidden real good. I never would have found it if I hadn't gone through the tunnel first." A tiny frown of worry touched her brow. "But why did you put it there, Papa? Do you expect we'll have to hide from Indians or something?"

He laughed. "No, Meri-berri. The only person you'll need to hide from is me if the Menaces make an appearance anytime soon. The passageway won't do you a lick of good, 'cause I know all its secrets. Even a few you have yet to figure out."

"Then why did you build it?"

He shifted his gaze away from his daughter and stared into the past. "The home I grew up in had one. We played for days on end, everything from pirates to ghosts to patriot spies. It's one of my best memories of childhood, and I wanted you girls to have that, too."

"Who is 'we'? Your sisters? They've always sounded too prissy to play pirates."

Tye's image rose in Trace's mind. A replica of himself with a patch over one eye, a red sash at his waist, and a wooden sword in his hand. Maribeth was three years old when they left South Carolina. She didn't know his twin brother ever existed, and he planned to keep it that way.

"Not my sisters," Trace finally said. "Just a boy who used to be my friend." Determined to change the subject, he asked her, "What are your sisters doing?"

"Katrina's playing on the swing out back and Emma's helping Miss Fortune in the kitchen. Papa, about Miss Fortune?"

"Yes."

"Can we call her Mama?"

The innocent question raised his hackles. Why, he couldn't

have said, but the instinct to pull his daughter close and hold her tight and safe all but overwhelmed him.

Maybe it was fear doing this to him. They'd called another woman mother, one who didn't deserve the title, and she'd hurt them terribly, whether they knew it or not. Neither Mari nor Kat remembered Constance and Emma's recollections were few, thank God.

Otherwise, they wouldn't have been so persistent about wanting a new one.

Jenny had been more of a mother to them in the past few months than their real mother ever had. Constance had been too busy reigning as queen of Charleston society to be bothered with her family. And he, fool that he was, had been too busy building a career to notice.

Well, he'd learned his lesson the hard way, and this time he intended to put his family before everything else.

"I reckon you can call her Mama if you want, Maribeth. If it's all right with her, that is." Trace couldn't see what it would hurt. After all, wasn't that one of the reasons why he'd married her? He'd wanted her to act like a mother to his children.

It was one of the few reasons he'd admit to. Even to himself.

A movement in a nearby doorway caught his attention, and he turned his head to see Jenny blinking back tears as she gazed at Maribeth, her face softened with a look of tenderness and love. In that moment, he knew a sense of rightness that did much to assuage the uneasiness he felt. Jenny wasn't Constance; he knew that.

But they had a saying here in Texas that he took to heart. Man is the only animal that can get skinned more than once. Trace had no intention of proving the tenet true. He'd go along with this pretense of home and family, but he'd always keep his guard up.

"Maribeth?" Jenny said, emotion choking her voice. "I'd be ever so proud if you chose to call me Mama."

He watched as his daughter ran to his wife and, laughing, threw herself into the woman's arms.

Yes. He'd always keep his guard up, and if she ever tried to hurt them, there would be hell to pay. Hell by the name of Trace McBride.

*It is always good luck to make a wish
under a new moon.*


## CHAPTER THIRTEEN


THE NEXT FEW WEEKS passed swiftly as the McBride family
settled into life in their new home. Trace completed the sale
of the End of the Line and placed an advertisement in the
*Democrat* announcing the opening of his office. Jenny divided
her time between Fortune's Design and the house, most often
managing to make her way home by the time the girls returned
from school.

Emma, Maribeth, and Katrina adored their new house and
were quick to invite school friends home. Proudly, they
pointed out the individual rooms. Embarrassment prevented
them from mentioning that sometime between their "good
nights" and "good mornings," they invariably ended up snuggled together in one of the sisters' beds.

Trace spent his days at his desk. Situated on the ground floor
of the three-story house, the office had a separate entrance for
business callers. Trace often gave potential clients a tour of the
house, effectively displaying his professional talents. When he
worked alone, he usually left the connecting door open so

family members could wander in and share the events of their days if they so desired, which they regularly did.

After much discussion and debate, the McBride family decided their new home needed a name. They eventually settled on Willow Hill, with Katrina being the lone dissenting vote. She'd had her heart set on Kat's House and refused to understand why it wouldn't be appropriate.

Jenny took on the task of furnishing the home, and as pieces began to arrive, Trace was impressed by her sense of style and the way she managed to stretch their budget. "You do have a knack," her told her one morning as she directed the placement of a rosewood parlor set before leaving for work. "If you ever want to give up the dress business, you could team up with me and decorate the houses I design."

She beamed with pleasure at his compliment, then proceeded to prove to him why they wouldn't make good business partners. Three potential clients left their cards at his office door during the two hours he spent with Jenny upstairs in their bedroom. She arrived at her shop to find four clients waiting anxiously beside the front door.

Customers had returned to Fortune's Design in droves, and now her problem was one of finding enough hours to work. After careful thought she decided to spend school hours at the shop, then bring work home with her so she could spend time with her daughters in the afternoons. Many of her evenings were spent in "horse training."

She was feeling fairly confident that they'd progressed to trot, walk, and stop.

A week following their one-month wedding anniversary, she sat at her worktable discussing a new design with Rilda Bea Sperry when the shop's welcome bell sounded and Jenny nearly fell off her stool in surprise. "Miss Baumgardner?"

The Dallas dressmaker wore a smart rust-sateen walking dress that was an out-and-out copy of a Fortune's Design. Jenny's temper flared. How dare that woman wear that dress to her shop!

"Good afternoon, Mrs. McBride." Ethel Baumgardner's muddy brown eyes gleamed maliciously as she glanced around the shop. "What a quaint little place you have here. It's too bad the light is so poor. That must be one of the reasons your stitches are so often uneven."

Jenny rose slowly to her feet, shocked at the woman's audacity.

"I'm in town to deliver the Harvest Ball gowns I've made for so many of Fort Worth's ladies," Ethel continued. "You know the dance is tonight. Or maybe you don't know. I don't believe you had any commissions this year, did you? Anyway, I wanted to see your little shop."

Rilda Bea scowled and said sotto voce, "Don't let her get too close, dear. I do believe she sharpens her nails rather than files them."

In a tight voice, Jenny said, "Miss Baumgardner, as you can see I am with a customer. Unless you are here to order a dress, I'd like you to leave now."

"Order a dress?" Ethel laughed as though it were the joke of the month. "Not hardly. I simply wanted to see Fortune's Design while I still could. You made a fine try at reviving your reputation, Miss Fortune, but after this latest trouble, there is no way your business will survive."

"That's Mrs. McBride." She wasn't about to ask what trouble, not that her lack of curiosity deterred good old Ethel.

She offered a patently false smile and said, "Of course, you might not have heard about it yet. I wouldn't know myself if I hadn't happened to be in the telegraph office when the note arrived. Mrs. Bowden, the operator's wife, is a customer of mine also. Anyway, poor Mr. Bowden was so shocked he simply couldn't keep the news to himself."

Jenny's stomach went sour. She stepped forward to escort

the woman from her shop, but before she could lay a finger on the troublemaker's arm, Ethel Baumgardner fired her final salvo. "The telegram came from New Orleans. Mary Rose Bailey Pratt has been horribly injured, and that means the Bad Luck Wedding Dress has now struck all the Bailey girls. I'd be worried if I were you, dear." She smiled like a cream-fed cat. "You're next on the list."

SEATED IN a woven rawhide chair in the Red Light Dance Hall and Saloon, Frank Bailey nursed a powerful case of anger along with his whiskey. The memory of the battle he'd waged—and lost—with his father early that morning festered like a thorn in his spleen. Damn that man for holding out on his promise. Damn if he wasn't crazy like everyone said.

Big Jack was sure as hell acting crazy today. *I ought to just shoot him,* Frank told himself as he slammed back his drink. Twenty-five thousand dollars plus a prime section of land—that's what his old man had promised if he'd come back to Fort Worth to live after his release from prison.

But Big Jack had reneged on his deal. This morning he'd signed over the land, but he'd left the money in the bank in an account with strings Frank didn't want to untie. Marriage. A grandson. Politics. The thought of it made him shiver.

No matter what he told his old man, he'd never intended to stay in Texas. Damned if Big Jack hadn't figured it out. Frank had railed at him, making every excuse he could think of to get that money released from the bank. "I'm a gunman, Pa," he'd said. "I rob stages, and I've done time in Huntsville. You think I could get elected to anything?"

The old man had given a droll look and said, "Now that's the dumbest thing you've said all day. This is *Texas,* boy. Of course you can get elected."

Scowling at the memory, Frank poured the last of the whiskey into his glass and signaled the bartender for another. He didn't want to get elected to anything. He didn't want his father running his life. As funny as it sounded, he'd gotten a taste of freedom while in jail, and that's why he'd intended to head north after doing his time. "I should have never looked back," he grumbled to himself. But the lure of easy money had called him, and here he was under his father's thumb once again. "Maybe I will shoot him, after all."

He glanced toward the nearby faro table where Big Jack Bailey placed another bet. Or maybe he wouldn't have to shoot him. As wild as his father was acting tonight, somebody else might end up killing him before the sun rose.

Big Jack seldom made the rounds down in Hell's Half Acre, so when he did schedule a visit to Fort Worth's tenderloin district, he made damn sure it counted. The clocks had yet to strike seven and already Big Jack had tossed back drinks at three saloons, enjoyed fistfights in two others, and danced a horizontal dance with a couple of girls at the Weatherford Tap. Now he'd settled into a game of cards here at the infamous Red Light, an establishment well known for violating every principle of decency and morality known to man.

"God, I love this place." Big Jack's voice filled up the hole in the noise left when the fiddlers declared a break.

Standing at the carved oak bar, his boot propped on the brass rail, one of the Lucky Lady's cowhands looked up. "You must've won big, boss."

The older man took the Havana from his mouth, leaned his chair back on two legs, and laughed. "Damn right, I did. Big Jack Bailey always wins. Right, boys?"

Bitter experience having proved the truth of that statement, Frank lifted his glass in mock salute.

The conversation between his father and the ranch hands flowed around him. He didn't bother to listen until a man approached the table and spoke in a harried voice. "Thank God, I've finally found you."

"Who the hell are you?" Big Jack's voice boomed.

Appearing totally out of place in the Red Light's surroundings, the wiry fellow adjusted his spectacles and withdrew a sheet of paper from his pocket. "Bob Bowden. I'm from the telegraph office. This came for you earlier this afternoon, and I sent a man out to your ranch. He learned you had come into town, and due to the nature of the message, we decided to track you down. We've had a devil of a time finding you."

As Big Jack reached for the message, a lanky range rider observed, "Don't know why you couldn't find us. Big Jack doesn't exactly leave a little trail."

Frank idly watched as his father read the telegram's contents. His interest sharpened when Big Jack's complexion paled, then almost immediately reddened with rage. He swiped his arm across the table, sending everything atop it smashing to the floor. His voice rose in a roar. "It's all that goddamned woman's fault!"

Frank snatched the telegram out of his father's hand and quickly scanned the page. It was from New Orleans. His youngest sister, Mary Rose, had moved there following her marriage to a railroad magnate.

The telegram was from her husband. M.R. injured in fire. Condition critical. Requests family at her side. Signed, Stephen.

Mary Rose was Frank's favorite sister. A deadly calm stole over him, a vivid contrast to his father's thunderous fury.

Big Jack cursed. He ranted. He raved. He yanked the gun off his hip and shot it into the ceiling, splintering a beam. "What time does that evening freight leave out of town?" he shouted to the hushed dance hall crowd.

"Nine-thirty," a dozen folks answered together.

Big Jack turned to Frank. "I should have known to expect trouble. The damned waiter at dinner set two knives beside my plate. That means death on the way every damned time."

"She's not dead yet, Pa," Frank snapped. "Don't anticipate."

Big Jack glossed over his objection. "I won't have time to get out to the ranch. I'll have to wake up my banker to get me some cash." He gestured toward the cowering telegraph operator. "You go with this fellow and send telegrams to your sisters in San Antonio and Waco. Tell 'em to get themselves to New Orleans the fastest way possible. After that, I want you to find that engineer and make damn sure he doesn't leave without us, you hear?"

Frank nodded.

Big Jack's brow wrinkled as he stared at Frank. After a moment, he nodded as if reaching a decision. "I want you to stay here. Mary Rose doesn't know you're out of prison so she won't be expecting you." He lowered a significant look on his son. "The Bailey family has some business here in town that needs taking care of. You follow me?"

No, he didn't. He shook his head.

Big Jack gave him a glare filled with frustration. "The dressmaker," he muttered softly. "I warned her. You take care of her."

Frank arched his brows. "Take care of her how?"

Rubbing his hand across his chin, Big Jack took a moment to think. "Permanently. I don't care how you go about it. Do as you please. It wouldn't hurt to make her suffer some, though. My girls have suffered a lot. Can you do that for me, boy?"

Frank folded his arms. If not for the news about Mary Rose, he'd have laughed. His pa had just handed him a gift. "Oh, I can do it, Pa. Although, for something like that I'll expect a reward. A substantial reward."

Big Jack drilled him with a look. "You're a sonofabitch, Frank Bailey. An opportunistic sonofabitch. Damn, but it makes me proud. Sure, I'll reward you. You do this for me, for your sisters, and you can have the money free and clear."

"No politics?"

"No politics."

Frank's lips curled in an evil smile. "Consider it done, Pa." He lifted his hat from the seat of the chair next to him and set it on his head. "You have a good trip, and give Mary Rose my love."

"Just get the job done."

Frank had a clear mental picture of the dressmaker's curvaceous form. A chuckle rumbled up from the blackest part of his heart. "It'll be my pleasure, Pa. My pleasure."

TRACE CHECKED his watch and glanced impatiently toward the staircase. He wished his wife would hurry. He wasn't looking forward to the Harvest Ball, but the sooner they arrived the sooner they could leave. If it were up to him, they'd skip the event, but Jenny was having none of it. She'd come home from the shop in a high temper, ranting and raving about bad luck, Big Jack Bailey, and "that dad-blamed Ethel Baumgardner."

Trace, biting his tongue not to laugh, had offered to teach her to cuss.

Of course, once she calmed down enough to tell him the story he was not laughing. Big Jack Bailey had been quiet since the wedding. He'd told an acquaintance of Trace's that by wearing the dress, Jenny had rightfully assumed ownership of the bad luck built into it. Would Mary Rose's accident change his way of thinking? Was Jenny once again in danger? He needed to talk to Big Jack to find out.

He'd wanted to ride out to the Lucky Lady as soon as Jenny told him the story, but his wife had pitched a fit. In a froth over what the Dallas dressmaker had said and done, she told him in no uncertain terms she expected him to escort her to the ball as planned, and he darn well better act the besotted groom. She intended to give the people of Fort Worth something to talk about other than Mary Rose's accident.

She had disappeared into the sewing room, and he hadn't seen her since. Under the circumstances, Trace couldn't help but be a bit nervous.

A door slammed above him, and since his daughters were in the kitchen with Mrs. Wilson, he knew his bride must finally be ready. He lifted his hat from the entry table, glanced toward the staircase, and froze.

"Good Lord, woman! What the hell are you wearing?" Trace knew the answer, of course. The dress all but screamed Miss Rachel's Social Emporium. She'd obviously made a few—just a few—adjustments to a dress she'd made for one of Rachel's girls.

The purple silk clung to her curves like a second skin, while the black lace sewn into the plunging neckline played upon a man's fantasies as much as bare skin. "You're not going out in public wearing that dress, Jenny McBride."

Their bedroom was something different, however.

"We need to say good-bye to the girls before we leave," she replied, ignoring his objection. "Are they still eating supper?"

He dragged out her name in a warning tone as he walked toward the staircase. "For-tune!"

Stopping two steps from the bottom of the stairs, she stood at Trace's eye level. Unleashing a saucy smile, she said, "Be brave, McBride. This is war." He came a hairbreadth away from sweeping her into his arms and carting her back upstairs.

Instead, he followed her toward the kitchen, groaning anew at the view of the dress from the back. "Jenny, you'll have every man at that ball drooling like a baby gettin' teeth."

Glancing over her shoulder, she showed him that smile again. "That's the plan. They'll see their wives in Ethel Baumgardner's gowns and imagine them in mine. I won't lose my customers, by gosh."

Trace sighed wearily as they entered the kitchen to find Mrs. Wilson placing a piece of green apple pie in front of each of his daughters.

"Mama, you look beautiful!" Katrina exclaimed.

Emma's eyes rounded and she gave a wistful smile. "I wish I could grow up half as pretty as you, Mama."

Maribeth spoke with her mouth full of pie. "Like your dress, Mama. Papa, I caught a black bass today and Mrs. Wilson said if I'm gonna bring 'em home, I'd have to learn to clean 'em. Would you teach me how to fillet a fish?"

"Don't talk with your mouth full, Mari," Emma scolded.

"That's right," Katrina added, snickering. "It sounded like you asked Papa to teach you how to *play* a fish."

Normalcy. Thank God for his daughters. His humor on the way to being restored, Trace frowned. "Once you learn the scales, it's not difficult to play a fish, Maribeth. Just don't ask me to tune a fish."

Jenny and Mrs. Wilson groaned. His daughters all giggled. With the sound ringing in his ears, Trace's step was lighter as he escorted his provocatively dressed wife to their carriage for the drive to Fort Worth's Third Annual Harvest Ball.

Pumpkins, gourds, and cornstalks decorated the ballroom at the Cosmopolitan Hotel. Dancing had yet to begin when they arrived, although a string quartet played in the background. The hum of conversation and occasional bursts of laughter drew to an abrupt halt the moment Jenny Fortune McBride stepped into the room. The silence lasted only a moment, then a tide of men surged forward, begging for a dance.

Trace managed, barely, to hold his temper.

Jenny didn't fare so well. Every time she turned around she saw or heard something that set her off. Amanda Tompkins's dress was a copy of one of her designs, as was Martha Clark's. Wilhemina Peters sported a silk gown of Ethel Baumgardner's design, and even Trace, who knew a fig's worth of fashion, said it was downright ugly. "Somebody needs to bell that woman," he said, eyeing the black-and-white monstrosity. "Bossie got loose from the pasture again."

"Trace McBride!" Jenny didn't put any heat behind her

scolding. In his own sarcastic way, Trace was defending her. Wilhemina was up to her old tricks again, spreading the news about Mary Rose and nonsense about the wedding dress. Seeing what was happening, Trace admitted to Jenny her strategy was sound. He told her he'd join the battle, but she'd owe him.

"Expect to pay up as soon as we get home," he told her, his steamy gaze dropping to the swell of her breasts, teasingly hid by the lace. "You can leave the dress on."

Then, although it obviously bothered him to do so, he abandoned his efforts to fend off her admirers and went to work. Jenny observed in amazement. Her husband was amazing. The twist he put on the story went a long way toward neutralizing the effects of the gossip. While it annoyed her that the townsfolk seemed to accept a man's word over a woman's, she wasn't fool enough to look a gift horse in the mouth—especially not one who'd advanced to the trot, walk, and stop stage.

Jenny smiled at her own metaphorical wit as she spotted young Casey Tate handing her husband a message. He frowned down at the note, then looked up, his gaze unerringly finding hers. He shrugged and tucked the paper into his pocket.

Jenny excused herself from the dance she was tolerating with Martha Clark's wandering-handed husband and crossed the room to Trace. She identified annoyance rather than concern in his expression, so she knew the note had nothing to do with the girls.

"What is it?" she asked upon reaching him.

"Nothing much. An old customer of mine at the End of the Line is traveling through town. He was looking for me down at the saloon. Wanted to have a drink."

An excuse to leave! Jenny almost kissed him right there in public. She'd had her fill of fending off both subtle and blatant masculine advances. "Wonderful. You can drop me by the house on the way to the Acre."

He took a step toward her. "You want to leave already? What happened? Did somebody bother you? Say something? What?"

My, the man looked fierce. Jenny smiled. She'd been right. They had progressed to the trot, walk, and stop stage. "Nothing. I—or I should say we—have accomplished what we came for."

He called for their buggy and retrieved their coats. They made the trip home quickly. As he helped her from the carriage, Jenny asked, "Do you think you'll be long with your friend? I need to prepare myself for my…punishment."

Emerald eyes blazed in the moonlight. "How long do you need to prepare?"

She shrugged. "At least two hours."

"I'll be home in an hour and a half."

He walked her to the door, then took her in his arms. Bending his head, he took her mouth in a thorough, yet gentle kiss. "One hour," he said, his voice low and rough.

Jenny smiled to herself as she entered the house. Seated on the horsehair sofa in the parlor, Mrs. Wilson looked up with surprise from the book she was reading. "Home already?"

"Yes. Trace had some business to attend to. I was glad to leave. Even though she wasn't in attendance, Ethel Baumgardner was everywhere I looked."

They talked about the ball for a few moments, the dresses the ladies wore and their reaction to Jenny's. Mrs. Wilson offered the news that the girls had conked out early and had all ended up in Maribeth's room that night.

The housekeeper departed for home and Jenny went upstairs. Peeking into Maribeth's room, she noted three shapes piled beneath the bedcovers. She stepped into the room intending to kiss them good night when the doorbell rang.

Mrs. Wilson must have forgotten something.

Jenny hurried downstairs, hoping to catch the door before the bell rang again. Katrina was a light sleeper and the chimes had awakened her upon occasion in the past. As much as she loved the girls, she looked forward to her husband's return. She'd rather avoid interruptions from a sleepy, doorbell-awakened seven-year-old.

The chimes sounded again just as she reached the bottom of the stairs. "I'm coming, Mrs. Wilson," she said a tad bit impatiently.

Jenny flipped the bolt on the lock and opened the door.

Right into the barrel of a gun.

THREE SHADOWS ran through the streets, keeping close to buildings and hedges in hopes of reaching their destination undetected. They raced silently and swiftly and managed to stay well hidden until the rising moon emerged from behind a cloud and illuminated three sets of pigtails.

Leading the way, Maribeth looked over her shoulder and said, "We're gonna get caught and Papa's gonna kill us."

Emma, in the rear, muttered, "Hush, Mari. We won't get caught if you run with your feet instead of your mouth."

"My tummy hurts," Katrina whined. "Can't we stop for just a little bit?"

"No!" her sisters cried in unison.

"Why not?"

At the murky mouth of an alley where darkness shielded them from discovery, Maribeth stopped short and whirled on her sister. "Because we have to get home! Mrs. Wilson might decide to do more than simply look in on us. Or even worse, Papa and Mama might come home early. They come kiss us every single night. They're bound to notice they're kissing our pillows rather than our faces."

"Let's go," Emma insisted, pushing past her sister. "Every minute counts. We've been awfully lucky so far tonight."

That much was true. Eagle-eyed Mrs. Wilson had actually been distracted this evening. Ever since the railroad robbery, she'd become a real problem, keeping tabs on the three of them with a zeal that bordered on religious. Lucky for them tonight she'd lost herself in the suspenseful pleasures of a novel she'd yammered on about most of the day. They'd been able to sneak past her with relative ease.

"I don't know why y'all are being so fussy," Katrina said, a whine in her voice as she clutched a squirming bundle to her chest. "Nothing bad happened. Sassy didn't hurt a thing."

Maribeth grabbed hold of one of her younger sister's pigtails and tugged her along, muttering in a whisper as they ran. "She would have if we hadn't gone to let her out after you told us you'd left her inside Fortune's Design. That was so stupid, Kat. That animal is not a house pet. She's an armadillo! They're night hunters, you know. She might have shredded Mama's midnight-blue silk with gold and silver threads!"

"Let me go! You're hurting me! And Mama keeps that bolt of cloth at home. I've seen it under hers and Papa's bed."

"Hush, you two," Emma snapped.

Maribeth ground her teeth in frustration as she hurried with her sisters down the black streets of the residential neighborhood. Knowing she was as much at fault as Kat made her feel miserable. It had been her idea to take the baby armadillo along on their visit to the Cosmopolitan Hotel to show Mrs. Raines. Kat would never have taken Sassy to Fortune's Design if Maribeth hadn't hauled it into the hotel first.

As they ran through the streets, she glanced into the sky, praying for a cloud to block the moon. They were bound to get caught; she just knew it. "Papa's gonna tan our hides for sure."

Emma would have told her sister to hush again had her lungs not been straining for breath after the run up the hill toward home. She tried not to breathe too loudly as she led the way along the side of Willow Hill. Abruptly, she stopped and her sisters piled into her. "Oh gosh," she whispered, staring in horror at the scene playing out on the front porch. "Oh, my gosh."

Hearing Katrina start to speak, she quickly shoved a hand across her mouth. "Hush, Kat," she whispered in her ear. "Fairy's promise."

Fairy's promise was an old McBride Menace tradition that meant something along the lines of "I'm being serious, and you need to pay attention to me."

Maribeth leaned forward as Katrina nodded. Emma laid a finger against her mouth, and in the dim light of the moon she watched her sister's eyes round with concern.

"What's going on?" Maribeth mouthed.

"It's Mama!" she hissed.

Just then, a man's threatening voice rumbled through the night. "Well, well, well, if it isn't the blushing bride. Just the person I was looking for."

Emma heard Jenny ask in a sharp tone, "Who are you? What do you want?"

"Who am I?" His sinister chuckle sent shivers up Emma's spine. "Don't tell me you don't recognize me, darlin'. Why, that purely breaks my heart."

Maribeth scooched next to Emma, peered around the corner, then whispered in her sister's ear, "Who is he?"

"I don't know."

"Neither does Mama." Katrina stated the obvious, her voice quavering.

The gunman said, "We met only once before, Mrs. McBride. Of course, you were Miss Fortune then. But I've heard a lot about you, more than I ever cared to hear, to be truthful. Now, I want you to walk with me out to the street nice and easy like."

"I'm not going anywhere. I don't have to. My husband undoubtedly has a gun pointed on you this minute."

"Your husband is down at the End of the Line, looking for someone who isn't there." He gestured for her to move along.

Jenny hesitated, but when he lifted the gun threateningly,

she did as he demanded. "Who *are* you?" she asked. "What do you want? Where do you think you are taking me?"

"I have a wagon waiting, and we're gonna enjoy a nice little ride out to the Lucky Lady."

"The Lucky Lady?" There was a moment's silence, then Jenny exclaimed, "That's it! You're a Bailey, the one from the train."

"You can call me Frank, darlin'. After all, considering the plans I have in mind for you, I reckon we should be on a first-name basis." He laughed softly.

The sound crawled down Emma's spine. She had the sudden notion she might hear it again in her nightmares. She watched fearfully as he gestured for her to descend the front steps.

Jenny took but a single step. "What plans?"

He said something softly that the girls couldn't hear, but their mother's reaction told them plenty.

"No!" she cried, lunging for the gun.

Bailey swept the revolver high above his head and out of her reach. Then he slammed her up against the house. Emma gasped, Katrina squeaked, and Maribeth murmured a naughty word. They didn't need to worry about being overheard, however, because the scuffle on the porch was becoming quite loud.

Jenny struggled with the Bailey man. She kicked and fought and grabbed for his gun, but he managed to drag her down the steps into the yard. He had one arm wrapped around her, and his hand covered her mouth. "Be still," he growled. "I don't want to hurt you now, but I will if I have to."

"Enough of this," Maribeth said, starting forward. "We have to help Mama!"

Emma grabbed her, holding her back. "You can't Mari. He's got a gun. Mama wouldn't want you to. We'll go get help. One of the neighbors."

Katrina tugged on Maribeth's blouse. "Let's go get Papa. He'll help."

"But—"

Her protest was interrupted by Frank Bailey's muffled cry of rage. "Goddammit. You little bitch!"

"She bit him!" Katrina exclaimed, clutching Maribeth's arm. "I saw her teeth. Did you see that? She bit him."

"He sounds so angry. Let's get help now. Come on!" Maribeth darted down the hill toward the nearest house and Katrina followed on her heels. Emma hesitated, sending one last glance in her mother's direction. What she witnessed in that instant was the worst thing she'd seen in her entire life.

It seemed to happen in slow motion. Moonlight glistened off the barrel of the revolver in Frank Bailey's upraised hand. Then, sneering evilly, he brought it down, butt first, whacking Jenny on the side of the head.

Like a puppet whose strings have been cut, she crumpled to the ground and lay still.

Emma followed after her sisters. The tears that spilled from her eyes and ran across her temples were the first she'd shed in six long years, the only tears she'd cried since the morning Papa told her their mother had died.

*A male cat with four different colors in
its fur will bring good luck.*

## CHAPTER FOURTEEN

JACKSON PETERS, editor of the *Daily Democrat* and Wilhemina's husband, threw down his cards in disgust as Trace raked in yet another pot. "I'd have been better off staying at that damned dance, after all. You know, McBride, if I didn't know better, I'd think you were cheating."

"Cheating? Me?" Trace's brows arched in innocence. "Now that's a dangerous accusation to make down here in the Acre. You throw that word around too much and you're liable to end up in your own obituary section."

Peters snorted and counted his chips.

Trace began another stack for his. One more hand, he told himself. That should give Jenny enough time to do whatever it was she had in mind. Imagining what it might be had kept him half hard since he left her.

He dealt the cards and picked up his hand, paying closer attention to the room around him than to his chance at a straight. This was the first time he'd visited the End of the Line since he sold it, and the twinge of bittersweet he experienced upon entering the building had surprised him.

The smell of the place was the same, the music was the same, and the people were the same. Trace was damned different. It made him feel strange as hell.

Not spotting his old friend, he'd concluded that he arrived too late and turned to leave. That was when Peters had called out, summoning Trace to his card table with a taunting remark about his bad luck marriage. At that point, Trace had decided to play cards.

His efforts to quell this bad luck business at the dance had worked all right, but he knew a little extra effort wouldn't hurt. Before the end of the first hand he discovered the newspaper editor kept a card or two up his sleeve. After all, Trace had known every card he dealt the man. No one ran card games for a living without learning how to cheat.

Peters continued to run his mouth, and Trace felt perfectly justified in his actions. Taking almost five hundred dollars off the newspaperman had soothed his temper—up to a point. But every time he about decided he'd fleeced the scoundrel enough, the fool would mention Jenny's name again, and he'd hang around for one more hand.

Peters called it quits first. "It's been a pleasure, gentlemen," he said, shoving back his chair and standing. "I do believe I'll have myself one last drink, then toddle back home." He appeared a bit green at the idea.

Trace watched him join a red-eyed cowboy at the bar and debated how long he'd let Peters suffer before offering him a way out of his misery. A ban on columns about the infamous dress and a few positive statements about Fortune's Design in "Talk about Town" would suffice nicely for the return of his cash, Trace decided.

Glancing at his watch, he calculated he had ten minutes to kill before heading home to Jenny. He allowed five of them to pass before rising to let Peters off the hook. Halfway to the bar a commotion in the front of the saloon snagged his attention. "What the hell?" he blurted.

Marshal Timothy Courtright held three squirming, twisting, hollering Menaces in his grip. "McBride!" the lawman called. "I ought to arrest you for neglect. I ran across this trio not half a block from here. I was looking for my deputies when these children of yours all but knocked me down and went to blabbering on about your wife's bad luck."

*The girls in the Acre on a Friday night? Oh, God.* Trace's hand gripped the back of a chair. His knuckles turned white, and fear threatened to knock his knees out from under him.

They all shouted, "Papa!"

As Trace headed toward them, Katrina slipped from the marshal's grip. Courtright scowled when Maribeth drew back her foot and kicked his shin. "That's enough!" he bellowed. "They're your trouble now, McBride. I've got enough of my own already. Some liquored-up cowboy has his former sweetheart cornered in a hotel dining room, and he's threatening to shoot her and everyone else in the hotel unless she marries him tonight." Giving the older two girls a shove toward their father, he turned to leave.

Emma whirled around and called after him, "Marshal Courtright, you can't leave! We need you!"

He didn't hear her over the clamor filling the saloon, and he didn't stop, disappearing through the front door.

A sick feeling replaced the fear gripping Trace as he took in his daughters' wild eyes. Something was wrong. Very wrong. "What is it?" he demanded.

"It's Mama," Maribeth cried as Katrina launched herself into his waiting arms.

"A bad man pointed a gun at her," Katrina added.

Then he noticed Emma's tears. *Oh, hell.* He extended a hand toward his eldest child and she grasped his fingers like a lifeline.

"He hit her, Papa. With the gun. I saw it. She fell down."

Maribeth's voice was full of fear. "He rode past us. He had her in front of him on his horse. He took her away."

He had to force the words past his fear. "Who? Who was he?"

"He said his name, Papa. It was Frank. It was Frank Bailey."

The name hit Trace like a fist. For the briefest of moments he closed his eyes. Then he asked, "What else do you know?"

"He said he was taking her to the Lucky Lady. You have to hurry, Papa. You have to save her."

*He had to save her.* The words echoed through his mind as he considered the situation. Courtright had his hands full; Trace would have to go alone. First, though, he had to see to the girls; he had to get them home. He could take them there himself, but that would eat up time. Someone else, then. Who?

Rachel. She'd do it if he paid for her time.

He rubbed his hand along his jaw. Maribeth's words had painted a scene that grieved him beyond words.

After pressing a kiss to Katrina's brow, he set her away from him. "I'll take care of it. But I need your help. I need you to promise me you'll stay here in my old office until I come get you." He paused a moment then added, "Fairy's promise, girls."

Their expressions showed surprise that he knew their private pledge, but each of them nodded their assent. He shooed them up the stairs and into his office, then handed Emma the key. "Lock the door behind me, Emmie. Don't open it for anyone but me or Miss Rachel, all right?" Outside he waited until he heard the lock click before hurrying down the stairs.

The scent of smoke hung in the air that swirled around the brawl spilling out into the street from the saloon next door. Trace ignored both the fight and the distant sounds of gunshots as he headed for Rachel's. He was quaking in his boots.

Frank Bailey had his wife.

JENNY FOUGHT consciousness, instinctively fleeing the fear poised to consume her. For a time, she battled successfully, but all too soon she awoke to find herself lying beneath a canvas in the bed of a buckboard, her wrists and ankles chafed raw by a tightly bound rope, her mouth gagged by a foul-tasting cloth.

Memory returned in a flash and, with it, anger underscored with fear. Big Jack wanted her punished for what she'd done to his daughters. How could that man be so insane? She'd sewn a dress, for goodness' sakes. A dress! Would they kill her because of a dress?

She was very much afraid she knew the answer to that one.

Cold seeped into her bones, and she realized her hands and feet had gone numb. From somewhere nearby a coyote howled, its thin, mournful note sending shivers up her skin. She had to do something. She couldn't lie here, meekly accepting her fate—whatever that might prove to be.

Was there any chance she could roll from the wagon without his detection? Would she even want to? The rate her luck was going she'd hit her head on a rock, then lie on the road as easy bait for the coyote.

Luck. That word made her want to scream. Being trussed in the back of a buckboard made her want to scream. So she tried, but the little sound that escaped the gag in her mouth sounded like a sob even to her own ears.

Frank Bailey called, "Whoa, boy." The wagon rolled to a stop. She heard the creak of springs and thud of boots against the ground as he descended from his seat. Desperation and a measure of fight brought her knees tightly to her chest and she curled into a ball. She wouldn't make this easy for him. He'd have to drag her from the wagon. If not for the gag in her mouth, she swore she would have bitten him again.

He hauled her from the backboard, then hoisted her over

his shoulder. She buried her fingernails in his back, despite the lack of feeling in her hands.

"Bitch," he snarled. "Dammit, aren't you smart enough to be scared?"

He stank of sweat and smoke and stale whiskey. He jostled her extra hard, pounding his shoulder into her stomach, and she thought she might be sick all down his back. She was scared, all right, but the flame of anger burning inside prevented the fear from overtaking her. Frank Bailey climbed a porch step then paused. Jenny heard the squeak of a turning knob. Hinges yawned as the door swung open.

She had the sensation of entering a tomb.

He carried her forward, into the inky darkness, then suddenly, she felt herself falling. She landed on something soft. A mattress?

A bed.

Jenny's anger deserted her as horror took its place. *Not that. Please, Lord, not that.*

A match scratched and flared, and soon the muted yellow glow of lamplight displaced the darkness. She gazed around the small room. Rough wooden walls, a thick coating of dust. This was obviously not the Lucky Lady's main house.

Bailey placed the lamp on a small bedside table and stared down at her, a sullen scowl on his brow. Jenny watched him intently. He appeared awfully unemotional for a man bent upon rape. Or murder, for that matter.

For some reason, it frightened her all the more.

What did Frank Bailey have planned?

His lips quirked up in a humorless smile. "Mary Rose lied to our Pa to save me from a whippin' one time. She'd bake peach cobbler for dessert once a week just because it was my favorite." He reached out and fingered a lock of her hair.

Jenny shuddered.

"Pa wants me to deal with you. He'll give me money, and

I want it to get the hell out of this state. Besides, there's Mary Rose." Leaning over the bed, he said, "I'll unwrap your mouth, but if you get too noisy on me I'll shut you back up. Got it?"

She nodded and he reached down and untied the gag.

Jenny wanted to spit but her mouth was too dry. "Water?" she whispered, ashamed to ask for anything.

He shrugged and left the small cabin, returning moments later with a canteen from which he poured water into a dull tin cup. She struggled into a seated position, then accepted the drink he put to her lips, hoping whatever was floating in it wouldn't hurt her. A nervous laugh clogged her throat. At the moment, bad water was the least of her worries. A bigger one concerned just what had Big Jack meant when he said "deal with."

Jenny worked up the nerve to ask him.

He removed his hat and hung it on a hook beside the door. Glancing over his shoulder, he said, "Pa wanted something permanent."

Permanent. Jenny swallowed hard. "You mean like a scar? Something that never goes away?"

His smile suddenly twisted. "Not exactly."

It made her wish she'd not asked any questions.

He approached the bed. "This place is the old homestead of the Lucky Lady. Back when I was doing stages, I'd hole up here for weeks and never see a soul. We keep it stocked with necessities—canned goods and bullets. Nobody ever disturbs the supplies."

"Why are you telling me this?"

He shrugged. "I took you away from town and prying eyes in order to have some privacy to do what needs doing. You need to know we're alone out here. No one will show up to help you. I can make this last a little while or a long time, depending on how you cooperate."

Fear swept through her like a cold, winter wind. He planned to kill her. She could see it in his eyes.

Extending a finger, he trailed it through her hair. Jenny shuddered.

"It won't be that easy for me, if that makes you feel any better. For all the stage jobs I've done, I've never killed a woman before."

The confirmation rocked her. She drew a deep breath, trying to calm herself, to think. Being afraid wouldn't help her survive, and that must be her first concern. She needed an idea. She needed a plan.

Quickly, she considered her options. He had superior strength, a gun, freedom of movement. All she had was her intelligence, but it gave her a chance. She'd have to outwit him. Her thoughts coursed like river rapids until she conceived a strategy. "Mr. Bailey, you need not necessarily begin with me. May I offer a suggestion?"

He laughed. "Gutsy woman, aren't you?"

"So I've been told. Nevertheless, I believe you can accomplish your objective quite simply." She licked her dry lips. "My husband is well-off financially. My parents are extremely wealthy. I don't doubt that between the two of them, they would be willing and able to provide a sum in excess of what Big Jack intends to give you."

He didn't speak. He hunkered down in front of the fireplace and busied himself with building a fire. Before long, a thin flame flickered in the hearth, the crackle of cedar sap sounding too much like gunshots for Jenny's peace of mind.

"Nope," he said finally, standing up straight. "I'm afraid that won't do. I have Mary Rose to think about." He walked to a chest that sat at the foot of the bed, inserted a key in the lock, and flipped up the lid. Jenny held her breath as he withdrew something sheathed in dark brown leather from its depths. A knife. A bowie knife.

She flinched when he leaned down and cut the rope binding her ankles, saying, "You're a pretty lady, Mrs. McBride. Real pretty. It'd be a shame to let it go to waste. I figure it's time for us to get down to the bargaining." He eased a hand up beneath her skirt. "Sure is a pretty dress you're wearing. Purple is just about my favorite color. And that black lace. It gets a man to wantin'." His touch along her thigh made her skin crawl. "Don't forget, the more you cooperate, the easier the dyin' will be."

His other hand ripped her bodice, and as he leaned for a closer look Jenny reacted instinctively.

She whipped her knee up and crunched his nose.

"Goddamn!" he shouted, as blood burst forth, raining down upon her.

He brought his hand up to cradle the injury and backed away from the bed as she kicked again, aiming for the knife. She missed.

With a roar of rage, he lifted the weapon, then rammed it downward. Jenny rolled, and the knife plunged into the mattress. She hit the floor, then scrambled to her feet. Her heart pounded mercilessly as she dashed toward the door, her mind racing. All she could think of was to get away.

She was halfway through the door when he caught her.

"You stupid bitch," he growled, wrapping his fist around her hair and dragging her back inside. "I'd have made this easy on you. Quick and painless."

Her scalp was in agony as he flung her back onto the bed. He'd abandoned the knife for a Colt revolver, and the cold hard metal seemed to burn her skin as he placed the barrel against her cheek.

He wiped his nose on his sleeve. "Not any longer. I'll make you hurt. I'll make you hurt bad."

Jenny waited, breathing hard, an awful anticipation seeming to freeze time as he loomed above her. She thought of her mother and father, of Emma, Maribeth, and Katrina. She thought of Trace.

*Dear Lord, she didn't want to die.*

Despite the gun, she moved. She rolled off the bed and fell hard against the floor, half-expecting to feel the bite of a bullet. Like an animal pursued, she reacted instinctively and rolled into the darkness beneath the bed.

His curse was ugly as he dropped to his knees. His blood-stained hand swept beneath the bed and reached for her. She recoiled as if it were a snake. Fear had its claws in her chest and she silently screamed for help. *Trace!*

She startled at his unexpected shriek. Frank Bailey yanked his arm from beneath the bed, howling and cursing in pain-laden agony. Jenny stared transfixed as his knees disappeared when he jumped to his feet. Something fell to the floor beside his boot. One, two, three, she counted. His boot lifted then stomped. *Thud. Thud. Thud.* Still, he continued to scream.

The distinctive smell billowed outward in an invisible cloud. Vinegar. Oh, Lord. Recognition hit her like a blow. People in West Texas called them vinegarroons. Twice the size of common scorpions, venom from that type of scorpion could kill a man.

Or a woman.

Her thoughts came like bullets. Her father had taught her about poisonous plants and animals indigenous to Texas. What did she remember about vinegarroon scorpions? Had he disturbed a nest? They usually traveled in pairs. She'd seen three, hadn't she? Was one lifting his tail to sting her even now? She lay still as a corpse, waiting.

A loud thud sounded as Frank fell to the floor moaning. Her heart pounded; she knew she needed to move. *Please, Lord.* She rolled from beneath the bed, anticipating a sting, her fear even worse than when expecting a bullet.

Nothing. She'd made it.

And Frank Bailey was in no position to hurt her. His screams had subsided and now he breathed small, pitiful whimpers.

Her arms still bound behind her, she wondered what she should do. "On fire," he moaned, his words slurred.

She licked her lips. Three vinegarroon stings. He'd die without help. He might die anyway.

He'd intended to rape her. Kill her. Was she actually going to help him?

Mud packs would help draw the poison.

It took precious time and a number of attempts, but finally she managed to position his knife so that it would cut the rope around her wrists. Blood seeped from the nick on her hand as she bent over him and touched first his nose, then his upper lip. "Mr. Bailey? Frank? Can you feel this? Does your face feel numb?" If not, she might still have time to help him. Numbness was one of the early symptoms of vinegarroon scorpion stings.

He didn't reply but simply looked at her with fearful, pain-glazed eyes.

Jenny grabbed a skillet by the handle on the way out the door. The creek ran some thirty yards to the east, and she raced toward it, ignoring the bite of sharp rocks and grass burrs that punctured the soles of her slippers. She dropped to her knees beside the water. Sinking her fingers into the slimy cold mud of the creek bed, she scooped up handfuls and soon filled the skillet.

She returned to the cabin at a run.

MOONLIGHT CAST eerie shadows in the darkness of the rolling, wooded land south and east of town. Trace heard a distant howl of a coyote and thought of times not long ago when a man had cause to question the source of such a sound.

He'd heard the stories repeated in his saloon, tales of when the Comanche had lashed the frontier like a whip. He'd listened as men spoke of nights like this one spent huddled in cabins made of logs. No light, no fire, no sleep—just a mother's clammy hand over the mouth if a child tried to complain. And always, the awareness that the screech owl's quaver could be your killer's call.

Trace thought of Comanche and settlers and screech owls and coyotes because he couldn't bear to think about Jenny. Dawn was half a night away. Would she be alive to see it?

He'd been on his horse for what seemed like forever, riding first to the Lucky Lady ranch house. A silent, thorough, and disappointing search pointed him toward his next destination. With a Comanche moon lighting the way, he'd started for the old homestead cabin. He should have reached it by now. With every minute that passed, his unease grew. What if he'd missed it in the dark? What if she wasn't even there? What if—

Trace reined in his horse. There, off to the right some hundred yards away, a light shone a welcome beacon in the cold, West Texas night. He released a breath as he turned his mount toward the glow. This had to be the place.

*Please be here, Jenny. Be here and be all right.*

Deciding it prudent to approach the rest of the way on foot, he slid from Ranger's back and tethered him to the trunk of a nearby elm. He walked quickly and quietly toward the light, anxiety heightening the tension inside him.

Built in the dog-trot style so common to the area, the cabin comprised two rooms separated by an open walkway, all contained beneath one roof. Light flickered in the window of the room on the left. The east wall of the cabin was solid without window or door, so Trace approached from that side. He rested his hand against the rough-hewn logs, standing stock still as he listened.

Not anything. Not a single sound.

Then, ever so faintly, he heard it. A whimper.

*Jenny.* His hand went automatically to his hip, reaching for the gun that wasn't there—a gun he had not worn since the night he shot his wife. He swore a silent curse. The vow he'd made never to kill again was as much a part of him as his love for his daughters. Yet the sound coming from inside the cabin made him question his pledge for the first time in years.

Could he kill again?

God, he didn't want to find out.

But he had to save Jenny.

Easing around the corner to the front of the cabin, Trace listened intently. Something about the tenor of the whimper struck him funny. The noise was pitiful, like a puppy repeatedly kicked by his master, but it was too deep-throated to be his wife.

Trace's heartbeat quickened. Maybe she'd won. Maybe she'd turned the tables on Bailey, and he was the whiner. If any woman could do it, Jenny would be the one.

Carefully, Trace slid along the wall to the window, then inched forward, positioning himself to peer into the cabin. The stench of vomit assaulted him.

Frank Bailey lay on the floor, his body jerking with convulsions. Jenny sat beside him, her ball gown in tatters. One hand clasped Bailey's, the other gently stroked his brow. Tears poured down her face.

"Jenny?" Trace stepped inside, his knees as weak as double-steeped tea. "Jenny, honey, are you all right? Are you hurt?"

She lifted a pale complexion and haunted eyes in his direction. "I couldn't help him. I didn't know what else to do."

Venom, Trace thought, his gaze sweeping the scene, lingering on the mud packs on Bailey's arm. "Snake bite?"

"Vinegarroon. Three of them."

Trace muttered a curse and went to his wife. Placing his hands on her upper arms, he thought to help her to her feet. "Come here, sweetheart. I'll take care of this."

"No. He's barely breathing. He's almost…" She couldn't bring herself to doom him with a word. "I don't think it will be much longer."

He resisted the desire to rip her away from the dying man and sat beside her, casting a dispassionate look on the sonofabitch soon to arrive at a well-deserved end, to Trace's way of thinking. God, this had been one hell of a night.

"Who is with the girls?"

Trace hesitated, not wanting to explain the entire story. "I arranged for Mrs. Wilson to come over."

They sat without speaking for almost five minutes before Frank Bailey's body convulsed again. It went on and on and on, and then grew still. Unnaturally still. Or perhaps, Trace thought, the most natural stillness of all. Jenny cried softly, rocking her body back and forth.

"Hush that, now," Trace said, weariness and relief adding a gruff note to his voice. "He doesn't deserve your tears." Hell, the man had kidnapped her and God knows what else. Her gown was tattered and stained. Trace had a knot of fear the size of a rock in his gut at the idea of what evils Frank Bailey might have played upon her in the past few hours.

Trace blamed himself. He'd relaxed his guard where the Baileys were concerned, believing the foolishness of the Bad Luck Wedding Dress had been finally put to bed. Instead, they'd hit hard and meaner than ever. The question remained just how mean.

Standing, he forced her to rise along with him. "Let's go get you washed up, sweetheart."

Jenny allowed him to lead her to the creek. She remained unusually passive while he removed her tattered gown and dipped her muddy hands into the cold creek water. She started shaking, whether from an inner or outer chill he couldn't say.

He wrapped first his coat and then his arms around her.

Hugging her tight, he spoke softly in her ear. "Can you tell me what happened, baby?"

He felt her chest expand as she drew a deep breath. "He came to the house. I thought it was Mrs. Wilson." She fell silent and a long minute passed before she spoke again. "He said he had to kill me, but I think he intended to…hurt me first."

Trace's stomach clenched. "Did he touch you?"

The minute before she spoke was one of the longest he'd ever lived. Her voice was weak, vulnerable, as she answered. "No. I broke his nose."

A sigh of relief whooshed from Trace's mouth. He closed his eyes momentarily as tension drained from his limbs. His Jenny was a fighter, thank God. She proved it time and again. He pressed a kiss against her temple. "You need to get some rest, honey, and I do, too. Can you handle sleeping in the cabin? I'll, um, clean it up a bit first, of course."

"No." She shook her head. "I want to go home."

Trace gently stroked her hair. "Not tonight. It's too far. It wouldn't be safe."

"Outside, then."

She burrowed against him and his arms clasped her tighter. It felt so right, holding her like this. Like a homecoming. And he'd been so damned afraid. "It won't be near as comfortable outside. It'll be cold."

"You'll keep me warm. And safe."

*Safe.* Trace's eyes closed and his head fell back. She knew the truth about him, knew what he'd done to Constance. Despite his having failed to protect her from Frank Bailey, she trusted him to keep her safe. *Why, Jenny? Why do you believe in me when I don't believe in myself?*

It was as if she had heard him. "I love you, Trace. I love you."

This time, the words did not pound him like hailstones. This time they sounded a warm, gentle rain that seeped into his skin and nourished his soul. Placing a finger beneath her chin, he tilted her face toward his. He brushed her lips softly with his. A fleeting contact. Once. Twice. A whisper of a touch. Then his mouth fused with hers.

Tenderly, he touched and tasted. His lips moved with velvet pressure. Offering, not demanding. Accepting what she proffered in return. With gentle passion, Trace told her with his kiss what he could not say with words.

Even to himself.

A CAMPFIRE FLICKERED, burning logs filling the air with aromatic smoke. Jenny lay spooned against her husband, wrapped in his arms and sandwiched between the blankets and mattress he'd pulled from the cabin's bed. Weariness tugged at her body, her eyes gritty as she stared at the starry sky.

She couldn't sleep. By all appearances, neither could Trace.

Beneath the shelter of a stand of hardwoods, he'd built a fire and fixed their bed before excusing himself to deal with Frank Bailey's body. Upon his return they'd shared food from his saddlebags and water from his canteen. Then he'd banked the fire and stretched out beside her. His body remained taut and tense.

Jenny's heart filled with yearning. Despite her fatigue, she wanted him. She wanted to lose herself in the pleasure of his lovemaking. To drive away the demons of this night with the promise of tomorrow, even if that promise was all pretense.

Or was it? She thought of the kiss they had shared. In the weeks since their marriage, they had kissed countless times, yet something about this kiss had been different. Special.

She wanted—no, she needed—to test it again.

She gently brushed her fingers up and down his forearm. Over and over, featherlight touches. Working up her nerve to try more. Instinct drove her during this, her first attempt to initiate their lovemaking.

His erection pushed against her bottom. Her pulse raced. Slowly, she wiggled her hips.

"God, Jenny."

His voice sounded rough as burlap. She turned in his arms, faced him, then lifted a finger to touch the velvet fullness of his lower lip. He groaned, nipped at her finger, then drew it into his mouth and sucked it. Flames raced through Jenny's blood. "Make love with me, Trace."

In the shadowed light, his eyes blazed as hot as the campfire. "I care for you, Jenny," he said, his voice a dry rasp. "God knows I want you, more than I've ever wanted another woman. But I can't tell you the words you want to hear."

She needed the words, but tonight, she needed him more. "No words. Just feeling. Give me the feeling, Trace. I need…"

He pulled her tight against him and fit his lips to hers, devouring her with his kiss. His mouth was open, his tongue diving and plundering. She sank her fingers into the thick, soft hair above his temples even as he rolled onto his back, carrying her with him.

He slipped his coat off her shoulders and chilled night caressed her skin, an acute contrast to the heat steaming between them. His hands stroked her buttocks, kneading her, cupping her, pressing her against the hard ridge of flesh that strained against his trousers.

And his kiss went on and on and on.

Jenny shuddered at the pleasure of it. He smelled of leather and sweat and that muskiness uniquely his own. She wanted to touch him, to feel his bare skin against hers. Boldly, she fitted her hands between them and attempted to loosen his buttons.

Low in his throat, he growled. In a flurry of motion, he moved from beneath her. His boots flew through the air, landing with a dull thud in the dirt. Cloth rustled and ripped, and then he was back, on top of her this time. Naked skin to naked skin. Damp and hot.

He kissed her again, hard and fast, then softer, trailing across her jaw to nip at her neck. She hummed and quivered. She burned.

He rose above her, his mouth moving lower. Slowly, ever so desperately slowly, he kissed his way down her body. His tongue circled first one nipple, then the other, bringing both to pebbled peaks.

Finally, he suckled her, murmuring in response to the small moan that escaped her.

She arched her back, giving herself up to that drawing fire that slashed from her breasts to the very core of her womanhood. Her hands gripped his shoulders as sensation bombarded her. Low in her belly, a knot of need tightened. "Trace…I want…I need…"

He rolled back on his knees. "Bend your legs. Open for me, Jenny."

Anything. She'd do anything. She lay aching, barely able to breathe. Expecting the pressure of his shaft, she was unprepared for the soft tickle on her inner thighs. Rough-soft and wet. The heated tracing of his tongue.

She whimpered and attempted to close her legs, but he anticipated her move, holding them apart, his fingers stroking the sensitive backs of her knees. "Trust me, treasure. Let me do this. I need to do this."

Treasure? The endearment settled on her heart like an angel's song.

Then his mouth dipped, touched her damp folds, tasted, and all rational thought fled. He lapped her, his tongue dragging across her most sensitive skin. Rough and silken at the same time. A whirlwind of escalating pleasure. Devouring sounds. Faster, harder. Plunging. Sweet torture.

Hot pressure coiled in her belly, stringing her tighter, shooting her higher than ever before. She teetered at the edge, unable to find her way over. She writhed upon the blanket.

Suction. *Oh, God.* Her thighs clamped around his head.

With a cry, she fell into the intense, swirling, exquisite storm of sensation.

Before she reached the bottom, he slid up over her and slipped into her. Lifting her hips, he withdrew and thrust, over and over again, demanding they climb the peak together this time.

His shout was throaty and harsh; hers a small, keening cry. He collapsed on her, his body quivering and damp with sweat.

He breathed a ragged pair of words that sounded like music in her soul. "My treasure."

*Carrying a buckeye in your pocket brings
good luck.*

## CHAPTER FIFTEEN

THE NIGHT MARKED a turning point in Trace and Jenny's marriage. The changes were subtle, but substantial, from her viewpoint. Trace was freer with his touches, his smiles were more intimate, their lovemaking was richer and more intense. One might say he'd progressed to the lope, trot, walk, and stop stage of training, she thought with a smile.

Upon their return from the Lucky Lady, she'd enjoyed a joyful reunion with the girls and attempted to return her life to normal. But her emotions were in flux, and she wasn't immediately able to put the incident behind her.

Jenny was angry it had happened, furious she'd been victimized. Yet the compassion she'd felt for Frank while he lay dying continued to linger. He'd died a horrible death. No matter how corrupt the man or evil his intentions, no one should have to suffer so.

Her emotions also vacillated where Big Jack was concerned. She both detested the man and pitied him. She understood his reasoning, faulty though it was. In his eyes his children had been hurt, and his orders to Frank had reflected a desire to protect those he loved.

Jenny didn't doubt that she would kill in a heartbeat to protect Emma, Maribeth, and Katrina.

What would Big Jack do when he learned his son was dead and she was still alive? Would he continue his pursuit of retribution? It was another worry that plagued her, one that didn't bear thinking about.

Trace thought about it, she knew. He'd assured her he would reach an understanding with Big Jack Bailey the moment he returned to Fort Worth. They would settle this bad luck business once and for all, her husband had declared. Under the circumstances, he thought she would be safe until then.

That no one outside the family knew about the abduction proved to be a blessing. The girls' efforts to seek help that night had failed because the neighbors were all at the Harvest Ball, and the few people they attempted to stop on the street had paid little attention to their babbling. The reputation they enjoyed ensured that nobody listened when the McBride Menaces were talking.

Trace stressed to the girls the importance of keeping the events of the previous night a McBride family secret. That idea had appealed to them, and they had assured their parents their lips were forever closed on the matter.

"Sealed like a can of peaches," Katrina said, snapping her lips shut.

Trace used connections in Hell's Half Acre to get word to Marshal Courtright of the body out at the Lucky Lady's homestead, and he and Jenny were relieved when Frank Bailey was buried at Pioneer's Rest Cemetery only two days after his death.

That wasn't enough for Jenny to put the incident behind her, however. In the week that followed, she suffered nightmares most every night. Visions of giant-size scorpions and gleaming knives and guns intruded into her dreams and sent her screaming from sleep into her husband's comforting arms. He'd hold her while she poured out the tales, offering comfort that often ended in lovemaking.

By the time a week had passed, life had settled down. Jenny concluded that their efforts the night of the Harvest Ball had fended off the worst of the gossip about the gown, thank God. Although Mary Rose's accident had stirred up some talk, Jenny still had customers flocking to Fortune's Design, and she still heard her dress referred to as the Good Luck Wedding Dress.

Now if that good luck would only hold after Big Jack returned from New Orleans.

Life at Willow Hill was good, family members for the most part happy. Not that they didn't fight upon occasion, because they did. All of them. All possible combinations of combatants. But they were normal family squabbles offset by normal family laughter. Jenny had never been happier.

Even though her mother had taken to dropping by Willow Hill unannounced.

Monique became a regular passenger on the Texas & Pacific run between Dallas and Fort Worth. She'd arrive at their doorstep unannounced and bearing gifts. Once she made up her mind to play the doting grandmother role, she went all out.

If only she'd be a bit more grandmotherly toward Trace. Jenny bristled at her mother's flirtatious behavior. "I wish she'd reconcile with my father," she told Trace in the privacy of their bedroom following one particularly annoying incident. "She could go pester him for a while and it would be just fine with me."

Trace paused in the act of brushing her hair, a task he volunteered for nearly every night. "Is she still angry with him for not coming to our wedding?"

Jenny nodded. "Furious. She hasn't spoken to him since. I don't know why she's acting this way. I'm the one who should be upset, not Monique. If I'm not angry, why is she?"

"Are you disappointed in your father for not attending?"

She was silent for a moment, then said, "Well, yes."

Finished, he set her hairbrush on the dressing table. "Remember last week when Emma was so disappointed for not winning a ribbon for her recital at the Literary Society festival? How did you feel about Mrs. Hander?"

Jenny wrinkled her nose. "That woman couldn't judge her way out of a wet paper bag."

His eyes gleaming knowingly, Trace simply smiled and Jenny got his point. "Why don't you go check on the girls," she groused. "I heard some suspicious bumping a few minutes ago."

He left wearing a superior smile. Ten minutes later, he returned with a frustrated frown. Climbing into bed beside her, he groaned. "If I live to be a hundred, I'll never understand those girls. All that noise I used to hear about wanting their own rooms. The bickering at bedtime—Katrina sometimes sings in her sleep and the older girls used to drive me crazy complaining about it. So what happens? I work my butt off to provide them what they've begged me for, and what do they do?"

He sat up and punched his pillow into the shape he preferred for sleeping. "They pile into Emma's bed like a litter of puppies."

Jenny laughed and snuggled up against him. "They've been together all these years, and I imagine they're lonely sleeping by themselves. I know I was."

He wrapped his arm around her and nuzzled her neck. "At times I used to envy them. It's nice to have someone with you when you fall off to sleep."

"See there, McBride?" She lifted her head and teased him with a satisfied smile. "Just one more problem I've solved for you. Now you needn't feel lonely when you go to sleep."

"Lonely, hell. I'm too exhausted to feel anything. Every night it's the same thing—'Kiss me, Trace. Make love to me,

Trace.' I'm telling you, Jenny McBride, if I'd known ahead of time what a demanding hussy you'd turn out to be, I might have thought twice about saying 'I do.' I can see it now engraved on my headstone." He extended his arm, palm out, and moved it from left to right as he said, "Trace McBride. His wife plumb wore him out."

She leaned over and nipped at his chest. "You did think twice. You thought twice at least two hundred times. And now I see where Katrina got her flare for the dramatic. Wear you out, hmm?" She laved the spot she'd just bitten and added, "Tell me, McBride. Can you think of a better way to go?"

The growl came from low in his throat. "Nope, can't say that I can." He rolled her over on top of him and said, "Kill me some more, treasure. Please?"

She proceeded to give it her best effort.

By Jenny and Trace's two-month anniversary, the McBride family had adapted well to the changes the wedding had wrought. They were settled into their new home. The girls were doing fine in school and causing relatively little mischief. Fortune's Design appeared to be well on the way to financial health. The girls were happy. Jenny was happy. Trace was happy.

It scared the hell out of him.

The fear was like a chigger bite that had taken weeks, instead of days, to fester. The itch came on slowly in the form of unease. As it bothered him more and more, doubt began to nag him. By the tenth week of their marriage, distrust and suspicion had him scratching like mad.

And that led to trouble.

He finished up his morning appointments early and decided to do a little work on the dollhouse he was building. Having gone to the mercantile to purchase the toy as a Christmas gift for the girls, he'd noted a lack of quality in the piece. Jenny had convinced him to create one of his own design, and he'd found he enjoyed the effort. Needing more wood for the trim, he left the house for the hardware store down on Main. Jenny was working in the shop that day, so after he made his purchase, he swung around by Fortune's Design.

It was closed.

That's strange, he thought. Although she'd cut back on her work hours, Jenny kept regular morning hours at the shop. It wasn't like her not to be here.

Big Jack. Trace shut his eyes, rocked at the thought. Aw, shit. No!

He raced to Marshal Courtright's office.

"No," the marshal replied in answer to his question. "I haven't telegraphed the news about Frank's death yet. Deputy Scott's brother lives in New Orleans and he's been visiting here in Fort Worth. He's offered to give Big Jack the word when he gets home. What does it matter to you anyway?"

"Are you certain he's still in New Orleans?" Trace asked, disregarding the question.

"Haven't heard otherwise. And you can bet he's not back in town or I'd damn sure know about it. Now what's put the burr under your saddle, McBride?"

Trace left the marshal's office without replying, his mind consumed with the question of his wife's whereabouts.

That chigger itch took to troubling him again, but Trace did his best to ignore it. Maybe she'd gone home. She'd done that a couple of times recently, showing up in the middle of the day for one of those tours they enjoyed so much. Trace nodded and headed for home.

But Jenny wasn't there. Neither was she at the dry goods purchasing new thread, or at the Fort Worth Literary Society meeting. He checked all the stores on Main, thinking she might be doing some Christmas shopping, but not a shopkeeper in town had seen his wife that morning. By the time he was done, Trace was feeling mean.

He went home and settled in to wait, old ghosts and demons riding his shoulder hard.

JENNY WALKED toward home in a daze. Although she'd had her suspicions, confirmation of her condition had sent her world spinning off its axis. A baby. A squirming, crying, hungry-all-the-time bundle of love.

She'd never been so happy in her life.

So happy or nervous or downright afraid. A baby. What would Trace think? They'd never discussed babies, but then that was no great surprise because they never discussed anything truly important. Did he even want any more children? He must have known the possibility—even the probability—existed.

He'd be happy. She knew it in her heart. Trace loved his daughters too much not to welcome another child into his life.

A baby. Jenny placed a hand over her stomach and smiled. What would the girls think? Would they be happy? Jealous? A little bit of both? She'd have to reassure them of her love and that her feelings wouldn't change with the new addition to the family.

The new addition. Questions bombarded Jenny like hailstones. How long before her pregnancy started to show? How long before she felt her baby move?

She stopped abruptly. How much longer could she and Trace make love before it might endanger the child?

She turned right around and returned to the doctor's office. Because she had to wait while he was out on a call, and because once she started asking questions she couldn't seem to stop, it was well after noon when she finally reached Willow Hill. Now that she had time to get used to the idea, she found she couldn't quit smiling. In fact, she'd hummed all the way home.

She entered the house through the back, accidentally allowing the screen door to bang shut. Taking a seat at the kitchen table, she propped her feet up on a chair, closed her eyes, and leaned her head back. Smiling, she imagined a green-eyed little boy with yellow curls.

"Where the hell have you been?"

Startled, she opened her eyes to see Trace standing in the kitchen doorway, a half-empty crystal decanter of whiskey in his hand. Jenny's brow lowered. She knew that bottle had been full when she left the house this morning.

She sat up. Oh, gosh. Had something happened to the girls? Were the Menaces somehow in trouble? A lump of fear clogged Jenny's throat and made it difficult to speak. "What is it? Are the girls all right? Is it Big Jack? Is he back in town?"

"The girls are fine," he said carefully, stepping into the kitchen. His voice a symphony of calm, he repeated, "Jenny, where have you been?"

She hesitated, wanting to save her news for the perfect moment, certainly for a more romantic place than the kitchen. "I was at the shop, of course."

"All day?" The light in his eyes altered, his expression turning mean.

Jenny didn't like it one bit. "Why are you questioning me?"

He yanked a chair from underneath the table, flipped it around, and straddled it. "I know where my daughters are. They're in school where they should be. I know where to find them if I go looking. They don't up and disappear without telling a soul where they're going. You know why? They don't have anything to hide."

Enlightenment burst like a bubble. He must have come into town for some reason and found Fortune's Design closed. Why, the big clod. She lifted her chin and folded her arms. "Are you insinuating that I have done something wrong, McBride?"

His expression grew stony and cold. "Insinuate, Mrs. McBride? That is your name now. You do remember that, don't you? You remember you're a married woman?"

She gasped with shock but he forged ahead, digging himself even deeper. "And I'm not insinuating anything, Wife. I'm asking it right out." He leaned forward, drilling her with a look. "Where were you, Jenny? I want the truth, and I want it now."

She almost reached across the table and slapped him. She was furious. She was angry. She was hurt. He thought evil things about her. It was written all across his face. "Just where do you think I was, *Husband*? At the Cosmopolitan Hotel perhaps? With one of my legion of lovers?"

He shoved to his feet and took a full step backward. The chair banged to the floor. He whispered, "Damn you."

That was more than she could stand. Jenny stood and advanced on him, her hands braced on her hips. "Don't you dare curse me, McBride. I have done nothing wrong and for you to even think it, much less accuse me, is an insult I'll not abide."

He didn't move. He didn't even blink. Jenny shivered at the chill that hung between them. She wanted to weep, but her pride wouldn't permit it. Nor would it allow her to explain. She'd not tell him of the child now and have what should be a special moment ruined.

She swept a hand toward the whiskey decanter he'd left on the table. "You've obviously already drunk yourself senseless, but if you feel obliged to continue, I'd appreciate your taking it down to your old haunts where it belongs before our daughters come home. Hell's Half Acre is a more appropriate venue for fools than Willow Hill."

Gathering her pride around her like an ermine cape, hoping it would keep her warm, Jenny walked toward the stairs and the privacy of a room in which to cry. Halfway up, she heard a crash as the decanter shattered against the wall, followed shortly by the slam of the front door.

Blinking furiously, she turned right at the head of the stairs, walking past her bedroom to the small, empty room across the hall. This would be the nursery. She opened the door and stepped inside. She gazed around the room, imagining a crib, frilly curtains on the window, and maybe a rocking horse in one corner. A father cooing at the infant in the cradle.

Jenny sniffed. Trace was acting the fool. A first-class top-of-the-line fool.

And that wasn't like him at all.

Suspicion flickered in her mind and she concentrated as the notion grew. This wasn't about her at all, was it? This was about something else. Someone else?

Jenny walked to the curtainless window and stared outside at the willows below, their drooping branches swaying in the breeze. Could there be any truth to her suspicions? If Constance had cheated on Trace, that would explain some of his more cryptic comments both before and after their marriage. She hated to think it, however. Trace McBride was a proud man. A wife's betrayal would hit him hard. It would also go a long way toward explaining his behavior today.

And what would it do to her chances of gaining his love?

Jenny sighed and lifted her hand to touch her stomach. A baby. Maybe a brother for her darling Menaces. Or another daughter. It didn't matter to her.

Turning away from the window, she returned her attention to the nursery. Another thought occurred and she couldn't stop a smile.

Somehow, she simply couldn't envision Monique changing diapers.

THE SUN HAD long since set by the time Trace climbed the spiral staircase and stood outside his bedroom door, working up the nerve to go inside.

It had been a long afternoon and evening. Self-examination was not one of his favorite pastimes, especially when he sensed he was in the wrong. If Jenny was innocent, then he'd acted like an ass. If she wasn't innocent, then he'd been a god-damned fool to marry her. He'd rather be an ass than a fool any day, and once he calmed down enough to think about it, he thought himself pretty safe on that score.

Their wedding night—or rather the morning after, in their case—had proved she'd had no lover before their marriage. He knew damn well he'd kept her satisfied in bed since the nuptials, so that wouldn't be a reason for her to betray him.

Of course, he couldn't allow himself to forget she was a woman and therefore didn't need a reason for duplicity. But the way she'd reacted—that outraged offense—reassured him. Jenny was capable of trying to brazen her way past guilt, but he didn't believe that to be the case this time. More likely, he'd angered her with his accusations, and she'd been too hard-headed to explain. That was more in character for Jenny Fortune McBride.

And besides, she didn't have a man sniffing about her heels and tempting her to betrayal. Tye McBride was half a country away from here this time. Thank God.

That thought gave him courage to step inside.

She'd waited up for him. Seated by the fire, she had knitting in her lap. Trace focused on that, and the wayward thought occurred that he had never seen her knit. Judging by her other skills, he bet her knitted creations were master-pieces. Maybe she'd knit him a nice warm blanket.

Depending on how mad he'd made her, he might need it for a cover wherever he ended up sleeping.

Shutting the door behind him, Trace said, "Hello."

"Hello," she replied, not looking up.

Silence hung between them like a heavy fog. He lifted a hand to rub the back of his neck. "I wasn't sure you'd still be awake."

"I wasn't sure you'd come home."

He sighed heavily. He hated it when she got snippy. "We need to talk."

Her knitting needles continued to click. "I'm listening."

"Would you look at me?"

Her hands stilled. He watched her breasts lift as she inhaled a deep breath. When she finally lifted her gaze and speared him with a glare, he felt the remaining weight lift from his heart. Jenny wouldn't still be so hot if she'd done something wrong. He hadn't been a fool, he'd been an ass. His lips lifted in a rueful grin. "I guess I owe you an apology."

She lifted her chin, and even though she was sitting and he was standing, she still managed to look down her nose at him. "Yes, you do. And I don't know that I'd be laughing about it if I were you."

"Ah, Jenny, I'm not laughing about any of this." Approaching the fireplace, he lifted the poker from the stand and stirred the dying fire. As it hissed, Trace fixed his gaze on the dancing yellow flames. "I'm sorry, sweetheart. I'm sorry I said the things I said."

She waited, watching expectantly, and Trace grimaced. The woman was out for blood. "And you were right about me drinking at home. That's not something the girls should see."

"It's not something *I* should see." Wrinkling her nose, she added, "Or smell."

Her sanctimonious sniff didn't wear well on him. "You're the one who told me to go down to the Acre."

Neither did the rolled-eye look. He rubbed his hand across his jaw. "You know, Jenny, all you had to do was give a little. If you'd told me where you were I wouldn't have stalked off."

Jenny stared at one of her knitting needles as if she contemplated plunging it into his breast. "Let me make sure I have this straight. All I had to do was to tell you where I was for an hour during the smack-dab middle of the day?"

"More like three hours."

"Three hours." She calmly laid her knitting aside, then rose to her feet. She braced her hands on her hips and stepped toward him, her head dropping back as she moved close. "Excuse me, McBride, but the country fought a war over slavery not long ago. I made certain promises to you when we married, but I don't recall 'accounting for each and every minute of my time' as being one of them."

Damn, but she was beautiful when she was in a temper. Her skin glowed with color and her eyes sparkled like sunlight on blue water. She was spirited, vibrant, and alive. He spoke without thinking. "God, woman, you make me want you."

She tossed her head, flinging her long blond tresses across her shoulder. "You make me crazy, McBride! Completely, totally, one-hundred-percent crazy." She reached for him and he expected to feel her hand strike him. Instead, her fingers tugged at the buttons on his shirt, opening them one by one. "What have I done to make you doubt me?" She yanked the shirt free of his pants. "What have I done to threaten your trust?"

She pushed the shirt off his shoulders, down and off his arms. Balling it up, she threw it away. "And what," she continued, pushing his bare chest with the palms of both hands, backing him across the room, "what makes you think I'd ever put up with having to account for every minute of my time? I'm a grown woman, McBride. I'm an independent woman. If you wanted to keep track of every tiny second of your wife's life, then you should never have married me!"

With that, she pushed him onto their bed and followed right behind him. She leaned over him, her unbound breasts grazing his chest. When her mouth was scant inches from his own, she said in her mellowest, sipping-whiskey voice, "But aren't you glad you did?"

They made love with a fierceness that surprised them both. It was a consensual taking and giving, commanding and surrendering. When it was over and they lay spent, sated, and re-plete, Jenny absently trailed her fingers across his abdomen and said, "I won't betray you, Trace. You can trust me."

For a long moment, he remained silent, a bittersweet emotion gripping his heart. With a sigh, he said, "That's the problem. I can't."

Her body, so soft and pliant a moment before, stiffened. Before she could protest, he laid a finger across her lips. "Shush, honey. You don't understand. It's not you at all. It's old demons that are riding my back with their claws sunk deep."

"What do you mean?" she asked softly.

He curled a strand of long blond hair around his finger. "I think it's beyond my ability to trust in anyone anymore. I know that's not what you're wanting to hear, but it's the truth—my truth."

"What happened? This must have something to do with your first wife."

His finger stilled. "I'll not speak of that woman while I'm in our bed with you." He rose above her and stared down into her face. "Don't worry about it, Jenny. I'll handle it from now on. Better than I did today, I hope." He sealed his promise with a quick kiss.

"Now, there's something else I want to talk about," he continued. "How would you like to take a little trip?"

"A trip? Where? When?"

He rolled onto his back and pulled her into the shelter of his arms. "Well, we'd need to leave tomorrow, actually. Be gone about a week. Definitely home for Christmas. I found out this evening that Hill County is about to decide on an architect to design their new courthouse. I'd like to have a go at getting the job. Counties all across Texas are in the market for landmark courthouses, and if I could get one commission, it might keep me busy for years. It's the type of work I love, to be honest. Not that I mind designing houses, it's just that—"

Jenny stopped him with a kiss. "Of course you'll go to Hill County, and they'll be fools if they don't choose you to design their new courthouse."

"I figured we could take the girls and make it a little holiday."

She shook her head. "This is a business trip. You don't need your family tagging along and tying you down. Besides, the girls have school and I have gowns to finish."

"No, Jenny. I'm not leaving you here alone. I can't. What if Big Jack were to return?"

Jenny considered the problem. It would be stupid of her to disregard the possibility of danger. Big Jack wanted her punished "permanently" because of the accidents his daughters suffered. The question returned time and again: How would he react when he learned his son was dead?

"Trace, you can't be with us all the time—"

"True, but I can be here when he gets back to town." His expression grew grim. "He won't bother us after that, I can assure you."

They sat silently for a time, each occupied with thoughts of Bailey. Then Trace gave Jenny a quick hug. "Never mind, sweetheart. I'll skip the trip. There'll be other courthouses."

"No. You need to do this. It's important. Besides, I have an idea. What if we hire a bodyguard while you're gone? Surely you know somebody who would be good."

She watched his expression as he considered it.

"Bart Rogers. He used to drink at the End of the Line."

After another moment's thought, he scowled. Jenny sensed he might be about to refuse, so she added, "We could ask Mrs. Wilson to stay the nights while you're gone. I know she prefers to keep this as a day job, but I'll bet she'd help us out for a week. In fact, we could have the bodyguard walk the girls to and from school. We could even arrange for someone to walk me to work and back if that would make you feel better. We'd be safer than if you were in town."

"Gee, thanks," he said dryly.

She smiled sheepishly. "You know what I mean. We'll be fine here, Trace. I don't want you to worry a bit. And, when you come back, I'll have a surprise waiting for you."

He arched a brow. "A surprise?"

She gave him her cat-'n'-cream smile. "An extra special Christmas present."

Sitting up, he studied her with a calculating expression. "What is it?"

She shook her head.

"Come on, darlin', give me a hint. Just a little one?"

Laughter burst from inside her. "You and your daughters are so very much alike. I've been hearing the same sort of thing from them for weeks. And you know what?" She gave his side a little pinch.

"Ouch! What?" He gave a mock ferocious glare.

She pretended to turn a lock on her mouth. "I don't tell them a thing. Just like I won't tell you anything about your extra special present—at least until you come home from Hill County with a commission to design their new courthouse in your pocket."

"What if I don't get the job?"

When he said that, she knew she'd convinced him. He'd hire this Bart Rogers in the morning and probably drive her crazy with instructions before leaving on the eleven-thirty train. "You will get the job. I have total confidence in you, Husband mine."

"Hmm." He lowered his head and nuzzled her neck. "Bet I can convince you to tell me what my surprise is now."

Her smile was a sweet, sensuous invitation. "You're welcome to give it a try."

Much later Trace fell back on his pillow, pleasantly exhausted. "You win," he said when he could catch his breath. "You fight dirty, but you win. You can keep a secret like no woman I've ever known before."

Jenny stretched languidly and purred. "What can I say, McBride? I'm good at everything I do."

Almost five minutes passed before he spoke again. When he did, his voice rumbled soft and low, without a sign of the banter that had flavored their previous conversation. "I know you're good. That's why, even after all this mess today, I'll be able to leave Fort Worth tomorrow without you. I have confidence in you, too."

She snuggled close to him. "You trust me."

She'd fallen off to sleep before he whispered, "I'll try, treasure. I surely will try."

SUNSHINE FILLED the sky three days later as Jenny stood behind the house wringing water from a wet window curtain. She'd worked at Fortune's Design that morning, until an intense desire for a nap sent her home.

Bart had proved to be a godsend. He did make her feel safer in Trace's absence, but she appreciated him just as much for the errands he consented to run. Like now, for instance. Bart was making a quick run to Fortune's Design for her. Once she decided to stay home this afternoon and help Mrs. Wilson with a few light chores, she'd asked him to fetch home the dress she simply had to finish by tomorrow. It was Mrs. Howell's tenth wedding anniversary, and for the special occasion she'd ordered one of the dresses Jenny privately called Miss Rachel's remakes.

Ever since Jenny had worn hers to the Harvest Ball, the gowns had been her biggest seller. A full half of the orders had been placed by husbands for their wives, also. Trace predicted a baby boom come summer as the result.

Jenny smiled at the memory as she draped the cloth over the clothesline. She scrutinized the ruffled yellow gingham for signs of blue paint and grimaced at the dark shadows she discovered. That Katrina. The child could destroy a cannon if she put her mind to it.

Pinning the curtain to the line, she tried to ignore the nausea churning in her stomach. It must be nearing two o'clock, she realized, wiping her wet hands on her apron. This child had begun to make his presence known as regular as clockwork. Three times a day at ten, two, and six, her stomach went to rolling like a ship in a hurricane. She swallowed hard, then quickly finished hanging the rest of the wash. She'd learned that if she lay down right away, she sometimes could hold off the worst of it.

She didn't mind spending a few minutes in bed, but she'd hate to spend her entire day that way. If Trace was here, that's exactly what would have happened. He'd have her tucked into bed round the clock.

It was a darn good thing she'd not made the trip, after all.

Lifting her face toward the sunshine, she closed her eyes and concentrated on calming her pitching stomach. She'd made the right decision by not telling him about the baby after she learned of his impending trip. She'd been afraid he wouldn't leave her if he knew. Now she hoped she'd be over the worst of the sickness before he returned. Otherwise, knowing Trace, he'd nurture her crazy.

She was placing the last pin on the last bedsheet when nearby, a man cleared his throat. Startled, she dropped the pin and whirled around. He stood beside the swing that hung from a branch of a nearby oak, and he wore a hesitant smile on his face.

"Trace!" she called with delight, running toward him even as she wondered what had brought him home early. She threw her arms around him. "I've missed you so much already." As he opened his mouth to speak, she closed it with a kiss.

And that's when she knew.

She wrenched away, shocked and shaken. She wiped her lips with the back of her hand. Her voice trembled as she backed away from him and asked, "Who are you?"

The rueful smile was just the same as Trace's. "Thackery McBride. Tye to friends and family."

As she looked closer she recognized the differences, slight though they were. He was a shade leaner than Trace and perhaps not quite as tall. Now she could see the small white scar above his lip, and she realized he parted his hair farther toward the left than did Trace. But the greatest dissimilarity was in his eyes. Oh, the color was the same, but the emotions were completely different. She detected wariness and caution. A hint of despair.

"I'm Trace's brother."

Jenny was speechless. Trace had a brother he'd never once mentioned? A *twin* brother? The nausea in her stomach churned fiercely. She lifted her hand to cover her mouth and rushed past him for the minimal privacy of the far side of the oak tree. Leaning over, Jenny was violently sick. It seemed to go on forever.

She felt his hands at her waist as he offered her support, and she was too ill to do anything but accept it. Finally, the spasms eased and she straightened. His arms dropped away and he took a step backward.

Embarrassment flooded her face as she accepted the handkerchief he offered. How humiliating, she thought, wiping her face. She meets her husband's brother and the first thing she does is lose her lunch on his boots. Sucking in a deep breath, she forced herself to meet his gaze.

His green eyes were mocking as he spoke in a dry, bitter tone. "I see by your reaction that my brother has told you all about me."

*Burning red onion peels will bring good luck.*

## CHAPTER SIXTEEN

STEAM ROSE from the spout of a porcelain teapot as Jenny filled two cups to the brim. Mrs. Wilson had taken one look at Tye, welcomed "Mr. Trace" home, then disappeared on an errand to the market in an obvious effort to leave the newly-weds alone in the house for their reunion.

Embarrassment hung between Jenny and her husband's brother like the sheets on the clothesline. Trying to get past it, she gestured toward a plate filled with different kinds of cookies. "Have one, please. The ginger cookies are Mari-beth's favorite."

"Trace's, too, if I remember right." He lifted a sugar-dusted cookie from the plate. "Lemon has always been my first choice."

Jenny smiled. "You'll have to fight Katrina for those. She positively adores lemon cookies."

Tye grimaced and pursed his lips.

"Too sour?" she asked.

"No. Not the cookie, anyway." He set down his sweet and

spooned sugar into his tea. "More like bitter memories." After a moment, he cleared his throat and asked, "How are the girls? I bet they've grown so much I'd hardly recognize them. I reckon Emmie finally grew a pair of front teeth?"

The awkwardness between them abated as they spent the next few minutes discussing the McBride daughters. Jenny relayed stories of the Menaces' shenanigans, and laughed along with Tye as he imparted a few tales of growing up with Trace. By the time he was done he had proved beyond a doubt where the McBride Menaces got the mischievous side of their natures.

"You mustn't tell the girls, Tye," she said with a groan. "Robbing a train was bad enough. My daughters don't need to know anything about explosives."

He leaned back in his chair and studied her warmly. "So, Mrs. McBride, how long have you and Trace been married?"

"Call me Jenny, please. Your brother and I married a little over two months ago."

"So this is your first baby."

Her cup rattled in its saucer. She leaned back in her chair and gasped at him. "How did you know? Trace hasn't even guessed."

"I always figured it out before Trace. Constance used to tell us…" His voice trailed off and he busied himself by spooning more sugar into his tea.

When he didn't quit, Jenny asked in a wry tone, "Care for a little more tea with your sugar?"

He stopped abruptly and gave her a sheepish grin. "I'm sorry. I admit I'm more than a little nervous."

Returning his smile, Jenny stood and retrieved a clean cup and saucer. She poured him a fresh cup of tea, saying, "That makes two of us, I'm afraid. I find this quite unsettling—you looking so much like my husband." She paused for a moment, working up the nerve to ask her visitor a question she'd wanted to ask his brother for months. "You mentioned my husband's first wife. Did you know her well? What was she like?"

He shook his head. "No disrespect meant, ma'am, but you need to ask your husband those questions, not me."

Jenny wanted to groan. What was it with these McBride men? They were worthless when it came to providing answers. It would serve them right if she sicced Wilhemina Peters on the both of them.

Unwilling to allow what appeared to be a golden opportunity to pass her by, Jenny tried again. "Trace refuses to speak of her. I know there was an accident of some sort, and that he feels responsible. But his reticence puts me in a difficult position. The girls wonder about her; they ask me questions they cannot ask their father. I'd like to know something I could tell them."

Slowly, he stirred his tea. He was obviously weighing her words. When he spoke his first sentence, she felt a surge of victory.

"Constance West was the most beautiful girl in South Carolina."

Ouch. Suddenly, Jenny didn't want to hear any more. Unaware of her change of heart, Tye continued, "She had a flawless complexion and thick auburn hair with streaks of red that shot fire in the sunlight. Big brown eyes a man could drown in. Once she set her cap for Trace, he didn't stand a chance."

Jenny's sour stomach returned as he spoke, and she knew it had little to do with her pregnancy. Jealousy was bad for a person's constitution.

"Constance had a way about her. Fire and ice, heaven and hell, all rolled into one. She knew just how to look at a man to make him—" Tye shrugged and laid his spoon down hard. "Trace is right not to talk about her. Believe me, Emma, Maribeth, and Katrina are better off not knowing about Constance."

"But she was their mother," Jenny protested. "They should know that she wanted them and cared for them. That she loved them."

He pushed his chair back from the table and stood to pace the room. "Trace won't lie to them, and you shouldn't either. Constance didn't love her daughters." Disgust laced his voice as he roughly declared, "Constance didn't love anybody but herself."

Jenny sat back in her chair. Tye McBride was a mirror image of her husband, right down to the pain flaring in his eyes. Was what he claimed true? And what about what he wasn't saying? What had happened to cause such a rift between the brothers? Why had Trace never mentioned Tye? Did it have something to do with Constance?

Jenny wanted answers. Trace had acted the jealous fool because of the "demons" in his past. Unless she was completely mistaken, one of those "demons" just stepped on a jack Katrina had left lying on the kitchen floor.

Tye sat in his chair and propped his leg over the opposite knee. As he yanked the metal toy from the sole of his boot, Jenny said impulsively, "You were wrong outside."

He turned his head and gave her a questioning look.

"Trace hasn't told me about you. In fact, I didn't know he had a brother."

Tye smiled crookedly and spun the jack on the tabletop. "That's more the way I figured it, to be honest. Last time I saw him he said he was severing all ties between us. Trace has always been a man of his word."

Jenny watched the toy smoothly whirl. After a moment it hit a cookie crumb and bounced, flying out of control until it fell from the table. A marriage could be like that, she thought. "Why are you here, then? To cause trouble?"

He scooped the jack up off the floor and tossed it from hand to hand. Then he caught it and held it trapped in his palm, his gaze capturing hers just as effectively. "No, I haven't come to Texas to cause trouble. I've come to make amends. Will you help me? Or will you stand in my way?"

"Trace won't be home for a week or two."

"That'll give me time to get to know my nieces again. And Katrina, of course. She was just a baby when Trace left South Carolina."

Slowly, Jenny finished her cookie. She suspected Trace wouldn't like her giving Tye access to his children and she told his brother as much.

"Listen, Jenny," Tye said, leaning forward and speaking intently. "Those three little girls are my family. That word means a lot to me, and to Trace, too, no matter what he says otherwise. I don't want to hurt them in any way, but I believe they deserve to know the McBride family—all of it. Not just me, but their great-grandmother and aunts. Trace was wrong to take that away from them. He was wrong about many things. He's had them to himself long enough. It's time for him to share."

She didn't like the sound of that. She opened her mouth intending to tell him when a child's scream pierced the sky. "Maribeth!" Jenny gasped.

Tye was out the door in a flash, Jenny right on his heels.

Katrina stood below the spreading branches of the huge pecan tree that stood halfway down the hill. Emma was running toward the house, hollering, "Mama, help," as Tye and Jenny hurried toward them.

"Mari's in the tree," the eldest girl cried. "She slipped and her leg is stuck. She's hanging upside down."

Tye stripped off his coat. He tugged off his boots and raced to the base of the tree. Grasping a low-hanging limb, he swung himself up. "I'm coming, sweetheart," he said.

"Hurry, Papa!" Katrina called, before grabbing Jenny's skirt and burying her face to hide her eyes.

Jenny's chest hurt from running. Maribeth's pigtails dangled straight toward the ground, and Jenny prayed the girl's head wouldn't plunge in the same direction. "Where's Bart?"

"We just played a tiny little trick. He'll figure it out soon, and it didn't do anything to hurt the dress he carried, Mama."

Jenny closed her eyes.

"Here we go," Tye said, wrapping his legs around a branch and reaching toward Maribeth. "Don't fight me now. I'm going to lift you toward me, and when you can, I want you to grab my neck. All right, Maribeth?"

"Y-y-yes."

Maribeth sounded as if she was in pain. Jenny wanted to cry herself. What if she'd wrenched her knee? What if she'd broken her leg? What if Thackery McBride had not been here to help?

Jenny breathed a sigh of relief as Maribeth's arms wrapped around her uncle's neck. Swiftly, but carefully, he descended the tree. Upon reaching the ground, he asked, "Mari, do you want me to set you down? Do you think you can stand?"

She nodded, and he lowered her feet to the ground, supporting her weight until she tested her leg. "I'm fine," she said, shaking off his touch and stepping close to Jenny. "Thank you very much for rescuing me."

Tye took a gentlemanly bow.

"Mari," Katrina said, her brow wrinkled in confusion. "Why are you talking like that to Papa?"

"That's not our Papa," Emma said, her hands clasped in front of her.

Tye grinned. "You're quicker than your mama. She had to kiss me first to figure it out."

Emma glanced at Jenny, then back at Tye. "I remember you. You're Papa's brother."

Maribeth glanced at her sister sharply. "You never told us Papa has a brother."

"I forgot."

Jenny suddenly needed to sit down. "My goodness, my knees are shaking. Maribeth McBride, you scared me half to death. What were you doing up in that tree?"

"I was just climbing. The tree called to me today." She dipped her chin. "I'm sorry, Mama. I didn't mean to get stuck."

Jenny lifted her face toward the sky and sighed. "You never go looking for trouble, but somehow that never stops it from finding you." Beneath her breath, she added, "Unlike Bart Rogers." He might be the best hired gun in the state, but he was lousy at managing Menaces.

"I'm starving," Katrina said, her eyes round as she stared at Tye McBride. "What did Mrs. Wilson make us today, Mama?"

"Cookies."

"I love cookies the mostest."

"I shouldn't let you have any."

"But you will, won't you?"

"Yes." Jenny shooed the girls toward the house, then gestured for Tye to join them.

Katrina glanced back over her shoulder as she walked. She plopped her thumb in her mouth, then spoke around it, her voice drifting clear as a bell to the adults who followed behind them. "He looks 'xactly like Papa. Am I suppose to love him?"

Jenny witnessed the effect the little girl's words had upon the man. Stark pain summed it up best and gave Jenny something to think about as she placed cookies on plates and fixed glasses of milk for her daughters.

Tye didn't join them at the table. Instead, he paused by the kitchen door and leaned against the jamb. Jenny watched him watching the girls as they washed up, his gaze all but drinking them in. He loves them, she thought. He apparently hasn't seen them in years, but he loves them no matter what.

Jenny smiled and said, "Girls, I'm afraid we have gotten things a bit backward here, but I believe introductions are in order."

"We don't need an introduction," Tye said, pushing away from the wall and approaching the girls. "I'd know these young ladies anywhere. Look at how big you've grown. And so beautiful. Emma and Maribeth, you look so much like your mother." He squatted down in front of Katrina whose eyes were round as a barn owl's. "Hello, Katrina."

She shuffled close to Emma as he reached out and gently touched her cheek. "Now you look just like your Aunt Penny, and she still wins the beauty contest at the county fair every summer. I knew the first time I saw you that you'd have the look of a McBride. You're just like I've dreamed." Shaking himself, he stood and backed away. "All of you. Just as pretty as I've imagined."

As Jenny would have suspected, Emma and Katrina beamed. Maribeth eyed him skeptically, then asked for a ginger cookie.

Tye McBride spent the next half hour charming the girls with stories of their family and censored versions of their father's youthful escapades.

"You were with him when he stole that pig?" Maribeth asked, shaking her head in wonder. "Why didn't Papa ever tell us that?" She looked at Jenny. "Why, Mama?"

Jenny lifted her shoulders. "I don't know, honey. You'll have to ask him that yourself when he comes home. In the meantime, I do believe it is time for you all to get to your homework."

"But Ma-ma!" they protested.

She waved her hand. "Shoo."

Katrina paused at the doorway, a milk mustache dotting her upper lip, and asked, "Uncle Tye, will you be here when we get done? Are you going to stay with us?"

He sat back in his chair, arms folded, and gave Jenny a questioning look. "Well, angel, that depends on your mother."

"Nothing like putting me on the spot," she grumbled beneath her breath.

He arched one brow, looking so much like Trace that Jenny blinked and looked a second time.

"Please, Mama?" Maribeth asked. "I want to show him the secret passageways. Maybe he can help me find the hidden doors Papa hasn't shown me yet."

Trace wouldn't like it; she could feel it in her bones. But Tye had come all this way. He'd saved Maribeth from what could have been a serious accident. And, he was right about family. The girls should know their great-grandmother and aunts. Hadn't she yearned her entire life for the type of extended family this man was offering her daughters?

But most of all, Tye McBride's presence in the house might provide answers to some of the questions Trace refused to deal with. She'd already learned a little about Constance and she wanted to know more. The more information she possessed, the better she could battle Trace McBride.

Because it was a war. He'd proven that the day before he left when he doubted her. She was engaged in a down-and-dirty, no-holds-barred fight for her husband's love, and she had every intention of coming out the victor.

"Do you have bags with you, Tye? I'll put you in the green room. Girls, since you are headed upstairs now, you may show him the way."

"Thank you, ma'am," he said with a nod, satisfaction gleaming in his eyes.

She lowered her voice to where the girls couldn't hear and added, "Allow me to state a warning. If you cause me one moment's worth of trouble, I'll show you the door myself."

"Fair enough," he said with a grin.

He rose from his chair to follow the girls when Jenny stopped him with a hand on his arm. "One more thing. You say Trace has severed all ties. What, in your opinion, will my husband do when he returns to find you in his home?"

"It's been six years." He glanced away as if looking into the past, then back at her. "Our grandmother seems to believe he'll be ready to listen to what I have to say."

"And what do you think?"

He shrugged. "Time will tell, Jenny. Time will tell."

She was still thinking about his answer a few minutes later when Bart Rogers marched into the kitchen, threw down Mrs. Howell's dress, and quit.

Jenny was glad to see him go. He had no excuse for using the words he did to describe her daughters. No excuse at all.

She poured another cup of tea. Sipping it, she considered how nicely problems worked out sometimes. Considering Bart Rogers had left them in the lurch, Trace would be so relieved when he arrived home to find his brother at Willow Hill.

*New Orleans, Louisiana*

BIG JACK BAILEY descended the stairs of Mary Rose's fancy town mansion and smiled with satisfaction. His baby girl had done good, damned good, even if she had married out-of-state blood. He'd known his son-in-law Stephen came from money, but until he caught a glimpse of his home, he hadn't realized how much. Gilt mirrors and crystal chandeliers, carpets that cost more than a section of Texas ranchland. Silver everywhere a fellow looked.

Jack detoured to Stephen's library and the Cuban cigars kept in a teak box atop the desk. Removing one, he slid it along his upper lip, inhaling the scent with pleasure. After twirling it between his fingers, he opened his jacket and tucked it into an inside pocket. Someone cleared his throat and Jack turned. His son-in-law and a stranger stood in the doorway.

"Afternoon, Steve," he said, not the least bit embarrassed at having been caught swiping a smoke. "I've just come from upstairs and a visit with Mary Rose and the baby. Finelookin' little boy we got. He's Bailey through to the bone. Now, have you had any luck in discovering who sent me that fake telegram?"

The young man shook his head. "Not yet. I'll be truthful with you, sir. With the baby coming early and then the trouble Mary Rose went through, it's not been my first priority."

"Well, get on with it, boy. We need to know, I want a piece of that fool's hide whoever he is. I was plumb scared to death about Mary Rose, as were her sisters. Whoever would do such a wicked thing should be shot, and I might just do it myself. Find out who did it, Steve. I hate being in the dark about anything." At that, Stephen and the stranger shared a look, causing Big Jack to scowl. Something was going on. "You gonna introduce me to your friend?"

His son-in-law spoke with obvious reluctance. "Allow me to introduce Bernard Scott. He has a brother who is a lawman back in Fort Worth."

Big Jack's brows lifted. "Scott? You talking about ol' Rufus?" At the man's nod, Big Jack observed, "It's a small world, ain't it."

Scott stepped forward. "It's a hard world, sir. I've just returned from a visit to Fort Worth, in fact." He took a deep breath, then continued, "I'm afraid I have some bad news for you, sir. Terrible news. You might want to take a seat."

Bailey grimaced and looked away. He shoved his hands in his pockets. "Why?"

Scott appeared to brace himself before speaking. "Mr. Bailey, I'm afraid your son Frank has met with an untimely death."

Big Jack heard a roaring in his ears and the room began to spin. "You want to repeat that, boy?"

"The marshal had the doctor examine your son's body. He's pretty sure it was venom from a sting of some sort—likely a vinegarroon scorpion. I'm very sorry, Mr. Bailey. You have my condolences."

Frank dead. His mouth cotton-dry, Big Jack worked to form his words. "What…where? Where did it happen?"

"At your old home."

Big Jack sucked in a breath. Sonofabitch. That's just where he'd have taken that goddamned dressmaker. "Was she with him?"

"She?"

"The dressmaker! Frank was to take care of her."

"If your son was somehow involved with a lady when he died, my brother never mentioned it."

Oh, he'd been involved all right, and somehow that goddamned dressmaker had turned the tables on his Frank. His only son.

It hit him then. Grief and rage and fury and anguish packed a punch that knocked his knees right out from under him. As he sank slowly to the floor, he seized upon one thought like a lifeline.

The woman. That goddamned bad-luck Jenny Fortune.

*She was going to pay.*

"PLEASE, EMMIE!" Maribeth begged. "Papa said there are five different entrances to the secret passageway and I've only found four. Uncle Tye showed me one, but he says I have to find the last one by myself. I've looked and looked and looked, but I can't find it. Please, Emmie? Uncle Tye says you knew the passage at the old house like the back of your hand. You could find this one for me. I'm certain of it."

"No, Maribeth." Emma looked up from the book she was reading. "I've told you before. I don't want to go inside those tunnels. They're creepy and I don't like them."

Maribeth put her hands on her hips. "How do you know? You haven't gone inside Willow Hill's secret passages once. How do you know you don't like them?"

"I just know."

"You're just chicken."

Emma tossed her head and returned her gaze to her book.

Maribeth put her hands in her armpits and flapped her arms, squawking, *"Bawk-bawk-bawk. Bawk-bawk-bawk."*

"Stop it." Emma slammed her book shut. She'd tolerate a lot from her sister, but being called chicken wasn't one of them. "Just because I think before doing something doesn't mean I'm not brave. It means I'm not stupid. I'd never climb a tree after pecans that weren't ready to fall, Maribeth. They're not good eating. It'd be stupid to go after them if you can't eat them."

Maribeth's eyes blazed. "Don't you be calling me stupid. I never said I was after pecans. You're just saying that because you're trying to make me forget that you're too much a 'fraidy cat to go into my secret passageway."

"It's not your secret passageway."

Maribeth shrugged. "Might as well be. I'm the only one who goes inside."

"That's what you think."

"What do you mean?"

"What about the ghost?"

"Ghost? There's no such thing. Besides, this is a brand-new house. We don't have any ghosts."

Emma lifted her chin and lied. "But this hill used to be a graveyard. Papa only told me because he knew you'd be scared."

"Scared? Me?" Maribeth laughed. "Now I know you're lying. Papa knows I'm never scared. I'm nothing like you, Emma. I'm no 'fraidy cat."

"If that's what you want to think, go ahead." Emma opened her book and acted as if she were reading.

Maribeth drew herself up regally. "Liar, liar, pants on fire. My secret passageway doesn't have ghosts. You're just chicken, Emmaline Suzanne." With another pair of squawks, she left the room.

And Emma fumed. She fumed for the rest of the day. Every

time her sister saw her, Mari did that chicken-wing act with her arms. Emma thought Katrina must be giving Maribeth lessons, because every squawk became more and more dramatic. It made Emma downright furious.

But it was the chicken feathers on her dinner plate that made her overcome her fear. She dared not allow Maribeth's challenge to go unmet any longer. Otherwise, she'd be hearing squawks and eating feathers for years.

Emma decided to plant a ghost in the tunnel.

She waited until after Jenny had tucked her sisters in bed and gone downstairs to share an evening cup of chocolate with Uncle Tye. Then, candle in hand, Emma gathered her supplies, clenched her teeth, and entered the hidden passage.

It smelled like new wood, not musty old dust, and this tunnel didn't seem near as big as the one in her memory. This one was kind of cozy, in fact. The steps leading downstairs didn't even creak.

In a moment of honesty, she admitted that she had been afraid to enter the tunnel. Every time she even thought about ducking into the spaces, she started to shiver. She didn't know why, exactly. It had something to do with her mother—her real mother—and the hidden corridors in the house back in South Carolina.

"Well, I'm not afraid anymore," she whispered to herself, hiking the coil of rope up higher on her shoulder. She'd rig the "ghost" near the parlor entrance. That was right below Maribeth's bedroom, and with any luck the sounds would wake her during the night.

Emma whistled beneath her breath and went to work, imagining how she'd scare her chicken-squawking sister half to death. She was almost finished when, from the other side of the wall, she heard Jenny's muffled voice mention her name.

Emma stopped what she was doing and listened for a moment. An old memory tugged at her mind and made her stomach hurt.

*Forget it, Emma. There is nothing to be afraid of here. It's just like the spy hole at the other house, only better because it goes all over Willow Hill.*

She lifted her chin. She'd venture into the passageway any time she wanted, by gosh. No stomachache ever got the best of Emma McBride.

TWO LOUD BLASTS of a whistle announced the train's approach to Fort Worth's Texas & Pacific station. While the axles turned, the brakes squealed, and a figure stepped out into the vestibule, waiting for the car to slow. He ended up jumping too soon, but he landed with catlike grace to the accompaniment of a railroad official's disparaging holler.

Trace didn't pause long enough to wave at the man or collect his baggage. He didn't even wait to hire a wagon. He'd been cooped up on the train since early that morning, and he could use a brisk walk. Besides, he could make it to Willow Hill in five minutes on foot. A ride wouldn't get him there any faster.

He was anxious to get home—eager to see his children and impatient as hell to bed his wife.

What would Jenny say about his success? He came home having been named the architect for both the Hill County and Wise County courthouses. Would she think the time away from home well spent?

Yes. Jenny was his greatest supporter. She'd be proud of him.

Willow Hill came into sight and Trace broke into a jog. The parlor windows glowed golden with light, a beacon in the deepening dusk. The wind that whistled through the trees carried the faintest hint of laughter, and Trace knew a warmth inside his chest that had nothing to do with physical exertion.

Home. Family. He missed it more than he ever would have guessed. And while it didn't paint him in the most favorable light, he wouldn't deny he liked the idea of his family missing him too.

After all, who else would help Maribeth with throwing a ball? Who else would play tickle monster with Kat? Who else would know when Emmie needed a daddy's proud wink? And who else would give Jenny a kiss to make her melt?

Trace misstepped on that last thought, and only a bit of good luck and a tree trunk handy for balance kept him from falling.

The front door opened beneath his touch with a quiet whoosh. Trace shook his head, determined to scold the ladies of the house about leaving the place unlocked. Stepping inside, Trace shut the door silently behind him, figuring to make his homecoming a surprise.

A low murmur of voices came from the parlor. Then, a laugh. Jenny's laugh. She said, "I can't believe you did that. Her husband must have been livid."

A low-pitched masculine voice replied, "Yes, he was, and rightfully so."

Bart Rogers. In Willow Hill's front parlor. Picturing the rough, hard-scrabble man trying to wield one of Jenny's little teacups made him grin.

The man's voice continued, "The woman made a fool of him in front of the entire town."

Trace's smile faded. *No. It couldn't be.* The warmth—the welcome—dripped from his bones like melting wax. He stood motionless, emotionless, while minutes passed as hours. Then the man's voice sounded once again and icy cold gripped his heart.

Fear. It was a monster that had breathed inside him all these years. A monster that propelled him toward the doorway where he halted unnoticed and gazed at the man he'd prayed he'd never see again.

Silently, he screamed, *Katrina...*

Aloud, in a voice as cold as his dying dreams, he said, "Thackery. I'd hoped I killed you."

Even as Jenny's stomach sank, even as dread skimmed

across her skin, she gazed from her husband to his brother, then back to Trace once more and marveled. She'd never seen two people look so much alike.

Right down to the murder gleaming in their eyes.

What was this? Tye had said he'd come here to make peace. Rising from her seat beside the fire, Jenny sought to defuse the tension vibrating in the room. "Welcome home, darling."

Trace ignored her, hurling his words at his brother. "Get the hell out of my house."

Tye settled against the sofa as though he owned it. "Not until I get what I've come for, brother dear."

Trace's hands fisted. "You goddamned stinking piece of—"

"Papa! You're home!"

Jenny looked toward the entry hall where she spotted three sets of feet scampering down the staircase. She glared first at Trace, then at Tye. "Watch what you say. Think of the children, for goodness' sakes."

Tye's casual pose disappeared as he shot to his feet and squared off against his brother. "I am," he said flatly. "That's why I'm here."

Trace spat a curse and lunged toward his twin.

"Wait!" Jenny called.

The girls barrelled into the parlor, the older two girls crying, "Papa!"

Katrina put her hands on her hips and shouted, "Don't you hurt my daddy!"

In the process of throwing a punch, both men froze, identical stricken expressions on their faces. A shudder of unease swept over Jenny. Something frightening was happening here. Something she didn't understand.

Stepping forward, she spoke to the girls in a voice that brooked no argument. "Go back upstairs, ladies. Your father will be up in a few minutes to say hello."

"No, I'll go up now." Trace stepped away from Tye, his

smoldering gaze never leaving his brother's as his daughters filed past him, curious and concerned expressions on their faces. "My girls come first with me—now and always. I want you gone by the time I get back downstairs."

Tye straightened the lapels on his jacket. "That's too damn bad. I've been staying here, you know. I've been getting to know the girls."

A muscle worked in Trace's jaw, and Jenny thought his glare looked lethal.

"I'm going upstairs with my daughters," Trace said coldly. "Don't be here when I come down. I'm not the same man I was six years ago. This time, I'll make sure you're dead." With that, he turned and followed the girls up the winding staircase.

For a moment, neither of them moved. Then Jenny reeled on Tye. "What in heaven's name is going on here? I thought you came here to reconcile with him!"

He wore the sullen look of an angry little boy caught in the middle of wrongdoing.

"Well?" Jenny said when he didn't respond.

He muttered a curse and raked his fingers through his hair. "He caught me off guard, sneaking in like that. And didn't you hear him? First time he sees me in six lousy years, all he has to say is, 'I'd hoped I killed you.' It touched a nerve. I reacted badly."

"'Badly' doesn't quite say enough." Jenny heaved a frustrated sigh. "If you two aren't just alike—bullheaded and hot tempered."

Tye shrugged.

After a brief moment of thought, Jenny crossed the room to a small secretary where she withdrew a ring of keys from a drawer. Removing one, she said, "This is the key to the apartment above my shop where Trace and the girls lived before we moved into Willow Hill. We've left many of the furnishings, so you should be comfortable there until we get this all figured out."

Tye shook his head. "I'm not leaving, Jenny. One way or the other, Trace and I are having this out."

"Having what out? What is going on between you two that I don't understand?"

He opened his mouth, then hesitated. "Maybe you're right. Trace never did listen worth a darn when he got riled." He accepted the key she offered and gave her hand a squeeze. "I'll go, for now. It won't take me long to pack. I guess it's probably better to give him a little time to get used to the idea of my having found him."

When he returned with his bags a few minutes later, Jenny stopped him in the entry hall. "What did you mean 'found him'?"

At the door, Tye paused and looked over his shoulder. "He ran off, Jenny. Took the girls and disappeared. You can tell him something for me. Tell him it won't be like last time. Now that I've found him, I won't let him vanish again. He and I have things to settle between us, and I won't rest until it's done."

On that cryptic note, Tye McBride left Willow Hill.

Jenny turned and gazed up the staircase, gripped by both weariness and apprehension. Unwilling to face the ghosts in the parlor, she slowly climbed the stairs. Questions whirled in her mind, piquing her temper. Why was it always questions where her husband was concerned? Would he ever provide answers?

Her head hurt and she slowly tugged the pins from her hair, massaging her scalp as she entered the master bedroom. She recalled the look on her husband's face when he gazed at his brother, and she shivered. In the space of a heartbeat, she had seen his fear. That frightened her more than any of the bitter words spoken by either man.

What troubles had she invited into their home along with Tye McBride?

"It's Trace's fault," she grumbled, taking a seat at her vanity and unwinding her braid. "If he hadn't been so secretive about everything, I'd have known what to do."

Lifting her hairbrush, she gazed into the mirror and saw in her features a reflection of the fear in her husband's eyes. When he entered their room a few minutes later, she'd reached a decision.

She'd ask her questions and have her answers. Tonight. No matter what.

But she was too slow and Trace asked first. "Why, Jenny? Why did you let him into the house?"

She twisted in her seat to look at him. "What reason did I have not to welcome him to Willow Hill? None that I know of, certainly. I think I'm the one who needs to ask the questions. Why did you never tell me about your brother, your *twin* brother?"

He didn't answer. Turning away, he stripped off his tie and jacket and pitched them to the floor. Yanking at his buttons, he opened his mouth, closed it, then opened it again. Still, he didn't speak.

"What?" Jenny asked. "You obviously have something on your mind, and I seriously doubt it's an answer to anything I asked. What is it?"

The question seemed to burst from his mouth. "Did you bed down with him?"

For a long moment, Jenny was speechless. How could he even think such a thing, much less say it? She pushed from her chair and advanced on him, the heat of her anger drying her tears in an instant. "Blast you, McBride! If you're not the biggest fool in Texas, then I shudder to think who is. Did I sleep with him? Arrgh!" She hit him with her hairbrush. "Stupid, stupid, stupid."

He grabbed the brush from her hand and tossed it on the bed.

"What is wrong with you, anyway?" she continued. "Didn't we have a similar discussion right before you left town? Did you leave your brain in Hill County? You make me want to scream!"

Jenny paced the room, waving her arms. "He's your *brother*. Why wouldn't I welcome him to your house? You've never told me any reason not to. You never even told me the man existed, for that matter." She stopped in front of him and declared, "I've given you no reason to be jealous, Trace McBride. No reason to be suspicious. I'm not a faithless woman and you know that. I vowed to love and honor you, to be faithful to you. I'm your wife." She thumped her chest with her fist. "Your *wife*."

He snorted, and she considered hitting him again. "And Tye is your brother, for goodness' sakes. Why would you walk into a room and see us drinking cups of hot cocoa and immediately assume we were involved in something illicit?"

"Because it happened before!" He swept up her hairbrush and threw it across the room where it smashed against the wall and fell in two pieces. "My *faithful* wife and my *devoted* brother were lovers."

Jenny stood paralyzed in the center of the room. Of course! She should have seen it before. All the clues had been there.

Trace approached her, his smile bitter. "I don't know how long it had gone on. Months, maybe. Once I discovered the truth—" his fists clenched repeatedly at his sides "—I killed her."

A painful knot tightened in Jenny's chest. "Oh, Trace."

"I came close to killing him, too," he said, a far-off look in his eyes. "The punch I threw knocked him against the fireplace."

He slowly shook his head. "God, so much blood in that room. Like the war all over again. He lay still as a corpse— still as Constance—and I died right along with him." He fell silent, his expression ravaged at the memory.

Her heart ached for him; her arms yearned to hold him. But Trace held himself separate, alone, and she sensed he would not welcome her touch. Moisture stung her eyes. "You thought he was dead until tonight?"

"No. Once I figured out he was breathing, that the blood on him was Constance's, I left."

"He told me you vanished."

Trace loosed a shuddering breath. "I thought my family was safe. After all this time, I quit looking over my shoulder. I thought we could have a real life."

Jenny could bear it no more. She went to him, clasped his arm. "Is the law after you?"

His brows arched in surprise. "The law? Why—oh, I see what you're thinking. Murder." He chuckled humorlessly. "No, I kept tabs on that. They ruled the shooting accidental because I was struggling with Constance when the gun went off."

"Then why—"

"Why are we not safe?" His expression turned to granite and his voice went hoarse. "Because of him. Because of that goddamn bastard brother of mine. I won't let him have her. We'll run again, only this time we'll go so fast and so far he'll never find us."

"What are you talking about?"

He squared his shoulders. "You don't have to come with us, of course. Fort Worth is your home." A thread of steel entered his voice. "But I won't let him take Katrina. I can't kill him. I already tried that, and I couldn't do it right. Our only choice is to run."

He actually thought he could leave her behind? The fool. The silly fool. Jenny clutched his shirtsleeves and shook him. "What do you mean, you won't let him have Katrina? What does Katrina have to do with all this?"

"She has everything to do with this!" he said through his teeth. "She's the reason it all happened. He wants to take her from me."

"How could he do that?"

His eyes grew stormy, turbulent, and gleamed with a sheen of tears. His anguished voice broke as he answered. "She's his, treasure. I'm not her father. Katrina is my brother's daughter."

*A new penny brings good luck.*

## CHAPTER SEVENTEEN

AT THE END of a near sleepless night Jenny awoke to a day dawned blustery and cold. Over her objections, Trace saddled up Ranger and left Willow Hill at first light, headed for the Acre to see a man who had connections in Mexico.

Jenny felt torn. Although she had assured her husband she'd follow him to the ends of the earth if need be, she'd argued against their leaving Fort Worth. She'd repeated Tye's statement that he'd find them should they attempt to flee. Trace had brushed off the warning, but Jenny wasn't convinced. She had observed the determination in his brother's eyes.

For all the secrets he'd kept since showing up in her backyard, Tye didn't strike her as the villain Trace painted him to be. She'd lain awake most of the night reflecting on the man's behavior during his visit, and she'd reached a number of conclusions.

Tye would not attempt to separate the girls, for one thing. He'd displayed affection toward all the children—not just Katrina. Secondly, she still believed Tye meant what he said when he claimed to want a reconciliation with Trace. Surely, if he wanted to heal the rift between them, he wouldn't be planning to rip Katrina from the bosom of the only family she'd ever known.

Trace was reacting to a threat that, in Jenny's opinion, didn't exist. He had refused to listen to any of her arguments, and by forbidding her to see his brother again, he'd made it easy for her to go visit Tye. She would give up most everything for the man she loved—she'd run to Mexico, if need be—but she would never abdicate her independence.

The day she allowed him to dictate who she could and could not see, who she could or could not talk to, would be the day she lost herself. She loved being Mrs. Trace McBride, but a part of her—that deepest, most basic part of her soul—would always be Jenny Fortune.

And Jenny Fortune decided to speak with Tye McBride.

She was buttoning her shoes when she heard a knock at her bedroom door. "Yes?"

The door cracked open, revealing Emma's worried frown. "Mama, can I talk to you for a minute?"

Jenny nodded. "Certainly, as long as you're quick about it. I don't want you late for school."

Emma shut the door behind her, then stood shuffling, gazing at her feet, her hands clasped behind her back. Jenny waited expectantly, then finally said, "Emma?"

The girl's head came up. Her eyes shone with guilt. She said in a rush, "Last night I was in the passageway rigging Mari's ghost and I heard you and Papa talking about Katrina. I knew I had to tell you, because last time I didn't, and all the bad things were my fault. I'm sorry I eavesdropped, Mama, and I promise to never, ever do it again. Please don't be mad at me!"

Jenny grimaced and closed her eyes in misery. Did she understand what Emma was saying? She'd overheard the truth of Katrina's parentage? This wasn't good. Not good at all. Katrina mustn't hear this news prematurely, and a secret of this magnitude should not be borne by a twelve-year-old. "Blast those hidden passages anyway," she mumbled.

"I'm sorry, Mama." Tears slipped down her face. "So sorry. Please don't be mad."

Compassion flared in Jenny's heart and she gave the girl a hug. "I'm not mad, darling, just worried. Now, you must promise not to say anything to your sisters about this. I have to think about what to do. It's getting late. You need to run on to school."

Her voice trailed off as she added, "I have to go somewhere myself."

Emma's tears didn't stop, and Jenny was at a loss as to how to deal with them. She was new at this mothering; she'd so much to learn. And a problem of this magnitude—a crack in the very foundation of her family—was more than she knew how to manage. "Your father will talk to you about this later, Emma. Go to school and try not to worry too much, all right?"

Jenny spoke to herself as much as to Emma. Trace would have to solve the problem of what their daughter had overheard. She planned to devote herself to avoiding a move to Mexico.

Donning a cloak, Jenny went downstairs to the kitchen. Trace had asked her to give Mrs. Wilson the day off, and she decided to accede to his wishes on this point. Only this point.

The housekeeper happily accepted the unexpected holiday and promised to see the girls off to school before leaving for the day.

A chilly wind whipped at her hem as Jenny walked toward the centre of town. Her stomach turned as she passed a small café, and the aroma of frying bacon and eggs swirled around her. She swallowed hard against the nausea and hurried on, concentrating on the arguments she intended to present to Tye.

First she would ask if what Trace had told her was true. She didn't want to believe that Tye had, in fact, betrayed his brother in such a fundamental way.

As she approached the building she noticed a light in the window above her shop. Good. Luck was with her in that he'd come here and not gone to a hotel. She didn't have time to check all the hotels in Fort Worth for a missing brother-in-law.

The front door to Trace's old quarters was locked, and Jenny rapped loudly on the glass, calling, "Tye? Tye McBride? I need to talk to you." She waited, and the hair on the back of her neck slowly prickled.

It's the cold air, she told herself as she glanced over first one shoulder, then the other.

She banged on the door again. "Tye? It's Jenny. Open up, please."

She heard a noise from inside, then the thud of boot steps descending the stairs. She opened her mouth to sound a greeting when she suddenly sensed the figure approaching from behind. Before she could turn around a hand gripped her upper arm, and the cold, hard barrel of a gun pressed against her side.

"Careful now, missy, or I'll blow a hole in both you and your husband right here."

Jenny's blood ran cold. Big Jack Bailey. *Dear Lord, not again.*

The door swung open and Tye stood on the other side. Bailey said, "Good morning, there, McBride. You shouldn't be letting your wife run around without a key. Never know when somebody might get the jump on her."

Tye's eyes narrowed. "Who are you? What do you want?"

Bailey gave an evil smile. "Who am I? Come now, McBride, don't play the fool."

Jenny licked her lips and said, "He's not Trace, Mr. Bailey. You're making a mistake. This is my husband's twin brother. You have no quarrel with him. You can let him go."

"Do you think I'm stupid or something, Dressmaker?"

Bailey asked, the gun barrel digging into her side. "Come along, now. I have a wagon waiting in the alley, and the three of us are gonna walk nice and peaceful-like around back."

"Why don't we go upstairs and discuss this problem," Tye suggested casually, eyeing the gun. "I'm in the middle of eating breakfast, and you're welcome to share."

"Nope. I've a job for you to do. Afterward, we're gonna return to the scene of your crime for a few questions and answers."

"Crime? What crime?" Tye gave Jenny a sharp, curious look.

She ignored him, all her attention centered on Big Jack Bailey. He can't know, she told herself. He might suspect the truth, but unless she confirmed his suspicions, surely he wouldn't hurt her.

Or would he? Jenny gave Bailey a sidelong glance and remembered the dressmaker dummy hanging from her porch.

Bailey motioned for them to move. "Come along, now. Daylight's a'wastin'. The four of us are taking a cozy little ride."

"Four of us?" Jenny asked quickly, her first thought of the girls. *Please let all of them be safe.*

They rounded the corner of the building, and she spotted a wagon with a tarpaulin covering the back. Bailey gestured with the gun. "You, me, your husband, and my boy. Damned sheriff buried him at Pioneer's Rest and I had to pay the mortuary to dig him back up. Frank needs to be at home at the Lucky Lady, and since you killed him, I figured you should do the burying."

"Jenny?" Tye asked.

She glanced at him and shook her head, not knowing exactly what she was denying. Silently cursing Big Jack's twisted logic, she closed her eyes and shuddered at the idea of traveling with Frank Bailey's body.

Big Jack told Tye to drive. He sat Jenny between them, his gun never leaving her side. "Take Throckmorton down to Fourteenth and head west," he said. "Just keep in mind that your wife will pay if you do anything to attract attention."

Bailey smiled and nodded to the people they passed. Jenny held her breath when Wilhemina Peters called out for them to stop. Bailey muttered to Tye to keep on going, then hollered back, "Don't have time, now, ma'am. Nice hat you're wearing today."

Once the wagon was away from town, Bailey climbed into the back and sat on the tarp-draped coffin. He shifted his gun from Jenny to Tye, then back to Jenny again. "You know, McBride. You should have known better than to marry her."

His evil chuckle sent shivers up Jenny's spine as he added, "Good Luck Wedding Dress, my ass."

TRACE WALKED into Willow Hill with five train tickets to Galveston in his vest pocket and a satchel full of money in his hand. He'd tried his damnedest to shut down his emotions, but entering this house knowing he'd be leaving it all too soon was a boot to the gut.

"Jenny," he called, pausing a moment to listen for her reply. Silence. He frowned and checked his pocket watch. Three hours yet before the girls finished school. He'd have thought she'd be here sorting and packing things to take with them. "I bet she's gone to the shop," he murmured, inspecting the kitchen. A conscientious woman like Jenny would want to clear off her books before leaving town. She wasn't the type to leave her customers high and dry.

He glanced down the hall toward his office. He didn't like abandoning his clients either, but a man had to put his family first. At least the timing of this was good. He'd made arrangements this morning to put the house up for sale, and the agent had advanced him a nice amount of cash. At least this time when the McBrides fled a town, they'd do so with a little money in their pocket.

He found the note in his bedroom telling him she'd gone

to the Rankin Building on an errand. Sure enough, he was right. She'd probably bring home half of Fortune's Design's fabric inventory with her.

He spent the next hours packing and trying to come up with a good explanation to give the girls for their abrupt departure. The entire time, he was conscious of his wife's absence and a niggling unease prodded his spine.

Had Jenny changed her mind and decided not to go? Maybe so, but she'd tell him straight to his face. It wasn't like her to dodge issues of any sort.

By the time his daughters arrived home from school, he had everyone's bags ready to go. He told his children the lie he'd concocted about a holiday, hoping to make their departure from Fort Worth a little easier to manage.

With everything ready and the train due to leave in less than an hour, he said, "I'm going to make a quick run down to your mother's dress shop. She must have gotten tied up with a customer and lost track of time."

Excited about the upcoming journey, the girls failed to notice his concern. He added a warning before leaving the house. "If she gets here before I come back, don't let her out of your sights, all right?"

"Sure, Papa," they agreed.

His unease grew all the way to town. He found Fortune's Design locked up tight with the closed sign hanging in the window. It didn't look as if she'd been there all day. Then he noticed the light burning in a window upstairs. Why would anyone be upstairs? Jenny had the only key other than his own. What would she be doing... *Tye.*

Anger surged through him. If she'd gone to Tye he'd kill them both. He tested the door and found it unlocked. Then he bounded upstairs.

He recognized the pair of revolvers slung over the back of a chair, and his gaze swung immediately toward his old bedroom. He started down the hall. He heard her voice in his mind. *Trust me, Trace.*

He was trying. Good Lord, he was trying.

He approached the bedroom door, his emotions a mixture of confidence and fear. Taking a deep breath, he stepped inside.

Relief washed over him like flood waters in spring. The room was empty but for an unmade bed and a man's clothes scattered haphazardly across the room. Tye never had learned to pick his britches up off the floor.

Just to be thorough, Trace checked the loft and wandered through the other rooms, pausing at the mess in the kitchen and the plate of flapjacks half eaten. He didn't like the look of that. Tye McBride might not pick up his clothes, but he never left a plate of pancakes half eaten. What was going on here? Where was his brother?

More importantly, where was his wife?

The name he'd done his best not to think about rose like a demon in his mind. Big Jack Bailey.

In his heart, he knew. Trace ran for the marshal's office. *Take care of her, Tye. Please, keep her safe.*

"THIS IS the prettiest spot on the entire ranch." Pride rang in Big Jack Bailey's voice as the wagon rolled to a stop atop an evergreen-dotted bluff overlooking the Brazos River valley.

Tye spied the iron fence that surrounded a small plot of land. Inside the rails, two monuments stood side by side, and he concluded that this was the family cemetery.

Bailey confirmed his suspicions by saying, "That's my Lilah Mae's resting place. The son she died aborning is laid next to her." He cleared his throat, then jumped from the wagon. "I want Frank on the other side of his mother." From beneath the tarpaulin, he removed two shovels. Tossing them to the ground, he used his gun to wave Tye down from the wagon. "Here you go, McBride. One for you and one for the little lady."

Tye scowled. "I'll dig your grave, Bailey. There's no call for Jenny to be doing that type of work."

"Nope." Big Jack shook his head. "She works, too. Hell, I wanted her to dig it by herself, but I figured we'd be here till Christmas if I made her do it alone. I don't have the time to waste; I'm needed in New Orleans. My daughter has recently delivered me a grandson, and I aim to make certain he is raised right. With his daddy's family connections, that boy'll be in the White House one day. Now, daylight's a'wastin'."

He glanced toward the sky. "Well, would you look at those clouds. 'Blessed are the dead the rain falls on.' I knew this was my lucky day. Get to digging."

Tye judged the distance between him and his captor, and impotent rage coursed through him. Damn. For all his apparent inattention, the man was canny when it came to keeping Jenny under his gun.

*Patience, McBride,* he told himself. This Bailey character would let down his guard sooner or later.

Jenny squeezed his shoulder as he helped her down from the wagon. "It's all right, Tye. A little bit of digging won't hurt me." She lifted one of the shovels and headed for the graveyard.

"Come on, man!" he protested, glaring at Bailey. "The woman's in a family way. She can't be doing hard labor like that."

Bailey shrugged. "Keep your mouth shut and get to work. Her condition don't mean squat because you'll both be dead by sundown. The only question remaining is how hard the dyin' is gonna be."

Rage rose like bile in Tye's throat. He shifted his gaze toward Jenny, trying to reassure her. He'd be damned if he'd allow this sonofabitch to kill them. He had no intentions of dying. Not now. Not when his family was once again within reach.

"Now, grab hold of Frank. You're gonna carry him over beside his mama. And don't get any fancy ideas. I'm keeping my Colt pointed at the dressmaker's heart."

Tye quietly directed Jenny to grasp the foot end. Taking as much of the weight as he could manage, he and his brother's wife unloaded the coffin and toted it inside the fence.

"You all right?" he asked as they set the burying box down. She nodded. "Let's just get this done."

Bailey scooped up the second shovel and tossed it at Tye. "Get to work, McBride. I want my boy buried before sunset."

Tye caught the spade, wishing he could fling it back at Bailey, but knowing he didn't dare. Jenny was still in harm's way. "Fine. But I'll do it. There's no reason for Jenny to dig—"

Bailey shot the dirt near Jenny's feet. "There's the reason."

Tye cursed beneath his breath, the need to fly at Jack Bailey nearly overwhelming. Jenny placed her hand on his arm, gave him a reassuring smile, and spoke in a low voice. "Actually, I don't mind the idea of digging a grave for Frank Bailey. I was with him when he died. Somehow, it seems right."

Tye snorted and buried the shovel in the soft dirt. She'd told him a little bit about the night the gunslinger died. In his opinion, the local folk should throw her a parade.

Perched atop the wagon seat, Big Jack's attention never wavered. He started telling stories about his children, from the time they were youngsters up to all the details of his new grandson's birth. Never once did he put down his gun.

Tye knew if he waited long enough and watched closely, the opportunity to catch the man off guard would arise. Perhaps when they lowered the coffin into the ground, he mused. Bailey was liable to be distracted then. It might well be his best chance.

He doubled his efforts and began to make good headway on digging the grave. Glancing over his shoulder to check Jenny's progress, he frowned. She looked as white and whipped as Sunday mashed potatoes. "Jenny?"

Her smile wobbled. "This is hard on a person's back, isn't it. But I'm all right, Tye. Don't worry."

Don't worry hell. If her back was hurting, could that mean something was wrong with the baby? He plunged his shovel into the dirt. Damn. He shouldn't have waited to make his move.

"Hey, Bailey," he called. "My side's deep enough. Mrs. McBride and I are going to trade places." Without waiting for a reply, he slipped beside Jenny. "Don't be afraid," he said softly. "I won't let him hurt you. If anything happens, hit the ground. It should be deep enough to shield you if bullets start to fly."

Jenny nodded and they worked for a few more minutes. Then, as he bent to shovel another load of dirt, he saw her grimace. "Jenny?"

Worry dulled her blue eyes as she looked at him and said, "I hope your moment comes soon, Tye. I'm a bit worried about my baby."

That's it, he thought. This nonsense had gone on long enough. He set down his shovel and lifted her into his arms, then laid her gently on the ground behind him.

"What the hell you doin', boy?" Big Jack Bailey called.

"She's done enough digging."

Tye prayed Bailey would let it go, but it wasn't to be. He jumped down from the wagon, his face mottled red with rage. "She'll never do enough to make up for what she's done. She killed my son!"

Tye shielded his brother's wife. "That's a lie, Big Jack. A scorpion got him. The doctor in town says so."

"The doctor doesn't know shit. She did it. She's a jinx!"

He approached the grave, his furious stare raking Jenny. "The first accidents were bad enough, but when I got that telegram about Mary Rose, I knew you had to be stopped. I sent Frank after you and what happens? He turns up dead."

His gun hand trembled with the force of his fury, and his voice cracked as he said, "Now I have a new grandson, one who has the chance to go places. I'll not allow him to be put at risk."

"You're wrong, Mr. Bailey!" Jenny said, rising to her feet. "My luck—good or bad—had nothing to do with any of the accidents that happened to your family."

"Jenny," Tye said in a cautious tone, worried at the look on the other man's face.

"Liar!" Bailey cried, raising his gun. He pulled the trigger and a bullet whistled past Tye's ear. "You're lying. You're just trying to save your skin. Well, it's too damned late for that. I have to stop you. I can't have you hurting my grandson."

Tye watched Big Jack Bailey's eyes glaze and reacted immediately. Muttering a curse, he lunged for Jenny. He grasped her by the shoulders and tugged her into the grave an instant before a bullet whistled by her head. He covered her with his body. Another bullet smacked into the ground behind them. "Keep as low as you can. To get the angle on us to shoot, he has to come closer. No matter what happens, I want you to lie flat. You with me?"

She nodded.

Tye gripped the shovel's handle and listened hard. He heard Jack Bailey approach. Sucking in a single deep breath, he gave a loud rebel yell and vaulted from the grave.

As he swung the shovel, he saw the gun swivel toward him. Pain slammed into him, and he smelled the coppery scent of his own blood even as the shovel connected with Jack Bailey's head.

The man fell like an oak. Tye bent over and tried to catch his wind. Glancing down, he saw the stain seep across his shirt. Well, hell, he thought, just before darkness consumed him.

A WRENCHING PAIN gripped Trace's shoulder as he left the marshal's office. *Tye.* His brother had been hurt. He knew it as well as he knew his own name.

The fear that had churned inside him since beginning the search for Jenny intensified. He knew in his gut she was somewhere with Tye. He knew in his heart that they both were in trouble. He'd done his damnedest to convince Courtright of the same.

The marshal said Bailey hadn't returned to Fort Worth. Courtright kept a pretty good eye on the comings and goings in town, but he couldn't know everything. Instinct told Trace Big Jack had Jenny, and instinct was telling him to ride for the Lucky Lady.

He'd extracted a promise from the marshal to take the girls to Mrs. Wilson's as a precautionary measure and begin a search of the town just in case Trace was wrong. He headed back to Fortune's Design to retrieve his horse when he heard someone call his name. Glancing over his shoulder, he winced.

Wilhemina Peters was scurrying after him, pad and pencil in hand. "Mr. McBride, oh Mr. McBride. Please wait."

He continued his pace for another moment before halting abruptly. Of course! He should have thought of her first. Wilhemina Peters made a career out of having her nose in everybody's business but her own. If anyone knew anything about Jenny and Tye's whereabouts, Wilhemina would be the one. Valiantly, he tried to hide his panic as he offered her a smile. "Good morning."

"Good morning." Lifting one hand to hold her spectacles, she peered up at him intently. "Dear, dear, me. This does make my job more difficult. Which one are you? The architect/saloonkeeper or the brother?"

"I'm Trace, Mrs. Peters."

"Good, good, good. It's you I want to see then. I have questions for my column, you see. Now, first of all—"

Trace interrupted, "Mrs. Peters, I don't have much time. I'm looking for my wife. Have you seen her in town today?"

Wilhemina wrinkled her nose. "Don't be so impatient, sir. We certainly know where the Menaces inherit that unattractive trait, don't we?"

"Mrs. Peters—"

"Your wife is part of what I wish to speak with you about." She poised her pen above her paper and shot questions at Trace like a Gatling gun. "Have the fences been mended between her and the Baileys? Has the family finally accepted the change in the wedding dress's status? Is that the reason behind your trip with him this morning? Or has he retained your professional services? Has he hired you to design a new home? What can you tell me about his reaction to the death of that gunslinger son of his? I never liked that Frank, you know. He had mean, beady eyes."

"You saw me with Big Jack Bailey today." A cold chill stole across his soul at the confirmation of his suspicions.

"Well, of course I did. Don't you remember, Mr. Bailey commented on my hat. You were right there. You looked—" she broke off abruptly. "Oh. I see. It must have been your brother with your wife and Big Jack in that wagon headed out of town. That's interesting." She wrote furiously on her notepad. "What business does your brother have with Big Jack? I met your twin yesterday. Have I mentioned how much I like the man? Why, he told me—"

Trace's mind was racing. The Lucky Lady's main house lay to the southeast. The old homesite where Frank had taken Jenny, to the southwest. "You say you saw them leaving town together?"

Wilhemina scowled. "Interrupted me again, just like those Menaces. If a person doesn't—"

"Mrs. Peters!" Trace shouted, his patience completely gone. "This is important. Do you know which direction they were going?"

She snapped her notebook closed and pursed her lips in a sour-lemon look. "West. Southwest, actually. I must say, Mr. McBride, you've demonstrated a surprising lack of manners."

He was already rushing away. "Sorry, ma'am, but I don't have time for manners," he called over his shoulder. "I'm afraid Jenny is in danger."

*When you find a horseshoe, spit on it,*
*throw it over your left shoulder, and*
*without looking back to where it fell,*
*walk away and you will have seven*
*years' good luck.*

## CHAPTER EIGHTEEN

BLOOD COVERED Jenny's hands like heated cream. Silence gripped the afternoon as she closed her eyes and centered her attention on defeating the panic that threatened to consume her. She would not surrender to fear. Tye needed her. This child growing inside her needed her. The girls needed her.

Trace needed her.

She trembled, shaking like leaves in a gale. She wanted more than anything to lie on the ground and sob.

*Be strong, Jenny,* the words whispered in her mind. In her mother's voice, in Trace's voice. In those of Emma, Maribeth, and Katrina.

And they did their job. Purpose flowed into her, replacing the numbing fear. She opened her eyes and resumed her efforts, ripping another strip of cloth from her petticoat and binding it tightly around the wound in Tye's shoulder. When she moved his shirt, she'd discovered the round hole marking the spot where the bullet had entered his body. On the backside of his shoulder, its exit had created a bloody, man-gled mess. She'd applied pressure to the wound until the bleeding had slowed, then flushed it with water from the canteen in the wagon. *Please Lord, let this be enough.*

What she wouldn't give for a needle and thread right now. She had no idea how much blood a man could lose before it caused his death. Tye had lost so very much. At least, that's how it appeared to her. His shirt, her hands, even her dress, were stained red.

Jenny swallowed hard as she scrutinized the makeshift bandage for signs of bleeding. A minute passed. Two. She breathed a tentative sigh of relief.

Now, to deal with Big Jack.

She remembered the rope he had used to secure the coffin in the bed of the wagon. Standing, she tried to ignore the ache in her back as she hurried to retrieve it. Tying Bailey's hands and wrists required a good amount of pushing and rolling his unconscious weight, but finally she accomplished the task. As she backed away from his prone body, she was breathing hard. "You won't get loose. My embroidery knots never fail."

She pressed her hand to her back as she considered what to do next. She glanced toward the wagon where the horses, still skittish from the gunshots, snorted and pawed the ground. Should she take the buckboard and dash for town and a doctor for Tye? Unless he awoke she stood no chance of getting him in the wagon, but the idea of leaving him alone with Big Jack Bailey—no matter how securely tied—filled her with unease.

She gazed up toward the sky, judging the time. They had an hour, possibly two, before sunset. The cloud hanging on the northern horizon likely meant weather on the way. Still, she believed they had time enough to spare for a little rest. Tye needed it and she did, too. Instinct told her to get off her feet.

She sat on the ground beside Tye. His complexion was parchment pale and she touched his face gently, wishing she knew more about the healing arts.

Ripping a clean section of cloth from his discarded shirt, she dampened it with water, then gently bathed his brow, humming a soothing tune. She'd gone through all verses of four different songs before she realized that the ache in her back had lessened, and relief washed through her.

Then a groan of pain from Big Jack Bailey reminded her of a problem rest wouldn't cure. His body rolled, his biceps flexing as he attempted to move his arms. Curses spilled from his tongue. Slowly, he opened his eyes and fastened his gaze on Jenny. "Christ, woman," he groaned. "Now your bad luck has rubbed off on me."

Temper flared inside her at his words. "I am sick to death of hearing about the Bad Luck Wedding Dress, Jack Bailey!"

Blood dribbled from the cut across his forehead into his eye. He blinked hard and dipped his head toward his shoulder in a fruitless attempt to wipe it away. Jenny gave an exasperated sigh and stood. Rag in hand, she moved closer. "No funny moves, Mr. Bailey. I'm the only one here to help you so you'd best be nice to me."

"Nice to you?" He laughed without amusement, then yelped in pain when she touched the cloth to his head. "You're the one who has caused all my trouble."

"No, I am not." She grabbed hold of his upper arm and tugged him to a seated position. Making certain she had his attention, she said, "I didn't make anything happen. Life made it happen. That's what life is all about. People make mistakes; they get hurt. People die. But good things happen to them, too. They win contests, laugh at picnics. They fall in love. It's life!"

"Shut up. Just shut up! It's your fault Frank's dead. You sent the telegram saying Mary Rose was hurt, when all she was doing was having a baby, and now you're trying to make me believe that Frank's death was my fault."

"Mary Rose wasn't burned?"

"No. You know that. You sent the telegram, and now you know I'm going to hurt you, and you're trying to talk your way out of it."

Jenny swallowed her denial and stepped away. She reached into her pocket and withdrew the gun she'd retrieved from his hand while he was unconscious. "You need to get a grasp on reality, here, Mr. Bailey. I'm not the one who is tied up. I'm not the one who is unarmed. You cannot do me injury, not any longer. As soon as we get back to town, I'm going to turn you over to Marshal Courtright. He'll see that you—"

His smirk stopped her. Belligerence shone from his face. Wasn't he threatened by the law even a little bit? By the looks of him, no. Jenny recognized the danger.

She considered her options. If she hauled him into town and turned him over to the marshal, he'd certainly go to trial. Kidnapping and attempted murder were serious charges. But such action carried a definite risk. She had no guarantee he'd end up in prison. Bailey had the money to buy every juror in town if he wanted.

Even if he were convicted and sent to prison, eventually he'd be released. He'd be a threat to her and her loved ones all over again. That she could not abide. This needed to end here and now.

What, short of killing him, would eliminate the peril Big Jack Bailey posed to her family?

She folded her arms and stared at the man whose superstitions had caused her such grief. From the shamrock pin on his hatband to the horseshoe designs on his boots, Big Jack was nothing but trouble. Why, he—

She broke off abruptly. Superstitions. Of course! Superstitions ruled his life. All she need do was to use that quirk of his nature against him to solve her problems. She absently rubbed the small of her back as she considered how to go about it. The idea that came to her was mean, true, but not as mean as killing him, which was one option. And it wasn't as if she hadn't tried to explain the truth. The man simply refused to listen.

For her family's sake, she needed a permanent solution. He had brought this upon himself. She would not feel guilty for what she was about to do.

Jenny took a deep breath and said, "I had hoped not to do this, but you leave me no choice. You said Mary Rose had a baby boy?"

Bailey's eyes took on a wary look and he nodded.

"It'd be a shame for any of the Bailey bad luck to rub off on the innocent little baby, now wouldn't it?"

Fear kindled in his gaze. "What are you saying, lady?"

"Have you met my mother, Monique Day?" she asked innocently. "She's French, you know, and when I was a girl we spent some time with her family in the Caribbean."

Bailey's body jerked and he gasped. "Voodoo?"

Jenny folded her arms and smiled. "You shouldn't have quibbled over the price of the wedding dress, Mr. Bailey."

He strained against the rope. "You put a curse on it, didn't you? I knew it. You're a witch. A blond-headed witch."

"I am a seamstress, Mr. Bailey," she replied with a laugh. "I sew all sorts of garments. Ladies' dresses, gentlemen's suits." She paused significantly, then added, "Children's clothes."

"I'll kill you!"

She stepped close to him, bent down, and snapped the chain and pendant from around his neck. Swinging the gold rabbit's foot from side to side in front of his eyes, she dropped it into the pocket of her dress. "If you ever cause harm of any kind to me or to any of those I love, I guarantee that a similar injury will return to you and yours tenfold. That's not a threat, Big Jack. It's a promise. Now, do we understand each other?"

His eyes were round as teacups and brimming with fear. Jerkily, he nodded. She turned away, intending to see to Tye, and he spoke. The bravado in his voice couldn't hide his fright. "If it weren't for the boy, I'd fight you."

Jenny looked over her shoulder. In all seriousness, she said, "Family is everything, isn't it, Big Jack? I do believe we'll all go to great lengths to protect our families."

At that, a sharp pain low in her back brought her mind back to matters at hand. "I need help with my brother-in-law. That dark cloud to the north is moving faster than I had anticipated, and I want Tye sheltered before the weather worsens. I'll untie your hands, and you are going to lift him and place him gently into the wagon. And don't doubt I'll shoot if you try anything foolish, Big Jack. I'm not in the best of moods right now, and I'd love the excuse to do away with you once and for all."

"Wait a minute," Bailey said. "What about my son? We can't leave him like that."

Jenny glanced at the coffin and sighed. A little rain wasn't going to hurt them, but it was beginning to look as if she'd be spending the night in the cabin, and she had to admit she'd sleep better if Frank Bailey were in the ground.

"All right, you may bury him. But try anything and I'll shoot you, Big Jack." Cautiously, she untied his hands. While he freed his feet, she sat beside Tye, keeping the gun constantly trained on Big Jack as he clumsily maneuvered the coffin into the ground.

Jenny glanced toward the sky. "Hurry with the dirt, Mr. Bailey. I'll give you another five minutes and that's all."

He shoveled quickly, glancing warily at her throughout his efforts, and he finished within the time she'd allowed. "Be gentle with my brother-in-law," she instructed. "Do you understand?"

"He's really not your husband?" he asked, stooping over Tye.

"He's Trace's twin, and that makes him part of my family. Don't forget my promise."

Bailey grunted as he hoisted Tye into his arms and placed him in the wagon. "Your curse, you mean."

Jenny kept the gun trained on Big Jack as he drove them the short distance down the hill to the homestead cabin. Small and stark, it rose from the ground like a nightmare come to life. The last thing she wanted was to walk inside those walls and face the memories of the worst night of her life.

No, that isn't true, she thought, following Bailey and Tye inside. Tears stung her eyes as she finally admitted her greatest fear.

The last thing she wanted was to lose her baby.

The ache returned as soon as she'd stood. If she moved too fast or jounced herself at all, the drawing pain intensified. Even if weather wasn't bearing down on them, she had no business riding a wagon on the bumpy road back to town.

Be glad this cabin is here, Jenny McBride, she scolded herself. Instead of her nightmare, it might be her salvation.

She shuddered a bit as she walked through the door and her gaze went unerringly to the spot on the floor where Frank Bailey died. It was obvious someone had cleaned the cabin since that awful night. The layer of dirt had disappeared and a quilt lay across the bed. She hurried to pull down the covers, careful to keep her gun trained on Bailey.

"Fresh linen, too. Good." She gestured with the gun for Big Jack to lay Tye down. Her brother-in-law groaned as his shoulder hit the mattress and Jenny took that as a good sign. As long as he was moaning, he wasn't dead.

And as soon as she could lie down and put her feet up, she wouldn't have any more cramps. She wouldn't lose her baby.

"Take his boots off," she instructed Bailey. When he'd completed the task, she added, "Thank you. You may leave now, Mr. Bailey. Go to Fort Worth. In fact, go all the way to New Orleans."

His brow lifted in surprise. "You're letting me go? Just like that?"

She shrugged. "I want you to take the first train or stage leaving town—after you stop by the doctor's office and send him out to me."

"But—"

"Did you know voodoo is a form of religion?" she interrupted. "I prefer privacy when I...pray."

"You're not gonna curse my grandson! You promised."

"It's a delayed thing, Mr. Bailey," she said with a smile, pulling his chain from her pocket. "I'll feel better about our agreement once it's in place. You see, I don't quite trust you not to have a change of heart and attempt to continue your vendetta against me. Go on now. Take one of the horses, but leave the wagon. And don't forget to send the doctor."

"You want me to leave now? But it's miles back to town and there's weather moving in."

"You'd best get a start on it then." She swung the chain in a circle.

"But—"

She pinned him with a glare. "Not all curses are delayed ones. I could change it to begin immediately." The gun still aimed at Big Jack, she laid the chain on the table and said in a chant, "Oh, Methumiasma, goddess of stomach ills..."

Big Jack disappeared through the door in a flash.

Jenny heard a weak chuckle from the bed. "Methumiasma?"

She whirled around. "Oh, Tye, you're awake. Thank God!"

"Why not this Methumiasma? She seems to work miracles. She got rid of a snake in the blink of an eye."

Jenny smiled. "Methumiasma is an ingredient in a recipe for a make-believe cake Katrina concocts for her tea parties. How are you, Tye?"

"Weak as twice-steeped tea leaves," he replied. "I sure don't feel much like moving. How bad is it?"

The light inside the cabin dimmed as she gave a brief description of the wound. She was explaining about the voodoo threat when a strong cramp gripped her womb and she gasped.

"What is it?" Tye asked sharply.

"Nothing," she lied. "Just a twinge."

"You're holding your back. Does it hurt?"

Her worry escalated to fear when a second cramp struck her. "Yes," she said softly. "I'm afraid my back does hurt. It comes and goes, though. I'm certain I just need to sit down."

He mumbled a mouthful of curses. "It's all that digging, goddammit. You need to lie down, Jenny. Elevate your feet. Here, this is a big bed. I don't bite." Tye grimaced as he shifted over to one side. "Let's take care of that baby, all right?"

Jenny didn't argue. What difference did appearances make when her baby's life might well be at stake? Tears stung her eyes at the thought.

Removing her shoes, she climbed into bed. Old nightmares of escape attempts and scorpion stings faded from her mind as she prayed for the health and well-being of her expected child. She loved this baby already, and it would kill her to lose him.

Imagine how Trace must feel at the thought of losing Katrina.

For the first time in a while, Jenny thought of the news that had sent her looking for Trace's brother that morning. She observed Tye as he plucked the bandage against his bare skin, making a face when the action obviously caused him pain. "Leave it alone, Tye," she said. "You'll cause it to bleed again and you certainly don't need to lose any more blood. Your complexion is frightfully pale."

"I'll be fine. I've been through worse incidents before. If I haven't died yet, I won't. Give me an hour or two and I'll be good as new." He looked at her, concern written across his brow. "I'm more concerned about you. Do I need to go for a doctor?"

Jenny shook her head. He couldn't ride a horse in his condition. He'd fall off before he traveled a mile. "I'm better already," she said. "I think I needed a bit of rest myself."

"Are you sure?" He tested her temperature with the back of his hand.

Jenny smiled and batted his hand away. "I don't have a fever, Tye, I have a backache. I don't need a doctor. I'll be fine, really." Reaching over, she clasped his hand in hers. "If you want to help, hold my hand. I like knowing I'm not alone. It's been an eventful day and fear takes a lot out of a person."

Tye studied her face. "Are you still scared, Jenny?"

"No." She blinked away tears as she showed him a weary smile. "Well, maybe a little." After a pause, she met his gaze and softly confessed, "I don't want to lose my baby."

"I don't want you to lose your baby, either." He gripped her hand tightly. "It's a god-awful thing to happen to a person."

Long minutes passed in silence. Jenny had heard the pain in his voice, and since the subject was now broached, albeit in a roundabout way, she chose to ask her questions. "Is it, Tye? I hear it happened to you. Is it true?"

He shut his eyes. "Trace told you about Katrina," he said flatly.

"Last night." She rolled over on her side to better view his face. "He thinks you've come to take her away from him."

Again, silence stretched between them. Tye's voice challenged her as he asked, "What do you think?"

"I don't think you're the type of man who'd rip a child away from her family."

"He did it. Am I a better man than my brother?"

"I think you love your brother."

He stared up at the rafters and she could almost see him thinking. Finally, he said, "I'm tired, Jenny. I need to sleep, all right?"

What could she do? She couldn't force him to talk about

Trace. Besides, she could use a nap herself. Maybe her back-ache would disappear as she slept. Then she'd be free to con-centrate on the problem of Katrina's two fathers without distraction. "All right, Brother-in-law."

He gave her hand a squeeze as if to say thank you, but Jenny shook her head and warned, "Get your sleep, but don't think this is the end of it."

"You're a stubborn woman, Jenny McBride."

"I do what I do for my family."

He sighed. "So do I, honey. So do I."

On that note, they both dropped off to sleep.

THE COLD FRONT hung in a blue line on the horizon. Trace eyed the sky, instincts ages old telling him to batten down, to join the rest of nature's children scurrying for the southern lee of trees or bushes or boulders. Time hung suspended, a sweaty hush of waiting for the hard shove of bitter, shuddering wind.

Trace wouldn't feel the cold. The temperature could drop forty degrees and it still couldn't come close to matching the chill in his soul.

He glanced down at the whimpering form lying huddled at his feet. The beating he'd administered to Big Jack Bailey had drained the rage that pounded through his veins since learning of Jenny's abduction, but the information that poured from the whining man's mouth had coated his soul with a numbing layer of ice.

Reality tunneled to a pinpoint as Trace's world altered to a jumbled confusion of past and present. Standing beneath the sloped roof of the lean-to, he gazed toward the rough-hewn walls of the Lucky Lady homesite and saw instead the brick facade of an overseer's cottage in South Carolina.

His brother and his wife were inside those walls.

He shifted his gaze from the cabin to his own right hand where the unfamiliar weight of a well-remembered gun lay cradled in his palm. The Colt was one of a pair, each engraved, their barrels glinting with gold inlays and their stocks adorned with mother-of-pearl. Years ago, he'd worn this gun holstered on his right hip; his brother had worn its mate on his left. He'd retrieved the weapons and the gunbelt from the Rankin Building apartment before leaving town. It was the first time he'd touched this gun—or any gun—since aiming it, barrel still smoking from the shot that had murdered his wife, at his twin brother's heart.

The present and the past overlapped as he tested the trigger's give. Constance and Tye. Jenny and Tye. Love and betrayal. Katrina.

Tye and Trace.

With a sweep of leaves and dust, the first big slam of cold hit. Trace lifted his face to the sky. An arched crescent cloud rolled high and fast upon him. Like sin on the soul, the blackness advanced, consuming all color in its path.

*If a white cat crosses your path you will
have good luck.*

## CHAPTER NINETEEN

TYE MOVED CLOSER to the warmth and continued to doze until the throb in his shoulder tugged him to consciousness. Slowly, he opened his eyes.

The storm had moved in while he slept, bringing darkness with it. Outside the wind howled, and inside the air on his face was an icy kiss. Were it not for the body snuggled against him, he'd be frozen half to death.

But Tye was comfortably warm. In fact, if it was any woman other than Jenny McBride plastered against him, he'd be downright hot.

He'd already desired one of his brother's wives. He'd be damned if it would happen again.

Intending to rise from the bed to light the fire, Tye rolled onto his side and blurted a curse. Pain rolled through him in waves.

"What is it?" Jenny asked in a sleepy voice. "Are you bleeding again?"

"No." He cleared his throat and unclenched his teeth. "I moved the wrong way, that's all. Sorry I woke you."

"Don't worry about it. I think we must have slept, though. A long time and soundly, too. I never even heard the storm sweep in, and that's unusual for me."

They discussed the weather as Jenny scooted up to a seated position and lit the bedside lamp. "I'll light the fire," she said, the chimney glass rattling as she replaced it on the base.

He placed a restraining hand on her shoulder when she moved to leave the bed. "I'll do it."

"But Tye—"

"No. I want you to stay right where you are." He paused, almost hating to ask but knowing he must. "How do you feel, Jenny? Better?"

The lamplight lit her face. Her smile brought a glow of warmth to the cold spot of fear in his heart.

"Yes, I do feel better. You were right, Tye. Sleep was just what I needed."

"No more backache? Cramping?"

Her skin flushed with embarrassment as she shook her head.

He blew a sigh of relief. "Good. I was worried about you."

"Well, to be honest, I was a little worried myself."

"So let's not rush things, all right? Give yourself a little more time. I can manage a fire."

She nodded and settled back against the pillow while he rose and padded across the room toward the hearth. "Dang this floor is cold," he grumbled. "I may as well be barefoot for all the good my socks are doing." Of course, the chill to his feet wasn't the reason for his grimace. The fire in his shoulder burned hotter than the one he lit in the grate.

He built a nice blaze, but when he bent to poke the logs one last time, a wave of light-headedness hit him. "Come back and lie down before you fall down," Jenny said. "I won't be able to lift you if you do, and that floor will turn more than your toes cold. Besides, I want to see your face while we talk."

"Talk?"

"Yes, talk. I believe you were about to tell me about Constance?"

"I was?"

She nodded. "Right before we slept."

"God bless, woman. Don't you ever give up?"

"No, not often."

Tye sighed. He didn't want to do this. He *really* didn't want to do this. "Jenny, you don't want to know this story, believe me. It's ugly."

"It's my family, Tye."

He cursed beneath his breath, then joined her in bed. "I darn sure don't have the strength to tell this story standing up. Give me some of that quilt. I'm cold. Some wildcat robbed me of my shirt."

Her voice was dry as she replied, "And lucky you are she did. Now, Mr. McBride, talk to me."

Tye winced as he lowered himself carefully to his pillow. "What has my brother told you about Constance?"

"He said he killed her. He never said how or why. I assumed it was accidental."

"An accident." He pursed his lips and thought about it for a moment. A bitter note entered his voice as he mused, "Hell, I don't know the answer to that one myself."

Jenny looked at him suspiciously. "You don't mean that, I know. Now, tell me how this tragedy came about."

Anguish lay below the surface of his flippant tone as he asked, "Which tragedy do you mean? My sister-in-law's death, or the fact that I slept with my brother's wife?"

"Oh, Tye."

The pity in her eyes damn near killed him. He shifted his gaze away and stared across the room toward the fire. The familiar guilt that plagued him, punished him, weighted his chest and made it difficult to draw a breath. When finally he spoke, his tone was low and weary. "I'm a sorry bastard,

Jenny. I betrayed him in the worst possible way. Are you sure you want to hear what I have to say?"

"Yes, I am." Her eyes pleaded with him to understand. "I must know before I can try to help. It's important to me, but it's also important to you and Trace and the girls. Especially Katrina."

"Katrina." Tye closed his eyes as a great yearning filled his heart. Katrina. A great wrong that somehow managed to be so perfectly right.

He cleared his throat and glanced at her. "It's a long story, but it'll make more sense if I start at the beginning."

"I'm not going anywhere."

He smiled sardonically and began. "Trace and I were boys when the war started, but before General Lee surrendered we saw our share of the fighting. Battle was...memorable."

Tye shook his head. Now, there was an understatement. His mind drifted back.

*He tiptoes over pieces of bodies strewn across a field. Where is Trace? He hasn't seen him since the battle began. "Halt." His captain reaches down, lifts a head—only a head— with his gauntlet-covered hands. "My brother," the captain said. "I believe that's his body up ahead."*

A tremor racked Tye's body. That memory would haunt him to the grave. "I started drinking and couldn't stop. It went on for years until Trace finally got tired of me and my excuses and my lies and decided to do something about it."

Jenny touched his hand and he grasped it, holding it like a lifeline. "What did your brother do?" she asked.

Tye smiled crookedly as he recalled the moment. "He abducted me. Stole me right out of a whore's bed and carted me off to a cabin in the woods. A very dry cabin in the woods, if you get my meaning."

"No liquor."

"Not even a brandy-soaked fruitcake. We stayed there for

two months. At times I truly wanted to die, but Trace forced
me to keep fighting." He paused for a moment, then added,
"No doubt he's regretted it since."

For the first time since starting his story, Tye met her gaze.
"I didn't take a drink for years. Not until Constance."

*Constance.* The name hung on the air like a bad smell.
Jenny pulled her hand away from his.

"Trace met her on the second day of a business trip to
New Orleans and married her before they left three weeks
later. Due to our grandmother's connections, we'd managed
to hold on to the family plantation after the war. Trace
moved his bride into Oak Grove and there we were, one big
happy clan."

Jenny questioned his sarcastic tone. "You didn't like her?"

"She flirted with me from the very first—just a shade past
innocent. I didn't think Trace noticed at the time, and frankly,
I loved it. I was happy for Trace and jealous as hell at the same
time. A beautiful wife, a successful profession, and soon,
Emma came along. I wanted children of my own."

"You never married?"

He shook his head. "No. I almost did once. In fact, it was
about the time Maribeth was born. By then, Trace and Constance had moved into Charleston. My fiancée was the daughter of a business partner of Trace's. But shortly before the
wedding, the lady decided she preferred a Yankee banker."

"The woman was obviously a fool," Jenny said with a dis-
dainful sniff.

"You're too kind, ma'am. You know what? Constance said
the same thing. She went out of her way to comfort her brokenhearted brother-in-law."

"Did you fall in love with her?"

"A little bit, maybe. But she and Trace were still happy
then, or at least, I thought they were."

Jenny shut her eyes and Tye knew this must be difficult for

her to hear. "Never mind, Jenny. Let's forget about this. How's your back? Are you feeling any better?"

She sat up and twisted her torso in a stretch. "My back is much better, thank you, and I want to hear the rest of it."

"You're like a puppy with a bone."

She nodded. "I'm very persistent."

Tye fiddled with the bandage on his shoulder. Damn but he ached—both in body and in mind. He'd almost rather take a bullet in his good shoulder than finish the tale. Sighing, he said, "Trace got caught in the middle of a Reconstruction political battle and his professional name took a direct hit. He damned near went broke. They sold the house in town and moved out to Oak Grove. That's when Constance went to work on me."

He fell silent for a time as memories rushed at him like a bitter wind. "She didn't like watching her pennies or being Mrs. Trace McBride when McBride wasn't the most popular name to be."

"You're a McBride."

"That's right. But I was a McBride with money. And Trace was acting stupid—dangerously dumb. He made enemies out of some powerful people, and the repercussions affected all of us. Politics—why he couldn't just let it alone I'll never know. The night they rode on Oak Grove and burned the fields I could have killed him."

Jenny opened her mouth to say something, then obviously changed her mind, instead making a neutral observation. "Trace is opinionated when it comes to politics even today."

Tye thought about the letter to the editor that had led him to his brother. "I guess some things never change."

"So that's when you and Constance became...close?"

His gaze fastened on the rafters and he recalled with shame how foolish he'd been. "I thought Trace was being an ass. I felt sorry for her. That's about the time Lord Howard showed up on our doorstep."

Jenny winced slightly as she asked, "Who is Lord Howard?"

Her expression worried Tye. Maybe the rest wasn't helping her backache after all. Maybe he should try to get to town. He was feeling better. Surely he could drive the wagon.

"Tye? Lord Howard?"

"Jenny, are you certain you don't need a doctor?"

"I need you to finish your story."

Now it was Tye's turn to grimace. "Lord Howard was a cousin, many times removed, from England. Baron of something or other. The title sent Constance into raptures. She wanted to host a ball, an old-fashioned southern ball to introduce the English peer to Charleston society and hopefully buy Trace's way back into good graces. I didn't see what it would hurt, and I offered to foot the bill. Trace took exception to that."

"I can just imagine," Jenny observed dryly.

"He was a real bastard about it, to me and to her. Later on, I came to wonder if something more was going on I didn't know about. But at the time I was still angry with him about his damned politics, and when she came crying on my shoulder, well, I let her."

Tye closed his eyes, remembering. A rainy afternoon. An empty parlor. A kiss. "It proved to be the beginning of the end."

Constance was like a black widow spider, drawing him in. He wanted her like he'd never wanted another woman—before or since. "She was my twin brother's wife. I loved him, I hated him. And I fell in love with her. She came to me one night, but I sent her away." He turned his head and stared at the woman beside him. "I sent her away, Jenny. I swear I did."

Her eyes glistened as she said softly, "I believe you, Tye."

"She and Trace had a battle royal before the ball—loud enough to shake the chandeliers. She came to my room, crying. Pleading for me to help her. She said he'd hit her."

Jenny stiffened. "Trace would never hit a woman!"

"I didn't believe her, either. I thought it was a ruse to get me to...well...she wanted me to send Trace away from Oak Grove, but allow her and the girls to remain. I told her that Trace was her husband, and that there could be nothing between the two of us. I sent her away."

Tye lifted his uninjured arm, bringing his hand to his brow as if rubbing it could rub away the memory of the pain. "It hurt; God, it hurt," he confessed. "I felt like my heart had been ripped out. I loved her, and I'd given her up out of loyalty to my brother—a brother I didn't particularly like at the time. I went downstairs to the ball feeling like a martyr for the cause."

"What happened?"

He chuckled humorlessly. "Good old cousin Lord Howard happened."

Jenny studied him, and he watched the certainty dawn in her expression. "He gave you a drink."

"He gave me a bottle," Tye corrected. "About halfway into it, Constance found me in the garden and showed me her bruises. On her arms. Her back. She said he only hit her where it wouldn't show."

"I don't believe it," Jenny said.

"Well, I was drunk as a skunk and I believed it. I was furious with Trace. I felt so bad for her."

He fell silent, remembering. After a long few minutes, he said softly, "She asked for comfort and I gave it to her. We did it there. There in the garden. And in the gazebo. And upstairs in my room."

Although Jenny didn't move an inch, he sensed her subtle withdrawal. No surprise, there. If he could have jumped out of his own skin, he would have.

"The next morning, I went to Trace. Of course I didn't tell him I'd pegged his wife, but I did ask him about the bruises."

"He didn't do it," Jenny said.

Tye nodded, the vision rising in his mind as clear as yesterday. A stone-faced Trace, swearing on their parents' grave he'd never laid a hand on his wife in anger. "That morning I hated him, and I hated her. But not near as much as I hated myself. I gave her some money, enough for her to leave him, and I left for Europe that very afternoon. I drank my way across the Atlantic."

Jenny wet her lips. "And Constance was pregnant. With Katrina."

Tye nodded. "And she never got around to telling my brother the baby wasn't his."

Pain lanced Jenny's heart. Her hand lifted to cover her womb as she shut her eyes and sighed. "Oh, Trace."

She had a sudden vision of Trace as Mr. Throw-Fish, frolicking with his daughters in the summertime water at Quail Creek. His love for his girls was as much a part of him as the color of his eyes. She could only imagine the depth of his pain upon learning that his brother had fathered Katrina.

"Constance eventually told him the truth?" she asked.

"Indirectly." Tye's face creased with pain. "More than a year passed before good old Cousin Lord Howard found me in Brussels. He sobered me up to the point where I'd listen to him, then dropped his little bombshell. Constance had recently delivered a daughter—my daughter—whom Trace believed to be his, and she had sent him with the demand I return home and claim my child."

Outside the wind continued to howl and Jenny slowly became aware of the even colder chill seeping through the cracks in the cabin walls' chinking. "So Constance continued to live with Trace after you left?" she asked, snuggling down into the quilt. When Tye answered her question with a nod, she added, "Because of Emma and Maribeth, of course."

"Not hardly," Tye scoffed. "It was at that point where my dear sister-in-law showed her true colors. It seems that a solicitor had contacted the family with information concerning an inheritance due the eldest offspring of the eldest offspring. I'm eight minutes older than Trace. Katrina, not Emma, was the McBride daughter who met the terms."

"Oh," Jenny said.

He nodded. "I didn't want anything to do with it. I'd already bedded my brother's wife. I wouldn't take his daughter from him, too. I told Cousin Howard to forget it."

A muscle worked in Tye McBride's jaw as he stared straight ahead and said, "That's when it got ugly."

The wind moaned through the chimney, the eerie wail seemingly a portent of things to come. Jenny waited for Tye to continue, almost wishing he wouldn't. "What happened?"

"It was a lot of money. A whole lot of money. Constance was determined to claim it on behalf of her daughter. So Cousin Lord Howard relayed her threat." Tye jerked himself out of bed and crossed to the fireplace. Ignoring the pain such movement caused, he lifted the kindling from the woodbox and chucked it into the hearth. Then abruptly, he turned. His eyes were tortured, his voice stark, as he looked at her and said, "If I didn't return to Oak Grove before Katrina's first birthday, she promised to kill the baby."

Shocked silence followed his declaration. To Jenny, the night had never seemed so cold.

She shuddered, her hand clenching the blanket, when she finally found her voice. "What? No, she wouldn't! You believed her?"

Heedless of his wound, he lifted his arms and held his hands palms out. His voice weak with pain, he said, "I couldn't be sure. After I thought about it, I began to suspect she'd set me up, that she knew about the inheritance before the night of the ball. If she'd gone to such lengths…" He shuddered at the memory. "I couldn't risk the child's life. So I went back."

A spot of bright red stained the bandage on his shoulder. "Lie back down, Tye," Jenny said. "You're bleeding again."

He sat next to her and took her hand in his. "I wanted to kill her, Jenny. For what she'd done to me and my brother, for what she'd threatened to do to the child. I'd dream of wrapping my hands around that slender, graceful neck of hers and snapping it like a chicken's. I always woke up smiling."

"My God, Tye!"

"She had seduction in mind when she met me in one of the old cabins on the plantation, a little place not much different from this, in fact. I played along with her for a bit, just to see how far she'd hang herself." A lopsided, sneering smile lifted his lips. "She hanged herself, all right. As soon as I related to her all that I'd been thinking for months, her temper exploded."

His eyes took on a faraway look. Jenny took his hand, sensing he'd welcome the connection to the present while lost in the misery of the past.

"She screeched at the top of her voice," Tye said softly. "She said the baby was mine, and that I couldn't deny her. I told her I intended to make certain she'd never hurt my daughter. I told her I'd take Katrina away from her."

Tye's eyes glistened as he looked at Jenny imploringly and said, "I intended to kill her, you see. I had my hands around her neck when I felt his presence."

"Trace."

Tye nodded. "Standing in the doorway. He never said a word, just pulled a pistol from inside his jacket and took aim at my heart. Constance shouted for him to stop—she wouldn't get the money if I were dead, you see—and she ran toward him. After that, I'm not sure what happened. Either she tripped or he jerked his aim, or something. She was in his arms when the gun went off."

Staring past Jenny, Tye cleared his throat. "I knew one of them had been shot, but they just stood there, frozen like statues. It took an eternity, but finally Constance folded to the floor. Her face. The bullet…"

Jenny closed her eyes.

"Trace stood staring at his hands. Covered in blood. I looked at him, and for just a moment I thought he was me back on the battlefield. He had that same look on his face that I carried inside me—that look that I used a bottle to wipe away. But then, he turned to me and it was like looking in a mirror."

Tye's voice caught. "He hated me as much as I hated myself."

"How awful for you both," Jenny whispered, lifting her hand to touch his cheek. She was crying, now. With him. For him. For Trace.

"He took aim at me again. I waited. Hell, I wanted to die, Jenny."

Sitting up, she wrapped her arms around him. She held him, rocking him like a child, as she offered her comfort and support.

His voice dropped to a murmur. "His hand shook—I'll never forget how it trembled—but he didn't do it. He flung the gun away and hit me instead, a solid chop to the jaw. It knocked me against the fireplace. I hit my head on the mantel and blacked out. When I awoke, he and the girls were gone."

Bitter cold swept into the cabin. Jenny looked up. Hinges squeaked and the door closed with a thump. A shadowed figure paused in the doorway, then slowly moved forward. She knew a sudden fear as thoughts of Frank Bailey's ghost flashed through her mind.

Lamplight reflected off the barrel of the gun in the glove-covered hand, and paradoxically Jenny found it reassuring. This ghost was of the earth.

As a boot thudded against the puncheon floor, a log in the fireplace rolled. Flames flared briefly, long enough to illuminate the face of the gunman.

"Trace?" Jenny asked, the gun in his hand causing her to doubt what she had seen. At Tye McBride's muttered expletive, she knew she'd not been mistaken. The tale of love and betrayal he'd just repeated burned like a brand in her mind.

Trace cocked the pistol, the click cracking like thunder in the room.

Jenny knew how the situation looked. She and his brother embracing on a bed. Tye without his shirt. Extending her hand toward Trace, Jenny simply said, "Trust me."

*Finding a ladybug brings good luck.*

## CHAPTER TWENTY

TRUST HER?

Trace sucked in a breath, bracing himself against the chaos of pain threatening to consume him.

Hell, no, he didn't trust her. She was his wife, goddammit! What more was required to doubt every lying, cheating word that dripped from her mouth? And if that weren't enough, he need only look as far as the dog she was lying down with.

Tye. His brother. His twin. Betrayal was the salt that spilled upon a wound both fresh and ages old. God, it hurt. His grip tightened on the gun, and when finally he spoke, his promise swept through the cabin like an ice-tipped wind. "This time I *will* kill you."

Tye pulled away from Jenny. "It's not what you think. Not now, and not then, goddammit!"

Trace almost laughed. "How do you know what I'm thinking?" he asked, scorn coating his voice. He walked closer to the bed, into the lamplight. He wanted his brother and his wife to see the disgust on his face.

He wanted them to see the murderous rage.

"Oh, I know." He snapped his fingers and showed them a twisted, mocking smile. "You think I'm recalling another time when I walked into a rustic cabin and found my wife and my brother in each other's arms."

Tye tried again. "Trace, I—"

"You could be wrong, you know. I might be thinking of another tender moment. You know which one I mean, don't you, Tye?" Trace flicked his words like a whip. "The one I didn't witness firsthand, but the one that haunts me every time I see the sunshine in my daughter's smile, every time I hear her laugh, every time I kiss Katrina good night. Surely you remember the occasion to which I refer, hmm? The time you—"

"I'm sorry, Trace!"

He paused. He lifted the Colt, aiming it at point-blank range at his brother's face. This man stole his woman. This man stole his daughter. Trace's hand trembled with the force of his fury.

His voice was flat and cold as death. "The time you fucked my wife and gave her a baby."

Tye flinched, his expression a stricken grimace. An unaccustomed pressure pulsed at the back of Trace's eyes. Silence yawned between them. Brother and brother, betrayer and betrayed. *Goddamn you, Tye. Why!*

"Trace?"

Jenny's voice surprised him, confused him, and he turned a furrowed brow toward the sound without shifting his gaze from his brother. For a moment he'd been lost between present and past.

"Trace, put down the gun. You don't need it." The tenderness in her tone beckoned him. Tempted him.

Trace resisted. "Yes, I do. I won't let him take Katrina away from me."

"He hasn't come to do that." She shifted her body, swinging her legs around to dangle from the bed. "Tye helped me, Trace. Big Jack had started shooting. He intended to kill me. Your brother saved my life."

She rose from the bed and stepped toward him, blocking his aim. He lifted a hand to shove her out of the way, and then he saw the blood.

It stained her dress from her breast to her thighs, and the tenuous hold he had on the present faded as he was catapulted into the past.

*My brother fucked you. He fucked you and gave you my baby! I killed you for it. Oh, God, I killed you.* "I loved you," he said, his voice cracking.

"You still love me," she said. "I know you do. You love me, and you trust me. You know I have not betrayed you." She reached for the gun.

Blond hair was black. Blue eyes, brown. He didn't believe her. He couldn't believe her. He yanked the gun back and away from her questing hand. "He betrayed me, goddammit! It didn't matter if you and I had problems, he shouldn't have done it. It's him I want dead. Him I want to kill. That blood should be his!"

"It is his!" she cried. "Big Jack Bailey shot him in the shoulder." She threw herself at him, wrapping her arms tightly around his middle. "Don't do this, Trace. For me. Believe in me, in us. I love you. I *love* you."

She lifted her face and gazed into his eyes. Blue eyes, not brown. Hair the color of Spanish gold. Not Constance, but Jenny. His Jenny. His treasure.

She gripped his lapels and implored him. "Listen to me, Trace. Time and again you have saved me. You protected me from the disaster of a marriage to Edmund. You gave me your name in order to salvage Fortune's Design. You'd have saved me from Frank if the scorpions hadn't got him first."

Tears trickled down her cheeks. "Most of all, you offered

me a family, your family. Something I've wished for all my life. You healed me, Trace. Let me help you in return, please?"

Trace looked toward Tye. His brother remained seated on the bed, unmoving, an enigmatic expression on his face. Their gazes met and held, and for the first time in years Trace felt the pull of the bond between them. He heard his brother's voice in his mind. *Kill me if you wish. It's your choice. Your right. I won't fight you.*

Trace's body trembled as Jenny touched his face, luring his attention. "I love you, Trace McBride," she said. "I have not and I never will betray you. Let me tell you what happened here this afternoon. Trust me."

*Trust me.* How could he? Did she have any idea what she asked of him?

*Kill me if you wish.* His brother. His daughter. Pain rent his heart in two.

Trace pulled away from Jenny's embrace, putting space between them. His heart pounded and his palms were damp. His breaths came in shallow gasps.

*Trust me.*

He'd been through this before. He'd given a woman his love, his trust, his faith. Look where it had gotten him—on the run and hiding from his family. Only now, his family had found him. Tye. Here to collect his daughter.

Oh, shit. Trace closed his eyes against the soul-destroying thought. His voice was just a whisper. "I won't give her up."

"Neither will I," Jenny insisted, imploring him with her gaze. "She's our daughter, Trace. Yours and mine. It doesn't matter who provided the egg and the seed. No one will break up our family, I promise you. Believe me." She extended her hand, palm up. "Trust me."

Trace stared at her hand and what it represented. Despite the chill in the room, sweat beaded on his upper lip. He glanced at his brother.

Tye had tears in his eyes. The brothers communicated silently: Trace's glare a challenge; Tye's a confusion of wariness, hope, and guilt. And maybe the faintest hint of love.

Oh, hell. Trace drew a deep breath, filling his lungs with air as his wife whispered his name. He looked at her and exhaled in a long, slow sigh.

He could drown in those eyes of hers, he thought. Blue as the Caribbean waters. Sparkling like fireworks on the Fourth of July. Warm as the emotion swelling in his heart.

He believed her. God help him, he believed her.

But what of the lessons of his past? What of the pain? Dare he give her that gift? Dare he offer her his trust?

*She is Jenny, your good Fortune. Your treasure. How can you do anything less?*

He holstered the gun.

Her smile chased the last rays of darkness from his soul and offered him a little piece of heaven. Trace lifted his hand, cupped her cheek in his palm, and voiced the words in his heart. "I love you."

Her eyes glistened. Her entire being radiated joy. Then, with the barest hint of smugness in her tone, she replied, "I know, McBride. I've been waiting for you to realize it."

She lifted her head as he lowered his. Their lips melded in a kiss filled with promise and with love. A kiss sweetened with the honey of trust.

NEITHER TRACE nor Jenny noticed when Tye hoisted himself from bed, his teeth clenched against pain both physical and emotional. Tugging the quilt along with him, he grabbed his boots and slipped outside.

The boards beneath his feet may as well have been ice, and bitter air hit him like a fist. Crossing the passageway between the shelter's two rooms, he told himself he'd rather spend the night in the outhouse than be a third wheel to his brother and his wife tonight. He'd played that particular role before.

Pushing open the door, he stumbled inside. "Black as a tomb," he muttered. It took a few minutes, but his eyes eventually adjusted to the darkness enough for him to make out the big stone fireplace on the opposite wall. Cast-iron skillets and a big Dutch oven indicated this room had served as the kitchen. Now to get a fire going before he passed out.

He found wood stacked near the hearth and matches on the mantel. Twice the pain in his shoulder caused him to halt his efforts, but finally he managed to create a small blaze. He tugged a rocking chair close to the fire, then gratefully sank into its seat. Spreading the quilt over his body, he sighed and closed his eyes.

For the first time in years, a flicker of hope warmed his soul as he drifted toward sleep. Trace had fallen in love again. Jenny Fortune McBride had helped to heal the wounds Tye and Constance had inflicted. She'd convinced him to trust again.

As he waited for heat from the fire to displace the chill of the night and of the scene just past, he acknowledged his deepest desire. Maybe Jenny Fortune McBride could work another miracle. Maybe she could convince Trace to forgive. Maybe she could help him get his brother back.

He floated in the haze between dozing and full sleep when the squeak of door hinges warned him he was no longer alone.

"Tye?" Trace whispered.

Too tired and too weak to face any more upheaval at the moment, he feigned sleep. He heard the sound of footsteps approaching, then the scrape of one log against another. Opening his eyes in a narrow slit, he watched as Trace added wood to the fire. One, two, three large logs. Lifting the poker from a hook mortared into the stone, Trace prodded the logs until the flames began to roar and warmth eased into the room like summer sunshine. He replaced the poker, then assessed the shelves built to one side of the fireplace. Removing three jars of preserved food, he turned to leave. Tye quickly shut his eyes.

Footsteps passed him, paused, and then came back. For more than a minute Trace stood beside the rocker, silent and still. Tye's mouth went dry as he waited; for what he didn't know.

A brush of a hand against his bandaged shoulder. A whispered curse.

Then gently, soundlessly, Trace McBride tugged up the quilt and tucked his brother in.

JENNY SAT ON THE BED waiting for Trace, knowing the time had arrived to tell him about the baby. She'd been married to Trace McBride long enough to know that the kiss they'd shared moments ago was, in Trace's mind, a prelude to love-making. Under the circumstances, they dared not indulge themselves, no matter how much they wanted to.

And Jenny wanted to. He'd told her he loved her, after all. Hearing those words had been her fondest fantasy while dreaming of how to tell him about the child. She'd pictured Trace verbally declaring his love while demonstrating it physically, after which she'd share her most special news.

Needless to say, her imaginings had never taken the route presented to her tonight.

He returned to the room with jars of food in his hands. "You found him?" she asked, referring to Tye.

He nodded and shrugged out of his fur-lined leather coat, tossing it onto a chair. "He's asleep in the other room. He'd started a fire and I added to it. He'll be fine. Rest is what he needs most."

Relief washed through her. "Rest and food," she replied, eyeing the jars in his hand. "We haven't eaten since breakfast."

"I come prepared as you can see." He twisted the lid off the jar of peaches and offered some to his wife. "I didn't see a spoon or fork. Can you manage with your fingers today?"

"I could manage with only my tongue."

The look he shot her could have set the bedsheets on fire. "I was counting on that."

The heat of a blush warmed her cheeks as she rushed to forestall any further suggestive comments by asking about the girls. His measuring expression told her he'd heard her unspoken request to slow things down.

"I'm a bit worried, to be honest," Trace replied with a shrug. "It's been a difficult day for them. It's been a difficult day for all of us."

"You didn't leave them alone?"

"No, the marshal promised to take them to Mrs. Wilson." He paused a moment then asked, "Jenny, there's nothing…wrong with Mrs. Wilson, is there?"

She licked the sweet nectar of peach juice off her fingers. "Of course not. Why do you ask?"

Trace tore his gaze away from her mouth. "It's just that I went through so many caretakers for the girls. I mean, some of them didn't last a day. And here's Mrs. Wilson, she's been as tickled as a two-tailed pup to watch over my Menaces since the very beginning."

"*Our* Menaces," Jenny corrected with a smile. She set down the peaches. "Don't worry about Mrs. Wilson, Trace. The answer is simple. She loves them. I daresay that after all your concern over providing them a mother, they'd have done fine without me as long as Mrs. Wilson was in your employ."

Trace scowled at her. "Don't think that for a minute, Mrs. McBride. All of us would be lost without you." He sat beside her on the bed and gently smoothed her hair away from her face. "Me, especially. It scared the hell out of me when you turned up missing."

Jenny turned her head to press a kiss against the palm of his hand.

"What happened, sweetheart? How did you end up in Jack Bailey's clutches?"

"It's a long story."

"I'm not going anywhere."

She smiled ruefully. "That's what I told your brother a little while ago."

He winced as if he'd tasted something extremely sour. "You know, Jenny, I said I trusted you and I mean it. My brother is another question entirely. Would you care to tell me why I found you two curled up in bed together? It wasn't that cold in here."

She tugged on his arm. "Come lie beside me. There's something I need to tell you, and I'd rather do it while I'm in your arms."

He rubbed his hand across his jaw. "Am I going to hate this?"

"Oh, no." Happiness put a smile on Jenny's face. "It'll make your heart sing, I feel certain."

He arched a brow. "My heart sing, huh?" He reached down to yank off his boots. "Well, don't say I didn't warn you if I find I'm overcome with lust."

In all seriousness, Jenny said, "Don't get too carried away. I'm afraid if we make love tonight we'll need to be somewhat inventive."

Trace froze. "Did Big Jack hurt you?"

"No, I'm fine now. I wasn't so sure earlier, though, and that's why you found me lying down."

"Talk to me," he demanded.

Jenny wanted to bite her tongue. She'd made a muddle of it, that was certain. "I didn't want it to be like this. Actually, I had almost decided to wait until Christmas. Remember I promised you that gift?"

"Jenny," he warned, looming over her.

She sighed. "Oh, all right. But you have to lie down. It seems more appropriate." He growled with frustration but rolled onto his back, pulling her on top of him as she had requested. Jenny lifted her head and grinned down at his long-suffering expression as she added, "After all, it's the lying down that got me into this trouble to begin with."

"What trouble!"

"Apron trouble."

"Apron trouble?"

"As in riding high. My apron's riding high."

His body stiffened. His eyes went wide. "Jenny? Are you…?"

"In a family way," she finished, her smile going wide. "Congratulations, Daddy. Perhaps it'll be a boy this time."

His hold on her gentled. "A baby? You and me?"

"You and me and Emma and Maribeth and Katrina."

"A baby." Wonder filled his tone and myriad emotions crossed his face—tenderness, happiness, pride. And love. So much love it brought tears to her eyes.

"Ah, treasure, you don't know how much this means to me."

"I know how much it means to me," she softly replied.

"God, I love you. Thank you, sweetheart." He pulled her head down to his.

Joy sang in Jenny's veins as she basked in the sweet sensation of her husband's kiss. It went on and on and on. More than a sharing of passion, this kiss was a uniting. It was as if a barrier between them had fallen, and only with its loss did she recognize it once had existed.

In the past, Trace had offered her his home, his family, and his desire. But tonight he offered her his love. He offered her himself.

Her heart overflowed. This was a sharing so beautiful, so fulfilling, she wept with the wonder of it and Trace kissed the tears away.

"Don't cry, baby. It hurts to see you cry." He brushed her hair off her forehead and said in a teasing tone, "Besides, I have enough salt on me now to keep a whole herd of deer happy through the winter."

She went along with his effort to lighten the mood by slapping playfully at his chest and saying, "You've told me before that my tears were sweet."

"I lied. They're as salty as your temper."

"You keep talking like that and you'll get a taste of my temper, McBride. You should have seen what I did to Big Jack Bailey."

As the joking light in his eyes died, Jenny wished she'd never mention Big Jack. "Trace, don't—"

"Tell me the whole story. Everything from how Bailey got his hands on you to why I walked in on what I walked in on."

"You didn't walk in on anything," she peevishly replied.

"Jenny," he warned. "Start at the beginning and tell me everything that happened."

And so she did. At times she thought he'd explode with anger. Other moments he grew so quiet and still she'd have thought he'd gone to sleep if she didn't know better. Only once did he interrupt, at the first mention of her backache and her fear she'd lose the baby. He tried to get out of bed, saying, "I'll be back with the doctor in a couple of hours."

"Wait, Trace. I believe there is a good chance Bailey will send the doctor our way."

"Why do you think that?"

She told him about the threats she'd made against Big Jack's new grandson. "Damn, honey. That was some pretty smart thinking."

"I'm ashamed at the idea, but I did what needed doing to protect my family."

Trace grimaced. "You did better than me, I'm afraid. I ran across Bailey on the way out here, and I'm afraid I didn't leave him in much shape for fetching a doctor." At Jenny's questioning look, he added, "I pretty much beat the tar out of him."

"Oh." She knew a niggle of shame over feeling great satisfaction at such knowledge.

"I'd best go for the doctor." Trace again made to leave.

She shook her head and insisted. "Not for me. If Tye needs a physician, fine. But I'm all right, now, I promise. I won't take any risks with this baby." Her lips twitched with a flustered smile as she added, "That's why I said we'd need to get inventive with our lovemaking."

"I won't touch you till he's born," he swore.

"Let's not go overboard," she replied, frowning. "I'm certain there are ways. You must know something about this. After all, you went through this three times with Constance."

"I don't want to talk about Constance."

Jenny squeezed his hand. "I think perhaps we should."

"No. I see no reason. That's the past, Jenny. Leave it there."

She rested her head on his chest. "The past is asleep in the other room of this cabin. Your brother and I talked about what happened while we were resting. He told me some things I doubt you know; some things I think you should be aware of."

"Ah, hell, Jenny."

She wouldn't be dissuaded. She told him most of the story Tye had told her—of Constance and her lies, of the inheritance, and how Lord Howard had contributed to Tye's downfall. "He hates what he did, Trace. He's sorry for it, and he wants your forgiveness. When he first arrived at Willow Hill, Tye told me he hoped for a reconciliation between you two. I still believe that's true. He hasn't come to take Katrina away from us. He wants you and all the girls to be part of his family once again."

"Forgiveness, huh?" Trace snorted. "He doesn't ask for much, does he?"

"He's your brother, Trace. Your twin."

"He's Katrina's true father!"

She wasn't surprised by the sudden savagery in his voice but by the words themselves. She would have expected him to condemn his brother for bedding his wife. Instead, his first thoughts were of Katrina.

And that, she realized, was the offense he could not forgive.

"It isn't his sin, you know. Tye isn't responsible for keeping the truth about Katrina from you. Constance did that. Tye didn't know about her until after she was born."

He shifted his gaze away from her.

Jenny reached up and turned his chin, gently demanding his attention. When finally his eyes refocused on hers, she said, "Blame him for being intimate with your wife, but don't hold him responsible for the fact you took Kat into your heart before you learned his seed, not yours, gave her life."

His jaw hardened, and she could see he didn't like what she'd said. But he'd heard it, and for now, that was enough.

*If you find a penny, pick it up and put
it in your left shoe for good luck.*

## CHAPTER TWENTY-ONE

DAWN BROKE in fiery splendor on a crystalline sky as Trace,
Jenny, and Tye prepared to depart the cabin. Telling himself
he preferred the cut of cold air to the idea of having his wife
exposed to Tye's bare chest any longer, Trace gave his
brother his own coat before making a pallet for him in the
bed of the wagon.

Next order of business was to extract a promise from Jenny
to inform him at the first sign of any ache or pain connected
with the baby. "Hunger pains don't count," he grumbled when
she voiced the matter for the tenth time since awakening.
"Y'all finished the last of the canned goods."

"Isn't there *anything* else I could eat?"

"Good Lord, Jen, didn't your mother teach you never to
ask that question of a man?" As color stained her cheeks, he
added, "No, of course not. Your mother is Monique Day."

He herded her outside and up into the wagon. She didn't
say another word about being hungry, not even when her
stomach let out a growl loud enough to frighten the horses.

Trace swallowed a laugh and flicked the reins, and the horses broke into a trot.

They spotted the doctor's buggy halfway to Fort Worth. "Either I didn't hit Bailey as hard as I thought, or you scared him more than you knew, Jenny," Trace observed. He stopped the buckboard, and the physician made a brief examination of Tye's shoulder, then listened intently as Jenny quietly outlined her symptoms.

Trace watched nervously as the doctor stroked his beard and frowned. He moved closer to overhear the conversation. "If you're no longer experiencing pain, Mrs. McBride, I doubt this bumpy road will cause any ill effects," the doctor said. "I'll follow you, and once I get Mr. McBride taken care of, we can discuss your symptoms in greater depth."

Trace's heart was lighter after that, and he even spoke directly to his brother twice during the second leg of the trip. Within two hours of leaving the cabin, they passed the outlying structures of the city of Fort Worth.

Trace didn't turn at the intersection that would lead to the Rankin Building where Tye had spent the night before last. When Jenny gave him a curious look, he shrugged. "It'll make the doctor's job easier if you're both in the same place. Don't make it out to be any more than it is, Jenny."

"Whatever you say, dear."

He glowered in answer to her smug, knowing smile.

The wagon rattled its way up Willow Hill, and by the time he pulled to a stop in front of the house, his daughters came flying out the front door. Maribeth and Katrina launched themselves at Jenny, hugging and kissing and laughing with delight. Emma hung back from the boisterous welcome, her complexion pale and her eyes watery. Trace wondered what was the matter. This wasn't like his eldest daughter at all. He decided that as soon as he saw his wife and brother settled, he'd have a talk with Emma.

A masculine, emotional clearing of the throat attracted his attention to the front porch where he was surprised to see Jenny's mother clinging to a man who could be none other than Richard Fortune.

The expression on both parents' faces clearly revealed the love they felt for their daughter. For the first time since he'd known her, Monique looked her age. How she'd known of the danger stalking her daughter, Trace didn't know, but the worries of the night were etched across her face. Richard Fortune, his complexion pale, the hand holding his wife betraying the slightest tremble, drank in the sight of his daughter. Jenny has his eyes, Trace thought.

"Honey?" Trace said softly. "Jenny, look."

She glanced up at him. "At what?"

"The house. We have visitors."

She swung her head around and gasped. "Mother? Richard?"

Then Monique was running down the steps, Jenny's father hurrying after her. "She's safe!" she cried. "Oh, Richard, she's safe."

Trace restrained his daughters from joining in when Jenny's parents swallowed her in an embrace. He watched closely to make certain they didn't unknowingly cause her or the baby harm.

Puzzlement colored Jenny's voice. "What's going on? How did you know about the trouble? Did someone telegraph you, Monique? Were you visiting Mother in Dallas, Papa?"

Richard Fortune's voice was gruff with emotion. "I came for your wedding, and stopped by Monique's on the way, thinking we might all spend Christmas together."

"My wedding!"

Monique gave her daughter another quick, fierce hug then stepped away. "My telegram said three weeks and he read three months."

Keeping his arm around his daughter, Richard frowned. "In

my defense, allow me to point out the fact that few people choose to conduct a large, formal wedding in three weeks' time. I believe I can be excused the oversight due to the unusual circumstances. And, since your mother has ignored all of my correspondence for some time now—"

"Almost three months," Monique interjected.

"—I had no way of knowing I'd made an error." He gave Jenny's hands a squeeze, saying, "I beg your forgiveness, Jenny. I've long dreamed of escorting you down the aisle. While in my opinion your mother is more at fault than I, it is conceivable that—"

"Hush, Richard," Monique snapped. "We haven't even found out if she's well."

"Of course she's well. Look at her." He looked more closely and frowned. "Oh, my. You are well, are you not, child? You look tired. Are you feeling all right?" He tossed a fatherly glare toward Trace. "My daughter obviously needs to rest. What are you doing standing there? Hurry, boy. Let's get her inside."

Trace opened his mouth to bark right back at Richard Fortune, but his intentions changed when he saw the expression on his wife's face.

Amazement. Delight. Unadulterated joy.

As Jenny stood on her tiptoes and pressed a kiss to her father's cheek, Trace swore to himself he'd never allow a day go by without showing his daughters how much he loved them.

The girls led the way toward the house, Jenny following, flanked by her parents, with Trace assisting Tye and bringing up the rear. In all the excitement, neither the girls nor Jenny's parents got around to mentioning the other surprise awaiting them inside.

Wearing a passably attractive dress, Ethel Baumgardner, her youthful face ravaged by signs of tears and worry, stood wringing a handkerchief in Willow Hill's front parlor.

Jenny stiffened visibly. "Miss Baumgardner?"

"Oh, thank God you are all right! You *are* all right, aren't you? Oh, please forgive me. You must forgive me. I never meant for you to be hurt." The Dallas dressmaker burst into a flurry of tears. "I just wanted to make you leave here. I never thought Mr. Bailey would go to such extremes. I am so sorry. So very, very sorry."

Trace breathed a curse under his breath as Jenny asked, "Sorry? For what?"

The dressmaker simply stood there, destroying her handkerchief and opening and closing her mouth like a fish.

Monique interjected. "The telegraph office in Dallas is run by the husband of the woman who trims my hair upon occasion. I discovered the truth and forced the witch to come along and confess. We never expected to arrive and find you missing!"

"What truth?" Jenny asked.

Trace's mind worked a little faster than his wife's at the moment. "She sent the fake telegram to Bailey about Mary Rose's being burned. And I'll bet she's responsible for a few other things, too. The paint and dead roses that decorated your house. Some of those nasty notes you received."

Guilt blazed across Ethel's face, reflecting the accuracy of his deduction.

"I didn't mean for anyone to get hurt," she said. "I just wanted you gone. I'm not as good as you are. I was trying to protect my livelihood."

After a moment of shocked silence, Jenny took a menacing step toward her. "Do you know what you've done? Look at my brother-in-law. You almost got him killed, Ethel. I almost lost my baby because of you!"

"Baby!" the McBride Menaces gleefully exclaimed.

"Oh, my." Monique gasped. "My baby's having a baby? Richard?" She clasped his hand. "Richard, quickly. Tell me my hair isn't gray!"

Jenny took it all in with a dazed look upon her face. Seeing her confusion, Trace laid a hand on her shoulder. "Honey, you need to go on upstairs and rest. I'll take care of this."

"Don't worry, Mr. McBride," Ethel Baumgardner said. "I'm leaving town. I'm leaving the state. I've decided to take my skills to California."

"Sounds like a good decision, ma'am," Tye observed. Trace heard the weakness in his brother's voice and knew he'd best get both his wife and his twin upstairs.

"I'll expect you gone within the week, Miss Baumgardner." Trace caught Jenny's gaze and cocked his head toward the stairs while he offered Tye a supportive arm. "You'll find it best to meet my expectations."

Then he dismissed the dangerous dressmaker from his mind as he helped his brother to his room. Later, once they were settled, he'd make certain the woman paid for her sins. Right now, his family was his main priority.

He then checked on Jenny. Despite his insistence, she refused to go to bed, although she did promise to take things easy. "We might as well get something settled from the beginning, Trace. I will not do anything to endanger our child. I know my body's limits, and I will not exceed them. You'll have to trust me on this. I won't be coddled for months on end."

Trace decided not to force the issue today. He'd damn well coddle the woman if he wanted to, but he wouldn't argue about it now. When she shooed him from their bedroom, he left after only a token protest.

Pulled to Tye's doorway by a force he wouldn't name, he observed from the hallway as the doctor tended his brother's wound. When he realized he'd lifted a hand to rub a sympathetic pain in his own shoulder, he gave a self-mocking grimace. His emotions were in a jumble as he watched the physician stitch the cleaned and medicated wound closed. As the doctor wrapped fresh bandages around Tye's shoulder, words seemed to pop right out of Trace's mouth. "Remember that doctor in the Fifth Regiment, Tye?"

Cautiously, Tye replied, "Yes."

Trace referred to the physician who'd attended him the day his thigh was sliced open by a Yankee bayonet. It would have been his neck had his brother not come out of nowhere and saved him. "He was a ham-handed sonofagun. Not at all like Doc Draper, here."

Tye nodded, and the doctor made a remark about the difficulty of practicing medicine during the war. Trace was inordinately relieved when Jenny arrived bearing a tray filled with sandwiches. The girls followed with fruit and lemonade. She addressed Tye. "Are you up for a little company or would you prefer peace and quiet?"

"Come in, please, all of you," he said, waving them inside. "Bright faces always make me feel better."

"Mama said we're having a picnic on Uncle's floor," Katrina said. "I've never heard of a picnic indoors before. Have you, Papa?"

"It's a new one on me, Katie-cat."

The girls hovered around Jenny until she and the doctor excused themselves to conduct a consultation. When she met her husband's gaze with a nod, he knew she intended to ask the doctor about the safety of continued marital relations considering yesterday's troubles.

Trace said a quick, silent prayer that the answers would be what they both desired.

When Tye finished his sandwich and set his bed tray aside, Maribeth approached him, her gaze intent. "Mama told us about you being shot, Uncle. Does it hurt? Was it gushy?"

"Maribeth!" Emma exclaimed. "Where are your manners?"

"I'm just asking. How will I decide if I want to be a doctor or not if I don't ask questions?"

Katrina sniffed. "You can't be a doctor. You're a girl."

"I can too be a doctor. I can be anything I want. Papa always says so."

Katrina folded her arms and gave her father a look. Trace smiled and said, "If Mari wants to be a doctor when she grows up, I'll do everything I can to help her."

The youngest child thought about it a moment and said, "That means you must help me, too. You must build me a theater, Papa. One with red velvet seats. I'm going to be an actress."

"An actress? I don't know, Katie-cat, that's not exactly the future I'd hoped for you."

"But you'll build me a theater, if I want it," she said matter-of-factly. "I know you will. I'll talk you into it."

He laughed. "I guess I can't argue with that. Tell you what. If I agree to build you a theater, I can promise it'll be the grandest theater on this side of the Atlantic."

She threw herself into his arms. "Oh, Papa, I love you the very, very, very mostest." Relishing the sensation of his daughter's fierce hug, Trace instinctively looked toward his brother. Tye's gaze was anguished, and in that moment, Trace wanted the question settled once and for all. Shoulder wound or not, it was time the brothers had it out over Katrina.

"All right, girls. Picnic's over." He rose from the floor and gathered up the quilt. "Why don't you take this stuff downstairs and put it away for your mother."

The younger two protested, but Emma shook her head forcefully. "Come on. We need to help Mama. It's very important that she's happy here."

The strange comment reminded Trace that he'd yet to have that talk with his daughter. As the girls exited the room he stopped Emma with a hand on the shoulder. "Want to walk with me for a licorice in a little bit, princess?"

She frowned. "Maybe, Papa. If Mama doesn't need me, that is."

She's my next priority, Trace thought as he shut the door behind his daughter. But first, Tye needed to understand what was acceptable where Katrina was concerned. He went on the offensive. "Jenny seems to think you didn't come here to break up my family."

Tye closed his eyes. "She's right. I don't want to tear anything apart; I never did. I'm hoping to put something back together."

Trace folded his arms and stepped toward the bed. Standing with his feet braced wide apart, he declared, "I'll never, ever, give my daughter up."

"I'm not asking you to," his brother replied tightly, his hands clenching the sheet. "I've seen how happy she is, how much she's loved. It would be selfish of me to take her away from all of this. I'll admit that I had some concerns, but now that I've seen her, seen you all, I know what's right."

Silence hung between them, then Tye added, "She's your daughter in every way that counts, Trace. I want you to know neither she nor anyone else will ever hear any differently from me."

Trace studied his brother's face and admitted to himself he knew in his heart that Tye spoke the truth. Relief coursed through him, washing away his fears and turning his knees to water. He'd been prepared to fight. Hell, he'd been ready to wage a damned war. Instead, his brother waved surrender before the first shot was fired, and the six long years of fear dissolved like sugar in lemonade.

Tye waited expectantly, but Trace didn't know what to say. Besides, he knew if he tried to speak right now his voice was likely to crack like young Casey Tate's. Under the circumstances, that would embarrass him like hell, so he nodded once and turned to leave.

His hand was on the doorknob when his brother's voice stopped him. "Trace, about that putting back together I mentioned? I'd like to talk about Constance."

Trace snapped to attention. "No need for that."

"There is a need," Tye insisted. "I need to say I'm sorry, so goddamned sorry. There is no excuse for what I did. I don't know why—"

"Forget it." His knuckles blanched white from the force of his grip on the doorknob. Trace swallowed hard before saying, "Let's just put it behind us. We need to let go of the past."

Yearning filled Tye's voice. "And the future? What does the future hold for us? Can you ever forgive me?"

Forgiveness. The all-important question. Trace's thoughts went to Jenny and the love she'd brought into his life, the lessons her love had taught him. He turned around. "Can I forgive you?" he repeated.

He walked over to the bed and touched his brother's arm. "I already have, Tye. I already have."

BY AFTERNOON the sun had chased the worst of the chill from the air and made the back stoop a warm, welcoming place to sit. Jenny had sent Emma there to shell peas, hoping the backyard swing would lure the girl and distract her from her worries.

She must be fretful over the conversation she'd overheard between her new mother and her father pertaining to Katrina, Jenny realized. From the moment the doctor had left, the child had been underfoot, requesting one chore after the other. When Jenny had mentioned the problem to Trace, he'd confessed his own concerns and declared he'd not allow a twelve-year-old to put him off any longer. Jenny observed from the kitchen doorway as he approached Emma and asked, "How about that licorice, Princess?"

Jenny was dismayed, but not surprised, when Emma shook her head. "I can't Papa; I'm sorry. I told Mama I'd help her."

"Your mama won't mind," he replied with assurance, giving his wife a wink. "We'll bring her back a piece of candy and that'll square everything. I have an important errand to run and I'd like to have you with me."

"Errand?" Jenny asked.

"The house," he said significantly. "I need to cancel something."

"Oh." Jenny remembered. He'd started to sell Willow Hill. "You'd best hurry, Trace. I don't want anything to interfere with that particular errand." Glancing at Emma, she added, "Except for a detour to the candy store. I've a real craving for licorice today."

"Bring me back some, too, would you?" Tye asked from the backyard.

Both Jenny and Trace glanced up in surprise. "What are you doing out of bed, Uncle?" Emma asked worriedly.

"Just enjoying the sunshine, honey," he replied. Stepping closer, he sought his brother's gaze and added with a chastising grin, "A house this fancy should have indoor facilities, Mr. Architect."

Trace shrugged. "The house is ready. The city is the hold up. The Fort Worth Water Department figures to dig out this far next spring. If you want to come for Christmas, I reckon our hospitality will be more hospitable." He looked at Jenny and added, "That reminds me, I have a case full of money to return to a man. Don't let me forget to do it today."

Pleasure at the invitation shone in Tye's face as he nodded, and Jenny would have jumped for joy were she not so concerned about Emma.

Sitting beside his daughter on the stoop, Trace asked, "Emmie, what's the matter? I can tell you have something on your mind. Talk to your old papa, would you?"

She shook her head, almost frantically snapping peas.

"How about if Uncle Tye and your mother give us a little privacy? Would that make it easier? Do you want your mother to leave, Emmie?"

"I don't want my mama to ever leave!" Emma cried, the bowl sliding from her lap.

Trace caught it before a single pea spilled. As he set it safely to the side, Emma's hands began to tremble. Then her shoulders began to shake, and soon she was shuddering as tears rolled down her cheeks. She threw herself into her father's arms. "I thought I'd killed her, Papa. Just like last time. I didn't mean to do it, I promise I didn't. Fairy's promise. I'd never hurt Mama. Never!"

*What in the world?* Jenny was astonished. So too was Trace, judging by the look he threw in her direction.

Trace set Emma away from him and gazed into her face. "I don't understand, Emmie. What do you mean just like last time?"

"Last time," she wailed. "My mother. My other mother." She gasped for breath between her sobs.

Trace pulled her into his lap, staring helplessly at Jenny, and then at Tye. Holding her tightly, he asked, "Sweetie? What are you talking about?"

Her voice was a thin wail. "It was just like before. I was in the passageway, and I heard you and Mama talking about Katrina's lie."

"Katrina's lie?"

"The one about her being Uncle Tye's daughter and not yours. It was just like the other time when that funny-talking man and Mother talked about the lie. I told her I'd been listening. Then she went away forever. MissFortune, I mean Mama, went away yesterday! Right after I told her I'd been listening." Sobbing, she buried her face against Trace's shoulder.

"Emma, calm down. I don't understand what you're trying to say."

"I wanted to tell Mama it was a lie, but she didn't understand. She said to wait for you. Then when she didn't come home, I remembered. That's why I hated the passageway. I told my mother what I'd done and she got mad. She hit me, Papa, and I wished she wasn't my mother. I wished she'd go away. I killed her! It's all my fault. I thought I'd killed Mama, too."

Jenny's heart was breaking. Her mother hit her? Constance hit her own child?

"Oh, baby." Anguish shimmered in Trace's eyes as he gestured for Jenny to come sit beside him. He rocked his daughter, slowly stroking her auburn plaits as he spoke firmly, but with a hint of tears in his voice. "No, Emmaline Suzanne, it doesn't work that way. You cannot wish a person dead. You are not responsible. Your mother died in an accident, and you had nothing to do with it."

"I was there when it happened, Emma," Tye said softly, his own tormented expression a duplicate of his brother's. "It was a horrible accident, but it had nothing to do with you. Don't think that."

The little girl looked up at her father. "Is that true? Really?"

"Have I ever lied to you?"

She nodded. "You told us you don't indulge in strong drink, but I've smelled it on your breath."

Trace winced. "I guess that teaches me, doesn't it? But listen to me, Princess. I'm not lying this time, fairy's promise. You are absolutely, positively not responsible in any way for anything that happened to your mother—good or bad."

She studied his face with a seriousness beyond her years, and slowly, belief transformed her expression. Trace sighed. "You've thought this all these years?"

"Yes."

"Why didn't you talk to me about it? It tears me up to think of your worrying about this." Trace hugged her hard.

"I'm sorry, Papa."

"No," he said fiercely. "You stop being sorry, do you hear? You may be my little thinker, but you needn't think you're responsible for the entire world. Right now, all you're responsible for is—" he paused, gesturing toward the bowl "—those peas."

"The peas!" Emma exclaimed, scrambling from his lap. "We'd best get them on to boil, Mama, or Katrina will be downstairs trying to talk you out of having them. I worked hard to shell them. I want to eat them tonight."

Smiling, Jenny stood and held out her hand. "Come along then, Emmie. I happen to know there's a pot on my stove just clamoring for peas."

They started up the steps when Tye said, "Wait a minute. Emma, can I ask you a question? You said you wanted to tell your Mama about Katrina's lie?"

She nodded.

"And the lie is that I'm Katrina's father?"

Again, she nodded.

"How do you know it's a lie, Emma?"

"'Cause I heard Mother say it."

Trace's gaze sought Jenny's as Tye prodded their daughter again. "Whom did she say it to?" he asked.

"That funny-talking man."

"Can you remember exactly what she said, honey?"

Emma shrugged. "That was a long time ago, Uncle. I was very little. All I really remember is how mean her voice sounded. It scared me."

"Your mother sounded mean?"

"I'd forgotten until I went in Willow Hill's secret passageway. That's what made me remember. It was her laugh that was so awful, you see. She laughed when she said she couldn't wait to see the look on my papa's face when she told him Uncle Tye had made the baby. She said it would destroy him to believe his daughter wasn't really his, and that he deserved to believe a lie."

Trace had grown very still. He stared intently at a beetle, crawling in the dirt near the bottom of the stoop. Jenny laid her hand on his shoulder. His muscles were as hard as steel. "What else, Emma?" she asked gently. "Do you remember anything else they said?"

She shrugged. "Something about a brilliant plan and lots of money. She said Papa should have stayed out of politics." After a moment's pause, she added, "I was so scared. When the funny-talking man left, I tried to ask her not to destroy Papa. Then she hit me. That's when I wished she wasn't my mother. That's all I remember." She opened the kitchen door. "We'd best hurry, Mama. Katrina's bound to wake up from her nap any minute."

"Certainly." Jenny's eyes were misty as she leaned over and pressed a kiss to her husband's head before going inside.

"I'll be right there," Trace said hoarsely.

He watched the beetle disappear into a tuft of green weeds, then looked at his brother. Tye's expression was similar to one he'd worn during the war in the aftermath of battle. Trace figured his own countenance must appear the same.

"It was all a setup," Tye said bitterly. "She set me up, and I fell for it."

"Why did she do it?" Trace asked, knowing but not believing.

"The money, of course. The inheritance went to the eldest child of the eldest child. It was a lot of money, a whole lot. Good old Cousin Lord Howard's finder's fee was probably enough to set him up for life. I'm eight minutes older than you. If Constance wanted that money, she had to go through me to get it. And I toppled like a rotten tree to her wicked intrigues."

Trace's voice trembled as he said, "Katrina is really mine."

Tye stooped and scooped a rock off the ground with his uninjured arm. He threw it hard, grimacing in pain. "I didn't get her pregnant the night of the ball, because *you'd* already done it. Howard told me the baby had been born a few weeks early, that she was little and sickly."

Trace shook his head. "Kat was the biggest of our babies."

"*Your* babies." Tye's voice cracked on the words. He cleared his throat before continuing. "There it is. I gotta tell you, brother, the notion tears at my heart. I love her, too, you know. Even though I never laid eyes on her until I knocked on your front door a couple of weeks ago, I've loved her since the moment I learned she existed. But she's not mine, after all. She's yours.

"Katrina is your daughter."

JENNY FOUND Trace in the extra bedroom she had adapted as a workroom. In one corner stood a dressmaker's form, and upon it hung the Bad Luck Wedding Dress. Seeing the gown, she said a quick, silent prayer for the health and happiness of Big Jack Bailey's new grandson. It was the least she could do, she thought. In a crazy way, Big Jack had brought immeasurable joy to the McBride family.

Trace stood before the dress. He was fingering the pearls. She wondered if his thoughts were similar to hers.

"Trace?"

He looked over at her, and the expression in his eyes twisted her heart. Grief. All-consuming, soul-wrenching grief. "What's wrong?" she asked.

"Me. I'm wrong. I've been wrong. I've been a goddamn fool. It doesn't matter. All these years, it's been my guiding force. I ran because of it. I ached because of it. I wouldn't trust because of it. If not for you being who you are, I'd have denied my daughters a mother because of it."

She went to him and wrapped her arms around his waist. "What is *it*, darling?"

"*It* is the seed that gave my daughter life. It took all of this for me to learn that it simply doesn't matter. I've always been Katrina's father. Hell, the king of England could have sired the child, but I'd still be her father. Always. It truly doesn't matter."

He took a deep, shuddering breath. "I have you to thank for my leap of understanding, you realize."

Jenny smiled up at him. "Me and the Bad Luck Wedding Dress."

The pain disappeared from his eyes, replaced by a glow of love so fierce it took her breath away. "No, not the Bad Luck Wedding Dress. Wilhemina Peters was right about that."

"Right about what?"

"This dress is special, but we were too blind to see it. It never has been the Bad Luck Wedding Dress, Jenny. It's been good luck right from the start. It's the Good Luck Wedding Dress." He stroked her cheek with his thumb and asked in a gravelly voice, "Wear it for me, treasure, would you? Now. Right now? Tonight?"

Jenny turned and locked the door. "You want me to model my design, Mr. McBride?"

"Yes. Oh, yes."

"I'm not a model, you understand." She undid the buttons down the bodice of her dress. "I'm a dressmaker."

"A very fine dressmaker," he said. "And an even finer figure of a woman."

She pulled her gown off her shoulders. "That's right. I'm a fine dressmaker. An excellent dressmaker. A master, in fact."

"Yes, ma'am." His voice was strangled.

"So, I'll model the Good Luck Wedding Dress for you on one condition, Mr. McBride."

She was naked now. "Condition? Honey, I'm willing to do damned near anything."

She picked up her tape measure and dropped to her knees before him. Licking her lips, she said, "Let me measure your inseam first?"

*Fort Worth Daily Democrat*
June 1, 1888
Talk about Town
By Wilhemina Peters

THERE IS AN OLD SAYING that All the World Loves a Lover. Livestock is another matter entirely.

Yesterday evening the people of Fort Worth were treated to the spectacle of another McBride family wedding. The event eclipsed every other social occasion in our fair city in the past five years, and will without a doubt provide fodder for discussion for years to come.

The bride, Miss Emmaline Suzanne McBride, was resplendent in her mother's gown, the Good Luck Wedding Dress that has brought Mrs. McBride such fame. The groom, Mr. Casey Tate, owner of the Lucky Lady Ranch southeast of town, appeared starstruck by his wife's beauty, as well he should have.

Attending their sister were Misses Maribeth Elizabeth and Katrina Julianne McBride, gowned in exquisite designs of yellow organdy. The church was filled to capacity, the flowers abundant, and the music superb.

It was such a shame the McBrides chose to allow their younger children to attend the ceremony.

In an apparent effort to eclipse the McBride Menaces' reputation for mischief, the younger children contributed to the ceremony in an unforgettable manner. Without a doubt, Fort Worth will recall this wedding for generations to come.

Whereas their sisters had turned mice and cats and dogs loose at their parents' wedding, these children decided to move to bigger barnyard animals. Immediately upon the completion of the vows, pigs, sheep, chickens, and a pair of long-horn cattle were ushered inside.

But, my dear readers, it wasn't the livestock that had the church pews emptying faster than a "Go in peace" on a windy-sermon Sunday. Allow me to say it in a word.

Polecat.

Yes, Fort Worth, you read it right. The youngsters turned a polecat loose at their big sister's wedding. Mr. McBride's shouted assurance that the family pet's protective essence had been medically removed did little to stop the exodus from the church.

This reporter feels compelled to comment. I ask you this, Fort Worth. Our fair city suffered through the mischief of the McBride Menaces for years. Are any of us ready for the second wave? Can Fort Worth survive the challenge of Trace and Jenny McBride's three boys, Bill, Tommy, and Bobby McBride—otherwise known as the McBride Monsters? Will luck be with us?

Keep your fingers crossed.

# HQN™

## We *are* romance™

Special Agent Cece Blackwell is smart, savvy and knows her way around race cars...and Blain Sanders.

### Award-winning author

# pamela britton

NASCAR star Blain Sanders can't believe that sexy lead investigator Cece Blackwell is the same drag-racing tomboy who used to dog his steps! But Cece has grown up, and while catching a killer is her main objective, she's not entirely above making the man who used to ignore her squirm just a little....

## Dangerous Curves

Two people on a surefire collision course...in love.
Available in February.